I0762090

An Old Woman's Last Prophecy

Book # 1

of the

Forsaken Elvish Scrolls Trilogy

by

J. A. Clark

"Many women have done excellently,
but you surpass them all."

Thank you, Shalamar.

Published by JMDC Publishing, Ltd, Colorado.

Printed in the United States of America

First Printing, 2016

ISBN-10: 0-9974911-2-4

ISBN-13: 978-0-9974911-2-8

ACKNOWLEDGEMENTS

There are many people close to this project who deserve special thanks. My wife is first on that list, for many reasons; her loyalty, guidance and feedback, and patient endurance through the entire writing process are beyond words. Her encouragement and support were so incredibly valued, she unequivocally has to be the first person thanked. My children are next, all of whom provided the never-ending fuel to see this project to completion. My father taught many principles necessary for crossing this finish line, especially the values of persistence and belief; for that, and much more, I am grateful. And my mother, having served in the Air Force, did her best to instill discipline, which took a bit longer to take root, but slow growing as it was, its absence would have doomed this entire project. Thank you to all my family.

I also owe a special thank you to Cornerstones Literary Consultancy for their expertise, and especially Dr. Sarah Quigley for her impeccable advice and editing. If others hear the true song of this story, it is because you helped it sing.

CONTENTS

An Old Woman's Last Prophecy

Chapter 1
A Prophecy Kept Secret

Limbs buckled under the frigid cold, crashing all along the distant tree line. But not a sound echoed into the old woman's cottage as destruction encircled her. The sudden shift in weather, the icy winds, the silence... she had seen the unstoppable force before: Its rage could be neither controlled nor contained. The horrible memories were as clear as the sight unfolding before her.

"Impossible," she whispered.

Someone would come for her, or rather, for her secret; she knew. But not this. Not now. This madness had ended centuries ago.

Maybe the frost is a coincidence.

She shook her head after a moment, sinking slowly into her chair, knowing coincidences could not be accommodated. It was too familiar.

A pair of glacier-blue eyes appeared out of the midnight darkness, hovering against the far wall. Their brilliance pierced her. She opened her mouth to say something, but a strange silence descended on the cottage like a thick, murky liquid. It stole her breath. She felt pinned to the chair as it crept down her shoulders and arms. Her heartbeat slowed. She fought to stay alert, blinking forcefully, but complacency tingled in her fingers and toes. Feeling a desire to forget the silence, she relaxed in the warmth wrapping around her, drowning helplessly in sleep.

The sapphire eyes rose silently in the shadows until the faint moonlight illuminated a pair of legs. They stood, defying the strangeness. One step forward, and a slender, lean frame separated from the wood stack.

"Do you feel the prickling of the night?" asked the voice.

The noise prodded the old woman back to consciousness. She blinked, surprised, searching for the sound.

"Listen to me, Dalis," she replied, still fighting the drowsiness. "I fear..."

Her voice faded as the tall, mannish figure emerged from the darkness of the corner.

"I fear something worse than death has arrived," she managed, weakly.

A lean silhouette emerged fully into the moonlight, but the figure was far from human. His slightly pointed ears slanted to the rear, and the shadows cut sharply across his face. His cloak blended perfectly with the bark of the chopped wood that was stacked half the height of the wall. He would have been invisible had the cloak not ruffled with his stride.

He lifted his strong chin, and the old woman felt a pulling sensation towards the back of her mind: the kind one feels when watched secretly from behind.

"Disgusting," he whispered, twisting away, his complexion ashen. "I can taste the foulness."

"You can taste death?" remarked the old woman. "I had no idea you knew its nuances so well."

"Not well enough," replied the voice quietly. "This is new. It is not a taste I would soon forget. Putrid, subtle, yet unmistakable. I would still be sleeping had you not woken me."

"I doubt that. We both know you were already stirring." The old woman stared at her friend and protector, her head nodding sleepily forward again. Her last sight was that of him watching the melted frost glide gently down the window, which was still warm from summer.

The sudden jolt of her chin hitting her chest revived her.

"Tonight..." she began. She struggled to strengthen her voice in the face of the stillness imposing its will on her with renewed vigor.

As she faltered, her head sank lower and lower for a third time, until a hazel flash of color danced in her usually chocolate brown eyes. She lifted her head in defiance, refusing to bend any longer. Her pupils narrowed into tiny circles.

"Dalis, I am afraid I underestimated their speed," she said firmly.

"Whose speed?" asked the protector, turning away from the water droplets drifting down the window.

The old cottage protested the question; the protector turned his gaze to the rafters as the old woman's eyes moved to the ramshackle wooden floorboards that creaked and groaned as if of their own will. The tiny cottage was ancient, but the noise was far from wholesome tonight.

"Forgive me," she continued, her eyes dancing up to the protector's. "I do not know exactly who is out there tonight, but I knew someone would come for us. I did not think it could be this soon, though."

Her words hung in the air for a brief moment. "I am afraid we are beyond escape."

The protector's acceleration was something few humans ever witnessed. The old woman had spent over two and a half centuries under his protection, but even so, she had never fully acclimated. She flinched.

"You mean to say you expected an attack and said nothing to me?" he asked, kneeling at her side with disbelief.

"I am asking your forgiveness," she replied, true regret and sadness filling her eyes. "For once, I tried to protect you. I am sorry I failed you, Dalis."

"My lady, we must depart." Dalis bent to help her stand. "We can still make our way out of this."

The old woman allowed her head to loll back, showing no intention of moving.

"My lady, this is no ordinary night," Dalis continued. "We have neither time to waste nor room for error. We must begin our departure immediately. I understand your aversion to being carried." He moved into a better position to lift her from the chair. "But you will have to allow me this night. We know not what hunts us, and I care not to find out while ensnared in its trap."

The protector's muscles tightened, ready to hoist the old woman, but she placed a gentle hand on his face, stopping him.

"No, Dalis. I do not wish to be carried anywhere tonight."

For the first time in Dalis's long life, the old woman felt frail to him. Her will was gone.

"What troubles you?" he asked, baffled. "It is not too late to escape."

"You are what troubles me," she responded, looking him dead in the eye, now without a care or fear in the world for what was coming for her.

"We *can* still escape," he urged.

"Can we?" she asked, shaking her head in answer to the question. "I have an important mission for you," she continued. "But there is something you need to hear first: a secret I have kept far too long."

"You can tell me your secret when we are far away from here," Dalis responded. "We are being encircled. We need to move."

The old woman pushed Dalis's arms away, fighting her way out of the chair. "What we need is another log on this wretched fire!"

Dalis exhaled, struggling to restrain the urgency coursing through his veins. Placing his hands on the wooden chair, he watched, painfully, as she gained her rigid feet. She shuffled to the stack of wood, visibly pouring all her energies into fighting the unnatural complacency sucking her down like a swamp.

"You need one more vital piece of information before setting out," she added, inching her way closer. "But my thoughts are scattered amidst this fuzziness. I knew they would come for me, and I knew they would not yield until my blood soaked the earth." She breathed in, trying to calm herself, fighting the raging sea of slumber trying to plunge her back into its comforting depths.

She tossed a small log into the dying red embers, and the flames enveloped it before she heaved another heavy sigh and, to Dalis's dismay, settled uncomfortably back into the rocking chair.

"They will kill me for the prophecy I have made," she said, quietly.

Dalis released a controlled breath, grasping for a handle, but it didn't stop the top of the old woman's chair from cracking under his grip.

"You have made no such prophecy," he managed with measured, restrained effort. "I assure you. That is my sole duty, and I have watched you every second for the last two hundred and fifty-seven years. You have uttered nothing even close to a prophecy, I promise. We have to move now. No more delaying!"

"Oh, not every second," replied the old woman, anticipating his response with a finger in the air.

Dalis stood, stupefied, taking stock of every unlikely revelation unleashed in a matter of moments: An unknown force gathered on their doorstep, after over half a century without anything remotely remarkable; an attack the old woman had anticipated but had said nothing about; and now came the most defiant, most outrageous claim imaginable: An unrecorded prophecy.

"Why would you say that?" Dalis exclaimed, bewildered. "Why now, amidst this attack?"

He released his grip on the chair and a fragmented piece of the decorated wood clanked to the ground. He exhaled again, moving to the window, trying to control the fury brewing inside him. How could she even imagine such a thought? It was insulting to think he might have missed a prophecy.

Surveying the clearing, his eye caught a movement above the treetops. Two blankets of clouds were speeding towards each other across the empty night sky, ready to clash in front of the crescent moon, which was the only source illuminating the night.

His anger channeled into sharp concentration as he watched the moon vanish behind a single mass of clouds, blossoming like an explosion high into the sky.

"Clouds should not move like that," Dalis remarked, amazed. "The forest is not our friend tonight. We may have better odds if we stay."

Destruction raged through the forest as Dalis observed frozen limbs dropping to the ground as if they were nothing more than feeble twigs. But only a howling wind, muted by window glass, entered their cottage.

"Dalis, they come *because* of the prophecy," she stressed. "I know our time is short, but you must hear me, even if it costs me my life."

The words drew his defiant, radiant blue eyes to her as if she had cursed at him.

She shook her head. "I am afraid I have destined you to an impossible mission."

Dalis lowered his gaze, shaking his head in return.

"No more secrets," he replied, calm but dangerous. "What is this prophecy? Who would be hunting us?"

"We should start at the beginning," she answered. "But first I would like to know the status of the tunnel. Is it complete?"

Dalis opened his mouth to reply, but stopped as a flock of birds took flight from the treetops on the far edge of the clearing.

"The tunnel is finished," he whispered sharply. "Two days ago..."

The birds disappeared after a few flaps of their wings, as if the night had opened wide and swallowed them into its black depths. No trace was left behind.

"They are controlling everything," Dalis whispered. "This is not the work of elves. We do not possess these kinds of powers."

"And the tunnel ends at the river's edge, yes?" she asked, unfazed, ignoring the remark.

Dalis made eye contact and nodded once, confirming the tunnel's completion.

"Very well then. Three summers ago, I asked you to check on an old friend; do you remember?"

Dalis turned and stared at her, speechless for a moment.

"The beginning of your deceit starts three summers ago?" he managed, quelling a wave of rising fury.

"Correct," she responded. "And another protector was sent to replace you in your absence. Do you remember?"

Dalis shook his head.

"Yes, I remember," he answered, allowing the conversation to move forward despite the things he really wanted to say. "The Council found it a most irregular request, but obliged all the same, considering your previous contributions to elf-kind. If memory serves, I was gone three days. But you could not possibly have kept a lie secret for that length of time."

"A fox can be crafty when necessary," she replied. "And you often forget that you live with one."

"I am very well acquainted with your craftiness, my lady," Dalis countered, pointing to the hidden entrance of the tunnel disguised behind a small bookcase. "Nobody in their right mind would spend two years aimlessly digging a purposeless tunnel. Yet here I am, still sane, and there is your purposeless tunnel." Dalis heaved another sigh. "What I do not understand is why you felt it necessary to lie to me."

"You will understand soon enough," she replied, nodding confidently. "But as for our story, that other protector was not as strong as you. I could tell it the moment I met him. It was all prestige in the beginning, but after a few hours, he found the task a bit bothersome. I could see the boredom overcoming him. It is why only the best are chosen, I suppose..." She stopped, as if distracted by some other thought.

"Yes?" Dalis prodded. "You have three years' worth to tell in a matter of seconds. Press on if you please."

"Of course," she replied, but seemed to still struggle to form her words. "As I said, I have a mission for you, a most important role I can entrust to no one else. For that reason, your duty is no longer here."

She paused, gazing expectantly into his icy stare.

"On the second evening of your departure, I had a mysterious sensation; a sensation that has gripped me only once before. Do you know of what I speak?"

Dalis studied the old woman for a long moment, but said nothing.

"You speak of urgency so quickly when I struggle to form my thoughts," gibed the old woman. "Yet what about you? It is a simple question: You know the sensation I speak of, yes?"

"I am considering whether it could be true," he replied, staring back stonily.

"Come, Dalis!" she exclaimed. "Who is wasting time now?"

"I am afraid the extra consideration is the cost a liar must bear. It is rather convenient this all takes place during the only three days we have ever been separated."

The old woman let forth a disgusted noise.

"Yes, the odds are unlikely to say the least, but perhaps you are not crediting the fates as much as you should. Your absence that evening opened what may be the only window for elf-kind's survival." She took a moment to breathe and calm her growing frustration.

"Sleep was coming fast that fateful evening," she pressed on. "And the other protector was already entertaining dreams. I did not want that lazy pile of coals reaping the prophecy that you had so diligently worked to record. So I opened my window and enticed one of the nightingales to watch over me. I asked her to sing me the story of what she may hear while I slept." The old woman paused, looking for a delicate way to continue. "But before I had a chance to hear the nightingale's response, I was taken into my stupor."

Dalis shook his head again with even greater disbelief. "The reprimands are so many, and the time so little."

"Rest easy, my friend," assured the old woman. "When I awoke, the nightingale was there to sing what she had heard. My initial intention was, of course, to relay you the prophecy upon your return, so that the natural order of delivering it could unfold. But after hearing the prophecy sung back to me that next morning, there was no way I could relay it... to anybody. Not until the time was right. It was too dangerous."

"Why dangerous?" asked Dalis, suddenly showing more interest.

"For many reasons," she answered. "Foremost, the Council would want to destroy it, along with anyone who knew about it. The messenger would have been killed, with my own death to follow shortly thereafter. Dalis, when you hear the prophecy, please understand I say all these things not about the elves I have come to love, but about those who are infiltrating the ranks of power."

A gust of wind blasted the window, rattling the small iron latch loose. The panes flew open.

"Four, maybe five of them," Dalis interrupted, the instant the chill hit him. The gust invaded the room like the dead cold of winter's night and his breath caught in his throat. He still expected the sweltering summer's heat. His cape and his long, black hair flew violently behind him as he forced the stabbing air through his nose.

"Wait!" He closed his eyes, breathing more deeply, letting the aroma settle around him. "Their scents are changing."

He took another deep whiff.

"Pine to grass," he continued, focusing harder. "And now to mint. They are blending into one. I cannot track them. I do not know how many there are." He turned incredulously to the old woman, his eyes darting back and forth furiously. "Who among us controls such power over the Earth? You said you anticipated this? Tell me who."

"Not this, exactly," replied the old woman. "They arrived much sooner than I anticipated. But as you can see from the events unfolding before us, my beliefs were well-founded when I said they would kill anyone who knew of the prophecy."

With this, unexpectedly, she faded into sleep again.

"Tell me everything!" Dalis yelled. He was at her side in a blaze, lifting her drooping head.

"Sorry," she answered, fighting to open her eyelids, clearing her throat. "Ever since that night, I refused to even whisper its existence, fearing something like this would happen before a solution presented itself." She began to nod off again. "Please hold my eyes open, Dalis. They are too heavy."

Dalis reached slowly and spread her eyelids apart with his fingers and thumbs.

"Much better." The old woman breathed a heavy sigh, relieved. "Thank you. With every passing day since that night three summers ago, the truth has been growing like thistles around my heart, reminding me this prophecy cannot be kept secret. I would like to think I endured longer than most..." She trailed off, falling into sleep once again, even though this time her eyes remained open.

"My lady!" Dalis yelled.

"But after a year," she continued, jolting back into consciousness as if nothing had happened, "I realized a solution was not coming to our aid. Or if it was, I would not last to see its arrival. I realized then, two summers ago, we needed to make our own solution."

She lifted an arm towards the fireplace and slowly swung it towards the half-sized bookcase concealing the secret entrance.

"The tunnel," Dalis exclaimed. "The tunnel is not a solution! Why did you not consult me? Whoever is out there hunting us can surely smell us."

"Not us," the old woman replied. "Just me. Your gifts of concealment are unmatched. You must escape."

"You are my duty and therefore our fates will be the same," he replied, releasing his fingers from her eyelids. "Can you manage?"

She nodded. "It is easier now. The onslaught is intense, but it has little endurance. I just have to weather the initial waves."

"Good," he replied, maneuvering his way back to the window for another view of the clearing.

"Dalis, listen to me," urged the old woman. "You must have understanding beyond the words of the prophecy. There is more happening than just this prophecy."

"Speak plainly," Dalis replied. "What do you mean?"

"For many years, I have feared the power-shift within the Council that is now before us. I sense darkness."

"How could you know such a thing?" He eyed her carefully. "You do not have contact with elves anymore, besides me."

"You know, as well as I," stated the old woman, "that my abilities of foresight are heightened in your presence, are they not?"

Dalis considered her words. "The High Council would be the absolute last among elves to kill the greatest seer of our lifetime," he refuted. "The prophets are too valuable, especially to them."

"I am afraid you are wrong, my dear friend," replied the old woman.

"No single prophecy is that important," Dalis countered, pressing the issue.

The old woman waved a dismissive hand. "Our time is short now. I used my own channels to relay this prophecy to the Council just yesterday." She raised a tired hand to try to calm the fury turning Dalis's fair skin shades of red.

"Please let me finish," she went on before he could speak. "You will not be able to save your race unless you hear everything."

"Our race," Dalis corrected.

"Never mind. It has been three years since the fateful words of the prophecy escaped me, and just last night, its thorns penetrated to the deepest core of my heart as those same words found their way onto paper. The prophecy cycle is complete, Dalis. There is no doubt as to its authenticity."

She released a burdened exhale.

"My lady," Dalis began with very measured effort. "My sole duty is to watch over you for the signs of a prophecy and deliver that prophecy to the Council. If what you say is true, if you are in danger because of this prophecy, the Council will assume we plot together as I did not personally deliver any word of it." He paused, letting the meaning of his words sink in. "Whatever mission you have for me, it must wait. Evading this current threat is our priority. Once you are safe, we can move forward."

He quieted as a faint whizzing sound approached the window. His legs gave way, and he collapsed to the ground an instant before a small, round object blistered through the open window on the back of the icy currents still whipping around the house. He snatched the thing with lightning speed. Feathers and wings sprouted through his lightly closed fist, and he rotated his hand to find a bird's head poking between his fingers.

"Ah, you found my messenger," exclaimed the old woman, life coursing through her once again.

Dalis stared at the delicately ensnared brown-and-blue feathered bird as it, too, stared back with baffled eyes at her captor.

"I am afraid your messenger has been coerced into some kind of unorthodox weapon," Dalis responded, still studying the creature.

The bird seemed to understand his words, and she reared back, pecking viciously in reply. Instinctively Dalis released her, but instead of flying away, she latched onto his finger and swung upright into a dignified position. Dalis extended his hand as the bird clucked and huffed at him, reprovingly.

The bird then stopped mid-screech and turned her attention to the old woman, pelting the room with a series of unnatural chirps and squawks far from the singsong melodies that commonly echoed through the forest. As the bird sang, the old woman's smile faded, and her eyes lowered heavily to the ground.

Dalis shifted his eyes between the bird and the old woman, while the bird waited patiently, looking expectantly at her perch with a cocked head.

"Unfortunately, conversing with animals has never been my strength," Dalis interjected, stealing a glance at the old woman. "Is she done?"

The question seemed to snap the old woman back to the moment, but her gaze lingered on the floor. "I am afraid our friend has brought terrible news. Although it is not unexpected."

With heavy effort, she released yet another painful sigh.

"That poor young elf we were just discussing—that other protector who took your stead to watch over me those three nights? He has just taken your stead once again. He is dead."

The nightingale flitted effortlessly, zipping to the floor. She hopped to the half-sized bookcase blocking the tunnel entrance, and plucked three tiny black seeds from a pile atop it. She gave one pleasant chirp to the old woman, and then flapped her small powerful wings against the gusting wind. Forcing her way through the window, she disappeared back into the night.

"It is an unfortunate sacrifice I felt compelled to make," the old woman continued. "The young elf was arrogant, and I knew he would be eager to deliver news of a second prophecy. I may pay for it many times over in the next life, but the sacrifice was necessary. I had to know if my fears were justified."

She pointed to the window.

"Our little messenger delivered the written prophecy by air just last night to this very elf, and with it were my instructions to present it to the Council. I then instructed the bird to wait until nightfall and deliver to me any news she might have heard." The old woman locked her eyes with Dalis's. "I am afraid my worst fears are confirmed."

"And what are those fears?" asked Dalis pointedly.

"Dalis, the elves I once knew would have delighted in such a prophecy. This prophecy can usher in a new and more glorious world than we have ever dared dream of: A world of humans and elves living together as equals. But I am afraid this defining moment in Elvish history has come at the wrong time."

She paused, trying to gather her thoughts.

"Just as it was with the first prophecy, you and I both know it takes only one to change the course of history. And that is exactly what I have spent the last two years doing: Preparing the way for another one."

"My lady, tell me the prophecy," Dalis urged, but the words had barely left his mouth before a piercing arrow sliced through his hand, stopping only as it penetrated the bone of his thigh. His head lashed backwards, a stifled cry escaping from his mouth. Blood began to pour down his leg.

In an instant, his face became like stone, detached from the pain. A stout, slender sword concealed within the layers draped over his back ripped through his shirt, flashing silver. It whipped around, catching the tail end of a second arrow. The sharp arrowhead plummeted into the floorboards, peeling back thick whittles of wood just in front of the old woman's feet. Severed feathers hovered to the ground as Dalis and the old woman locked eyes for a brief moment.

Two more arrows screamed through the window, one narrowly missing Dalis's shoulder. It dug into the wall, while the second ricocheted off the sill. Dalis's hand, pinned to his thigh with an arrow, poured with blood. Swift and true, his blade seared between the narrow space and sliced the shaft with a clean snap. Dalis dropped below the windowsill for cover. Wrenching the broken arrow from the back of his hand, he watched its Blackwood brother buzz ominously across the room.

The old woman gained her feet. Watching her shuffle to the fireplace, Dalis wondered at the odds of a decorated Elvish Warrior succumbing to an arrow before the slow and withering woman. The hawk-feathered weapon emerged delicately from the back of his hand as he decided the odds were colossal. He studied the masterful craftsmanship. The dense Blackwood was extremely difficult to shape, but its trajectory was always true. Dalis threw it away, disgusted. It was the work of highly trained elves.

Dalis checked the old woman, trying to distract himself from the pulsing pain in his leg; the familiar scratching noise of feather tip on parchment was working frantically. Dalis proceeded to dig the sharp end out of his thigh and quickly extracted a large leaf just as the blood-drenched tip emerged. With two fingers, he pushed the lively plant into his mouth, and after precisely eight chomps, retrieved it. The mutilated mess now sparkled with yellow flecks along the edges.

Veins throbbed in his neck as most of the leaf entered the gaping hole of his thigh. The ferocious silence in his eyes soon began to spread across his face; the gushing blood stopped within seconds. He exhaled. Pushing the last bit of leaf all the way through the oozing wound in his hand, a yellow shimmer appeared at the center of his palm.

Dalis regained his feet, leaning against the wall for support. He tested his injured leg, but didn't wait for the pain to register before darting to the fireplace.

"My lady," he whispered. "Move to the tunnel and wait for me there."

The old woman scribbled her last few words and turned with the parchment in hand.

"The boy must be saved!" she cried. "That is your mission!"

Before she could let out another word, a thunderous roar besieged the night, shaking the walls of the house. The crack lasted only a split second before dying away, but the violent shaking clung to the cottage like a disease, growing in strength. The roof groaned and protested, raining dust and debris.

A brief, quiet moment followed, just long enough for Dalis and the old woman to exchange a worried look. The silence weighed heavily on both of them; the storm was still bubbling beneath the quiet. The thought barely had a chance to enter Dalis's mind, that staying in the cottage may have been a mistake, when it happened: The walls ripped apart from each other, exploding into hundreds of pieces.

In an instant, the open night sky flashed as splintered fragments of the cottage hurtled in every direction into the clearing. The old woman flew into Dalis, knocking his feet out from under him. He scrambled in mid-air, instinctively trying to find his feet again, but a large boulder shaped like the corner of the fireplace stole his very last thought as it came tumbling towards his outstretched arm, braced for impact. Dalis recoiled just in time to see the boulder pummel the floor, leaving three uprooted floorboards in its wake. He pulled the old woman close; there was no more time to adjust. The sharp, daggered floorboards awaited their arrival as he held her even more tightly, embracing the unfamiliar sensation of hope. She didn't resist. Dalis's spine hit the hard, uneven earth, breaking the old woman's fall.

He opened his eyes, waiting for the sharp, piercing pains of the floorboards to register, but they never did. To his disbelief, he'd managed to miss every last broken shard. The mayhem rumbled over them as he squeezed the old woman into his chest, waiting for the last of the carnage to dissipate into silence.

An icy cackle echoed from the tree line. It was followed by the faintest of footsteps emerging from the clearing's edge. The footsteps had a soft, padded timbre to them, and they were moving quickly.

Unmistakably Elvish, Dalis thought.

He checked the shimmering yellow herb protruding through his palm; it had turned a dark purple, indicating that it was nearly finished. The purple turned a fleshy color before his eyes, and then the hole in his hand was gone. There was not the slightest trace of the bloody injury. He flexed his hand. No pain. But they needed more time as he felt his thigh and immediately flinched.

He lifted his head, searching for the bookcase that concealed the hidden entrance to the tunnel. The same putrid stench that he had first tasted now danced and swirled even more strongly. A shadow flickered on the outskirts of his vision as he found the bookcase; it was almost unrecognizable. Their door to escape now lay amidst a section of the ceiling twisted around it. If a chance still existed, Dalis knew their window was small.

"We can still make it," he whispered to the old woman. "Come with me now!"

He rolled her off to the side and gently wrapped her arm around his neck. But the smell of something burning wafted across his face and he stopped; smoke was emanating from the old woman's hand. The coals from the fire had scattered in the explosion, igniting the parchment still clutched in the old woman's hand. It glowed red, smoldering at the end. Dalis snatched the paper and, dampening the slow burn, stuffed it into his chest pocket.

He popped his head up with lightning speed to see how much time they had. Several small fires flickered, licking at the splinters scattered throughout the clearing. They had to move now. He hoisted the old woman onto his back, but his injured leg crumpled after one step. He collapsed to the ground, cursing.

The footsteps were growing louder. There was no more time.

Dalis lifted his head again. The enemy moved effortlessly behind columns of sooty, black smoke, shadows dancing and taunting their imminent approach.

Dalis secured the old woman's arms with one hand and heaved forward, crawling with his other arm. But they barely moved half a body length. The discouragement rested like a sack of rocks on his back as he readied for a second attempt. But then he stopped again. The old woman felt heavier; she neither resisted nor helped.

Dalis quickly slipped the old woman off.

It cannot be, he thought, reaching a hand to check for any sign of breath. There was none. Dalis clung to hope, pressing on her chest, but the woman uttered nothing: nothing except the deep, penetrating peace that Dalis knew all too well from the battlefields.

Grief threatened to overtake him. He felt the coolness already sweeping her away as he kissed her forehead lightly. With an intricate looping pattern, he placed the mark of safe passage on her forehead.

"Travel safe, old friend."

He wiped the soot from her brow, removing any trace of the sign as he rose to a crouch. The wound on his thigh reflected a slight tinge of purple. Then it turned to a fleshy color, just as his hand had done.

He placed his full weight on the injured leg and committed to one last hope. Diving towards the opening of the tunnel, he slithered to the huge chunk of fallen roof that concealed his body as he rose to a seated position. He fought to peel open the now flimsy entrance to the tunnel, but the door was pinned tight. With a heave, he pried it open just enough to squeeze through and crawl inside, embracing the dank tunnel full of crawling insects. A brief moment of relief washed over him; the tunnel was intact. The blast hadn't destroyed it. He reached back to close the door, but froze as the first elf emerged ahead of the others into view. In one fluid motion, Dalis pulled his arm back and disappeared into the darkness.

He closed his eyes, collected his energy, and prepared for a quick, quiet attack. The open entrance was hidden amongst the debris. But if they studied the bookcase closely enough...

"Where is she?" the elf in view demanded. He cackled again; it was the same high-pitched noise from seconds earlier. He was standing hunched at the shoulders, his neck craning forward over a bloated stomach. His scraggly arms and sunken cheeks made Dalis wonder if he hadn't eaten in months.

The elf vaulted a pile of rubble, exactly where the front door used to exist. Purple eyes surveyed the wreckage, cutting through the darkness like lanterns. Dalis remained silent, perched like a snake ready to strike. His blood screamed to release the attack that had taken form in his hand. Usually, it would have appeared like an orb of light, waiting to be unleashed. But with Dalis's gift of stealth, it hovered at the ready, as dark as the night itself. He wanted nothing more than to obliterate the vile thing posing so victoriously.

He steadied his breath. The wisdom of refraining proved its worth almost immediately as the satisfaction of killing the one would have been short-lived: Two more cloaked in black emerged out of the smoke. Dalis considered the odds, weighing how fast he could rebuild for another attack. He decided better of it. The odds were not in his favor.

The shadow of an arm moved across the jagged carnage, and the remainder of the fireplace obliterated into a hundred small stones, just as another thunderous crack split the night.

"We need to find both," commanded a fourth elf, entering the opposite side of the clearing. "No trace of anything should be left behind."

"There is the old hag," screeched the elf, pointing a sharp piece of floorboard at her, "with a stick in her back!"

Dalis watched the elf summon another piece of broken floorboard into his outstretched hand. The elf then threw the two spear-like splinters in quick succession at her exposed, defenseless body; Dalis's blood burned as the shards struck the old woman's back.

The dark orb in Dalis's hand pulsed, ready to fly; it screamed to be released. He was on the verge of succumbing to the temptation when a deep, confident voice spoke.

"I know I tagged the protector."

In the silence that followed, Dalis felt the eyes of the four assassins pressing into the debris, searching for him. The dark orb disappeared instantly as Dalis transferred all energy from a quick attack to invisible stealth. The ability to not be seen was his true gift, and he put every last thought behind it. The shadows melded into him, welcoming him like a long-lost son.

"There!" said one, running in Dalis's direction. Dalis remained still, watching the purple in the elf's eyes grow larger; he didn't know what kinds of gifts these elves possessed, but he liked his odds of getting at least two of them, especially if they expected him to be wounded. *Maybe a third, if I can draw one into the tunnel first,* he thought.

His concentration began to slip towards building for another attack. *Almost there... three... two... one...*

At the last second, the elf veered left of the tunnel and stopped, almost within arm's reach. Dalis, less than a breath from unleashing every last orb he could muster at the creature, silently watched the elf scan the distant horizon; he could reach out and snatch him into the tunnel if he wanted.

The elf yelled over his shoulder. "Something is moving through the woods, I think."

Dalis reunited his efforts toward stealth again, releasing every bit of focus dedicated for the attack. Something was very wrong. The elf paced right in front of him, but couldn't find him. *What elf is incapable of sensing another from a mere breath's distance,* he wondered. It was a skill all elves were born with; they could feel each other.

"He is on the run," screeched the voice. "After him!"

"No," commanded another with authority; his full shadow emerged into view opposite the others. Dalis still couldn't see the leader, but he could hear his rugged forceful voice.

"We have new orders," the leader continued.

The high-pitched voice screeched in protest, but he only managed that single sound, before he was consumed in uncontrollable fits of coughing.

Dalis watched the elf gasp for breath, clawing at his neck. It was a long, uncomfortable moment before something yielded, allowing the sickly elf to suck air back into his wheezing lungs.

"Interrupt me again, and see the limits of my patience," bellowed the gruff voice.

The elf continued to struggle with his breath, but the fearful look in his eyes said there would be no more interruptions.

"The protector no longer concerns us," continued the leader. "Once we kill the boy, it is done. Dalis's next move will not matter." The ensuing quiet dared the scraggly elf to say something, but there was only silence, until the rough voice resonated again.

"Latest news from the Council is that the Greco team botched the boy's execution. The family is running. The boy and his parents were last seen in the south, fleeing further southward towards the human village of Bellington. We are assigned clean-up once finished here. We travel by night, leaving immediately. Expected contact is midday tomorrow. Any questions?"

Barely a second had passed before muffled footsteps landed atop the tunnel above Dalis. Dirt rained down, and then began to sprinkle along the length of the tunnel. The others disappeared out of view, following the footsteps.

Dalis shook the dirt from his hair and turned in pursuit, grateful he had dug a straight path with plenty of headroom. Memories bombarded him from the many countless days spent digging for the old woman as questions raced through his head. *Who were these creatures? Were they really elves? What could the old woman's prophecy possibly be?*

His last image of her flashed vividly into his mind. It was the last thing the old woman had said: *The boy must be saved! That is your mission!*

Her frantic look was seared into his mind's eye. He had never seen her overcome with such hopelessness. They should have had more time. Dalis willed his legs to move faster as he sprinted along the underground trail. There could be no doubt about the boy these creatures hunted. It had to be the same one the old woman mentioned. Elves did not care about humans, nor did the humans even know elves still existed.

As Dalis approached the exit to the tunnel, he slowed, emerging just enough to break the barrier of sight. The wind rustled through the treetops, and the forest was again coated in the blue hue of the crescent moon. The clouds had all but disappeared as Dalis shot a glare at the traitorous sky, listening for the telling footsteps once again.

Seconds turned to minutes, as his ears strained to hear the tiniest hint of activity. Eventually, the moments turned into too much time gone. The tunnel was a straight shot to the river's edge, and he expected to beat them to the crossing, but not by this much. Despite the one elf's sickly appearance, these elves were young and fast. The odds of arriving so far ahead suddenly plummeted. Dalis waited a few more seconds to be sure; maybe a situation had arisen, delaying their progress.

Nothing. The forest was silent.

Dalis took one step outside the entrance, resigned to the fact that precious time was slipping away. The squad had to be advancing at an incredible rate. But then a blinding violet flash broke the skyline, halting him dead in his tracks.

In the far distance, across the river, four tiny silhouettes were illuminated against the dark horizon. Their shadows danced and weaved through the air as another thunderous crack assaulted the night. The image of the flying four burned into Dalis's eyelids. The creatures moved with the same unnatural, icy currents that had broken into the cottage, and that now coursed of their own will through the treetops.

Dalis rested on his knees, pondering on any way to save the boy: a boy he had only moments ago discovered in a prophecy kept hidden from him for the past three years. The old woman's paper rustled in his chest pocket as the wind ruffled his shirt.

"I am sorry, my lady," he whispered.

He withdrew her last written words and began to unfold the charred paper, handling it carefully, peeling back one layer after another until only one folded crease remained. But then he stopped. Something made him look back to the dark horizon where the flash of shocking purple remained like a picture painted in his mind. The old woman's voice echoed again: *The boy must be saved!*

His chin dropped; he was lost as to how to outmaneuver these creatures. He had no idea how to reach the boy before them.

To his bewilderment, he found his fingers working of their own accord, folding the piece of paper back into its original shape. Then they placed the parchment into the protection of his chest pocket again.

Dalis wanted nothing more than to see what could have caused such chaos. The greatest prophet in Elvish history was dead, disposed by an unexplainable attack, delivered by the very ones sworn to protect the prophets against all harm. He couldn't fathom it.

The flickering orange glow from the flames lit up the forest behind him, and he turned to look at the cottage's remains being eaten by the fires. The feeling of helplessness transformed itself immediately. The vigor was unstoppable, uncontrollable, and instant. He knew the feeling was unstable. It was anger: pure, sharp, explosive anger. If he unleashed it, there would be no recourse, no control over what happened next.

Yellow flared in his eyes; soaring across the river in a single bound, he landed at a dead sprint. The rage burned hotter inside, devouring him, fueling him. He had no choice: He would kill those soldiers. Tonight.

Chapter 2
Nine Years Later

"Pay attention!" yelled the short, plump teacher over the ruckus of chairs scraping on the old, wooden floorboards. Her red, frizzled hair appeared orange in the afternoon sun; it bounced wildly as her freckled arms waved to catch the students' attention. "Remember, no classes for three full weeks. The beginning of the Harvest Festival is tomorrow!"

The Harvest Festival was a very special time of year: It marked the end of autumn. And it was especially exciting for the children, because they were all granted time away from their studies to help bring in the town's crops. Mr. Hallings's cornfields were the children's first, and favorite, stop. The farmer grew rows and rows of corn on the western slopes, with stalks that seemed to touch the sky. His fields burst with enough ears to feed the whole town for an entire winter. He boasted that the secret to making his corn the sweetest corn on this side of the river was the way the morning sun struck his fields. Of course, since most of the town never traveled outside the village, no one really knew for sure if it was indeed the sweetest. But the children loved starting the harvest in his fields; there was no denying it was delicious. They would sneak an ear here and there, and Mr. Hallings never cared. He was happy to see their smiling faces. The villagers always had more than enough to carry them through the harsh, rugged winters in the mountains.

Ms. Weely's expansive clover fields were also an impressive sight. Waves of wind rippled through her clover pastures that stretched the width of the valley. It was like a massive lake of emerald green on the eastern side of their town, which they called Cleargar. The waves of wind crashed on the gently sloping banks of her clover fields, which then rose steeply into towering, jagged snow-capped mountains that guarded the north and south sides of the village. The entire town stretched the length of the valley between the two mountains. Within the valley, rolling hills protruded far apart from each other in the otherwise smooth, grassy expanse. Sometimes the townspeople also called Cleargar *The Narrows*, because even though it was wide and spacious, the enormity of the two peaks dwarfed the lush green channel spanning between them. Homes dotted the mountainsides with farms winding down the grain of the valley. And Ms. Weely's secret was also well known: For the most delicious honey, the clover flowers had to be so ripe they were almost jade blue, even if it meant waiting until the very last days of the season before releasing her bees.

The story was the same for all the villagers; each had their own secrets for the perfect crop or service. Storages were filled with apples, honeys, oats, corns, and beans from all across the valley.

But there was another reason why the Harvest Festival was so important: One villager, named Mr. Bodock, harvested a mixture of flowers, roots, and barleys to make something quite extraordinary. Until three years ago, Mr. Bodock was nothing more than a simple pub owner. But that year, something changed. He took the same, simple ingredients, as he had done every year prior to that one, to make his less-than-mediocre brews, but now those simple ingredients were transformed into the most sensational draughts, bubbling with all kinds of flavors. The flavors by themselves were good, but not nearly as interesting as the especially odd effects.

Three autumns ago, upon drinking one of Mr. Bodock's master creations, partakers found themselves glowing, each a different color of the rainbow. The townspeople also found they could change their color simply by thinking different thoughts. The drinkery had been filled with happy, lit-up customers bobbing with riotous approval into the early hours of morning. Mr. Bodock's dirty old pub, with its caved-in roof and its awful food, transformed that autumn into the most spectacular place in the valley. People unearthed their stores of extra oats and beans for trade, and they came in droves until the brew was all gone. That first year, the stock only lasted for that one night. But of course it was only Mr. Bodock's very first year and very first batch. The town chattered for the rest of the year in anticipation of the next season, and the next year the township was not disappointed: Mr. Bodock's line of brews tripled.

It is worth noting: Two of the townsfolk made annual trips down the mountainside to barter and to exchange news every year, but they seldom came back with more than a few rare foreign trinkets and moderate material for gossip. But that next year, the two townsfolk returned with something the village had not seen in a generation: Travelers.

The wild stories of their small mountain village had reached a party of three older gentlemen and a younger stout boy, all of whom arrived with skeptical grins, talking in whispers and snickering. During usual times, the town didn't particularly like visitors. They brought unnecessary trouble. Farm tools would mysteriously go missing, and bartered items would, more often than not, disintegrate into broken heaps soon after the foreigners departed. However, the Cleargar folk were not keen on listening to foreigners badger and poke at what all the town had fiercely come to love in just one year. So the four travelers wagered a handsome deer pouch, filled with rare rocks and glistening stones, betting that every last story about the magical brews was rubbish. If the travelers were right, they would get to have a free wagon made by Mr. Bullberry, the township's wood carver, and the townsfolk agreed to load it full of anything the travelers desired from the village storages.

The travelers readily agreed, with wide toothless grins. But that second year of the mysterious magical brews, the effects went far beyond emitting the simple colors of the rainbow. A couple of batches in particular had extraordinary effects, with tiny old Miss Hankle probably the most famous example. The old woman, of a rather great age, lifted a table of eight grown, full-bearded men, all piled and wrestling atop it—four of them, of course, being the travelers, who were fighting to keep their pouch of stones. The sight was still the topic of many late-night conversations, when gossip and rumors exhausted themselves. Mr. Bodock and his pub had since become something of a local legend, and a landmark for travelers.

After that second year, which featured the heroics of old maid Hankle, Mr. Bodock launched the very first Harvest Festival, specially designed to showcase his newest brew creations. And while everyone knew Mr. Hallings's secret to sweet corn, and Ms. Weely's clever ways to produce unrivaled, perfectly floral honey, not a single person had uncovered Mr. Bodock's mysterious trickery.

"Your homework, when you return," said the teacher, still waving her arms frantically to get the children's attention, "is one full written parchment, neatly scrolled, about your favorite brew."

"Yes ma'am!" rang out the children's scattered voices.

Students hurried to stuff their books, papers, and quills into small sackcloth bags and cinched them tight, running for the door as they heaved the bags onto their backs. But they didn't make it far; a boy at the back tripped over a chair and stumbled. Throwing a hand out to brace himself, he fell into the backs of his classmates, and the mob of students, all dressed in drab gray school robes, surged forward. They piled into each other, flooding under the cracked, granite archway crafted by the local stonemason, Mr. Friar. Then they spilled into the sprawling schoolyard, scrambling to keep their feet.

"My goodness! Students!" yelled the teacher over the ruckus, appearing under the shade of the gray stone overhang just a moment after the last student had escaped into the blue-skied afternoon. With her face buried in a colorful piece of parchment, the teacher remained oblivious to the tumult until the huge bell in front of the school echoed with a deep thud. She looked up, startled to see students toppling into it.

"Remember," the teacher screamed, trying to ignore the mayhem of children running into each other, "I forgot! The festival starts tonight!"

Seeing the giant mess of flailing arms and legs piling up, she couldn't pretend not to notice any longer.

"How many times must I say to be mindful of the bell?" she bellowed over the noise, scrunching up her face and clucking disapprovingly. Her rosy cheeks, pale skin, and fat round nose gave off a rather piggish appearance, which sometimes opened the door to unsavory remarks, especially when given advice to *be wary of the bell.* The children were all quite aware of the bell's location, but somehow two things always managed to happen: Last-minute announcements after being dismissed, and ensuing collisions with the poorly positioned bell. The children furthest away nursed bumps on their heads and bruises on their elbows. Then a boy's voice suddenly carried a bit further back to the schoolhouse than he would have liked.

"That's quite enough of that," replied the teacher over the mass. "Now settle down!"

She glared at the boy with an especially large, tawny brown eye. He smiled nervously. The teacher's look was ill-timed, though, as it somewhat enhanced the boy's unsavory remark and caused a few snickers. The children tried their best to stifle giggles as the protruding eye roamed, looking for those who thought it was funny.

After a moment of fruitless searching, she blinked both eyes and returned to her usual buoyancy.

"Mr. Bodock has graciously decided to open his pubbery one full week sooner than usual for the second straight Cleargar Harvest Festival." She cupped one hand around her mouth in secrecy. "And I heard he has three new brews this year."

Her eyes sparkled as the children chattered excitedly.

"It also says here," she continued, "that the New Original Brew recipe is supposed to make you glow all over!" She clapped frantically and gave a quick hop in place. "And rumor has it the glow should last the entire walk home, even if you live as far away as Broomstead Hills." She winked at a little girl who jumped excitedly while two boys slapped hands.

"We'll be able to see ourselves on the way home this year!" one of the boys' voices rang out.

"Will you be there, Miss Flubber?" asked a girl's voice. "Tonight?"

"If I'm not, send the township for me!" she exclaimed. "I wouldn't miss a pint of my favorite Butterfly Honey Drub for anything!"

"We love the Honey Drub!" screamed a group of giggling girls. "It's my favorite!" squealed another.

The kids began to disperse, running excitedly in all directions towards their various family farms that snaked along the mammoth valley. Every home across Cleargar featured bright blue forget-me-nots, proudly planted above the main doorways; the town had decided to make the flower its flagship, guiding travelers to their increasingly famous village of brews. Their attitude towards travelers was definitely changing: Foreigners brought more interesting news from further away, every year, and the goods they bartered were no longer anything to scoff at.

Enthusiastic comments rang out amidst the retreating clatter, such as, "I can't wait to try the new ones tonight." But once the teacher disappeared back inside, it was: "Uck! The Honey Drub is much too sweet. Old man Bodock should toss that whole recipe."

"He should not!" replied a girl fiercely. "It's perfect! And you can run super-fast after only one pint."

"Good night!" replied the tall lanky boy, who was guilty of the offending comment. He held his large boney arms up in submission, while his thin black hair swayed with every movement. His hooked nose protruded with a certain vulture-like quality, but the effect was softened by his nervous smile and olive skin.

“You win,” he said, laughing nervously. “Does that mean you’ll be in the race, Mara?” His smile widened; clearly he was happy to gain her attention. “Everyone knows it works better on girls. Annalin won last year, you remember?”

Mara’s cheeks blushed red, and the fierce girl-warrior disappeared behind innocent blonde curls and big, blue, blinking eyes.

The boy’s smile widened in relief. He puffed out his chest and attempted to say something else, but suddenly deflated into squirming fits of laughter. His fixation on the girl had left him unaware of the stealthy, darting movements behind him.

A boy appeared sneakily out of the departing mass, latched onto his ribs, and began tickling him ruthlessly.

“Why do you care, Meric?” demanded the stealthy boy, refusing to cease the onslaught. “You said you’d be my partner for the Hoppy Brew tryouts. You aren’t abandoning me, are you? I need your big, gangly legs.”

At this Meric released a high-pitched scream and yelled at the boy to stop between fits of laughter.

“I... MEAN... IT!” he cried, getting a good breath. Twisting and wriggling away, he turned with flustered fists towards the unknown assailant.

The new boy had thick, fire-orange hair, which stood on end, spiked like an untrimmed lawn growing in every direction. Reaching an arm around Meric’s neck, he smiled from ear to ear. He was lean, with a freckled face bronzed from the late summer sun, and although he was a full head shorter than Meric, his piercing green eyes glistened confidently. He was thoroughly pleased with himself at foiling Meric’s meeting with the girl.

"The races are at the same time tomorrow, you see," continued the boy with the fire-orange hair, "and you cannot possibly be in both races at once." He shook his head, like a parent correcting a child for lack of planning.

The girl giggled and quickly stepped away from the two, running to rejoin the other girls.

"Perfect, Ector!" cried Meric, his long stringy hair dancing all over the place. "You scared her away! Do you know how long it took me to introduce myself properly?"

Ector hesitated. "Er, well, unless I'm mistaken, that remains unaccomplished."

"Thanks to you!" Meric bleated, throwing his hands out towards the fleeing Mara.

"No thanks necessary," Ector replied, feigning modesty. "I could tell you were stunned by her viciousness. I was, too."

Meric fumed, his hazel eyes blackening with anger.

Ector shrugged and smiled. "You have to admit, old mate, she did rather look like a snake there, in the beginning, when she cried like that." His eyes sparkled like brilliant jasper-fern stones in the afternoon sun, as he searched for a sliver of agreement. "The Butterfly Honey Drub *is* much too sweet, like you said." Ector placed his hands high on his hips as Miss Flubber would have done. "By the way, I'm quite sure Mara knows who you are. We've all gone to school together since we could walk."

"That's not the point," Meric replied, angrily raising a finger.

"Right you are," Ector interrupted, mirroring Meric's posture with an equally forceful finger. "The point is you were dangerously close to risking our second straight title as the Harvest Festival's Top Hoppers."

"Why can't we try something new this year?" Meric whined, dropping his large head and slim shoulders, his eyes returning to their usual golden-speckled hazel. He had tried backing out all year, but to no avail.

"Because," Ector urged, flexing his fist, "I've heard rumors. Some boys from Bellington are attending this year. They want to steal our title!"

"Where did you hear that?" Meric asked, lifting his head, annoyed. He and Ector were both twelve, but different in almost every other way. Ector was short, lively, and ready for adventure. His thick, unruly, sunset-orange hair was as vibrant as his emerald-green eyes. His appearance contrasted starkly with Meric's tall, lanky build; the dull brown of Meric's hair and his hazelnut eyes seemed to absorb light rather than reflect it. When Ector charged forward, Meric was right there to drag his extra large feet through the mud in futile resistance. Ector knew it was always only a matter of time before Meric eventually gave in.

"I did hear it!" replied Ector. "And the competition has some rather thick legs, if you know what I mean."

"That's ridiculous," Meric responded, growing more annoyed. "You can't have heard anything. You've been in the fields for almost a full month, every day after school. Old man Bodock made you start harvesting early so he could get his brews cooking for the festival."

Meric lumbered away towards the schoolhouse, veering off to the side and around the back. "And you haven't been over to the farm in two whole weeks," he added, over his shoulder.

"So you tried to trade me in for a girl?" Ector asked, astonished. "Some mate! Look, I hear stuff in the fields as people walk past. Word of old man Bodock's brews is spreading like pollen. I heard a few folks might even travel all the way in from Bueford, from across the river!"

Meric shook his head, unimpressed by the news. "The pollen is spreading into your ears, mate. Even old man Bodock doesn't remember the last time he saw travelers from across the river."

Ector made a disgusted noise. "And to think, I was on the verge of teaching you how to properly introduce yourself. Makes me glad I didn't."

"I know how to properly introduce myself!" roared Meric, turning and launching himself at Ector. He looked like a long stick jumping into a ball of fire, but instead of being consumed in flames, the stick tackled the flame to the ground.

"I've been carefully planning that moment since last harvest season!" Meric cried, rolling with Ector in the long, golden hay-grass alongside the dirt road. Meric finally rose to his feet with Ector's bright carrot head tightly secured under his armpit.

"Say fudd-muddle-fickles!" Meric panted, shaking the hair away from his eyes.

"Fudd-muddle-*stickles*!" Ector managed with a blue face, snatching a stick from the ground and stabbing Meric's rear.

"Ow!" Meric released Ector's head and shot straight up into the air. "Hey, that's not fair!"

Ector leaned on his knees for a moment, letting the blue ebb away as Meric waddled around, grabbing his hind parts. Gathering himself into a dignified position, Ector shook the broken stick, which now hung only by a thin thread of bark, at Meric.

"Well, I hope you've learned your lesson," Ector coughed, still breathless.

"Yeah, I learned my lesson alright," Meric shot back. "I'll be at the Honey Drub starting line tomorrow!"

"No! Everybody knows it only works on girls. Besides, any girl that can turn from a snake to a flower that quickly is dangerous." Ector paused and smacked himself on the forehead. "No, I forgot! The old man said to pick five bushels of yellow forest flowers today! He needs them for one last brew he's finishing up." Ector kicked the tall hay-grass. "Can you help me?"

"Sorry, mate." Meric looked to his sore bum and then back, rubbing it tenderly.

Ector dropped his shoulders. "Really?"

"Yes, really. Pappy says I need to clean the horse shed before the sun disappears today."

"Great," Ector mumbled, snatching a few strands of the grass blowing around him.

"Well, last time I tried to help," Meric continued, "old man Bodock ran into the fields, waving and roaring like a wild animal." He flapped his arms, imitating the old man.

Ector looked towards the far hills and saw the last of his classmates running into their homes.

"Yeah, he's odd sometimes, especially with those recipes. He keeps them locked away good and tight, wants everything done the same way every year. You know, between you and me," Ector continued, watching everyone disappear, "I don't think old man Bodock knows exactly how he does it."

"How he makes the brews, you mean?" Meric asked.

"Yeah. I mean, ever since I picked his crop that first year, he's kept everything the same: He cleans the big oak barrels, seven swipes around for each barrel, same direction. And he won't let anyone clean them except his wife. He walks back and forth behind the bar two times before opening the front doors, just like he did that first season."

Ector paused for a moment, quietly considering the old man's bizarre behavior.

"The worst part though," he continued, "is that he won't let anyone help me with the harvest. That first year was manageable, but now that the brews have grown every year, it's all I can do just to get the cursed fields harvested without missing half the school year! I wish he hadn't used me to pick his crop that first season." He shook his head, annoyed.

"Yeah, that's bad luck, mate," Meric replied.

"Can you at least come to the pub tonight after you're done?" Ector pleaded.

"Maybe, I'll have to ask the Pap."

"Don't fool around!" Ector added, pointing a stern finger. "We can get a few practice rounds done tonight. The Bellington boys probably won't arrive until tomorrow. We'll have the advantage."

"Alright, alright." Meric turned once again towards the distant barn behind the school. "I'll meet you at the pub just after dusk."

He jogged towards the big barn towering in the distance behind the school, but after a few paces he stopped.

"Hey, look there!" He pointed to the edge of the forest that crept along the base of the northern slope, but the late afternoon sun was already on its downward descent, diving towards the treetops.

Ector shielded his eyes. "What is it?"

He followed Meric's finger pointing towards the forest jutting halfway out into the valley.

"Just inside the forest," Meric hollered back. "There's a patch of yellow flowers."

Ector squinted harder, this time focusing on the ground until faint shimmers of yellow reflecting in the afternoon light finally caught his eye. They sparkled like stars against the dark evergreen forest bed.

"See, one bushel of flowers down!" Meric yelled over his shoulder. "And *you* are welcome!"

"Right," Ector mumbled, dragging his feet towards the forest line.

Cool air gusted out of the forest, and the warmth of autumn vanished instantly as he crossed the threshold into the mountainous shadows. The forest was very different from the dusty fields that made his eyes water and his throat itch. The air was crisp and cool, and he drank it in deeply. Every breath was wholesome and easy.

Most of the forest towered with sharp pine trees. But an enormous fallen pinewood caught his eye as he surveyed the forest for signs of movement. The downed reddish-wood giant was now covered in moss, and a wide beam of sunlight cut through where it used to stand. The surrounding shadows appeared even darker next to the majestic rays slicing into the forest. Ector squinted, trying to gaze into the shadows stretching up the draws and into the saddles. But only a few scattered purple vines growing up the trunks jumped out in the otherwise looming, monstrous landscape.

Ector stepped with care, walking between low branches and avoiding dead limbs. Even though the wind rustled through the canopy, he tried not to add extra noise; a single twig snap seemed likely to echo forever in here. He danced to the patch of yellow flowers shimmering just on the edge of the sunbeam. Clearing the last spindly branches that threatened to tear his clothes, he studied the bed; it flowered barely to the thickness of his boot sole and was so dense that the plant looked more like a yellow moss than a flower.

Ector decided on brute force. He wrestled with the first handful, but its roots had no desire to leave the ground. Twisting and heaving, he threw his legs into the haul, and the quick release sent him stumbling backwards. To his disappointment, he watched the war-torn flowers and bent stems fleeing in the wind. Old man Bodock specifically ordered undamaged flowers, and absolutely no missing petals. Ector cursed, tossing the rest of the useless flowers into the breeze. He needed five whole bushels of these weeds.

By the time he had finished his first bushel the sun was considerably lower. Through sheer luck, he had found a sharp stone, useful for hacking at the base of the dense plant, but it took him the entire first bale to figure out that they released more easily when cut near the roots.

Now on his second bushel, working his way around the base of the tree, he caught a glimpse of two more yellow patches a little deeper inside the forest. His eyes had adjusted to the intense contrast of bright sunlight surrounded by dark shadows, and he felt a burst of excitement; he might just finish before sundown. He made quick work of the third patch, sawing all the yellow flowers and pear-shaped leaves as close to the ground as possible. The leaves blew away in the wind and he kept what was left: A beautifully yellow, intact half-bushel ready to be tied with the others.

Satisfied, he whistled while trekking to the next two patches. But halfway there, the wind gusted again, this time downright frigid. The sparse, twinkling gold aspen leaves fluttered, straining to be free of their white branches.

Ector retreated back to the two harvested bushels and removed his school robes, wrapping it around them just as some of the precious petals threatened to blow loose. Gray clouds began to form above the enormous canopy hole, blocking out the sun. Ector watched as the clouds began to pour through the opening and fill the forest like a levitating fog. The shadows turned even chillier. Ector pinned each corner of his robes on the ground with a small stone to keep the wind out, and rushed back to collect the final patches.

He immediately began hacking at the flat, dandelion-like blossoms, swinging relentlessly as the first flakes drifted gently onto his bare neck. He looked at the sky again. An entire blanket had now rolled into place above him.

He made quick work of the large patches and wrapped them together with a vine creeping from the forest floor. Dashing back to stack the two new bushels neatly alongside the others, he draped the robe back into place just before the wind intensified, pulsing erratically.

This time, Ector turned and ran. Twilight was settling throughout the forest, and a shimmer of yellow flickered in the corner of his eye as he hauled the last two away. Sprinting to three perfectly formed patches growing almost on top of each other, he threw himself into a squat and rested against a tree, carving once again, but faster this time, anxious to be done.

Thoughts of a second straight Hoppy Brew Championship descended upon him, and he savored the familiar place in his mind. Since he worked alone most of the time, he went there often. But the sweet indulge was abruptly interrupted as the snowflakes began falling in droves. Throwing an annoyed look at the sky, Ector picked up the pace, and it only took a few minutes before the last bushel sat, tied and bulging.

He stood and stretched his arms, but then suddenly froze: There were footprints in the snow. Someone had walked past.

Ector peered around the large tree trunk and followed the line of fresh tracks leading straight to his four bushels, still sitting protected under his snow-covered robes. He stepped away from the tree for a better view. His blood turned cold; a hooded man, cloaked in black down to his boots, stood hovering over the haul. Covered in the recesses of his hood, his head moved ever so slightly as he studied the harvested flowers.

Ector retreated swiftly behind the protection of the tree, fear clamping down on him. The snow was cold, but something about the man sent unnatural chills through his body. He couldn't stop the uncontrollable shivers that followed. He wasn't sure what the man wanted, but picking another five bushels from scratch wasn't an option. The snow was only going to get worse. He couldn't stay out here much longer. Ector took a deep breath, trying to calm the shivers, and even though it didn't work, he mustered the tiniest shred of courage to step out from behind the tree again. He prepared as best he could to holler at the stranger, but the instant he opened his mouth, his voice caught: The man was gone.

Ector surveyed the forest in both directions, but nothing stirred; nothing except the rustling of snowy branches. Lifting his head and standing on the tips of his toes, he looked for more footprints. But even the initial faint tracks were now buried under the pouring snow, no longer distinguishable between the ruts and foliage distorting the uneven ground. There was nothing.

Ector cautiously approached his school robes, which now looked like a tiny, white hill. Not a single footprint dented the snow in any direction anymore, except his own.

Another gust burst through the forest, causing the falling snow to spiral up into several swirling vortexes that dropped from the canopy all at once.

Ector dropped to one knee, bundled all five bushels into his arms, and wrapped his robes tightly around them. A bare patch of ground was left in stark contrast to the completely white forest as he stood. The strange tingling began to creep up Ector's spine again and something inside told him to run! Hugging the bushels tighter, he sprinted for the forest's edge; the unease felt like eyes watching him.

The dead limbs and twigs he had been so careful to avoid on his way in snapped all around him, while dried leaves crunched and sloshed beneath his churning feet. The stiff pine needles pushed through his clothes, sticking into his bare arms.

Breaking through the last row of dense pines, Ector immediately felt the warmth of autumn hit him full in the face. There was no trace of snow whatsoever. The sight of the valley basking in fall colors and sunshine slowed him to an uncertain jog. He turned back to the forest, blinking, wondering if it was real. Icicles had already formed on the branches along the edge, which rained with melted snow. All evidence of the frosty attack retreated before his eyes, leaving the tree bark sopping and the purple vines and lush evergreens of the forest returning by the passing second. Ector looked to the sky, searching for the source of the storm, but not even the tiniest hint of a gloomy cloud remained. The sun lightly kissed the treetops, shining just as radiantly as before. It wasn't twilight at all; the last sign of the storm hung for a moment longer just under the canopy, in the form of a misty fog, but it, too, was quickly dissipating.

Ector checked his haul to make sure the flowers had survived the flight. A few of the petals danced to the ground. He would take however many lashings the old man wanted to dish out, because no amount of pain could make him go back into that forest. He shook the melted snow from his hair and scanned the tree line one last time for the mysterious man. The forest continued to drip, but nothing moved.

Then the tingling shot like a fountain through his spine. Ector's reflexes instinctively tightened his grip on the bushels, causing even more petals to flutter to the grass. But it didn't matter. Sprinting the entire mile back to the pubbery, he didn't look back even once.

Chapter 3
Shadowy Strangers

"A funny feller, dressed in black, tore up me flowers?" asked old man Bodock, his eyebrows raised. His fat, balding head and scrunched forehead glistened with sweat under the booming fireworks that lit up the sky through the hole in the backroom of the pub. The old man had refused to fix the roof because of '*how many grains it would cost for that thief of a repairman, Donnells.*'

Customers had already begun to arrive in hordes, and the ruckus of the festival suddenly spilled into the narrow backroom. The old man gave a high-pitched laugh as he tried to herd the people back outside. Once the last person had crossed the threshold, he slammed the door and latched it to prevent another interruption.

"No!" cried Ector, exasperated. He'd told old man Bodock twice already what had happened in the forest, and was now undertaking his third attempt. The old man wasn't interested in hearing it, though. The tattered bushels spoke louder than anything Ector could say; the flowers hadn't survived the flight back to the pub and now sat atop the table, wilting and mostly bare.

Ector jumped back against the wall as Mrs. Bodock rolled two huge oak barrels toward the door and out to the guests. One label read "Grasshopper Ale" and the other, "Butterfly Honey Drub".

"Never mind," said Ector, turning to leave.

"You're not getting off that easy!" threatened the old man, wagging a fat finger. "I said I needed five of those bushels, and I got maybe one and a half! How am I supposed to make me special brew with this? The whole batch is rotten!"

He slammed his fist into the bushels, all of which rested on a long wooden bench bolted to the wall; the remaining petals exploded into the air on impact. Ector had a temper to match his fiery hair, and it had got him into trouble on several occasions. He felt his skin getting hot.

"Just because you live here," roared the old man, building up a head of steam, "you think you can do what you want? Ignoring me when you feel like it?"

Ector thought back to his earliest memories of living with the pub owner. The happy memories were few and far between, and actually didn't involve the old man at all.

"And now you're off in la-la land, not even listening to a word I'm saying!" hollered the old man, slamming his fist down on the table again. But it was one assault too many on the rickety bench. The last two rusted bolts gave way and the table came crashing to the ground, followed quickly by the old man himself.

At the sound of the commotion, a massive, hairy dog with drooling jowls barreled into the room. His wagging tail sent pots and pans crashing throughout the kitchen as he ran excitedly to Ector, barking thunderously. A large white paw, roughly the size of a small bear's, stepped squarely on the old man's face.

"Blast that animal!" cursed the old man under the strain of its weight. Bathing Ector in affectionate slobber, the dog moved to the side, leaving a muddy paw print smeared across the old man's cheek. Bodock rolled from side-to-side, flailing on the floor like a capsized turtle.

"That's it! Out!" he screamed, finally finding his knees. "I ought to use that furry menace in one of me brews! OUT, Rahms!"

Just as the dog turned to leave, a rumbling gurgled in Rahms's stomach. The animal locked eyes with the old man for a brief second; the old man scowled in reply. Staring stupidly, Rahms lifted his tail and released a foul wind in the old man's face.

"Curse that dog!" spat the old man, trying to wave the smell away from his nose.

"Come on, Rahms," said Ector, grabbing the dog by his harness. He left old man Bodock coughing, gasping for air and beginning to turn a sickly yellow. The dog's tail whapped the old man in the face as they exited out back.

"I'm not finished with you yet!" came old man Bodock's distant voice as Ector let the door slam shut.

Ector fought to hold his tongue. He released a slow deep breath, and gave Rahms an appreciative scratch behind the ear for saving him. Rahms had been with Ector for as long as Ector could remember. Before the old man had *allowed* Ector to have a room inside the pub, Ector had been forced to sleep in the shed located out back towards the base of the mountains. Ector thought back to those many cold winter nights when Rahms would sleep curled around him. He didn't have to think that far back because, even now, Ector preferred the dog's warmth in the shed to sleeping in the shabby old closet in the kitchen. Ector wasn't sure what had happened to his parents, but one thing was for sure: old man Bodock certainly wasn't his father.

As Mrs. Bodock told it, Ector arrived one summer's night on their doorstep, just a toddler. He was carried on a tiny wooden sled latched behind Rahms. Mrs. Bodock had heard a scratching at their front door in the middle of the night and found the huge cinnamon-spotted dog, then a much younger Rahms, sopping wet. Ector was fast asleep on the sled, nearly frozen to the bone, despite the summer's warmth.

The Bodocks, in all their generosity, had straightaway put Ector in the dank shed out back. It had originally been designed as a lodge for travelers, so it could have been worse, but even if travelers weren't something of a rarity in these parts, no one would have willingly stayed there. There was no reason for people to pass through a valley located this high in the mountains, and the Bodocks knew it, so they didn't bother keeping the guest lodge in good condition.

As Ector had gotten older, he'd made small improvements to the old shed, eventually turning it into what it was today: The best room on the old man's lot. The now spacious shack featured a plush, heaped pile of hay-grass for a bed in the corner, plumped and restocked every few nights; a stall for Rahms, fitted with a water pail; three meat-drying racks positioned to absorb the streaming morning sunbeams on one side, and the afternoon rays on the other wall from a window carved out by Ector; and a sturdy, self-made stool and long table for wood-crafting, stone-carving, and scroll-writing projects to keep him busy when he wasn't harvesting. If old man Bodock ever cared to pay Ector a visit, he probably would have confiscated the renovated shack on the spot. But luckily the old man had resigned himself to thinking nothing in the world could salvage the once-dilapidated hut, especially now that Ector had lived in it.

The Bodocks previously tried to keep the dog chained up on the back side of the pub, but Rahms refused. It was a game to him; he would wait until the old man's eyes were off him, then break free and take flight to the shed at the first chance. It infuriated the old man to no end. No matter what he tried, the dog always broke free of the leash the moment the old man disappeared. It was never a mystery where Rahms had gone, though. Old man Bodock would kick in the door to the shed, back when he did still visit, to find Rahms at Ector's side. Finally, the old man had let the dog stay in the shed and became resigned to simply complaining about it at every chance.

"Ector!" rang out a voice from the laughing crowd, which had gathered outside the pub. Ector suddenly realized he had been lost in his thoughts, rooted just a few paces outside the pub for who knew how long. A slight smirk spread across his face as he realized the old man hadn't even bothered trying to chase him down.

It was dark now, but the outside was well lit with several poles as tall as the houses, topped with bright fires in iron baskets. The night was about to begin! Ector could see a tall, lanky arm waving to him.

"Good boy," said Ector, ruffling Rahms's cheeks. He gave the dog a hug around the neck. "Go have fun in the woods! I'll bring some Grasshopper Ale to the shed tonight, eh?"

The dog barked his approval, gave Ector one last lick, and ran towards the forest at a full sprint.

"Ector!" came the voice again, louder this time. "I've been looking for you everywhere. Where have you been?"

"I've been getting an earful from old man Bodock about those forest flowers," Ector replied, walking over to Meric and proceeding to tell him the whole story of the stranger and the bizarre weather.

"It was snowing?" Meric eyed Ector with an uncertain look. "Inside the forest?"

"Yes!" Ector exclaimed, thankful somebody finally believed him.

"Well, there's your first problem, mate: You need to think of a better story." Meric laughed. "Everyone knows it never snows inside the forest; the canopy is so thick nothing ever gets through."

"You're not listening!" Ector replied, immediately boiling over. "I know it never snows in the forest! What I'm saying is the storm formed underneath the trees. I've never seen anything like it!"

"I don't know. I've never even heard of anything like that happening." Meric held his hands up defensively at seeing Ector's frustrated face. "Look, I'm not saying I don't believe you," he continued. "I'm just saying, if I hated you to begin with," he nodded towards the back of the pub where old man Bodock's muffled voice could still be heard carrying on about the broken table, "then this wouldn't be something that changed my mind."

"Well, if he hadn't slammed his fist into the bushels and destroyed every last flower!" roared Ector in reply, more to the back of the pub than to Meric. He took a deep breath and lowered his voice to a normal level. "Then, I'd tell you to go poke your head in there, and see that I know very well how to pick forest flowers."

He took another deep breath, angry at having to constantly defend himself.

"And another thing," he added, unable to stem the flow of raging thoughts. "Why would I run all the way back here after spending three hours collecting all of them, just to have them ruined while running back for no reason? I wouldn't have wasted all that time picking a bunch of shoddy stems just to make up a story like that. I would have simply said I couldn't find any, taken the usual lecture and beatings for being lazy, and gone on with my merry night!"

"Alright, alright," said Meric, trying to calm Ector down. "I believe you. All I'm saying is that a snowstorm inside the forest, a strange traveler who leaves no footprints in the snow, and then it all melts before anyone else in the entire valley notices? You have to admit; any one of those would be pretty hard to believe, and they all happened in the same story. You show up with a bunch of stems instead of flowers, and that's how you explained it to the old man?" He shook his head. "Personally, I would have lied. I probably would have gone with a bunch of flower mites ate them or something."

"Forget it." Ector shook his head. Why should he have to waste his energy inventing a dull lie when something bizarre had actually happened?

"Look, on a different note, you were right," continued Meric, pointing a thumb back to the crowds. "I've been asking around all evening, and I can't find anyone from Bellington. We've got the edge on them. You ready for a round of Grasshopper Ale?"

"Am I ever," replied Ector, glad to be finished recounting the story. "Have any other travelers arrived yet?"

"You better believe it!" cried Meric. "A crowd from Bueford has already arrived." He gave a quick glance over his shoulder and lowered his voice. "And the girls are very pretty!"

"Oh-ho!" Ector replied. "What about all that time you spent prepping yourself for Mara?"

Meric's back hunched as he looked over his other shoulder. "She's been laughing and making friends all night with that boy, Fenodor. You remember him? He's the tall one with long, wavy black hair and a big chest. She can't seem to get enough of him. He left school last year to start his own little farm on the back part of his father's oat fields. The great oaf started growing red berries, but he planted the wrong ones and nearly poisoned himself!" Meric scoffed and shook his head. "Now that he's gone from school, though, all the girls can't seem to stay away from him."

"Cheer up, mate." Ector clapped him on the shoulder. "If he likes poisonous things, he'll get a taste of Mara's venom soon enough."

Meric shot him a sideways glance, clearly not agreeing with the sentiment. But Ector's smile widened.

As the boys made their way over to the brew stands, strange faces hovered on the outskirts of the crowd, watching the festivities. Ector was accustomed to seeing leery travelers after the last two years; people would travel in for the first time, wondering if the stories were true, and then just wait to see what happened once the barrels were tapped.

"Two pints of Grasshopper Ale," yelled Ector over the noise, slapping down two tiny pouches of grains as Meric searched frantically to find his stores. The two had agreed last year: The first one to buy the first rounds at the beginning of every year got to pick the first event for the year. A wide, brimming smile spread across Ector's face under the light of several more fireworks exploding overhead.

"Looks like another year at the Hoppy Brew tryouts!" yelled Ector, over the clamor and clapping. "You buy the next round!"

Meric cursed loudly, clearly having clung secretly to one last-ditch effort for backing out of the tryouts.

"You should be thankful when someone buys you something," Ector continued, smiling victoriously. "Especially a gift as delicious as this!"

He raised his pint in a toast, and then took a deep draught of the golden, fizzy drink with yellow foam. It tasted like sweet berries and tickled his nose. The wonderfully crisp, light liquid hit his stomach, and immediately he began to feel lighter. He bounced effortlessly from side to side, hanging a little longer in the air with each hop.

"Oh, the batch is good this year!" Ector exclaimed. "Let's see what those gangly legs can do." He pointed to Meric and lifted his mug in another toast. Meric looked down into his glass, and it only took a second for all signs of dejection to disappear as he, too, took a deep swig.

"I'll bet you can't clear one of those fire poles!" Ector dared, still bouncing lightly from foot to foot.

"I'll bet I can," Meric retorted with growing confidence. "What's the wager; the first event?"

"Absolutely not," Ector replied, not falling for the quick-tongued trickery. "I don't know why you still want to do that silly Butterfly Honey Drub sprint. You were made to be a Hoppy Brew champion!"

Meric accepted the compliment with a nod, bowing his legs out to the side and recoiling for a leap. His leggings hiked halfway up his shins, and his rear was almost touching the ground before he unleashed a ferocious jump. The flames atop a lit pole licked his flailing legs as he flew past with screams of delight. He toppled to the ground several seconds later, but quickly rolled to his feet, regaining his balance. The crowds clapped and roared with approval. Ector laughed and applauded with the rest, feeling better about their chances tomorrow against the rumored Bellington boys. He and Meric would show the competition they had no business competing against them.

Meric was bathing in the applause with bows and excited waves, when suddenly something caught Ector's eye: A dark figure moved slowly in the dim, flickering light behind Meric. Normally, such a sight wouldn't have drawn Ector's attention, but the man was clearly watching Meric with a strange sort of interest. The flames from the nearest fire pole leapt a little brighter, just enough for Ector to see a black hood, disguising a very familiar-looking silhouette. The man's neck craned forward, just like the stranger he had seen in the forest.

Ector wanted a better look. He stopped his idle bouncing and gave a leap that carried him several paces from the brew stands. The man was definitely watching Meric. Ector tried to dismiss the anxious prickling dancing up his spine; after all, the extraordinary leap had left nearly everyone staring spellbound at Meric. But then he saw the stranger's hand was clasping a very sturdy-looking metal object. The man's cloak obscured what it was attached to, but the dark outline of the long, metal handle in his clutches looked exactly like the hilt of a sword.

"Meric!" Ector shouted. But even the people closest to Ector couldn't hear his yell; he sounded like everyone else cheering Meric's name. Then Mara appeared; she grabbed Meric's hand out of nowhere, and they both began laughing.

Perfect! Now I don't have a chance in the world!

"Meric!" he shouted again, straining to make his voice heard.

The dark figure continued to move slowly towards Meric, and Ector felt the same fear overcome him that had seized him in the forest. He tried to calm his racing mind, searching for any other possible reason for the stranger's behavior, but as he looked around, not even the wariest of travelers could resist the temptation to try a pint. The brew stand was packed and growing larger by the second. More and more people began to pop out of the night, glowing brilliantly with every shade imaginable as they bought pints of the Original Brew. Everyone was captivated by the magic of the drinks. All except for this stranger, who had eyes only for Meric.

From behind the makeshift counter, Mrs. Bodock called out to the masses of people crowding closer. Her husky voice was so loud, Ector found himself distracted by the announcement.

"If this is your first time, we recommend the Original Brew, the one that started it all!"

She fielded a few more questions out of Ector's earshot before yelling again.

"What you see here is what we have tonight! We should have the full line available tomorrow!"

Ector couldn't suppress the worry any longer as he fought to bring his undivided attention back to the stranger; if the previous year was any indication of what to expect, all the foreigners who witnessed this sight for the first time would either join in or depart immediately. There was no middle ground. And there was certainly no reason for a stranger to be that interested in Meric, when everyone could experience the same thing for the price of a small pouch filled with beans.

Ector had seen enough. He ran towards Meric, but at the first step, the brew's altering effects sent him almost flying through the air. He tried to drag his feet a few paces in front of Meric, but he was moving too fast. He skidded, trying to dig his feet into the dirt and slow his momentum, but the force was still too much. A cloud of dirt blossomed into the air as Ector knocked both Mara and Meric to the ground, along with everyone else close by.

Fenodor rushed to the scene. "Are you alright, Mara?" The brute helped her stand as Ector was forced to endure Mara's huffing and puffing about how dirty her blue dress was.

Ector finally managed to clasp on to the ground with spread arms and legs to stop from bouncing away. He remained latched like a spider to the grass, making sure he had control before daring to move again. He lifted his head in search of the hooded man, but the stranger was nowhere in sight.

Ector heard gasps from the crowd. He rolled onto his back and scanned the perimeter, looking for signs of the man. Still he found nothing. There were just a bunch of fingers pointing at the commotion: the commotion he had caused. The crowd began to separate as a voice cut through the night.

"What's all the fuss?" came a very familiar, yet very unwelcome bellow. Ector cringed, knowing old man Bodock would not be happy to see him like this.

He grabbed at Meric's shirt, trying to stand as they both struggled to regain their feet. "Meric, come on, we have to get out of here!"

An awkward silence fell across the crowd; Ector lifted his eyes to see the big, beefy man grinning with crossed arms.

"I might have known. I have just the thing for you two."

After being dragged inside the pub and up the stairs, the boys stumbled into a newly added guest room on the second floor at the end of the hallway. The old man stood menacingly, blocking the light out of the doorway.

"You two are gonna stay right here!" he said. "And I'll deal with you once the night is over."

The door slammed in the boys' faces, and the sound of keys jingling echoed on the other side of the door. Then the outside lock clicked. The old man had installed an extra set of locks on the door's exterior to prevent old customers from simply wandering into the rooms without paying. A rash of lost keys had cropped up last autumn, which were discovered some months later hiding on certain travelers revisiting and helping themselves to the rooms. But Ector never thought the extra locks would be used to lock someone inside. The old man's muffled mumbling faded down the stairs, and the last thing Ector heard was something about "*trying to ruin the festival.*"

"Listen, Meric..." Ector turned to explain, but he felt two fists suddenly close on the front of his shirt.

"You just can't let me talk to Mara, can you?" Meric's long thin hair trembled with fury. "Not one little second, huh?"

"Meric, listen to me," Ector continued, calmly trying to wrench his shirt from Meric's grasp. "It was the man from the forest. He was there tonight, right behind you. I tried calling out, but you didn't hear me."

Meric released his grip and shoved Ector away.

"Now she's out there with old Fungle-dor." Meric mimicked Fenodor's deep voice, doing his best oaf-impression with his bottom lip puffed out, pretending to assist someone. "Oh, can I help you stand?"

"Get a hold on yourself!" Ector cried, kicking the door.

"I hope the old man chokes on his festival! We always get blamed for everything!" Meric bleated.

"Look," Ector continued, trying to rein Meric back to sanity. "This is more important than Mara. That traveler was closing on you. It looked like he had a sword or something."

"Closing on me, eh?" commented Meric, pretending to entertain the idea. "Well, you know what? Next time, don't do me any favors!"

"I'm sorry," repeated Ector. "I really didn't mean to knock you both down."

Meric proceeded to tear into Ector for every wrong that had happened since they were little. Ector rolled his eyes, resigned to let Meric exhaust himself. He was used to this specific tirade; Meric kept a running list of every way Ector had wronged him since they'd first met as children.

But his attention was diverted to the loud barking ringing out from the grounds outside the pub; he recognized the deep, heavy growls. Moving to the window while Meric continued to berate him, Ector saw Rahms jumping feverishly, snarling at their window.

"What's he doing?" Ector wondered aloud. "I told him to go to the woods..."

Dread zipped through his spine again as a cape fluttered on the second story of the pub and disappeared around the corner.

"Meric, he's here!" Ector cried. "He's scaling the wall!"

"Don't even try it," Meric replied, unfazed, continuing down his list. Ector grabbed Meric's shoulder and dragged him to the window.

"He's right there!"

Ector thrust a hand out the window, but the tailcoats had vanished out of sight.

"I don't even know the word for you!" Meric screamed, boiling mad.

"You hear Rahms barking, don't you?" Ector replied, defending himself.

Ector knew he wasn't going mad. All three times tonight he'd seen the dark stranger, but not a single person believed him.

"Next time he comes around," Ector retorted, "I'll just stay back, shall I? Let him get his hands on you, so you'll believe me? I doubt I'll have to wait long. He seems pretty determined."

Meric fumbled with frustrated fits of noises before managing a coherent sentence. He uttered each word with slow deliberation.

"Ector, why would a traveler sneak up on me?"

Ector shrugged. "I'm quite sure I don't know. But he did start towards you once you made that leap over the fire pole. Maybe he's from Bellington?"

Meric breathed more slowly, considering the thought.

"It was an incredible jump, mate," Ector continued, determined to keep the topic changed, now that he had a hold on Meric's tantrum. "No backing out of the race now. They want our title, and they're playing dirty."

"You think?" Meric replied.

"He was lurking around the forest, wasn't he?" Ector couldn't believe he had distracted Meric from his fury. "Probably trying to figure out how old man Bodock makes his brews. Then, he sees you make that unbeatable leap and moves in to eliminate the competition! After I foiled his plan, he tries to climb up here, where he knows we're locked up good and tight." Ector pounded the wall in disgust. "Good ol' Rahms sounded the alert and scared him away though."

Shaking his head, Ector felt himself getting worked up, even starting to believe the made-up story.

"Maybe." Meric nodded. "But maybe he's just a crazy wanderer."

"Maybe," Ector replied, happy to settle the discussion there.

Suddenly the doorknob rattled. Both boys turned on instinct and moved to the far wall as the locking mechanism clicked. The door swung open. A hooded traveler, cloaked in black, stood in the doorway, blocking the light. He had high boots and a leather satchel draped to one side.

The boys moved closer together. Ector couldn't see the man's face, but he immediately searched for the weapon. The man made to remove his hood, but the sudden movement caused Ector to raise his fists.

The man dropped his hood slowly, and the shadows receded to reveal fair skin and smooth black hair pulled tightly backwards. His hair draped down like a horse's tail in the back.

"My apologies, young masters," said the traveler. His voice was sturdy and confident, but welcoming. His eyes shimmered like a deep glacial river, accentuating his strong jawline. "The keeper must have provided the wrong room." He laughed, but it didn't carry to his eyes, which remained firmly fixed on the boys. "Please pardon the intrusion. I will inform the keeper the room is already filled and relock your door for you."

"No!" blurted Ector, surprised by his own voice. "Er, I mean, that's no trouble at all. We'll get the door."

The man looked at Ector a long moment. It felt as if the man was penetrating his thoughts; Ector didn't like it.

"As you wish," he replied after a moment, smiling. He turned swiftly, and the boys heard his footsteps fade, clunking down the stairs.

"You almost had me," Meric said, letting out a relieved sigh. "For a second, I almost believed everything you've been saying."

"Well, you should! That wasn't him," Ector replied defiantly. "The other stranger had a sword or something on his waist. It was clearly visible. And the other stranger didn't have a traveling bag."

"Clearly visible, eh?" commented Meric. "Clear as a man dressed in black on a dark night?"

"Go ahead and poke fun," Ector shot back. "But who's the one who thought fast and had him leave the door unlocked?"

"Yeah, smart thinking," mocked Meric. "I guess if it's between you and someone that plants poisonous berries across an entire mountainside, you're the victor."

Ector punched him in the arm. "Come on, let's get out of here before the old man realizes he rented out the key to our escape."

He checked the window one last time before leaving; both Rahms and the mysterious pursuer were long gone.

Escaping out the back door, Meric swiped one of the New Original Brews, which turned him an incandescent yellowish orange, and he departed for the distant barn. Tomorrow night's race was too important to squander. Ector watched Meric's light bounce from side to side back up the valley, remnants of the Grasshopper Ale still lingering in his body.

Ector grabbed another Grasshopper Ale, as promised for Rahms, and slipped off to the shed for the night. Crossing into his shack, he poured the brew into Rahms's trough and peered through the window at the huge crowd roaring through the thin walls. Tomorrow would be the biggest turnout yet, and the whole town would see them win.

He looked one last time for any travelers lingering on the outskirts of the party, but there wasn't a single flicker from the fire poles still capable of reaching the edge of the crowd.

Ector began counting the number of people closest to the shed, but soon moved over to the thick haystack piled in the corner, giving up. There had to be more than twice the number of travelers to townsfolk already. The bizarre traveler floated through his mind again, but the image quickly left as the hay began to warm up.

Before drifting off to sleep, he registered heavy panting, and a distant, almost dream-like Rahms crawled through a dug-out hole beneath the back wall; the hairy beast sniffed Ector, gave him a lick, and then followed his nose to the foamy treat still dancing with bubbles and fizzing.

Chapter 4
The Harvest Festival

The next morning unfolded uneventfully. Old man Bodock, so pleased with the number of travelers, completely forgot that he'd locked Ector and Meric in the upstairs room.

"Go tell Mr. Hallings I need five more barrels of his corn," he said to Ector, during their midday meal.

Ector stopped mid-bite and looked up to see the old man immersed in a pile of parchment. The papers glistened with greasy fingerprints as he finished off the last bites of his boar chop. Ector sensed trouble brewing. The old man must have been double-checking the brew stock available for the week ahead and saw a shortage in the making.

Ector cleared his throat.

"Uh, Mr. Hallings said he's not selling any more corn this year." Ector quickly swallowed the last bite of his oats mixed with cold water, bracing himself for the backlash, knowing it would probably be the last bit of food from the old man's table for the day. "Mr. Hallings is running thin on his winter supplies and said he can't afford to trade anymore this year."

He exhaled, pleased with himself for finishing an entire bowl before tasked out for some pointless chore, or more commonly, commanded to leave for no apparent reason.

"Bird droppings!" cursed the old man. "Look, you tell Hallings he can have three free brews on top of what I usually give him. We used fifteen barrels more than I expected last night, and we won't have enough for the final night." The old man leaned closer to Ector and dropped his voice to a dangerous growl. "You tell him I *need* those barrels. I ain't gonna turn people away!"

Old man Bodock shook a fat finger at him, as if Ector somehow imposed the minimum limits on Mr. Hallings's corn reserves.

"What do you want me to do if he says no?" Ector asked, fully expecting this to be the case. Mr. Hallings was thin and wiry, with deceptive strength achieved from working the cornfields most of his life. He was an old, quiet man, but Ector knew he wasn't intimidated easily, least of all by old man Bodock.

"If he says no," replied the old man, getting worked up, "ya tell him to stick that there corn stalk up his ol'..."

"Mr. Bodock!" reprimanded his wife. "Take care to watch your mouth around a lady." She spun and took her sturdy torso out of the kitchen.

Ector stifled a scoff. Much worse had come out of old lady Bodock's mouth, especially when it came to Ms. Weely's "*over-priced*" honey. Mrs. Bodock had few reservations when it came to Ms. Weely forcing her to pay more for honey over the past couple years. But somehow old lady Bodock always managed to overlook how much her honey consumption had increased, now that they had ample stores to trade with.

Old man Bodock leaned closer still. "You tell that ol' corn bag to hand over me corn, or I'll visit him personally!"

Perfect, thought Ector. Anytime the old man threatened to get involved personally, it always ended badly—but mostly for the old man. It was good for a private laugh, usually, and it meant Ector wouldn't have to waste his afternoon trying to talk Mr. Hallings into trading. Ector had tried three times already and been denied every time. Bad blood was brewing.

Last year, old man Bodock trudged up the valley, enraged at Mr. Hallings for not letting Ector pick the corn. So after that, Mr. Hallings tried to keep track of how much corn left his fields, down to the ear. With so much corn pouring into the brews now, the winter storages for the whole community were becoming much tighter. At first, Ector had neglected to tell the old man about not picking the corn, because he had been rather glad for the break. But after the brews from that batch were finished, something went wrong. The brews didn't make the old man or Mrs. Bodock glow. The Bodocks always tested every batch to make sure it worked before barreling, so they were wise to its lameness immediately.

The old man had worked himself into uncontrollable breathing fits, jumping to the conclusion this was the end of his magical brew business. He backtracked through the entire process, scrutinizing every miniscule detail that might have possibly gone wrong, until Ector could bear the sight of the old man's helplessness no longer. He tried to explain that Mr. Hallings pre-picked everybody's rations that season, because of the corn shortage, but it didn't matter.

The ensuing punishment certainly made Ector think twice before going out of his way to help after that. Old man Bodock stomped to those cornfields in a fit and tore into Mr. Hallings like Ector had never seen. Mr. Hallings's farm was located at the end of the valley, but Ector saw every one of the old man's fat finger wags through the shed window. Mr. Hallings eventually let Ector go back and pick another batch, but he made old man Bodock pay again, for which, of course, Ector was punished as well.

Later that same evening, the old man had found a grasshopper in the lame batch. Guessing that could have been the problem as well, old man Bodock mixed both batches of corn together, and when the next brew was finished, its magic had miraculously returned. The old man eventually decided the grasshopper had been the problem, but he never gave a second thought to apologizing to Mr. Hallings. And Mr. Hallings never forgot the encounter. Consequently, getting enough corn supplies for both types of Original Brew this year had been much more troublesome.

Now, working his way over to Mr. Hallings's cornfields yet again, Ector looked on in amazement at the entire town bustling with activity under the midday sun. Villagers bartered their specialties, some being satisfied just to trade for stories, while others traded for furs, mountain boots, beaded jewelry, dried meats and fruits. Old man Bodock may have had a knack for rubbing people the wrong way, but the whole township, including Mr. Hallings, knew their winter storages were significantly more bountiful because of the Harvest Festival. It brought travelers to Cleargar, and the travelers brought plenty of goods with which to trade.

Although Mr. Bodock never shied away from crediting himself as the root of all the flourishing businesses in the village, truth be told he had as much intention of helping others as he did of giving Ector second helpings at mealtime. The real truth was that Mr. Bodock absolutely refused to change anything about the brew-making process since that first year, and unfortunately that consisted of only Ector and Mrs. Bodock being used for help. This also meant only so much could be made every year. And to ensure enough brew reached the week's end, the old man implemented a rule: The first barrel of every evening would not be tapped until the bottom of the sun touched the horizon.

Excited travelers, coming from afar and anxious to try the brews, were now left waiting in anxiety for evening to hit. At first the locals were also upset, itching to partake in the festivities just as the travelers were, but there was an unintended consequence of Mr. Bodock's rule: Travelers became trapped customers during the days, waiting for the festivities to start. This meant the days became for trading and the nights for celebrating. Nearly all the town had warmed to the idea by the first day's end of that first season, and compared to last year, nearly every Cleargar farmer and storeowner had become much more skilled at parting travelers from their monies.

As Ector moved through the crowded valley, he couldn't help but notice even more people today than the night before. Travelers wearing the same dark cloaks and high boots lingered throughout the masses, but none of them drew any particular attention like the one from last night. Ector wondered if he was drawn to them simply because they were wearing cloaks and hoods. It was not uncommon for travelers to wear such attire.

Lost in his thoughts, Ector bumped into someone. He turned to apologize, but the tall man was deep in conversation, inquiring about the children in the village. The traveler didn't even seem to notice Ector had knocked him.

"Well, I don't quite know how many exactly, sir." Ector heard a woman's voice respond merrily. It was Mrs. Bullberry, the wife of the village wood carver. "I suspect we have a dozen or more between the ages of ten and twelve. Are you interested in a gift for your young one?"

The stranger mumbled something Ector couldn't discern, and then he turned swiftly, disappearing into the crowd, walking with unusual purpose amidst the meandering masses. Suddenly a hand clasped Ector's shoulder, startling him.

"Good afternoon, young master."

Ector turned to see a man garbed in a dark brown cloak, with tall mountain boots and a leather strap crossing his chest supporting a bag that hung at his hip.

"Yes, sir?" asked Ector.

"Ah, you do not remember me?" asked the man with a chuckle. "Probably for the better. I was worried I upset you and your friend last night. I still feel rather dreadful for barging into your room. You must have been tired from traveling here."

Suddenly Ector recognized the man as the one who had burst into the upstairs room last night; he looked different in the sunlight, but his dark hair was still pulled into the familiar-looking horse's tail in the back.

"Oh, that wasn't our room. My uncle, the owner, locked us up there for *disturbing the festival,*" Ector explained, still perturbed even after a good night's sleep.

The man looked taken aback. "What could a couple of fine lads possibly have done to deserve such a thing?"

Ector shrugged, feeling a little embarrassed. "My friend and I had gotten an early start on a couple Grasshopper Ales. I suppose I made a bit of a scene after my mate cleared the lit pole."

"Oh, that was your friend?" asked the man cheerily. "I saw that amazing jump! I presume that was an early teaser for the Hoppy Brew tryouts later today?"

Ector nodded, noticing the traveler knew something about the festival already; he tried to remember if he'd seen the man last year.

"And you said your uncle locked you up there?" reaffirmed the traveler, pointing to the pub. "I guess that makes you two locals then. And your uncle is the keeper of the inn?"

Ector nodded again.

"Well, then," the man continued, folding his hands and bowing slightly to Ector, "I stand in the presence of the great Harvest Festival heir. Shall I call you Nephew Bodock?"

"No, no," Ector replied, refusing the polite gesture. "My name is Ector, and I will inherit none of this. The brews are very sensitive. I help my uncle, but without him there would be no brews."

"Ah, I see." The man nodded with increased interest. "Well, Master Ector, tell me; I have heard many great stories, but this is my first festival. What brew would you recommend?"

"The Grasshopper Ale," Ector replied without hesitation. "It's the best of the brews by far, if you haven't tried it yet! The oats are the key; the far north side of Mr. Flubber's fields gives the brews the highest jumps! And that's the only place I visited this year..."

"Oh, so you are the master creator of the brews, then?" asked the man with a look of surprise. "Is that how you help?"

"No, no," Ector answered, deflecting the question as passersby overhearing their conversation began to stop and look. "I just help my uncle. He is the brew master. I only pick the ingredients."

He was suddenly wary at giving out so much information to the stranger. He felt oddly comfortable conversing with the man, but he had no idea who he was. He was suddenly struck by the traveler's distant demeanor; the man was guarding something. Ector imagined asking the traveler all these same sorts of questions and got the undeniable impression the man would not have obliged with answers.

The man seemed to sense Ector's sudden apprehension.

"It would be wise, young master," he said, dropping his voice so that only Ector could hear, "not to tell too many people of this. There are strange people in the area this year. The fame of your uncle's festival travels on the wings of birds, attracting all kinds of people. Be careful tonight." He winked and began to move with the crowd. Ector stared after him and saw one gloved hand rise into the air.

"I will be sure to try that Grasshopper Ale tonight!" said the man, waving farewell before disappearing completely into the masses.

By the time Ector had perused the markets, running into a couple of schoolmates along the way, the afternoon had dwindled away to early evening. The visit to Mr. Hallings's cornfields had, predictably, ended in another miserable failure. The corn farmer had barely allowed Ector two words before slamming the door in his face.

Now, returning empty-handed and none too eager to relay the bad news to old man Bodock, Ector decided to hike one of the many rolling hills on his way back to the festivities. The sun grazed the horizon, and he couldn't resist the temptation to see if any more travelers had arrived into the valley.

Cresting the hill, Ector saw the township packing up their displays and waving hurried farewells as the crowds migrated towards the sprawling fields in front of the pub. The fire poles were already being lit as two-dozen barrels of every flavor were rolled out to a long-table tappery. The old man had recruited several more servers this year, and they began to unplug the first six barrels of each flavor. The distant cheers echoed off the mountains as the crowd surged towards the high counter, all of them anxious to be among the first partakers.

Ector rested a moment, watching the first colors explode in a brilliant display across the sky. The fireworks rained down in different shapes on the valley to another roar of clapping and laughter. Then, just like the fireworks, people began exploding into different colors right before his eyes: deep crimson, violets, sunset orange, and sparkling yellows dotted the mass of people. Ector's eyes caught old man Bodock laughing, shaking hands with everyone surrounding him. Ector still hadn't decided how to phrase the disappointing news, but he felt quite certain it would only dampen the old man's spirits.

Tonight isn't worth it, Ector decided. *It can wait until morning.*

The first calls for the Butterfly Honey Drub race registered as he descended the hill. Another enormous wave of hollering rose, and the crowd separated to reveal a wide swath of juniper grass spanning between the two rows of fire poles. At one end, Mrs. Bodock laid a thick piece of hay twine on the ground, and then unrolled it across the entire width of the field.

"This is the starting line!" she bellowed. "Racers may partake of no more than two pints. But choose wisely," she warned. "One pint will get you on your way sooner, but two pints will stay with you longer!

Forfeiting a little time upfront may prove a wiser decision. Do not start sipping until the race begins!"

The participants jumped and clapped, some chattering nervously with their friends.

"Participants must run all the way to the town limits where the two pines tower above the rest." Mrs. Bodock pointed westward, towards the distant entrance of the valley where the two mountainsides appeared to narrow towards each other. At the base of the mountains, two enormous pine trees marked the town's gateway, clearly visible even from where they stood.

"Racers will pay for their pints now, please!" she instructed pleasantly, holding out her hand as the Butterfly Honey Drub trolley, marked especially for the competition, rolled up. Ector saw several people reach for small pouches, anxious to reserve their spot in the race.

"Ector!" cried a voice behind him.

He turned to find old man Bodock working his way closer and felt his stomach drop at the unexpected encounter.

"Where's me corn?" asked the old man, approaching with a baffled look and searching Ector as if he might have hidden the five barrels in his pockets.

"No good," Ector replied, holding his arms out empty-handed.

"Blast that man!" Bodock roared, forgetting himself. Several people turned at the outburst, to which he quickly responded with a smile and began patting Ector's head.

"Listen!" he continued in sharp whispers. "You go tell that old wind bag I'll be visiting him tonight, *after* the festival is done!"

"But the Hoppy Brew tryouts are about to begin!" Ector pleaded. "I've been waiting all year. Meric and I have to defend our title against some Bellington boys."

The old man raised an eyebrow. "Bellington, eh?" He narrowed his eyes with interest. "Had a traveler from Bellington stiff me last year." He looked as if he were entertaining the idea of excusing Ector from the errand.

Ector decided to push his luck. "I barely got two words out to Mr. Hallings before he closed the door on me. If I warn him now, it'll just give him time to think up a reason to turn you down. He'll be more likely to give you the corn if you surprise him."

The old man nodded, puffing out his black mustache and caressing the thick gray stubble on his chin.

"You let me know if you see a tall man with yellow hair from Bellington," he replied, agreeing to Ector's idea. "He's got big bulging eyes. He owes me from last year."

Ector nodded excitedly as a group beckoned for the old man to come over. The old man obliged with a smile and, to Ector's immense relief, stepped away before he could change his mind.

"The Hoppy Brew tryouts are beginning!" announced a man's voice a short distance away. Ector turned and saw people already leaping in high arches, warming up their legs to compete for one of the eight slots in the tryout round. Ector searched frantically for Meric. They had to be together to register.

"Ector, I'm here!" came Meric's voice, emerging from somewhere in the crowd. "Hurry! There are only two spots left!"

Ector ran to him, digging in his shirt for a tiny pouch of grains to pay for the brews. But then he stopped, feeling his heart drop like a stone into his stomach. He hadn't returned to the shed after visiting Mr. Hallings; he didn't have anything to pay for his pints.

"I don't have my stores on me!" Ector cried, wide-eyed.

"NO!" Meric replied in disbelief.

"I'll pay you back, mate. Can you cover me?" Ector pleaded.

"I only brought enough for me!" Meric exclaimed. "We're going to lose our spot. We have to go now!"

"Split it!" cried Ector. "You have enough for four pints, right?"

"Yeah, but..."

"We only need two pints a piece for this first round," Ector cut in. "After we qualify, I'll pay for the next four pints, and then we're even."

"We have to pay for everything up front!" cried Meric, shaking his head. "They won't let us enter if we don't pay in full."

"Bollocks they won't!" Ector shot back defiantly. "I didn't harvest an entire month in the fields to miss this. Every oat that went into that Grasshopper Ale, I've had my hands on. They'll make an exception for us. Come on!"

Ector marched up to the registration table. The man was hanging two nameplates on a large wooden pallet, which stood behind the table. Both names were being placed on the *Team #7* hanger.

"Here, give me your stores," said Ector, holding his hand out to Meric. Meric obliged, albeit reluctantly.

"Excuse me, sir!" said Ector boldly, stepping up to the table. "Meric and Ector in the last slot, if you please."

"Ah, of course!" said the short frail man with a toothy grin. It was Mr. Bullberry, the village's wood carver. "Was wondering if you two were going to make it! You like the new board this year?" He pointed proudly at the hanging wooden pallet. In the flurry to reserve a slot,

Ector actually hadn't noticed its beautiful construction until now. Curving lines bordered the enormous work of art, and every letter of the title *Hoppy Brew Championship* had been masterfully crafted.

"That must have taken you all year to make!" Ector said with sincere awe. "It's great!"

"Oh, no," Mr. Bullberry replied, shaking his balding head, which was crowned with spiky silver hair on the sides. "The idea struck me just last week. Now let's see..."

He bent and reached under the table, searching for something. Ector could hear the sound of wood scraps clunking together before Mr. Bullberry pulled out two very special nameplates: He turned and hung them in the last slot for *Team #8.* Their style and craftsmanship matched that of the board and stood in stark contrast to the rest of the teams' names written in chalk.

"In honor of the returning champions!" shouted Mr. Bullberry, so that everyone could hear. Polite clapping and a few cheers leapt from the crowd behind him. Ector couldn't believe it! No one had ever made anything special for him. Mr. Bullberry smiled at seeing the look on Ector's face.

"Now, how 'bout those grains so we can start this frog hoppin' race!" he continued with delight.

"Oh, uh, right," Ector stuttered, feeling shame settling over him. "Listen, Mr. Bullberry..." He leaned in, talking more quietly. "I have a favor to ask."

"Yes?" Mr. Bullberry also hunched over the table, mildly surprised and curious.

"Well, you see," Ector began, feeling terrible for even suggesting the request, especially after Mr. Bullberry made that exquisite placard for him.

"I don't exactly have the right amount of grains on me at the moment," he whispered. "Can we pay for just the tryout round, and then I'll bring more stores for the other four pints as soon as we're done?"

"Oh, Ector," Mr. Bullberry replied. "I don't think I can do that. There were a lot of people hoping to play this year. Look." He pointed over Ector's shoulder at the disappointed people stuffing the tradable goods back into their pockets. "The purpose of this race is to make people excited and want to buy Grasshopper Ale. I don't think your uncle would approve of such favoritism."

"I know, but..."

"And where is your partner?" Mr. Bullberry interrupted. "I might have been able to oblige for the returning champions, but a riot would flip this table if the crowd saw me allowing just one participant to enter!"

Ector turned on the spot, searching for Meric. *Where had he gone? Why would Meric leave?*

"I'm sorry, young Ector," Mr. Bullberry continued sadly. "But unless..."

"Got 'em!" Meric blurted out, completely out of breath, slamming another four pouches of grain on the registration table.

"Well, there we go!" Mr. Bullberry replied with a wink. "Fine timing, young Meric. You'll both do well to be a little more organized next year, I presume?"

"Yes sir, we will!" Meric replied, still huffing.

"Where did you find another four bags?" Ector asked, reeling from all the different emotions crammed into such a short space of time. He had gone from determined, to honored, to ashamed, to helpless... he clapped Meric on the shoulder, glad to end on relief as the last emotion.

"They're yours," Meric answered. "So we're even. I took off for the shed the moment I handed my pouches off."

"How did you know where my stores were hidden?" Ector asked, taken aback.

"I didn't," Meric replied, bracing himself on his knees, trying to slow his breath. "Rahms told me. He was in there sleeping."

"What do you mean Rahms told you?" asked Ector, looking confused. "Rahms is a dog."

"I know," Meric replied, shaking an annoyed hand at the question. "I mean, I was talking aloud to myself, and then Rahms got up and started pawing at the loose boards under the table next to your window."

Ector squinted, questioning Meric with a silent stare.

"Look," Meric continued. "All I know is, he scared the shivers out of me, cause I didn't know he was in there, but I found your stores, so let's just get our pints. Shall we?"

"Alright." Ector held his hands up, but still shook his head with disbelief. "I'm burying my stores in a new spot after tonight, though."

"I wouldn't tell anybody where it's hidden!" replied Meric, insulted. "You don't trust your best mate?"

"Nope. Don't trust anyone," Ector retorted, turning for the tappery table. "Maybe Rahms, but I'm reevaluating that now."

Meric scoffed. "That's sad, mate."

Ector ignored him and ordered the first four pints for them to split. They each grabbed two frothy Grasshopper Ales and made their way to the starting line for the Hoppy Brew tryouts. Only one other team was from Cleargar: Fenodor, and another boy from their school named Grigor. Grigor was a couple of years older than Ector, and tall like Fenodor, but quite a bit thicker in the mid-section. He always missed classes at school for some reason. Oddly enough, his face reminded Ector of an angry bullfrog; he had a lazy sort of stance, a wide mouth that stretched all the way to his ears, and narrow, bulging eyes. Even his voice had a raspy croak to it. Fenodor pointed at another team, and the two began to snicker loudly.

"Team One, take your marks," yelled Mr. Bullberry, coming out from behind the table after placing the finishing touches on the magnificent competition board.

"Jumps are scored two ways, which is why we have teams of two!" Mr. Bullberry explained as the first team stepped up to the line. "The highest jump between teammates will be scored, as well as the longest jump between teammates. You can choose to drink one or two pints, but no more than two!"

"Look at those cheats," whispered Meric, pointing towards Fenodor and Grigor as they guzzled their first pint, pouring it down like water through a drain. "I saw them sneaking pints not even half an hour ago."

"What?" cried Ector, outraged. "You should say something!"

"It's no use," continued Meric, shaking his head disgustedly. "It's my word against theirs; two versus one. Plus, they're bigger, and I'm not in the mood for an oaf-sized fist in my gut tonight."

"And one last thing," finished Mr. Bullberry, dropping his voice back to normal and turning to the eight teams huddled around him. "Mind this starting line! If you step even a toe over the line, I shall be forced to disqualify you for that leap. Simple enough?"

Mr. Bullberry made sure to see everyone nod before turning back to the crowds.

"We're ready," he called excitedly, raising his hands. "Let the races start!"

The crowd roared with approval, excited to see the competition get underway.

Fenodor wiped away the foam from his mouth and prepared to make his first leap as the other seven teams moved away from the starting line, giving the first participants plenty of room. Fenodor bounced at the ready, building momentum in his legs with several practice squats before unexpectedly giving a gigantic leap that sent him soaring through the air. He passed the first lit pole with ease and even slapped it as he flew by.

"He didn't go very high," Ector whispered. "He must be their distance man."

Meric stifled a laugh. "He didn't go very far either. He's not exactly bird material, is he? Maybe they should've started cheating a little sooner in the day, eh?"

Ector clapped a hand to his mouth as a couple of foreigners shot ugly glares at Meric and him, probably assuming they were laughing at Fenodor's effort. Ector felt a twinge of guilt, because that wasn't entirely the case. But Meric was right: Fenodor flying through the air looked about as natural as old man Bodock running for fun.

"One full head above the pole!" yelled Mr. Bullberry, walking back to the table to record the score underneath *Team #1* on the board. He wrote a large number "*4*" with "*H*" next to it, designating the height score. Then he turned and began marking off the distance from the starting line to determine how far Fenodor had jumped.

"Seven points for distance!" announced Mr. Bullberry. He hustled back to the table to write an equally large "*7*" with a big letter "*D*" next to it, indicating the score for the distance portion. Ector had to give it to Mr. Bullberry; it certainly was a good system to make sure the scores didn't get mixed up.

"Alright, laddie!" yelled Mr. Bullberry enthusiastically, clearly feeling the excitement of the competition. "Let's see what you can do!"

Grigor stepped up to the line. He may have looked like a bullfrog, but he definitely didn't move like one. Bouncing in place several times, he tried to mimic how his partner prepared for the leap, but it didn't look natural at all. Ector watched with a grimace, slightly hoping Grigor could find a rhythm before springing through the air. But it was too late. The wave of embarrassment that rolled over him as Grigor launched and began tumbling head-over-heels through the waning evening light was too much; Ector turned to the laughing traveler next to him, feeling obliged to explain that not everyone from Cleargar jumped that way.

"Two full heads below the fire!" yelled Mr. Bullberry, disappointed. "I believe that is an all-time low score of one point."

After rolling to a stop, Grigor got to his feet and kicked the fire pole in frustration. Red embers and ash rained on the crowds.

"Mind your temper!" yelled Mr. Bullberry, hopping around, patting at the small flickers briefly igniting his arm hairs. "Perhaps you'll do well to remember we have rules for a reason: Drinking more than two pints weighs you down," he explained, indicating that he already had an idea about the extra pints sloshing around in Grigor's belly. He began to step off the distance and tallied the height score. "Let that be a lesson!"

"Who said I drank more than two pints?" Grigor demanded, catching on to Mr. Bullberry's implication rather quickly and looking affronted. Ector shook his head as Grigor searched the crowds for the culprit.

"Your pitiful leap says you drank more than two pints," answered Mr. Bullberry over his shoulder, counting the paces aloud. "Ten, eleven, and a generous twelve!"

Mr. Bullberry turned, and the two locked eyes for a long moment; Grigor still feigned insult from the accusation while Mr. Bullberry simply stared at him, displeased.

"You're welcome," added Mr. Bullberry, breaking the uncomfortable silence. "I should have stopped at eleven, but I'll give it the benefit of the doubt."

"Hmpf!" Grigor trotted off, angrily. "I'd hate to see you when you're stingy!" he mumbled.

"Next team! Take the line!" Mr. Bullberry announced, deciding to ignore the comment. The low score was punishment enough, and Ector was glad to see *Team #1* reap it for trying to cheat.

Mr. Bullberry recorded a large "*9*" with a big letter "*D*" next to it on the board. He compared both height and distance scores for the two jumps before circling Fenodor's better height score of "*4*" points, and then Grigor's marginally better distance score of "*9*" for a team total of "*13*" points in all.

Mr. Bullberry announced the score for all to hear and wrote the total out to the side.

Thirteen points will be easy to clear, thought Ector. *Meric alone can get over half that with one good leap.*

All the teams rotated through in succession. Ector and Meric waited, anxiously watching the competition record jump after jump. The best team so far had bounded one-half body length above the fire pole, and twenty-seven strides down the straightway. It belonged to the two boys from Bellington, confirming the rumors Ector had overheard in the fields. Mr. Bullberry drew a large number "*29*" for their total team score, and a very special placard engraved with the word "*LEADERS*" hung next to the slot for *Team #2* with "*Bellington Boys*" written in chalk underneath it. Ector stole a glance at the stout lads, both of whom looked undeniably smug with the work they had put forth so far.

Ector reassured himself that Meric would pull through for them. Meric jumped for height, and nobody today could even come close to what Ector had witnessed of Meric, even last year, when the ales were weaker. But Ector was the distance-man in their duo, and twenty-seven strides would be a stretch to beat.

Meric finished the last sip of his Grasshopper Ale and wiped the foam from his mouth. Stepping up to the starting line, he squatted low into his signature stance, pants hiked all the way up to his knees this time. He continued to squat even lower, until his rump almost brushed the ground. Ector watched Meric's legs tremble as he fought to control the jump frantically trying to unleash itself. Meric only managed to hold for a second longer before shooting straight up into the night, hollering with delight. Ector had to shield the firelight from his eyes to see Meric disappear one full body length and another half above even the tallest flames.

"We have a new Harvest Festival record!" declared Mr. Bullberry, jovially pulling out his tall measuring stick to estimate the height. He then began calculating the score on his fingers. "Our very own young Meric has scored nine points for the height portion!"

The crowds surrounding the pitch boomed their applause. Mr. Bullberry shook his head with disbelief and laughed as he stepped off the distance.

"And another nine paces down the stretch," said Mr. Bullberry, turning and scurrying back to record a meager distance score of only eight points.

"How do you think he tabulates these scores?" asked Meric, staring befuddled at his distance score.

"I don't know, mate," Ector replied, wondering the same thing. "He has to use math for his carpentry, so I guess he knows what he's doing. Maybe he does one point for every three strides." He pointed at the *Team #1* score. "Grigor got one point more than you, and jumped three strides longer."

Meric shrugged, still looking a bit disappointed at his distance score.

"Hey, cheer up, mate!" Ector added, clapping him on the shoulder. "You just set a new height record!" He took the last few sips of his second pint before continuing. "We decided this ahead of time, remember? You only worry about jumping high, and I'll only worry about jumping long. They can't beat us if we stick to the plan."

Meric perked up, remembering their strategy as Ector strode to the starting line. They had planned it all summer, and now it seemed so simple. They often fell into assuming other teams would have the same strategy, but most tried to jump both high and long in the same leap.

Ector stopped about ten paces short of the starting line and gauged where the Bellington boys had landed; he estimated it a few paces shy of the second fire pole. He felt the bubbles dancing happily in his stomach, making his legs light and springy. Stepping to the side, he found his halfway point. Too high, and the wind would catch him and slow him down. But he needed an angle that could stretch twenty-seven-strides down the fairway. He decided to aim for a height equal to the fire poles. Running through all the calculations, he decided no matter what, it would be tough.

Ector threw all his weight into every step, running as hard as he could. Launching headfirst from the starting line, he felt the wind coursing through his orange hair, making his head look like a flying ball of fire. He pinned his arms, ascending higher and higher. The first pole grew larger by the second. Exhilarated, he kept an eye on the fire pit, watching his halfway target carefully. Waiting for it to come to eye level, though, he started to descend before reaching the right height. He strained his body straighter, fighting to keep parallel to the ground, trying to shed all resistance. Most would tuck their legs and brace for impact, but not Ector. That was his secret. He stayed unprotected until the very last second for those few extra strides.

The blades of grass magnified larger by the fraction of a second as he rained to the ground like a hailstone. Disaster beckoned, salivating, but Ector denied it, tucking his head and rolling head under feet. He sprang into another ferocious leap, soaring, arms and legs spread wide, feeling the wind slow his pace.

The ground found him again, and he latched on with all four limbs this time. The crowd cheered, but it sounded distant. He hadn't gone as high as he wanted, but still, it felt like a good leap. The shuffle of Mr. Bullberry's footsteps grew louder. Ector rested, trying to catch his breath while excitement coursed through his body. His nerves suddenly returned, tightening his stomach as Mr. Bullberry walked up to the spot where Ector first landed.

"Twenty-eight strides!" roared Mr. Bullberry.

The nerves transformed into sheer disbelief and ecstasy. Ector sprang to his feet, bounding back in short leaps to the starting line where Meric waited for him. He roared like a victorious warrior, arms raised to the night sky.

"That was incredible, mate!" Meric exclaimed, just as Ector returned from the other end of the pitch.

"Hopefully those Bellington boys don't have anything left." Ector grinned, grinding to a halt, breathless. "I don't think I could've mustered much more!"

The boys laughed as the scores were tallied. The Hoppy Brew tryouts allowed for eight teams to compete, but only four of them would continue for the final round later. Everyone waited anxiously for the last score to be announced.

"In first place, with a total of thirty-three points," announced Mr. Bullberry as the night danced with growing excitement, "is Team Eight, Meric and Ector!"

Mr. Bullberry removed the wooden "*LEADER*" placard hanging next to *Team #2,* and instead placed it next to *Team #8.* Enormous applause erupted, echoing off the dark mountainsides and up to the first stars of the night.

"In second place, with a combined score of twenty-nine," continued Mr. Bullberry, "is Team Two, Nettles and Hattry, from Bellington!"

More cheering followed, but Mr. Bullberry didn't wait for it to die away before pressing on.

"Third place is Team Three, Vory and Cappers from Bueford, with a score of twenty-one." He began ruffling through his sheets of parchment, glancing over the remaining scores one last time. It was now too dark to see the scores on the hanging board clearly, but Mr. Bullberry, prepared as always, kept a back-up tally on several pieces of small parchment.

"And finally," he concluded, wearing a bewildered look as he prepared to announce the last team earning a spot in the final competition, "is Team One, Fenodor and Grigor, with a score of thirteen."

Mr. Bullberry flipped through the parchment again, double-checking the other scores to be sure. Equally astonished, Ector thought back: The other teams had had a hard time mustering leaps with good distance, and that was definitely where the bulk of points were earned. Last year almost every team had decent long jumps, with the difference being height scores. But not this year.

"Yes, these are your four finalists!" Mr. Bullberry reiterated, putting the papers back inside his pocket, smiling. The crowds cheered again, and this time Mr. Bullberry let them have a good roar before continuing.

"The final round will take place at the end of the night! In the meantime, enjoy a pint of Grasshopper Ale and see where you stack up against our four champion teams!"

The crowds leapt at the chance, forming queues right away. The shadows were already beginning to stretch longer into the night as the dozens of fire poles illuminating over half the valley were restocked with fresh logs. The merry atmosphere was contagious, and Ector felt the excitement from winning the trial round swelling. The crowds eventually moved from sampling each of the brews to dancing and singing.

"Come on!" Meric said, laughing. "Let's go see who won the Butterfly Honey Drub races."

Ector snatched a pint of regular Original Brew off a nearby trolley and tossed a small bag of beans into the collection sack; having already stopped by the shed to grab plenty of sacks after the near-disaster of missing tryouts, he counted twelve remaining pouches.

The server obliged with a smile and a tip of his hat. At first sip, Ector's skin began to glow bluish-purple. He laughed and clanked glasses with Meric, who was already half finished with a pint of the New Original Brew and was glowing a bright bloody red color. The difference was clear: The new recipe gave off a drastically richer glow. The two boys maneuvered through the crowds, inching their way closer to the finish line of the Butterfly Honey Drub races.

As they passed through the crowded mass of people, Ector couldn't help but notice the edges of the crowd shifting uneasily. People in dark, hooded traveling cloaks straggled there. They blended into the night and were only noticeable when they moved. It was impossible to see their faces, which were hidden in shadows.

"Look there," Ector said, throwing a thumb towards two stragglers occupied in discreet conversation. "You ever see so many foreigners hold back before?"

"Where? What are you talking about, mate?" Meric asked.

"Those travelers over there." Ector pointed again. "You ever see anything like that? Most people are long gone by now, if they're not interested in the festivities."

He surveyed the entire crowd under the firelight. The flickering made it hard to see any details, but one thing was perfectly clear: All the travelers hovered along the edges and were dressed in the same black traveling cloaks, with hoods pulled over their faces at almost exactly the same angle. They even stood in the same unnerving manner. Staked out on all sides, most of them stood like statues, but occasionally a few moved their hooded heads and shadowed faces.

"Probably just late arrivers," answered Meric, shrugging it off. "It does take a little while to acclimate to this sort of sight. Look at you!" he exclaimed, laughing. "You look like a forget-me-not that should be planted above a door!"

He grabbed Ector's blue arm and began dragging him along, hastening their progress towards the finish line.

"Hey look!" cried Meric excitedly. "There's Mara!"

He released his grip on Ector and ran over to her. Ector couldn't help but scoff indignantly. At least he knew where he stood on Meric's list of importance: Somewhere below Mara.

He shook his head, watching for a lingering moment; from a distance it looked as if she were laughing, but as he took a couple of steps closer, the violent sobs became clear.

"It's alright, Mara!" said one of her friends, trying to console her. "You ran really well!"

"It should have been me!" Mara cried, pounding her fists into her thighs. "Why does she always get to win?"

Ector followed Mara's vengeful stare and found another returning champion basking in the praises of the crowd. Ector hadn't spent much time around Mara, but he got the distinct impression she didn't like losing. Ector broke away and let Meric turn all his attention towards Mara, deciding that, especially after last night, any type of interference probably wouldn't end well. Instead, Ector worked his way through the raucous crowd towards the returning victor.

"Hey, great job, Annalin!" Ector smiled, squeezing between two foreigners.

The girl turned to see who'd said her name; she had long brunette hair that touched her shoulders, a thin, pretty face, and sapphire eyes.

"Thanks, Ector!" she replied, smiling back. "How did you and Meric fare at the Hoppy Brew tryouts?"

"We managed alright. Meric had a personal best, but it'll definitely be a battle in the finals later. There's a team from Bellington this year that can really jump! It looks like you handled the competition fairly easily though." Ector threw a look over his shoulder towards Mara, who was now working herself into even greater fits of frenzied sobs, barking at anyone trying to offer consoling words. Ector couldn't stop his smile from widening for Annalin's victory.

"I presume that means you took first place again?" he asked, wanting to hear her confirm it.

"It was close. Mara led the whole way, until the final stretch. Before the race started, I suggested she drink both pints, but she wouldn't listen." Annalin's smile faded as she shrugged indifferently. "She only drank one, wanting to get a faster start. She puttered out on the last leg of the race. I learned that the hard way last year."

"But you won last year," Ector commented, confused.

"I did, but not easily. The girl who finished second wasn't exactly built for speed, but she drank two and had plenty of leg left at the end. It took a lot of grit to hold her off."

A nasty word suddenly echoed over the crowd, and Ector turned, astonished to see Mara glaring at the two of them. Ector was speechless. His shock gave way to anger.

"Don't. She's just upset," Annalin interjected, grabbing Ector's arm before he could say anything. A retort had been on the tip of his tongue, and he was a breath away from yelling it out before Annalin continued. "She called me worse before the race started, when I recommended the second pint. Better to let it go. She'll calm down in a bit."

Ector looked back over his shoulder, still fuming at the remark, but his anger was diverted as he watched Fenodor push into the picture and place an arm around Mara, forcing Meric aside. Ector watched Meric sulk away back into the crowd, not even putting up a fight. Now Ector didn't know whom he was angrier with: Mara for being a venomous snake, or Meric for liking her.

"Well, I better go," said Annalin. "Give my congratulations to Meric, too, in case we don't bump into each other before the finals tonight."

"Thanks, I will," Ector promised, glad Annalin was there to make him mind his manners. "Wait, hang on."

He retrieved a small pouch from his shirt and plopped it onto another of the passing trolleys carrying an assortment of brews. He snagged an Original Brew and handed it to Annalin.

"For your victory, and for being a better winner than I would've been." He toasted his own pint, lifting it high in the air. Annalin tried not to laugh while nodding her thanks. She took a sip and immediately turned a pinkish-orange.

"When does the final Hoppy Brew competition start?" she asked, wiping the foam from her lips.

"It's the last event of the night," he replied. "Will we see you there?"

"Wouldn't miss it." She was unable to stop a laugh this time as Ector's arm remained awkwardly in the air, pint still toasted. His purplish-blue glow changed closer to Annalin's pinkish-orange as he lowered his arm, embarrassed.

"Good," he replied, clearing his throat. His plum aura began to return as he regained confidence. "I might need a good pointer or two in handling some sore losers!"

Annalin laughed as they parted, and waving goodbye, Ector turned to fight his way through the crowd in search of Meric.

Chapter 5
A Dark Night

The night wore on, with no sign of Meric. Ector returned to the shed and settled on the haystack for a few minutes, watching the movement of the crowds through his window. Rahms, snoring, didn't even notice him enter.

Ector poured the rest of the Original Brew into the dirt and let his lavender glow fade. He was grateful he'd avoided the New Original Brew, which left people glowing for hours on end. The idea of drawing extra attention to himself left him uneasy; he wanted the advantage of not being seen, should so many travelers continue lingering outside the light of the fire poles.

The crowd ebbed and flowed like a sea of colors as Ector allowed his head to rest. His thoughts turned to Meric again; he had never seen him this upset over a girl. He wondered what Meric saw in Mara: a slimy leech, salivating at the ready, floated through his mind.

Wondering if leeches had fangs, he felt his thoughts turning fuzzy in the warming hay. Visions of another Hoppy Brew Championship twinkled. The crowds cheered and celebrated. Sailing high, watching the ground stream past, he twitched at the announcement echo faintly.

He blinked several times, confused. Rubbing his eyes, he scanned the dark, quiet shed.

No!

Ector scrambled to his feet and bolted to the door. The crowd danced and swirled every direction as Ector weaved into the nearest opening and followed a current moving towards the Hoppy Brew starting line.

"Sorry, mate," Ector yelled, breaking through the crowd. Jogging over, he slapped Meric on the back and blinked hard, rubbing the sleep out of his eyes. He sighed, relieved to see the other teams milling around, still waiting for the signal. "I fell asleep right after we left the Honey Drub race." He yawned, shaking his head. "Guess that first jump really took it out of me."

"Yeah," Meric mumbled, not even bothering to turn around.

"Come on, mate." Ector suddenly remembered he was searching for him earlier. "Are you still upset about Fenodor?"

Saying nothing, Meric didn't look up.

"Here's the time to get back at him," Ector continued. "Fenodor and Grigor got the worst score, so they'll go first, right? We go last, which means we'll see what we need to beat."

Meric continued to stare sullenly at the ground, hands in his pockets.

"Come on, mate," Ector prodded, refusing to relent. He clapped Meric on the back again. "I can't do this without you. I can't jump another twenty-eight strider. That means we need to make it up on the height. Can you do it?"

"I guess," Meric muttered.

The frustration returned as Ector remembered he was angry at Meric for even wanting to be in the same space as Mara.

"I will never understand why you like her, but at least show Mara what she's missing, if she decides to hang around that big oaf."

That seemed to do the trick. Despite rumors that the New Original Brew could last the whole night, Meric's already-faded glow changed from dark royal blue to magenta as his spirits lifted from the mud.

Ector slapped his shoulders, excitement building.

"We have a thoroughbred jumper, right here!" Ector declared into the noise of the crowd. "Not a thoroughbred dimwit who plants poisonous berries!"

A few glanced Ector's way, but he didn't care. All that mattered was rebuilding Meric's confidence.

One final call for the Hoppy Brew Championship rang through the night, just as the last team emerged from the crowd. It was the duo from Bueford.

Huddling closer to the edge of the field, every neighbor vied for the best view as extra logs were spilled into the hovering baskets, fueling the flames to light all sides of the field.

The tension settled in Ector's stomach again. Thoughts of disaster suddenly raced through his mind. What if he tripped? What if the Bellington boys gave only a half-hearted leap last time?

He shook the nerves out of his legs and took a deep draught of the first ale Mr. Bullberry handed him. The happy old man made his rounds to all the teams, handing out two pints a piece to every competitor.

"Good luck, boys," Mr. Bullberry cried, his eyes twinkling in the fires.

Ector nodded his thanks, breathing deeply. He thought his racing heart was going to pound right out of his chest. Looking at the other teams, one of the Bellington boys stared back and whispered something to his teammate, which made the other snort.

The friendly competition suddenly took a turn towards disdainful as Ector felt the fire of competition burning hotter within. He wanted nothing more than to show why they should have chosen a different race.

"You ready for this, mate?" Ector yelled, turning to Meric. Meric had finished his first pint and was more than idly jumping. "Whoa, easy." Ector signaled not to jump so high. "Go slow on the second one, so it's fresh."

"No worries here, mate!" Meric replied. "We earn more points for jumping longer. I'll clear the competition. You just make sure you log another twenty-eight strider!"

"Right," Ector muttered, feeling the pressure sinking on him again.

Grigor sailed through the air just as Ector looked up; giving several extra hops mid-leap, he tried to push himself higher.

Awkward, but interesting, Ector thought, amazed that Grigor had come up with such an idea. On those rare occasions Grigor did show up to class, he hadn't developed a reputation as a "thinker."

Grigor soared past the first lit pole, chin stuck out. The effort was much improved from his first leap, but still significantly short of the leaders in both categories. Mr. Bullberry dutifully stepped off the distance.

"One full head below the fire pit, for a score of three!" Mr. Bullberry announced. "And sixteen paces distance, leaving us a score of ten!"

The crowds whistled, but it was too dark to see the board, so Mr. Bullberry jotted the notes on his pieces of parchment instead.

"Ha! Fenodor needs to jump over thirty paces to even come close," Meric cried. "Good luck, mate!"

Ector had witnessed two versions of Meric tonight, and between the two, he preferred the over-exuberant one, without a doubt. But another thought did cross his mind.

"Uh, quick reminder," Ector chimed delicately. "We're focusing on beating those Bellington lads, right?"

"Why can't we set our sights equally on everyone?" Meric asked innocently, pretending like he hadn't been obsessing over Fenodor all evening. His reddish glow deepened, reminiscent of the hue earlier in the night before he unleashed the unbeatable jump. Taking it as a good sign, Ector stopped pushing his luck.

"Excellent point!" Ector agreed, abandoning the attempt to refocus him. "And you've figured out Mr. Bullberry's scoring methods, have you?"

"No, why?" Meric asked, looking confused.

"Well, how do you know he needs to leap over thirty paces?" Ector replied.

"Oh, that's just a guess." Meric shrugged, waving off the question. "He certainly can't beat us with anything less."

Fenodor loosed a roar of a belch, startling Ector, and stopped about six long strides behind the line.

"Alright, young Fenodor, whenever you're ready," Mr. Bullberry encouraged, bouncing on the balls of his feet.

Fenodor sprinted forward, launching himself through the air with an incredible push.

"Good night!" Mr. Bullberry exclaimed, beginning to march out to where Fenodor landed, less–than gracefully.

"Twenty-three, twenty-four..." counted Mr. Bullberry, just as the crowd started chanting with him. "...And twenty-eight for a second time tonight!"

"No way!" yelled Ector, but his voice was drowned in the roaring. He craned his neck, trying to find the impact site, but giant shadows flickered across the area, making it hard to see. Ector would have bet his last pouch of beans Fenodor had gained an extra two strides after bouncing forward on the landing.

"That's a mighty generous mark," Ector commented, still trying to find the flattened grass.

"Fenodor's not as dumb as he looks," Meric replied. "He must've watched you during the trials, because he tucked his legs just before landing and got those extra strides, just like you."

Ector couldn't believe it.

Meric craned his neck as concerned murmurs floated around the crowd.

"What's happening?" asked Ector. "Can you see?"

"Looks like he's hurt himself," Meric replied, towering over the surrounding people on the tips of his toes. "He definitely wasn't prepared for the landing, that's for sure. Actually, they ought to deduct a couple points for that atrocious sight."

"Team One's much improved final score," Mr. Bullberry bellowed, hanging on to the last word for a long, agonizing second, "is twenty-seven points!"

The crowd erupted anew as Fenodor hopped to his feet and waved to the crowd, hobbling off.

The first boy from Bueford took the last gulp of his Grasshopper Ale and, placing the empty pint on the ground, readied himself at the line. Sizing up the field, he flung himself through the air from a dead standstill.

To Ector's relief, the boy barely reached the bottom of the fire pit as he soared past, flying in a low arch that didn't carry him very far. Ector turned to Meric and breathed a bit more easily knowing that they could both top that.

The second Bueford boy, visibly disappointed with his partner's effort, quickly stepped up, eager to redeem the team. Stepping backwards several paces, he let his arms dangle for a moment. But then, like a flash of lightning, he sprinted full speed and launched himself long like an arrow, clearly going for distance.

"Disqualification!" Mr. Bullberry yelled.

Ector, captivated by such a stellar launch, searched confusedly for Mr. Bullberry. Partially hidden in the recesses of the shadows, Mr. Bullberry pointed at a clear footprint denting the grass, stretching halfway over the starting line.

"I'm sorry, laddie," Mr. Bullberry continued as the boy bounded back, yelling. "You can give it another try if you like, but once your one good jump is out, we've yet to see anyone outdo it on their second attempt."

Ector couldn't understand the boy's thick accent, but one thing was clear: He was boiling mad.

"You'd have to drink another pint," Mr. Bullberry answered, clearly much better at understanding him. "But we can't keep the last two teams waiting. That's why I told you to mind the starting line. It wouldn't be fair to make the other teams wait, letting their brew lose its spring, while you prepare for another turn."

The boy kept arguing, but Mr. Bullberry simply shook his head.

"No, that won't do either. That's why the teams that jump the best get to go last. If you jump after them, it takes away the advantage they've earned. This isn't our first Harvest Festival, laddie!" Mr. Bullberry turned his back and announced the next team while fixing the trampled line.

"You two heard?" Mr. Bullberry asked, turning towards the Bellington team. "I don't want to make that call again, but I will if I must."

The first Harvest Festival had been riddled with cheating and disorganization, but Mr. Bullberry was having none of it this year. The Bellington boys nodded nervously, seeing that the old man meant it.

The first Bellington lad stretched his arms wide and took five gigantic steps backwards. Digging his back foot into the ground for better traction, his stocky legs shoved forward with quick, choppy movements. Taking Mr. Bullberry's warning to heart, the boy sprang a full foot's length behind the line. It was a small price to pay as he went soaring like Ector had only ever seen Meric do. His upward pace was good, and his head cleared the flames before his torso and knees followed into darkness.

Ector watched, stunned as everyone cheered. The boy landed, giving three more medium-sized leaps down the pitch before meandering back to the starting line with a smile from ear to ear.

"One full body above the fires!" Mr. Bullberry cried, ecstatically. "And a height score of seven!"

The pressure returned.

Mr. Bullberry announced a distance score of ten as the second Bellington jumper pounded his chest, lining up even further back than Ector's previous ten paces. The boy hesitated barely a second before charging like a bull. Arms pinned at his sides, he flew straight as an arrow, head first. Following Ector's example, he didn't protect himself on the descent, but unlike Fenodor, his hands flew out to brace for impact at the last possible instant. Tucking underneath his shoulders, he tumbled head under feet and rolled to a magnificent standing pose several bounds later.

"Eighteen, nineteen..." Mr. Bullberry shouted, bellowing the number of strides as the crowd joined in. "...Twenty-seven, twenty-eight, twenty-nine, thirty!"

Ector couldn't believe it. Blocking out the rambunctious hollering filling the night, he turned to Meric.

"This is your race, mate!"

"We have a new distance record!" Mr. Bullberry cut in. "With a distance score of twenty-seven points!"

He didn't even bother announcing the height score; the boy had barely flown half the height of the fire poles down the field.

"Team Two has a total of thirty-four points in all!"

The noise from the crowd made Ector's ears ring as Meric bounded up to the starting line in large leaps, teasing the masses. Ector took another large gulp of his last pint, fighting off the nerves.

"Whenever you're ready, son!" Mr. Bullberry yelled over the chanting of Meric's name. Meric paused for a moment, searching the crowd. Ector watched Meric crane his neck, and he tried to follow his line of sight. Then he found her: Mara. Standing with Fenodor, her eyes were locked on Meric. She looked torn between Fenodor's affection, and the contestant who had the entire crowd's attention.

Apprehension swelled. Meric's spirits couldn't sustain another trip through the mud; there was no way they stood a chance at winning without Meric.

Ector's eyes shot to him; he feared the worst. But Meric was already down in his signature stance, pants hiked up to his knees, legs trembling even more ferociously than during the tryouts.

The leap that followed was incredible. Meric hurled himself so high, he almost completely disappeared into the night; only the tallest flame, of a much larger fire than before, could shed light on a pair of boots gliding past.

Several long seconds later, Meric landed amongst a thunderous applause that swallowed any sliver of silence in the valley. Ector looked to the mountains, worried they might start to crumble. When he glanced back, Mr. Bullberry's voice didn't have a chance to cut through the noise, but Ector saw his mouth form the word "*ten.*" Beginning to step off the distance, Mr. Bullberry stopped a few paces in and waved off the exercise, jovially. With a broad smile, he turned and waved Ector over to the starting line, already savvy to their plan that Ector would go for the long leap.

Approaching the line, and still fighting the sourness in his stomach, he suddenly caught sight of Mara. She flung herself out of the crowd trying to touch Meric as he passed. He gave her a wink, but continued strutting back to the line.

Now Mara had eyes only for Meric, and he smiled, knowing it. "One jump to go, mate!"

Ector laughed, which eased the tension.

Yeah, one jump to go, he thought, loosening his legs. One last swig of the Grasshopper Ale and he felt the spring in his step lighten even more. He set the empty pint on the ground and bounded forward, stopping twelve long strides behind the starting line. Arm out, he lined up the exact spot where the Bellington boy landed; if he could just manage to reach that same general area, Meric's score would edge them to victory.

Satisfied with his aim, Ector swung his arm back for a boost of momentum and bounded forward. Pushing with everything his legs could muster, he moved with the lightest of ease. The starting line was fast approaching, and he made sure to step carefully.

The fear of disqualification drifted away, along with the ground, as he sailed effortlessly, the wind ruffling his thick hair like never before. Soaring past the first fire pole, and still heading upwards, he felt the excitement surging. Never had he flown this fast before. But no sooner had the thought entered his head than the wind cut sharply across him. All the air supporting him suddenly disappeared, and he dropped in mid-air, feeling his momentum slow. Already on the descent, he fought the wind torquing him to the side as it gusted through the open field. Glimpses of the crowd trying to hold their hats and coats in place caught his eye.

Ector strained his body straighter, shedding the resistance, but the gust started whipping around him, faster and faster, changing trajectory and direction so quickly, he couldn't counteract it. The wind made its final turn, facing him head on, and the downward pressure was too much to bear. Ector felt himself forced to the ground. It all happened so fast; he landed in a crumpled heap, just managing to raise an elbow and roll side over side, doing his best to keep tucked. The ground slowed him to a halt.

The dull pain only lasted a few seconds, before it was pushed to the back of his mind. He didn't want to open his eyes. The crowd didn't cheer, and the eerie silence only confirmed his worst fear.

Lifting his head, he was surprised to find sleek black boots standing in front of him. The musty, stained leather reeked of mold and stalled his breath for an agonizing moment. Ector recognized the pointy-ends, which had stood next to his snow-covered bushels the day prior. He arched back his head to see a familiar black traveling cloak, ruffling and flapping in the wind as it coursed around the tall figure. Masked in the shadows of his hood, the man's motionless head gazed at him.

"Nineteen, twenty. Make way if you please," shouted Mr. Bullberry, stepping out the measurement. "Twenty-one!"

The crowd murmured.

"Did you see that?" exclaimed one observer, voice cutting slightly above the crowd's noise.

"Just popped out of the air, he did!" cried another.

Ector got to his feet, retreating a couple of paces. The man watched him silently, following his every movement. Looking around the clearing, Ector saw several more figures, dressed exactly the same, beginning to appear out of the crowd. The man was at least twice Ector's height, and he reached slowly with gloved hands to remove his hood, but the on-lookers gasped as the man – no, not a man – revealed a head of long, silvery hair pulled tightly around elongated, pointy ears. His skin was blotched green, reminding Ector of a rotting cucumber. Glimmering purple eyes emanated like beacons into the night and locked into him. The creature's lips curled into a smirk.

"What is it?" asked a lone child. Silence gripped the crowd as the creature looked to the distraction, snickering.

"Fools!" His voice rumbled in a low growl. But he didn't waste time answering the question. His head was already swiveling back to Ector to study him once more.

"Indeed, he does bear the mark of evening's light," the voice continued, but softer, as if talking to himself.

Ector sensed others drawing closer. He stole a quick glance around and found the shadowy figures bleeding from the crowd's edges beginning to form a circle around him in the open field.

"This day is long overdue," rasped the creature, not to himself this time, but clearly to Ector. Ector saw his gloved hand reach for something silver, slung at his hip.

"You ask what it is?" came a different voice from somewhere in the crowd, responding to the lone child's question still hanging in the air. The creature's pulsing fuchsia eyes danced along the crowd, searching for the distraction.

"They have no name!" continued the man, louder this time, but still hidden somewhere in the masses.

The creature's eyes narrowed to a glare as his search intensified. But he didn't have to look hard as people began to shift, making way for a tall traveler. The mysterious stranger stepped to the edge of the crowd; the flickers from the fire poles made it hard to see him clearly. The voice sounded familiar.

"They are vile and despicable!" answered the voice, even stronger now as he took another step, separating himself. The traveler emerged into full view, and Ector saw the silhouette of a man with tall boots, and a round, brimmed hat, which concealed his face in the shadows, even when the light did flicker on him fully. His traveling coat draped to his knees and ruffled in the wind behind him. Those encircling Ector all turned their attention to the newcomer.

The creature standing before Ector seethed, baring his teeth at the man.

"In due time, old friend," he rumbled, with a hint of a smile. "First, we must finish old business."

The translucent violet eyes returned to Ector, but they didn't have a chance to lock onto him again. Ector felt two hands latch onto his shoulders and hoist him high into the air; flying over the encirclement before he knew what was happening, Ector heard Meric's voice.

"Gotcha, mate!"

They tumbled to the ground several paces away, outside the circle. Ector rolled to his back; the henchmen had already turned, closing the distance as Meric bounced away into the night, out of control.

A ball of light suddenly leapt into the air from the hand of the brimmed-hat traveler and streamed into the center of the empty encirclement, exploding into a rage of fire. A wave radiated outwards, knocking Ector and everyone else flat to the ground.

The crowd erupted into chaos. Several more balls of light appeared in each of the cloaked henchmen's hands, as all regained their feet. The night flashed with explosions in all directions as huge columns of black smoke started rising high into the air. The smoke soon glowed orange with small crackling fires, and the largest sprang to life on the pub rooftop and quickly spread to the nearby fields parched from autumn. A high-arching orb of blue light illuminated the night and then landed dead center on the pub. The scattered fires united into one huge blaze as the wooden roof burst into flames. Hazy light flooded the darkness amidst the thick smoke rolling throughout the valley like a dense fog, obscuring everything.

The brimmed-hat traveler appeared out of the smoke before Ector. "Come with me if you want to live!"

He removed his hat, and Ector immediately recognized the man's icy blue eyes. It was the traveler with the horse's tail in the back: the one he'd met earlier in the day, and the one who'd granted his escape from the pub. But something started to happen to the man. His eyes were the same, and his hair was still midnight black, but his ears began to grow, pointed at the tops like the creatures that had encircled him. His skin remained fair though, without any green blotches that plagued the other one.

"What are you?" Ector yelled, fighting out of the man's clutches.

"My name is Dalis," he replied, helping Ector to his feet. "I am an elf."

Ector felt the thing's other arm wrap around his mid-section and begin leading him towards the mountainous forestside. "I will explain more after we escape."

"Wait, we can't leave the others!" cried Ector, resisting.

"Oy!" came Meric's voice, finding his way out of the smoky chaos. "Take your hands off him!"

Meric lunged at Ector's captor, but Dalis effortlessly shrugged the attack off, sending Meric rolling into a bed of shrubs and bouncing away; the uncontrollable effects of the Grasshopper Ale still coursed through him.

"This is quite a mess you created," Dalis remarked, picking Ector up off his feet and bolting with unbelievable speed to where Meric was fighting his way down from a low growing tree.

"Me?" cried Ector. "The night was going just fine until you..." He paused, realizing to whom, or rather to what, he was talking. "Did you say you're an elf?"

"As I said, young master," Dalis replied, holding out a hand to prevent Meric from bouncing away. "I will explain more, once we are further away from here. These are no ordinary elves that come for you tonight. Forgiveness, young Meric."

"How did he know my name?" Meric asked, climbing down, looking to Ector for answers. "Why are these things chasing you, mate?"

"I don't know," Ector replied, while Dalis herded them both deeper into the woods. "I have no idea what's happening right now."

"Did he say he's an elf?" Meric asked, bewildered. "Elves aren't real!"

"Well, I've never seen a human that looks like that," Ector whispered.

"Keep your voices down!" hushed Dalis. "We will not survive another attack. You are lucky to have made it this far."

"Why would elves come after you?" Meric pressed on, apparently not comprehending Dalis's instructions. Ector shrugged, at a complete loss as Dalis continued to push them deeper into the woods.

They climbed over dead logs, snuck between outstretched limbs, and ducked beneath branches, until Dalis pulled everyone down into a dense bush.

"What about the others?" Ector asked. "We can't just leave everyone back there."

"Their fate is unfortunate," replied Dalis, checking for pursuers. "But we cannot go back."

Screams echoed off the mountains and up into the night, rising like the smoky fires consuming the village.

"They are burning everything, searching for you," Dalis explained.

A twig snapped off to their left.

In a flash, Dalis disappeared towards the sound.

The boys waited several seconds before Ector left the protection of the bush and chased after the elf. Meric followed close behind.

They didn't have to travel far. A short distance away, Dalis held his hand cupped over a sobbing girl's mouth and a knife to her throat.

"Stop!" yelled Ector, but quickly bit his tongue at Dalis's deadly stare. Ector hurried over to them, tip-toeing along the soft brush. "She is a friend. Her name is Annalin. She is with us."

Dalis re-sheathed his knife onto his belt, but kept his hand firmly secured over her lips. His waist was laden with all sorts of pouches and sheaths; Ector couldn't even begin to guess what they might contain, but he saw at least a second knife hidden beneath the traveling cloak.

Dalis kept his hand secured over Annalin's mouth, but turned her around so she could see the single finger held to his lips that wanted absolute silence from everyone.

The wind suddenly gusted through the forest.

"Quickly, into the bush!" Dalis hissed, corralling the three under a nearby shrub with sharp leaves.

Ignoring the pricks and scratches, Ector shoved inside to make room for the others. The gust howled even louder as Dalis threw himself in last, and stretching his cloak out wide, he wrapped all of them in utter darkness.

The sucking noise died, and in the silence that followed, Ector heard soft footsteps roaming close by. Dalis's crystal sapphire eyes glowed right in front of them under the cloak; they moved from side to side, signaling all of them to remain absolutely silent and still. It was an unnecessary gesture as Ector felt the cold fear of being hunted grip him. The padded steps crunched in circles, closer and closer.

"They were here," a husky voice said. "Look at these tracks. You see the elf prints?"

"There are too many prints," replied a scratchy, higher-pitched voice. "Dalis would not have bothered rescuing any of the other beasts. He just wants the one."

"But the tracks disappear right here," continued the husky voice, standing beside the bush, merely a step away from them. "Can you not see the elf prints?"

"Yes, I can," replied the scratchy voice, impatiently. "But in case you forgot, we combed this area last night looking for Dalis's hut. These are our own tracks."

A long moment of silence followed.

"We need to return," the scratchy voice said, sounding agitated. "The torturing is about to begin. Loramis is furious that we lost the boy again. If these animals are hiding him, they will turn him over."

"And if the boy has already fled?" asked the husky voice.

"Then he will not last long, will he?" replied the other, sounding annoyed with the questions.

The deeper voice grunted his agreement, but then stopped.

"Wait!"

Ector sensed the creature inspecting the area, prying into every nook and shadow. The silence was almost unbearable.

"Do you smell that?" murmured the voice. "Smells like humans, very near. I think I hear the thoughts of one, too..."

A loud, unexpected whack cut the night. Ector flinched.

Fortunately, the elf's painful yelp masked the slight rustling as Annalin clasped a hand to her mouth, stopping a scream just before the scratchy voice returned again.

"I told you—stop wasting time. Of course I smell it! The whole valley is rife with their stench. It is an infested swamp."

"This smelled closer," threatened the husky voice, bristling at the discipline.

"You are new to our ranks, and so forgiven for your ignorance, but when I say we are finished, it means we are finished!" The scratchy voice paused, almost daring the other to test him. "We are finished," the elf reiterated slowly.

The last scratchy words had barely left his mouth, before the howling sprang to life again. It swirled, kicking up dead leaves, twigs, and anything else not rooted to the ground. Through Dalis's cloak, the faint outline of both elves began to lift into the air. They disappeared with the wind.

Waiting under the cloak for several more seconds, Dalis stepped out first, emerging from the bush.

"That was incredible!" Meric exclaimed, rushing out after Dalis. "How did they not see us? We were right in front of them!"

"Very strange," Dalis commented, looking between Ector and the other two for a moment. "They should have heard your thoughts and detected your scents, but..."

"But what?" Meric asked, about to overflow with excitement.

"I suspect their deformity is to blame," Dalis continued, searching the area for others snooping close by. "It would not be the first time their dark magic has left them blinded to what was right in front of them."

Dalis stopped and stared intensely at Ector for a moment, but then quickly resumed scanning the area again, muttering something that sounded like, "*Perhaps it is something different.*"

"That one said he could smell us!" exclaimed Meric. "And hear our thoughts!"

"Yes, your scents are rather thick," responded Dalis. "And your thoughts annoyingly loud; both are problems we will deal with soon, but not now. We need to first move away from here, and quickly."

Annalin spoke for the first time, whispering.

"What makes them different from you?"

Dalis turned, visibly displeased at the question. "You cannot tell the difference?"

The scared look in Annalin's eyes penetrated Dalis's chilly demeanor, and his glare softened as she began to sob quietly.

"You will have to forgive me, young ones," Dalis continued, apologetically. "I forget how strange this all is for you. Judging by young Meric's earlier remark—that elves are not real—it seems we have, indeed, become a myth among you."

"I can't believe you're real!" Meric exclaimed, unfazed by Annalin's sobbing, staring wonder-eyed at the mystic creature.

"You looked different the other night," Ector interjected, taking Annalin's courage to heart and braving a question of his own. "Your ears—they looked like ours before tonight. They weren't pointy."

Dalis nodded.

"Elves are born with various gifts. Mine is that of concealment; the ability to blend in with my surroundings." He gestured towards his face.

"That includes matching the appearance of humans, when I am close enough and choose to do so."

"Why are they attacking us?" Annalin demanded, still fighting the tears welling up. "What did we do to them?"

"I am afraid that answer requires more time than we have at the moment," Dalis replied, turning to advance deeper into the forest, away from the smoke and flames devouring the village. He waved for the children to follow.

"We can't just leave the town burning!" Ector cried, astonished that the elf expected them to simply walk away. "We have to fight them! We know those people! They said they would torture everyone until they find us!"

"No, not us," Dalis corrected, continuing on his way. "Just you, Ector."

Ector held his arms out, stopping Meric and Annalin from following the elf.

"Why are they after me?"

Dalis stopped and turned to face Ector, clearly not appreciating the attempt to hold their forward progress hostage.

"We have no idea who you are," Ector continued, feeling his voice shake as the elf's threatening stare penetrated him. "Maybe you're leading us into a trap."

"They are after you, because they are sick in their minds," Dalis answered. "And they will return to search these forests once they discover you are not in Cleargar." He turned and took a few more paces before stopping again. He shook his head, realizing they still weren't following.

"They will never stop hunting you, young master." Dalis turned to face them again. "You must follow me, now, if you want to live."

Never in all his life had Ector fought so hard to muster the courage for a simple question as he did now. His arms felt heavier, begging to drop under the weight of the elf's piercing stare boring into him.

"Why do you keep calling me master?" Ector managed, scraping together every last shred of gumption.

"Because I serve you now, as I have for the last nine years, hiding you from them," Dalis explained. "And I can either tell you some of the story now, and risk us all dying once your scents reach them again, or we can move a safe distance from here, and I will tell you everything."

Every last fiber in Ector's body wanted to follow the elf to a safe place, away from these monsters, but something inside refused to budge.

"We cannot leave the others!" Ector insisted, surprised by the force of his words.

"Keep your voice low!" Dalis ordered. "Their dark powers are difficult to outmatch one-on-one, let alone in numbers."

Ector knew he risked Annalin's and Meric's lives by delaying. His arms dropped. Balls of light continued to rain and explode on everything he knew so well as he turned for one last look at their home. The trees spanning the edge of town burned, along with the fields, and the stores and houses; all the people he had ever known in the whole world were trapped in a circle of fire. Because of him.

"They torture your people, because the battle most important to them was lost. You. And not only that," Dalis continued, backtracking all the way to stand next to them. "But they lost this battle for a second time. If you return, they will kill you, and swiftly."

His words hung heavy in the air.

"Isn't one life better than an entire village?" Ector asked, unable to bear the thought of what was happening behind the flames separating him from Cleargar. His stomach turned on itself, making him sick.

"Your selflessness is admirable," Dalis replied, sounding slightly surprised. "But your ignorance leads you to foolish conclusions. They will destroy the village regardless, because they hate all humans."

Again, Dalis let his words rest on them for a moment.

Why do elves hate humans? We didn't even know elves were real.

"You are their prize," continued Dalis, watching with the children as the valley was destroyed before their eyes.

"I don't understand. What do they want from me?" Ector asked.

"Some years ago, I lost a dear friend because of too many questions," Dalis responded. He was so quick that Ector was stunned, staring disoriented up at the ground. It took a second to realize he had been lifted effortlessly and was actually staring down at the ground, bent over Dalis's shoulder and being carried away deeper into the forest.

"I will not make that mistake tonight," Dalis continued, walking with Ector draped like a sack of beans over his back. "If you two want to live, it is time to move."

Annalin and Meric stood stupefied; the elf apparently had no qualms leaving them to die.

But Dalis had barely made it three steps before a very large and hairy animal blind-sided him. The collision knocked the elf to the ground, and Ector rolled into a very prickly bush. Before Ector could find his bearings, a familiar snarl told him everything he needed to know: Rahms.

The dog stood menacingly over the elf, threatening to clamp down on his throat. But as quickly as Rahms had launched himself out of the darkness, he settled and began to sniff curiously. Dalis didn't move a muscle and allowed the dog free rein.

The sniffs turned to wet licks, and then Rahms settled to the ground, panting without a care in the world.

"Thank the fates!" whispered Dalis, rolling to his knees, dripping in slobber. "He has the worst eyesight and nose I have ever witnessed of an animal."

Ector stopped short of challenging the idea that the elf somehow knew Rahms; Rahms never eased on a threat, almost to a fault. Yet here he sat, idly panting.

"How could Rahms know you?" Ector asked, shifting his eyes uneasily between the two.

"Come with me," Dalis responded, gaining his feet. "Before we are found. This way—my dwelling is just over here. I built it close enough to the village to keep an eye on you, but far enough away to not be discovered accidentally."

Ector scanned the area skeptically; he'd visited this part of the forest dozens of times. Not once had he found anything even remotely close to a dwelling.

"Quickly now!" urged Dalis, waving for the children to follow as he stepped briskly, marching deeper into the dark forest.

A persistent nagging urged Ector to return to the village and fight. But as he looked over his shoulder again, and saw the unnatural wind twisting the flames, creating vortexes that sucked the fire, swirling them higher into the sky, he hung his head. These things had powers he had never seen, had never even imagined.

"Ector," beckoned Dalis. "You must choose your battles. Tonight is not the night."

The screams rose louder, and Ector hated himself for agreeing. He took a step towards the elf, and one foot followed the other until they were all stepping at Dalis's hurried pace, heading much deeper into the woods. It seemed like only seconds before the cries sounded distant.

After several minutes of silent scolding, Ector planted his foot to double back. Rebellious thoughts of rescuing the village had overcome him. But before breaking away, a peculiar tune rang softly in Ector's ear. The elf whistled it lightly, directing it with cupped hands.

A mysterious jostling rumbled underfoot as Ector stretched out a hand, clinging to a tree. The tremors died as quickly as they began, but in its wake, a glow from below the surface of the ground flickered faintly. Dalis knelt next to the enormous Blackwood tree, from where the source emanated. He whistled again, a bit louder this time.

The light crept along the gnarled veins running up the tree's trunk, but then the roots of the tree demanded all attention as they opened wide and parted the earth. The glow expanded to reveal stairs leading down into a large underground opening; the hole in the earth was big enough for them to pass through.

"Quickly, if you please, before we are seen," encouraged Dalis, waving to the three of them.

Rahms raced down the steps first, almost as if he had been there before. Meric and Annalin quickly hurried in afterwards, and Ector, too, found himself following. Having barely cleared the level of the forest floor, Dalis was already on Ector's heels, whistling the same peculiar tune again. The soil filled the gaping hole, and the roots quickly contorted back into their original shape before Ector's very eyes.

He wanted to say something, wanted to protest, but he had nothing new to say. They had already been over the matter, and tonight was not the night to challenge these creatures. But he couldn't stop himself.

"We shouldn't be here! Not while everyone is out there dying!"

Dalis didn't respond, but instead passed him on the staircase. The children followed and descended into a round, cozy room with a roaring fire. Ector hadn't noticed how cold he was until the warmth reached his icy hands.

"I am afraid we do not have the means to defeat them, young master," Dalis replied, hanging his timber-colored traveling cloak on a root that crawled along the earthen wall. "In all honesty," he continued, turning to face Ector. "It is rather amazing you survived a second time. You were incredibly lucky the first time, and even luckier tonight."

Ector's only response was to stare confusedly. He had no clue what the elf was talking about.

"I don't understand. What do these things want with me? And how do you know my dog? This is the first time I've ever seen anything like you, or them. We should be out there fighting them!"

He pounded on the wall with frustration.

Dalis didn't say anything, but simply watched as a long, uncomfortable moment passed. Meric and Annalin clearly felt the awkwardness as well and diverted their attention to taking in the new surroundings, making noises of surprise.

"This is fascinating!" Annalin exclaimed, putting a little too much effort into sounding awestruck as she looked around the enchanting underground home.

"It was a rather difficult piece of magic," Dalis replied kindly, though his eyes remained fixed on Ector.

"And you are tired," Dalis continued, nodding to Ector and ending their uncomfortable moment. "You must get some rest. The sun will break the horizon in four hours."

The mere mention of rest made Ector's body feel twice as heavy. On any other night, he would have been asleep hours ago and would gladly have taken the offer.

"I can't sleep," he replied, to the immense disappointment of his body's tired muscles. "Not while people are being tortured because of me."

"Well, you must become acclimated to it and quickly," countered Dalis matter-of-factly. "They are not the first to die for you, nor will they be the last."

The words were harsh and unexpected. Ector thought about arguing; perhaps they had the wrong person? But there were too many strange coincidences: Could the dark henchmen also have mistaken him? *Maybe*, he decided. But there was still no explanation as to why Rahms felt at ease around this... *elf*. Ector found it hard to use the word, feeling silly even thinking it to himself.

"I don't understand what any of that means! You're the first *elf* I've met!" Ector exclaimed, shaking his head, deciding just to embrace the word. If Dalis wanted to call himself an elf, then so be it. "Until this moment, all the elves I've heard of live in bedtime stories."

"Not true, on both counts," Dalis replied, studying Ector with unflinching eyes. "You really have no idea, do you?"

Ector stared blankly in response.

Meric raised a hand to chime in. "Actually, I think I may have seen an elf once."

"Doubtful," Dalis replied, cutting Meric off. "We tend not to care about humans."

The blunt statement was a visible disappointment for Meric.

"Nothing like this has ever happened before," Ector emphasized, hoping that if he said it enough times, they might all realize this whole ordeal was one huge mistake. "You said this is the second time I escaped; are you absolutely sure you have the right person?"

"You were only a youngling when the first attack happened," Dalis continued, taking a seat in a rather uncomfortable-looking wooden chair. "Please, sit."

He pointed to a stack of cushions piled in the far corner of the room and then reached for three wooden bowls. Pouring steaming hot liquid into each, he placed the bowls in front of the fireplace where he motioned for the children to sit. Annalin retrieved the cushions for everyone as Rahms plopped down beside the elf, panting.

"That is how your dog knows me—I aided in your escape when your family was first attacked, which is why Rahms did not try to rip me to shreds when he found me hauling you away."

Ector watched the elf stroke Rahms's coat. The scent of pine and berry wafting from the bowl in front of him was irresistible. He sipped the steamy liquid and found it strangely delicious and satisfying.

"I was there the night you escaped," Dalis continued. "This animal saved your life."

Seeing Ector's baffled look, the elf leaned closer. "Perhaps it is better if we start from the beginning; drink, it will help."

Dalis waited for everyone to settle into a comfortable position before pressing on.

"Almost nine years ago, I left from a distant part of the forest in search of these elves that found you tonight. It was a strange night. The season was warm, but the wind blew cold. A frost besieged us."

"Wait," Ector interrupted, remembering the bizarre storm that struck the forest just an evening ago. "The other day, I was harvesting flowers on the other mountainside, when the air turned cold, and it began snowing *inside* the forest. I saw a strange traveler cloaked in black, just like the ones out there tonight."

"Yes." Dalis nodded. "That is their signature: The chill."

"But if they mean to kill me, why didn't they?" Ector asked. "I was all alone in the forest."

"All I can tell you is that they once came for me, too," Dalis replied. "But they are blinded by something. There is no way either of us should be alive, talking with each other tonight. I do not pretend to fully understand it, but just know: this is not the ordinary magic of elves."

"Ordinary magic?" Ector asked. "How do you tell the difference?"

"It is a bit difficult to explain," replied Dalis. "If you were more familiar with our kind, you would understand my meaning."

He thought for a moment, visibly struggling with where to begin.

"Let us take my gift as an example," he offered. "My gift is that of disguise. I can conceal myself almost anywhere." He stood up and moved to the far side of the room. "Watch carefully," he said, before stepping into the shadow of the corner. The children watched.

"I don't understand," Meric commented, looking baffled. "I can still see you. You're right there."

"Yes," remarked Dalis. "You can see me, because I drew your attention to me beforehand. Look away to the fire and then try again."

They all looked at the fire for a brief moment. Then, just as Dalis requested, they returned their gaze to the corner, but the children all gasped: He had disappeared.

"I am still here," came Dalis's voice; a pair of nearly invisible pants ruffled for them to see.

Ector made out the faint line of the elf's body in the shadows after that.

"How did you do that?" exclaimed Meric.

"Only when I draw your attention to me can you find me," Dalis explained, stepping out of the recesses and returning to his seat.

"But how did you disappear?" asked Meric again.

"I told you. It is my gift. But as you all could see, I did not in fact disappear entirely. I only camouflaged myself with the surroundings."

"Well, how is that different from what those other elves are doing out there?" asked Annalin.

"I will get to that in a moment, lady Annalin," Dalis answered patiently. "But first you should know that, just as all elves have a gift of some kind, elves can sense when another elf is near." Dalis paused, looking expectant, but the children only stared blankly back at him.

"Do you remember when we hid in the bushes just now?" asked Dalis. "Those elves were only a few paces from us. Knowing now that we can sense each other, is it not a bit peculiar they had trouble finding us?"

"Well, it was your gift," said Meric. "Right?"

"No," replied Dalis, shaking his head. "My gift does not supersede our innate ability to sense each other. They may not have been able to see me, but they should have known an elf was there."

The children looked confused.

"Humans are even worse," he continued. "Your scents are very strong to us. It is what helps us avoid you when we desire it, which is almost all the time."

"Why didn't they find us then?" asked Annalin.

"As I said, something blinds them," explained Dalis. "I think it is related to this magic they wield, but I need more time."

"More time for what?" asked Ector.

Dalis rolled the question around before answering. "Elves have a very foggy past, you could say," he replied finally. "There are certain events, certain scrolls, which our elders have tried at all costs to destroy. The true accounts of what happened around one thousand years ago and before are unknown to us, or at the very least, have been concealed." Dalis pondered on his words for a moment. "I need more time to research," he continued. "More time to see if these dark powers are hidden somewhere in our forsaken histories."

"How are you going to do that?" asked Ector.

"There is a body that rules over all elves," Dalis explained. "It is called the High Elvish Council. I believe your kind has what are called kings, yes?"

The children nodded.

"It is similar to that," Dalis continued. "You could call it an Elven Kingdom of sorts. At any rate, there is a chamber that contains many of our past secrets; it is rumored to be a library of our past."

"What do you hope to find?" asked Annalin. "What could a library possibly tell you about these elves out there?"

"There might be something," Dalis responded, still deep in thought. "Something that could explain this. There is much to your story, master Ector, before the night your parents died." Dalis lifted his gaze to meet Ector's. "The one I once swore to protect spoke of a dark power infiltrating our Council before she died. And she was the only one still alive with first-hand knowledge of those distant times."

"From one thousand years ago?" exclaimed Meric. "She was over one thousand years old?"

"What happened to her?" asked Ector, seeing Dalis nod solemnly in response to Meric's question.

"I failed her," Dalis replied simply. "These same dark elves flew in the dead of night on the back of the wind. They ambushed us, and then they came for you, young Ector."

Dalis's words struck hard. Ector wanted to vomit.

"Is that their gift?" asked Meric, excitedly, oblivious to the somber moods settling throughout the room. "To fly on the wind?"

"It may not seem like dark magic, young Meric," Dalis replied. "But to control the wind—to bring a storm like they did on the night of your parents' death, Ector—it is very dark magic indeed."

The wind howled just then, squalling even through the dense ceiling of soil overhead.

"I have yet to fully discover the source of their power," Dalis continued, ignoring the interruption. "But the reason it is considered dark magic is because it cannot be controlled. As young elflings, we always heard of the rumored dark magic, but not until I saw it with my own eyes did I understand, or even believe it was real."

Dalis got to his feet.

"If we are to continue this, we must eat." He walked to the other side of the room and retrieved a large plate. Filling it with hardened breads, nuts, dried berries and cheeses from a shelf brimming with food, he took a couple of slices for himself, and then placed the tray in front of the children, gesturing for them to eat. None of them needed a second invitation; they began devouring the food, famished.

"Much like elves have become myth among your kind," Dalis explained, while the children ate, "dark magic has become the same for us. It is a myth, in large part I suspect because of the forgotten histories. I thought the dark magic was nothing more than old elf-tales, until nine years ago, when I caught up with these elves just as they reached you, two leagues due east of Bellington."

Ector stopped mid-chew, stunned to see the story turn so close to Cleargar. Two leagues east of Bellington would have been a mere day or two from their valley.

"There was a ferocious storm the night your parents died," Dalis continued, leaning in closer to them. "A storm these dark ones created." He pointed to the ceiling where the large roots moved and shifted, adjusting in the ground to support the massive tree protecting them from the unnatural wind outside.

"Purple lightning filled the sky as the largest vortex I have ever witnessed destroyed the forest. Frozen raindrops, sharpened to a point, sliced through the air sideways, cutting us deep. Your mother and father fled for their lives as Rahms raced ahead of them, carrying you on a wooden sled."

Dalis paused to refill his bowl with another helping of the hot pine-needle berry drink and then did the same for the children's half-empty bowls. The gravity of his words hit Ector as his earliest memories returned.

"Mrs. Bodock said I was nearly frozen the night I arrived in a wooden sled," he said, aghast.

Dalis nodded. "I watched from a distance to make sure Rahms found refuge that night. He fled to the south, and I made sure you had not been tracked. I watched from the cliff of this very mountain. There was many a night I considered taking you, but I could not risk exposing your whereabouts. It was simply safer to watch you grow up in secret. The older you grew, the better your chances for survival. The safest and most optimistic outcome would have been to see you become a full-grown man, oblivious to all of this. And we almost made it."

Dalis trailed off, looking as if he regretted the decision to remain hidden this whole time.

"What happened to my mother and father?" Ector asked, feeling a fountain of other questions gushing inside him as soon as the words left his mouth: *What did they look like? Why did this elf know more about them than he did? Why were his parents stolen from him?*

Dalis took a deep breath, looking squarely into Ector's eyes. "They fought bravely. Especially your father, who was just a human."

"What do you mean, just a human?" Ector asked.

Dalis looked puzzled for a moment, until realization dawned on his face.

"Forgive me. I forget how little you know." He fiddled with his bowl and took another sip before continuing. "Your father, he was human, and as I said a very brave one. But your mother was an elf."

Ector's breath caught.

"You are what we call an elf-man, or a halfling," Dalis continued. "And you are very rare. I have only known one other halfling in all my long life. Both of you physically appeared like humans, but have certain Elvish qualities... Elvish abilities if you will."

Ector stuttered, shaking his head in disbelief.

"I don't... I don't have any abilities. I'm just me!"

"You think an unremarkable inn keeper, in all his lazy glory, created that concoction out there?" Dalis allowed the question to hang in the air before continuing. "Until you turned up on his doorstep, there was nothing special about him. And that remains the case today."

"That can't be right," Ector replied, rejecting the idea. "I told you earlier today when we met at Mrs. Bullberry's wagon; I don't make the brews!"

"You might not make the brews," Dalis countered, "but as you said, it was your task to harvest the ingredients. Have you noticed the brews getting stronger every year?"

Ector thought about it. "Well, yes, but that's because the old man has been trying different..."

"Your abilities are getting stronger," Dalis interrupted. "And every year, it has drawn more attention, including that of the elves. Travelers from all around know of your brews. Do you remember what I said to you earlier tonight? When you wondered how I could change my appearance?"

Ector nodded. "You said being around humans allows you to look more like us."

Dalis nodded in reply. "Your gift works similarly."

"You mean if I stop living around humans, I'll stop looking like them?" Ector asked, almost shocked.

"No, that is not your gift," Dalis clarified. "Remember, I said we all have different abilities. Your gift is with plants, and when you touch them, something magical happens." Dalis pointed to the corner. "Just as I am able to match the shadows over there, or the appearance of humans when surrounded by them, likewise you become more like an elf when surrounded by us. Your gift becomes stronger in our continued presence. The same was true for the other halfling I once knew."

Ector felt dizzy. "But I don't understand. The elves showed up just tonight. How could the brews have been getting stronger if they just now showed up?"

Regret fell across Dalis's face. "Living here in the forest, I have always been close to you, and it has clearly affected you. I considered moving further away to reduce the signs of your gift, and thus reduce your risk of being found, but..." Dalis let his voice trail off again. "With these dark elves tightening closer every year, it would not have made a difference. Their presence would have caused the same outcome. These dark ones have searched tirelessly for you ever since they failed to assassinate you."

Exhausted, Ector struggled to piece everything together.

"Your gift is two-fold, which is rare, even among elves," continued Dalis, settling back into his chair. "First, your touch releases a magic that lies dormant in plant life. But second, and more intriguingly, you seem to have the gift of unlocking this magic for humans to experience."

Dalis studied Ector carefully for another moment.

"I have watched you relentlessly and knew you had no idea of your gift. But I could not figure out how the brews continued so consistently every year. Not until our encounter earlier today. The old man was dimwitted in most regards, but he was savvy enough to keep the entire brew-making process the same, year after year. I should have realized it sooner."

Both Annalin and Meric looked at Ector as if he were a diseased vagrant.

"There has to be some other explanation!" responded Ector defiantly. "I can't be the reason all those people are dying!"

"You are not the reason," countered Dalis. "Those dark elves are the reason. And I am also to blame; the festival attracted more attention than I expected. I knew the dark elves were hunting you, but I muddled the years away in indecision at how to deal with the growing fame."

Quiet fell on the room for the first time since they arrived, as each of them took in the events of the night and of the past years in stunned silence. After a few moments, Meric raised his hand as if in a lesson at the schoolhouse.

"Er, I'm still confused about the dark magic. Why is it forbidden to make the wind blow?"

"Ah, yes," replied Dalis, returning from the depths of thought. "We need to finish our story. When I arrived the night your parents died, young Ector, a treacherous tornado swept the forest. The lightning lit every corner of the sky, flashing bolt after bolt. Rahms bounded ahead of your parents, navigating the snow much better than they could. Despite being an elf, your mother was the first to lose her footing."

Ector's earliest memories flashed into his mind. Purple lights, and a woman's voice calling out.

"Your father commanded Rahms to keep running," continued Dalis, looking down at the dog, now nine years older. "I remember seeing Rahms stop. He wanted to come back and help. But at your father's order, he ran as hard as he could for the mountains, pulling you along in a sled behind him. The snow was so deep you could barely be seen. Rahms churned the snow in all directions, covering you from head to toe. It is a miracle you did not freeze to death, being so young." Dalis shook the thought away, reliving the entire disaster. "Your father threw himself in front of your mother, while she used her magic to cover your tracks. Then a tree came crashing down..."

Dalis stared blankly into the crackling fire.

"Your mother cried out," he continued. "And just before your father perished... I am sorry, young master."

Ector felt the longing inside rising like an unstoppable wave. Why did his family have to be ripped from him like that?

"Your mother," Dalis continued, sighing. "She protected you with her very last breath, until the storm raged out of control. There was no recourse once the dark elves lost their handle. A lightning bolt pierced your mother, and then the storm turned, devouring the entire forest in all directions. It killed everyone, including the dark elves. Everyone except you, me, and Rahms here."

Ector didn't know if the anger or the sadness was swelling faster, but he felt about ready to explode with one of them.

"I raced down the ravine in pursuit of you and Rahms, staying on the outskirts. I watched from afar as the storm lasted for three long days. I believe the locals still talk about it, even today," he added, sounding almost disgusted. "I did not understand the type of magic I was dealing with at the time, and I still do not to a large extent. But what I do know is that we three were all lucky to walk away alive." Dalis stared into Ector's eyes, unblinking. "I eventually found you, hours later. Rahms was very clever. He saddled your sled and ascended the northern mountain, traversing the barren, rocky crags by night where the snow was unable to fall. He left no footprints to be tracked, once escaping the storm. Then he descended the other side and found the old man's pub in the early hours of morning, where you have been hiding ever since, unbeknownst to even yourself."

Dalis turned back to Meric.

"Attempting to harness the wind is considered dark magic, because it is uncontrollable. It leads to catastrophic events. The wind is a force of nature meant only for the Earth to use as she sees fit."

Ector could barely keep his eyes open any longer. He found Meric and Annalin already lying on their cushions in front of the fire.

"Are we safe here?" Ector asked, intending only to rest for a moment before trying again to persuade the elf to go out and rescue the others.

Dalis responded by pointing to the ceiling, and Ector recognized for the first time that the night sky was staring down at them.

"This enchantment allows us to see outside," Dalis explained. "But to anyone outside staring down, all they see is the forest floor. And your scents are well-guarded here. We are quite safe, I assure you."

Dalis rose and retrieved three blankets piled next to a small wooden bin. Giving one to Ector, he draped a blanket each over Annalin and Meric, both of whom had fallen fast asleep even before Dalis had finished answering Meric's question.

"Thank you," Ector said, taking the blanket. "For saving us. I'm sorry if I haven't sounded grateful. I am."

Dalis smiled and gestured for him to sleep.

Nodding his thanks again, Ector settled on his cushion next to the others, and he had barely nestled under the blanket before extreme exhaustion, aching in his muscles, overtook him. He caught one last fleeting glimpse of Dalis reclining into his chair, pouring another cup of pine-berry soup, and just before a dreamless sleep washed over him, Ector saw snowflakes descending out of the enchantment. But they never reached him.

Chapter 6
The Flight

Ector awoke to midday sunbeams striking him full in the face. Shielding his eyes, he squinted up at the sky, confused. He braced on his elbows and found the tiny room from last night still surrounding him. There was noisy rummaging in the kitchen area behind him, and Dalis's voice rang out.

"It is amazing you humans still exist," he said, talking with Annalin.

Rolling onto his stomach, Ector saw them preparing a meal at a tiny table meant for only one.

"With as much sleep as you require," said Dalis, "it is a wonder the wolves have not eaten you all."

"Don't you sleep?" Annalin asked.

"Sometimes," replied Dalis; judging by the look on his face, he didn't quite know how to respond to the question. "But only for a few minutes at a time. Never for half the day."

Ector rolled back over, exhausted. Staring up at the enchantment on the ceiling, he felt nervous, as if anyone could walk up to the cavernous hole and look inside.

"We have to go back," he called out groggily. He pretended not to notice the stiffness in his back as he made his way over to the kitchen. "We have to see if anyone else escaped."

"The dark ones will expect your return," Dalis replied. "They will likely use the villagers as bait to draw you out."

The idea brought the horrible sickness into Ector's stomach all over again.

"And good morning, by the way," Dalis continued, handing Ector a bowl of berries, leaves, and nuts. "We need to teach you something of manners before long. But first, eat. You cannot venture anywhere like this."

Ector looked at the strange assortment of foliage piled in his bowl. It didn't look appetizing.

"I know you are not used to this food," Dalis continued, acknowledging Ector's hesitation. "But it will serve you well."

"I'm not hungry," Ector responded. And it was the truth; the thought of people suffering pushed all thoughts of food to the back of his mind.

"Hungry or not, force it down," Dalis replied, refusing to accept the bowl back. "We will escape at nightfall; it is a long trek to where we go. You will need your energy."

Grudgingly, Ector shoveled a bite into his mouth. To his surprise, it went down easily, and even settled his stomach a bit. The thick, furry leaves tasted of cucumber, and the yellow berries exploded with a refreshing, slightly sweet juice. The nuts energized his aching muscles and left him feeling more solid as he crunched his way through the firm purple and white cabbage-like leaves.

"Where are we going?" he asked. "Why can't we stay here?"

"If the dark elves are not already scouring the mountains, they will be soon." Dalis handed a full bowl to Annalin. "As soon as they realize you are not in the village, they will follow our tracks to the foot of this tree, which is where your last step disappears. Time is limited, and the sooner we depart, the better."

"We can't leave before checking for others," Ector countered, refusing to fold this time. He regretted his decision to leave everyone the moment he took that first step deeper into the woods last night. He wasn't going to make that mistake again.

"Yes," Annalin agreed, moving to stand beside Ector. "We can't leave without searching for anyone who might've escaped."

Dalis stared at both of them a long moment.

"I want to hear a promise from all three of you, right now," he replied firmly. "No matter what we find out there, we will leave this place forever, with no second thoughts. Is that understood?"

Ector and Annalin nodded, and Meric meandered up to the tiny table just in time to sleepily agree as well.

"It is settled then. Once you are finished eating, it is time to prepare for our long journey. We will use the cover of night once the sun drops below the horizon."

Dalis stepped away from the table and walked to the only tall cabinet in the spacious circular room. He opened the door. As Ector craned for a better look at what was inside the hideaway, he saw every shelf was stuffed and almost overflowing with food.

"I have sensed the dark ones closing on you for some time and made preparations," Dalis explained. "But I did not anticipate trekking with more than one additional body. We will have to ration our food as we go."

"Where will we go?" Meric asked. "I've never been outside the valley."

"Neither have I," said Ector and Annalin together. The three looked at each other, uncertain as to what awaited them beyond the boundaries of the guarding mountains. The thought was daunting. Ector felt like one of the brews, bubbling over with all kinds of different emotions: Guilt for leaving the others, gratitude for still being alive, and both excited and scared.

"We are headed close to an Elven city," Dalis replied. "A place called Lannonoir; it is very close to where I used to live." He looked up through the ceiling almost longingly, deep in thought. "Where we are headed, we will be in hiding. You must be strong. All of you. Because where we go will likely be just as dangerous."

"Why can't we stay here, then?" Meric pleaded.

"Because certain death awaits us here," Dalis answered. "And I need an answer that can only be found in the Room of Revelation, deep within the Great Elven Libraries: an answer about you, Ector."

"What do you want to know?" Ector asked, baffled. "I'll tell you anything about me."

"It is not an answer within you," Dalis replied, turning to stuff his pack with a blanket. "I will tell you in due time, but not now. Prepare your packs, as I am doing, and when the sun disappears, we leave."

Several hours later, Ector, Meric, and Annalin all sat waiting for night to fall, each of their traveling packs loaded with a blanket and all the food from Dalis's tall storage closet. Having seen the food divvied up between the four of them, Ector couldn't help but think a couple of good meals would clean their rations down to nothing.

As dusk finally disappeared, the children moved to the foot of the staircase, ready to head back and look for survivors. Ector felt every heartbeat pumping through his veins. His mind raced at what they might find in the valley.

The crisp night air suddenly gusted coolly through the enchanted ceiling, ruffling their coats lightly. Dalis had handed out every last one of his spare traveling cloaks, and while Meric's fit quite nicely on his tall, lean frame, both Ector and Annalin swam in theirs.

"It is time," said Dalis finally, starting to ascend the staircase, but then he stopped halfway and turned to face them. "We cannot go into the village. It is too dangerous."

"But that's where the people are!" Ector exclaimed in disbelief. "You promised! We have to at least look!"

"We will, but from the edges of the forest," Dalis assured him. "Stay concealed in the brush, and if you see anyone alive, signal to me; I will retrieve them."

"What do we do if you're captured?" Meric asked, a sudden look of terror gripping him. "Or killed?"

The thought was beyond unsettling. The idea of trying to escape from these things without their new friend sent shivers down Ector's spine.

"Do not worry," Dalis replied. "I have no intention of being captured or dying tonight."

"Well, we didn't intend to discover the world of elves last night," Ector retorted, "but it came crashing down on us all the same!"

He scolded himself for not holding his tongue; his frustration was getting the better of him, and the thought raced out of his mouth before he could stop it. The look on Dalis's face left no doubt that he was not amused.

"What he means to say," interjected Annalin delicately, "is that you said yourself, just last night, you don't understand their magic."

"And here I thought you were sleeping," Dalis remarked with a slight smile.

"How can you be so confident nothing will happen?" she asked.

"Because I have evaded them before. And to your dismay, we will not linger long or rescue anyone beyond our grasp." He paused to look directly at Ector. "No matter what their condition."

Ector bit his tongue, trying to stop the rebellious thoughts fighting to get free.

"Ector," Dalis continued, interrupting the mutinous thoughts running through his mind. "Before we leave, look at Meric. Look at Annalin. If you decide to do something foolish once we are outside, you are condemning your friends to torture and death."

The weight of Dalis's words slammed into him.

"I will let them die to ensure you live," he continued, not caring that Meric and Annalin could hear him. "Do you understand?"

Ector looked at both his friends, both of whom shared looks of horror at the elf's words.

"Do exactly as I say, and you will all be fine," Dalis reassured them. "I know this seems harsh, but you do not understand the gravity of what is happening right now. Your death is unacceptable, Ector."

"Why?" Ector shot back. "Why am I more important than anyone else out there?"

"Your modesty will serve you well, young master," Dalis answered, leaving Ector unsure if the elf was reminding him of his manners again or truly paying him a compliment. "But once again, your question stems from ignorance. As I said earlier, you will understand more once we are far away from here, but until then, regardless of your feelings for me, trust me and know that I will die to ensure you live."

Ector knew that Dalis sensed his anger and frustration, and yet the elf still pledged his life. Ector couldn't fathom why. Appreciation suddenly washed over him, causing his thoughts to finally become calm. Ashamed at lashing out, he buried every last mutinous thought and nodded.

Dalis looked at Meric, Annalin, and lastly Rahms, who sat panting at the ready in the rear of the group.

"Let us move quickly!" he urged, ascending the steps two at a time.

Ector followed close behind, but as they approached the enchanted ceiling, Dalis didn't whistle the peculiar tune that made the entrance appear. He just kept bounding up and up. Ector wondered if the elf had forgotten, but then Dalis ascended through the enchantment into the clear, starry night. Leaning into his climb, Ector pushed through the invisible barrier as well, but a blinding white blizzard accosted him at the first step outside. Ector lost his balance as the wind knocked him to the ground, face first. The snow was so cold it burned.

"Quickly!" Dalis shouted above the howling wind, waving for Ector to regain his feet.

Ector got to his knees and held out an arm for Annalin as she cleared the dwelling's opening. He hoped to spare her the same fate of tripping face first, but it was futile. She barreled into him, and they both toppled back into the snow. Then Meric piled on top two seconds later.

"I thought the enchantment showed us what was happening outside!" Ector yelled.

Annalin braced her weight against the tree, trying to stand. The air was so cold, she gasped for breath.

"It is the dark magic," Dalis replied, returning for Meric, who had flown a good distance forward after tripping. "It behaves unexpectedly."

Leaning on Dalis's arm, Meric was almost on his feet, but then he collapsed back to the ground as Dalis disappeared in a flash. Silver shimmered through the racing snow, followed by the sound of clashing metal. Ector squinted through the whiteout, straining to see the flicker again; the racing winds paused for a breath, long enough to see Dalis masterfully dismantling a dark silhouette.

Leaving Annalin, Ector trudged over the building snow to Meric and reached out an arm to help. But he fell back against the enormous Blackwood tree that had housed them for the night as the brisk wind of a black arrow grazed his face. Ector stared wide-eyed at Dalis holding the bow, until a soft noise crunched in the ice behind him. Turning, he saw a black hooded figure fall to the ground an arm's distance away. Thick scarlet blood spilled from the elf's chest as Ector felt his cheek and flinched.

Returning to the Blackwood tree as quickly as he had disappeared, Dalis aided Meric to his feet again.

"How did you know he was there?" Ector yelled over the howling wind.

Even with the creature lying just a pace away, Ector could barely see the corpse through the racing snow.

"I told you," Dalis cried back. "Every elf is born with the gift to sense another, even if they have turned dark. And their stench is horrendous." He moved closer, dropping his voice. "It is a simple part of being an elf," he added. "But they sacrifice it so willingly for these dark powers."

"Why would they sacrifice it?" Meric asked, staring down at the disfigured body in horror.

"Once the darkness takes root in them," Dalis explained, "their obsession blinds them to what they have lost."

He corralled them closer, blocking out the wind.

"Listen to me, all of you. I know I promised to look for others, but we are in graver danger than I anticipated."

Even huddled together, Ector could barely make out the words as the dead, gruesome creature lying at his feet pushed all thoughts of protest entirely from his mind. It looked nothing like Dalis; the face was thin and starved-looking. A twisted nose accentuated the blackening eyes. The top lip curled up at one side to reveal the same sharp, yellowed teeth Ector had seen on the other elf last night. A few long strands of hair on the elf's balding head blew wildly in the wind. And the weed-colored splotches covering his skin made it look as if a disease were overtaking him.

"Why do they look like that?" Ector asked, pointing at the corpse. "Does the dark magic do that to them?"

"I think so," Dalis answered. "And there is something strange about their diet, too. I have never seen a single one eat an elf's meal in the last nine years."

"Are they really elves?" Annalin asked.

"They were, once," Dalis replied, looking on with disdain. "The deterioration is slow in the beginning. Like what we saw last night with that newly joined dark elf; he could still hear your thoughts, apparently.

But as they progress further down this dark path, their ability disappears entirely."

He paused, looking long at the dead body.

"These new ones are just as dangerous as the more seasoned ones."

"How?" Meric asked.

"We were almost discovered last night in that bush, because he heard your thoughts. We cannot risk that again. He was the first I have ever seen that retained an ability to hear another's thoughts after the transformation. He must have been very gifted before he joined."

A worried look overcame his face just then.

"Come. We must move now, and quickly." Dalis nudged them forward, leaving the dead body blowing over with snow.

"Wait!" Ector cried. "What about the others still in Cleargar?"

"There is no life over there anymore," Dalis replied, turning to face him. "They did not even bother prolonging the torture, as I feared they might, in an attempt to bait you back to the village. They summoned this storm to track you instead."

Dalis's meaning dawned on Ector, as he looked down and saw the trail of footprints left in their wake.

"Rahms!" cried Ector, seeing a separate set of four-legged paw prints denting the snow in the opposite direction, leading back into the distant rising smoke.

"Quiet yourself!" Dalis ordered. Turning, he beckoned them closer. "Rahms knows how to keep safe. No more talking; I can smell the dark elves preoccupied a short distance that way." He pointed towards the two towering pines guarding the gateway to the valley.

Following his finger, Ector stared through the dense forest, wondering if he might catch one last glimpse of anyone. The howling wind and torrential snows suddenly calmed again, and Ector could see thick black smoke billowing from the other side of the trees. His village still burned, even amidst the blizzard. Calls for the Butterfly Honey Drub echoed in his mind as he searched fruitlessly for any signs of life. Turning back, he found tears welling in Annalin's eyes.

"We have to do something about your scents," Dalis continued, guiding them under the protection of a nearby pine tree. "With all the humans now gone, they will be able to track you more easily. Reach up and grab a handful of these pine needles, young master Ector." Dalis gestured towards a low-growing branch. "We will use your magic to disguise all of your scents."

Uncertainty filled Ector. He still didn't know if he believed he had magical powers. There was a small voice inside that continued to hold out, saying it wasn't possible. *But this will prove it,* he thought. *Maybe then, they'll realize they've all been mistaken.*

He suddenly became anxious to prove it, to himself, to Dalis, and to all the dark elves out there hunting him. They simply had to have the wrong person.

"Wait," said Dalis, placing a hand on his shoulder, just as Ector started to reach for the pine needles. "Alright, now go. You still have little control over what your magic does. I will guide it."

Ector hesitated, feeling his doubtful thoughts beginning to weigh even more heavily, but he did as instructed just as the wind began to whip up again, swirling the snow in every direction. He held up a hand to block the ice flakes and hailstones from pelting his face. As he ripped a handful of pine needles off the branch, he paid special attention for any unusual signs. But they didn't feel special in any way whatsoever.

"Since your gift is unlocked by touching the plant life," Dalis continued, "we will transfer the charm similarly to how you gave creation to the brews, but a bit differently. Place the pine needles in your mouth, and chew them precisely eight times. No more and no less."

Ector looked up, baffled.

"Then, you will hand them over to Meric," Dalis finished, ignoring Ector's shocked look.

"Why?" asked Meric, clearly not keen on the idea of handling Ector's half-eaten mess. But Ector quickly shoveled the pine needles into his mouth and began chomping, aware of Dalis's stone-faced stare.

"Use only two fingers to pluck them out," Dalis continued, "and then hand them over." He turned towards Meric. "Rub them all over your face and neck. Anywhere there is exposed skin."

"My face?" asked Meric, aghast.

Dalis nodded. "And your hair."

"My hair?"

"Do it!" Dalis commanded, jolting Meric into action. Meric immediately retrieved the half-chewed, soggy mess from Ector's two fingers and began frantically rubbing it all over.

There was no doubt that Meric definitely smelled more like a pine tree, thought Ector. But if this was the type of "magic" he possessed, handing a bunch of chewed-up pine needles over to make someone smell like the forest... Ector felt his ears warming, anger simmering. His decision to follow Dalis any further was in the balance.

"Perfect," Dalis said, searching for something in the air as he breathed deeply. "Your scent is completely gone; there is not a trace remaining."

He gave a nod to Ector. "You will do very well, once you have some training."

"That's not magic," Ector responded. "That's disgusting, and of course he smells like a pine tree now. I can smell it, too."

"I am not talking about the pine aroma," Dalis replied. "The pine will dissipate in a few minutes, but Meric's scent will remain masked. It is difficult for you to understand, I know."

Ector heaved an unconvinced sigh. "I still think you've got the wrong person."

"You want proof, do you?" asked Dalis.

That small voice inside of Ector suddenly cried out, *Yes! I do want proof!* But he thought it best to hold his tongue. He was feeling more certain about the mistaken identity by the second now.

"Once you realize you've got the wrong person, this will all go away," Ector continued, feeling his confidence growing.

"I am afraid that is not so," Dalis replied. "The damage to your village cannot be undone, nor can the lives that have already died for you return. But to put your mind at ease, I will prove it to you."

Ector nodded, conceding his agreement to be convinced.

"First, do for yourself and Annalin as you did for Meric just now." Dalis placed his hand on Ector's shoulder again. "And then I will show you."

Ector reached up with both hands, plucked two handfuls of pine needles, threw them both into his mouth, and began chewing.

"Remember," Dalis reminded him, "it is very important to only use two fingers when you remove it from your mouth, and to only chew the needles eight times."

Ector nodded his understanding and, after a few seconds, extracted the mess with the same two fingers. Offering one-half of it to Annalin, he stared apprehensively at the remaining half. He felt sorry for Annalin and Meric; the only thing worse than this would be enduring someone else's masticated mess.

"Can you smell us anymore?" asked Ector, rubbing the strongly scented wet needles all over his face and neck and sporting globs of ponderosa pine in his honey bronze hair.

"Not even a hint, young master," Dalis replied, smiling, taking a moment to breathe deeply just as he had done with Meric. "But we still need to cover our tracks there. See?"

Ector turned back to the trail of footprints leading away from the Blackwood tree, straight towards them.

"Grab some more needles and line your gums," Dalis instructed. "This time, we will use our combined gifts to make you walk as light as a feather over the snow, leaving not a trace."

Now they were getting somewhere. There could be no doubting after this, Ector thought. Anxious to show the elf his mistake, Ector plucked another handful and tossed the pine needles into his mouth, lining his gums just as Dalis said. They prickled fiercely, but he cleared his throat to disguise the discomfort. No matter how many stabbing pine needles it took, he would prove the elf wrong.

"Go ahead then," Dalis continued. "Chew eight times, and then place it back along your gum line."

Ector collected the pine needles with his tongue, and after precisely eight chomps, he placed the prickly mash back into place.

"Do not forget the top," Dalis added.

Ector felt his heart drop; he knew it would sting even worse on the top. But without flinching, he followed directions and spread the stabbing mouthful over the entirety of his gums.

"Good," Dalis remarked, releasing his grip on Ector's shoulder. "Head back to the base of the tree now."

Ector did so, staring down at his feet along the way: But they were still making imprints in the snow!

"Ha!" Ector yelled, accidentally spitting out a few needles. "See?"

"Keep your voice down!" Dalis hushed. "We have wasted too much time here already. Look behind you, foolish boy!"

Ector stopped, and to his surprise, there wasn't the tiniest trace of a footprint anywhere in his wake. He quickly checked where he stood and found the trick of his shadow deceiving him.

Ector took a few more steps and watched carefully. What he thought had been his normal footsteps denting the snow now disappeared the moment the moonlight struck it fully. He looked up at Dalis, stunned.

"Keep going," Dalis whispered with urgency. "All the way to the tree."

"I believe you!" Ector hissed back, awestruck. "I don't need to go any further."

"Yes, you do," Dalis stressed. "You are in charge of covering our tracks. Do it quickly!"

"How am I supposed to do that?" Ector asked, still reeling.

"Step into a track," Dalis explained, dropping his shoulders and sighing. "And then step out again."

Baffled, Ector found a nearby set of footprints. He stepped over to them lightly, making sure the magic was still working, and then placed one foot into the imprint. The magic slowly unfolded; the snow seemed to stick to the bottom of his boot, releasing only when it rose level with the surface again. Ector couldn't believe it.

"You need to step into all of these tracks before we can move ahead," Dalis continued, waving for Ector to get on with it.

Ector spent the next several minutes stepping into every last footprint, including the tussle marks left by the encounter with the dark elves that still hadn't blown over completely. Eventually he picked up the pace, but every magical step was even more unbelievable than the one previous. Finally, he danced back to the shelter of the pine tree, all his work finished.

"You do not need to walk like that," Dalis commented. "Just walk normally. You could jump in the snow, and it would not matter right now."

Ector excitedly proceeded to test it out, bending his legs to spring, but Dalis placed a hand on his shoulder.

"Do not," he said, struggling to stay patient. "I have instructed Meric and Annalin to step only in my footprints from here forward, until we are out of the blizzard. We will move faster if you do not have as many tracks to cover. Do you understand your job?"

Ector nodded.

"Then move silently. Give the dark ones no reason to abandon their search on the other side of your village."

Turning swiftly, Dalis set off at a brisk pace through the snow. Meric followed first, then Annalin, and finally Ector, watching every last footprint continue to disappear before his eyes.

The clouds began to part a short distance into their trek, and the bite in the air dissipated. The wind slowed and, for the first time since they had emerged from the protection of Dalis's home, the snow stopped completely, leaving the forest sparkling like winter in the moonlight. They continued on for almost two leagues after that in complete silence, stepping quickly and dodging spindly branches that could betray their whereabouts. Then the darkness started to give way to the dawn.

The snow had abruptly ended about a mile back, and Ector's gums were raw from the pine needles cutting into them. Having resisted the urge to reposition them for fear the magic would stop, he couldn't continue for much longer.

"May I take these out now, please?" Ector asked, making an extra effort to use his manners.

Dalis slowed his pace and turned to face him, considering the question. He scanned the area quickly for any signs of danger, and then gave a curt nod. Ector quickly spat the prickly mess to the ground, grateful to have it out.

"Be sure to cover it up, so no one finds it," Dalis added.

Ector did as he was told, burying it into the muddy ground.

"How did you know I needed to place the pine needles along my gums for it to work like that?" Ector asked, intentionally ignoring the blood seeping from his mouth. "It seems like an odd place."

"Your saliva makes the magic more potent," Dalis answered. "That is how elflings are first introduced to their gifts, and I wanted to see for myself how you compared. You were clearly born with enough gift; it might have even worked simply holding it in your hand."

"Why didn't you say something sooner?" Ector's shoulders dropped with disbelief, every thought of using his manners disappearing. "My mouth is torn to pieces!"

Dalis slowed his pace again and allowed Ector to fully catch up with him.

"First, and foremost," Dalis responded matter-of-factly, as Ector strode up next to him, "I was uncertain how much ability you possessed, and I had to use caution. But secondly, and perhaps more importantly, it should serve as a reminder for you: I understand you have doubts and many questions; this new world came flooding down upon you just last night. But remember, there is a time and a place for asking those questions. Let the pain inside your mouth be that reminder that when our lives are at risk, it is a time to follow my directives, without hesitation. Had we departed sooner from the tree, we might have been able to experiment and find a more comfortable way to release your gift."

The lesson was hard for Ector to swallow, but he did so, along with his pride mixed with the taste of blood.

"I swore an oath to protect an old friend," Dalis continued. "And shortly before she died, she transferred that oath to you. I protected her for over two hundred and fifty years. But now my sole duty is to protect you, young master."

He reached into his pocket and extracted a broad, lively basil-green leaf, which he handed to Ector.

"Chew this exactly eight times, as before, and spread it over your wounds," Dalis instructed.

Ector cautiously took the leaf. It was crisp and sweet, but after only two chews, immense relief began to spread all over his gums. The tiny cuts were starting to heal instantly. By the time he reached the eighth chew, his mouth was completely healed.

"I hope you will trust me," Dalis continued. "And remember that when you feel the rebellion rising inside you, if you let it win, the pain you have felt this whole time is but a snowflake in the blizzard of what you will inflict on others. You are not like the young ones you have grown up around. We were fortunate to have encountered only two dark elves back there, and even more fortunate to have surprised them. Judging by how they were spread out around your village, it appears we encountered a small force left behind to cover their rear. Most of them were scouring the opposite mountainside."

As they crossed deeper into the northern mountain rage, the air suddenly began to warm. They trekked in a brief moment of silence, as the sun streamed through the thinning autumn forest. It was amazing to think that the storm hadn't even remotely touched any part of this terrain.

"I thought we were heading north," Meric interjected, striding up to join Dalis and Ector. "Why is it getting warmer?"

"The blizzard that struck us last night spawned from their dark magic," replied Dalis. "It was not of the Earth. The dark elves started that storm by tampering with the wind, until it raged out of control, transforming into that blizzard we witnessed. They broke the balance that keeps the wind harnessed. Once that balance is broken, no one controls what happens next. It is too early in the season for the snows; what you feel, now, is how it should be throughout the land."

Meric looked around, taking in the late autumn warmth, which they had all basked in but days ago.

"So, making the wind blow is dark magic," Meric reiterated, "but when Ector covers our tracks in the snow, that isn't?"

"Again, if you had prior knowledge of our magic, you would better understand," Dalis responded. "The fruits of our gifts are different from the meddling of things beyond our control. For example, when the winters arrive," he continued, pointing back towards the blizzard that still raged with blinding white in the far distance, "the Earth is ready for rest. It is the appointed time for everything to sleep, just as you sleep at the end of the day."

He stopped fully to look back at the storm.

"But these dark ones," he continued, looking into the distance with disgust, "what they do is very dangerous. The world in which we live is completely intertwined. When the balances tip, they have no ability to stop the disasters awaiting them, and for that matter, awaiting all of us. The weather belongs to the Earth, and to Her alone. Meddling with it is forbidden."

Dalis turned back, suddenly, herding Ector, Annalin, and Meric behind outstretched arms. He reached slowly for the sword hilt protruding over his shoulder.

Taking Dalis's unspoken warning to heart, Ector ducked and pulled Meric and Annalin with him into a crouch.

A ball of luminescent, cyan light appeared in the distance, just like the orbs the dark elves had used to destroy Cleargar. Ector's eyes widened with fear as the distant light launched itself towards them. Unsheathing his sword, Dalis deflected a streak of light that arrived upon them like a bolt of lightning. The delayed clang from his sword registered loudly, well after the orb had ricocheted off his blade, singeing the tree nearest them with a smoldering red wound.

"Stop!" Dalis cried out. "It is Dalis of the Wood Elves!"

"Dalis!" A faint voice echoed. "Thank the fates! Come quickly!"

"Follow me," Dalis said over his shoulder, sprinting ahead of them.

Ector was by far one of the fastest in Cleargar, but Dalis pulled away almost instantly. Annalin followed not long afterwards, sprinting past him as well. Stunned, checking his legs to make sure they worked properly, Ector watched helplessly as she began to widen the gap. Dalis raced with unfathomable speed, leaving Ector and Meric to follow in Annalin's wake, trying desperately to keep up. After a good minute, Ector arrived with Meric close behind to find Dalis behind a dense bush talking in a low voice with another elf.

"You should be banned from the Butterfly Honey Drub race," Meric panted, throwing his hands to his knees, looking at Annalin. "That's simply not fair."

Annalin smiled, her breathing already slowing. "Why? Just because I'm a girl and faster than you lot without it?"

"Well, yes actually," Meric responded, unashamedly. "Ector, how many other girls do you know who can run like that?"

Ector shook his head. "Met the first one who's ever beat me just now!"

"Well, we don't stand a chance against him, do we?" replied Annalin, pointing a thumb to Dalis, who was still talking half-disguised behind the bush.

They didn't stand a chance against any of them, in any capacity, thought Ector, agreeing by shaking his head.

"You have humans with you!" exclaimed the new elf, surprised. "I could not even smell them!"

The new elf stepped to the side, and the children got their first good look at him: He had wild yellow hair, much shorter than Dalis's shiny black hair still neatly tied in a horse's tail. But the elf did share Dalis's bright blue eyes, fair skin, and pointy ears.

"How many of you are there?" Meric blurted out, apparently overwhelmed at the sight of yet another elf.

"More than you realize!" exclaimed the new elf. The children stared in amazement and listened as the elf returned to talking with Dalis.

"I have found more of their kind. They nearly soiled themselves when they first saw me. I started a fire to warm their chilled bones. By their looks, they ran themselves straight into exhaustion."

"This is Melowin," Dalis said, turning to face the three of them, acknowledging their blatant eavesdropping. "He is an old friend."

Ector, Meric, and Annalin stared with wide eyes at the new acquaintance.

"And these are not just any humans," remarked Dalis, continuing his discussion with the new elf. "This is the one."

Melowin stared, aghast, quickly stepping aside for a better look.

"By the Great Oak!" he exclaimed. "You mean to say, this is the one they desire? The one they hunt?"

Dalis nodded slowly.

"Dalis, this is very irregular!" Melowin continued with a stern, fatherly look. "Considering our profession, I am sure you do not need me to tell you this prophecy should have been reported to the Council..." He paused, searching for words. "Years ago!"

Dalis shook his head. "Besides these three, you are the first to know of its existence."

"This is preposterous!" Melowin roared, immediately clapping a hand over his mouth. The outburst caused the children to jump.

"Sorry, I know, self-control," Melowin whispered, waving off what looked like a pent-up lecture waiting to be unleashed at Dalis's wagging finger. "But why have you not reported it?" he went on, sounding genuinely shocked. "There should be fanfare and celebration throughout the land at news of her second prophecy!"

"I am afraid there is a bit more to the story with this one," Dalis replied.

"Well, which boy is it?" Melowin asked, stepping closer to the children for a better view. "Ugh, they look just as drab as the other ones. Pipe up, you lot! Which one of you is it?"

Melowin studied Meric and Ector in close detail, but suddenly turned to face Dalis's unflinching steely eyes aimed at the back of his head. The two elves exchanged a long look: long enough for Ector to wonder if they were able to talk without speaking. The elves' eyes remained deadlocked for several more moments before either one spoke.

"Quite," Melowin finally replied, turning to stare directly at Ector. "I see your predicament, Dalis." There was another pause as Melowin turned his attention back to Dalis. "And did you say dark elves?" he asked incredulously.

Dalis cleared his throat, looking agitated.

"Well, in any event," Melowin continued, turning back to the children again, "you will be happy to know we found more of your friends. They seem to be about your age. Come this way if you please."

Melowin turned on his heel, and Dalis didn't hesitate to follow. The children had little choice but to do the same, as the new elf led them a short distance further northward. They continued on for a few minutes before Ector overheard Dalis ask how Melowin had managed to find the others.

"Miraculously enough, they escaped on their own!" Melowin answered. "We were journeying back from Anathia when we saw the terrible storm, and then we found three of them about one-half league south of here."

"We?" Dalis asked cautiously. "Who else is with you?"

"Not to worry, I sent them ahead." Melowin replied. "We saw the great storm take shape as we cleared the Western Ridge yesterday. I told the comrades I would investigate and then rendezvous with them in three days."

"Very good," Dalis replied, heaving a sigh of relief. "Well, what news is there from the great city of the west? Did you encounter any Wood Elves?"

Ector couldn't help but notice the sudden change in Dalis's voice when he asked the question; he sounded hopeful, almost longing.

"I want to hear more about these dark elves," Melowin replied in a very serious tone, choosing not to answer Dalis's question. He waited for Dalis to agree with a nod before continuing.

"Your Wood Elf kin are still scattered in the far western territories," Melowin replied. "A few clans remain, but most families fled after the last Great War. You know the stories, of course."

Ector could only see Dalis's back, but there was no mistaking the disappointment in his nod.

"I had hoped they would return by now," Dalis responded, dejected.

Melowin placed a consoling hand on Dalis's shoulder. "In good time, old friend." He lowered his voice yet again and asked what Dalis knew about the storm. Ector strained to listen, but couldn't catch anything coherent after that. He turned to Meric and Annalin.

"I think they can talk through their thoughts," he whispered. "I was wondering about it a few seconds ago, and then, Melowin looked right at me, and..."

"And what, mate?" asked Meric excitedly.

Ector felt silly putting words to it. "Well, he answered my thought!"

Meric immediately bought the idea, gasping with awe.

"I don't think so," Annalin said after a silent moment. "If they could, why bother talking in low voices at all, like they are right now?"

It was a good point; Ector watched the two continue their dialog, unable to think of a response until Melowin's voice rang out.

"It is because your new friend wishes to keep a secret from me!" Melowin looked over his shoulder, a mischievous grin clearly aimed at them in reply to their whispered discussion. "He pours too much focus into guarding his thoughts, though. Thus we talk in low voices."

Melowin turned fully to the children, his smile widening unabashedly. "Your thoughts, on the other hand, you all may as well trumpet them out to the world!"

Dalis cursed at Melowin. "Keep your voice down!"

"Come now, old friend," he gibed, elbowing Dalis. "How can I compete against one whose native skill blocks my efforts so easily?"

"Not easily enough," Dalis retorted, breathing a hair easier, cracking a slight smile of his own. "You have improved beyond your natural abilities, significantly."

"Well," replied Melowin, suddenly serious, "when you learn how I had to pry the information out of these unwilling souls I have lived with for the past few months, you will understand why. Stubborn and deceitful to the end, they were!" He paused with a sigh. "It was a mission better suited for Fenilmir or better yet, Lowen. But both were already tasked on a mission, so they sent me. Elves with their gifts are in curiously high demand these days."

"Well, I am sure you did just fine," Dalis replied. "I cannot imagine enduring that level of mental bombardment for any length of time."

Melowin laughed. "False flattery is insulting, old friend. Time may have kept us apart, but my memory is as strong as ever. You cannot expect me to believe that you, Dalis, the only great Leighmoor who has ever withstood Iglasias's unrelenting mental assaults, have problems deflecting my feeble attempts to acquire from your mind what I want."

"You say your memory is strong, yet you still waste your time trying?" Dalis asked in reply, with an ever-widening smile.

"I have found great success in the quick, unsuspected attack," answered Melowin excitedly, dropping his voice closer to a whisper, as if sharing some valuable piece of insight. "Of course, it has yet to be tried on a target of your caliber—until now, that is. Glad to see you are still sharp."

Melowin turned and clapped Dalis on the back, waving for him to follow as he began leading the way towards a distant waterfall. Dalis slowed, staring after him for a long moment, clearly pleased to have run into his old acquaintance. But he allowed his pace to slow to a halt, choosing not to follow. Instead, he turned to the children and waved them closer.

"Melowin has a point," Dalis commented, dropping his voice. "We will need to use your magic again, Ector."

The sores along Ector's gumline had healed, but he could still feel the phantom pains throbbing in his mouth.

"Why can't we use your magic this time?" Ector asked. "I don't want to tear my mouth apart again."

"I will help guide your gift, as we did before," answered Dalis. "But no pine needles this time. Pine needles would not be a good tool for this."

"What is the magic for this time?" Meric asked.

"Melowin is right," Dalis replied, turning towards Meric. "The old woman never had a problem keeping her thoughts to herself, but it is not so with you," he explained, turning back to Ector. "You have inherited that trait from your human father."

He turned and searched the surrounding forest for something.

"Ah ha, this one here will do." Dalis held a finger to a wiry vine with waxy leaves growing up a tree close by. "Quickly, Ector, if you please."

The leaves had a thin, purplish lining around their edges, but the leaves themselves were actually quite thick. Ector snapped off a small piece of the vine.

"What do I do next?" he asked, holding it lightly in his hand.

"Intertwine it around your fingers, like so." Dalis plucked a separate piece of vine and, winding it in between each of his fingers, he demonstrated what he wanted Ector to do. "Be sure to wrap a piece of vine around each hand. When you are finished, hold hands with Annalin and Meric."

Ector did as instructed. Feeling Dalis's hand firmly latch onto his shoulder once again, he waited for something to happen as he grasped Meric's and Annalin's hands. But nothing did. He looked up at Dalis, wondering if this was like the scent-masking charm, where the elves would notice a difference unbeknownst to any of them. Dalis's eyes remained closed for a long spell, deep in concentration, muttering something soundless and incoherent.

After a minute, he shook his head disappointedly and opened his eyes.

"I am sorry, young ones," he said. "I had hoped to spare you the unsavory task, but it is unavoidable. Ector, if you please, once more: Pick a fresh strand of vine, and after eight chews, hand it to Meric and Annalin."

Meric's shoulders dropped with disbelief, clearly not wanting to endure another disgusting bath. Even Annalin looked noticeably dejected at the news.

But again, Ector did as asked. The eight chews couldn't be finished soon enough this time; the leaves were chewy with an oily taste that was far from pleasant. Using only two fingers, he plucked the mash from his mouth, anxious to have the bitter taste off his tongue. He extended it to Meric and Annalin, and she was the first to take the plunge, clearly ready to be done with the chore. Then Meric heaved a sigh and lumbered closer for his share, leaving Ector with the last portion. After a disgruntled look at the suspiciously larger pile of masticated mess left over, Ector decided he couldn't blame them. Rubbing down his face and neck, he noticed a very different sensation from the pine-needle-spit concoction. His thoughts quieted, but he could still think clearly. It was as if every passing thought now crossed his mind with padded footsteps.

Meric's dejected state transformed quickly into excitement as he made another awe-inspired noise, apparently feeling the same effects.

"That is very good, Ector," Dalis said, astonished. "Elves your age could not have done a finer job. It will take time before you can control it through other, cleaner methods, but do not worry."

Despite the disgustingness, the words of encouragement helped.

"That other elf said you were guarding your thoughts," Annalin interjected. "What were you trying to keep secret? You don't trust him?"

"Well," Dalis replied, folding his arms across his chest, "I can see this second charm has worked quite well; I can no longer hear all the inquisitive thoughts running through your mind anymore, young lady Annalin."

Ector saw Annalin blush slightly, but she didn't say anything more. She looked hopeful for an answer.

"I trust him implicitly," Dalis responded, "but there are things which I must keep to myself."

"About the prophecy?" Annalin pushed. "It's about Ector, isn't it?"

Dalis heaved a sigh. "I understand you have your concerns, as you should, but none of you are ready to hear this prophecy yet."

"Why not?" Meric asked, standing behind Annalin, his confidence growing noticeably—at least while Annalin stood as a shield in front of him.

"Our town was slaughtered by these monsters," Meric continued, "and every stranger we've met over the past two days seems to know of Ector because of this prophecy!" He dropped his eyes sheepishly at his own forwardness, but taking his cue from Annalin, he managed to not waver too much and brought his eyes back up to face Dalis's. "Why are you keeping it from us?"

"When the time is right," Dalis replied, "you have my word, it will be revealed to you. But for now, there are crucial pieces of the puzzle that need solving. Primarily among them, learning more about our enemy."

"I thought you said you'd been watching the dark elves for the last nine years?" Ector responded, astonished. "How much more time do you need?"

"Their dark magic dates back long before just nine years ago," explained Dalis, dropping his voice so as not to be overheard. "We elves have very dark things in our past: things which have been forgotten; things which have been destroyed by our leaders, so that certain events would pass from memory and not stain our reputation."

He paused, looking over his shoulder to make sure they weren't being overheard.

"There are many elves that think we are the Earth's favored creature," he continued softly. "Once upon a time, they would have been right. But we have fallen far from grace since the Warring Ages. Some elves still cling fervently to this idea of superiority, but their numbers are dwindling, or so I thought, while I protected the old woman."

He gathered his thoughts for a brief second.

"Our fall was so devastating, it is not even taught in Elvish history," he continued. "The leaders struck it from the scrolls, hoping to make it a blemish forever forgotten. The only records that now exist are buried deep within the city of Lannonoir. They have remained hidden for hundreds of years, beneath the Great Elven Libraries."

Annalin's arm suddenly shot straight up into the air, which was met with a quizzical stare by Dalis. Meric reached up and pulled her arm down.

"This isn't school, Annalin," Meric muttered. "Just ask."

Annalin blushed slightly. "Right. Er, well, if it isn't taught anymore, how do you know about it?"

Dalis nodded appreciatively at her shrewdness. "It is good to see you humans at least have the capacity to pay attention. You remember the one I protected? The old woman?"

The children all nodded.

"She was the last living witness from the second Great War. She told stories that would have led to her assassination long before it happened, had the Council known she were sharing them. She lived to be over one thousand years old, if you can believe it."

"Wow!" exclaimed Meric, shaking his head in awe. His brain looked ready to explode right through his ears. "Was she an elf? I want to hear more about this Great War!"

Dalis ignored the question, but not before his eyes shot conspicuously to Ector. "Come, we must rejoin Melowin, now that the charm is in place."

"Wait, I forgot," interrupted Ector before they started off. "How do you know which plants to use? In case we need another charm," he paused at the word, feeling a bit silly, "to protect us."

Dalis laughed at the idea. "You will learn for yourself," he replied, "once we get you to an Elven Circle."

The children looked at each other, confused.

"Come," Dalis said, waving to them. "I will explain more as we go. But first, let us see who these other humans are."

When the four of them finally caught up with Melowin, he was standing much closer to the towering waterfall they had seen from a distance. The forest all around basked in bright rays, as if autumn didn't even exist here. The air continued to warm up the further from the storm they went.

"Well, I would have much rather found your lot," Melowin exclaimed to Dalis, as they approached. "You have a much livelier bunch! Not a drop of hesitation in letting their curiosities run wild!"

"I thought the charm blocked our thoughts," Meric whispered to Ector.

"They do, laddie!" Melowin bellowed back with complete disregard for Meric's attempt to be discreet. "But we also have very fine ears, if Dalis has not told you already. You want to hear more about the Great War, do you?" he asked, answering the question that should have been too far away to hear. "Perhaps one day, if time allows, I will tell you many stories of our battles! Reminiscing on Dwarvish defeat never gets old."

"In the comforts of a place far removed from easily offended ears," Dalis cut in, implying something that Melowin seemed to understand. Melowin allowed a subtle scoff to escape, and mumbled something that sounded like, "*Let them hear.*"

Waving for them to follow, Melowin led their group deeper into the greening forests, along the base of the snow-covered peaks. It was an oasis of juniper amidst the distant, golden countryside. Ector turned his gaze upwards to the towering mountains, jagged with cliffs, and got his best view yet of the spout crashing down the sheer mountainside, spraying a rainbow of mist before them. He arched his back to find the source of the water emerging from a crevice in the rock face. The magnificence of the underground river spilling out of the crag utterly captivated him, until soft chatter reached his ears. It was coming from the foot of the falls. Melowin picked up the pace, leaving Ector, Annalin, and Meric running to keep up. Bounding between large boulders dotting the shallow river, Ector saw three distinct silhouettes beginning to take form: An oaf of a figure; a tall, slouching blob; and then the very familiar, bouncy curls of Mara.

Meric recognized them first and blurted out Mara's name excitedly as he gave a grand leap to the next boulder, waving at her. If the forest didn't know Mara before, it certainly did now.

"Er, sorry," Meric managed, clearing his throat. He threw an awkward look back in Ector's direction, but then started swinging his arms wildly, fighting to keep his balance against the momentary wave of embarrassment that threatened to knock him from the boulder. Watching him devolve and struggle to stay put on the slippery platform, Ector leapt to the next closest rock. The river below was crystal clear, and it didn't look very deep, but the quick-moving rapids coursing around the boulders looked nothing to be trifled with.

Meric managed to regain his footing, though, before Ector could extend an arm, and he quickly leapt for the next boulder, anxious to get to Mara. Or perhaps it was to hide his fiercely blushing face, which Ector had indeed noticed. Ector and Annalin were left staring with raised eyebrows as Meric bounded away from them.

The rest of that day progressed mostly the same way. Meric, apparently too love-struck to keep his wits about him, continued to make a fool of himself at almost every turn. But Ector was too tired to care; the night's travel had been long, and after the first hour of blunder after blunder, even Annalin seemed to stop paying Meric any attention.

Unfortunately, to Ector's greater concern at this point, the unfolding of the past night had started a new routine. The plan seemed to be: travel by night, rest at day. Ector struggled to relax at first, lying under the glaring midday sun, but after he found some shade to shield his eyes, the day disappeared in a series of naps.

Feeling somewhat better rested as night began to fall, Ector joined the others who were all gathered closer to the waterfall. The air was noticeably crisper than when they had arrived that morning, as one by one, the stars began to shimmer in the crystal clear sky above them. It seemed as if only seconds passed before the sun dipped completely out of sight and hundreds of stars emerged out of nowhere.

A skinned rabbit turned slowly over a small crackling fire, guarded with unwelcoming looks from Fenodor, the oaf figure Ector had seen, and Grigor, the blob. They sat, towering on either side of Mara, opposite Meric and Annalin and now Ector as he sat down beside them. The smell was glorious; Ector could do little to hide the rumblings in his empty belly. Grigor shot Ector an especially ominous glare at the sound.

Disgruntled, Ector reached for his pack and retrieved a handful of dried berries and crumbled bread that hadn't survived the journey intact. Deciding it was better than nothing, he threw the meager handful into his mouth, not even bothering to hide his longing as he stared at the fat rabbit, which had more than enough meat for everyone to get a decent meal.

Just then, over the fire's crackling, a heated discussion between Dalis and Melowin broke out; they were standing a short distance away with their backs turned. Dalis's voice rose above the fire's snapping, just loud enough to hear.

"We cannot stay! It is not safe here!"

Melowin's voice shot back. "We are in no condition to travel with humans!"

"Can you not sense our enemies circling closer?" Dalis pressed.

"I am expected in Lannonoir in three days," replied Melowin, not answering the question. "And I have already spent a day here idle with these humans—not to mention, now they clearly know we exist. How do you plan to explain that to the Council?"

"The fates of elves and humans are about to collide," replied Dalis. "There is no use avoiding the humans any longer."

"Well, if you are relying on news of a delayed prophecy to make that case for you, I do not think it will help your predicament." Melowin looked grave.

"The prophecy is no secret to the Council," Dalis continued, equally as seriously. "They will sacrifice everything to find him."

Out of the corner of his eye, Ector caught Dalis tilt back his head and survey them all huddled around the rabbit. Ector reached his hands closer to the flames and flexed his fingers, pretending to be concerned only with staying warm.

After a moment, Dalis returned his attention to Melowin, and a small object exchanged hands between the two.

"I have not told you the prophecy yet," Dalis said in a low voice. "Just that there is one, about the boy. This piece of paper—this is why the old woman died. She kept it a secret until her last breath, even as agents of the High Council descended upon us."

A long silent moment passed, and then a flame jumped. In that instant, Ector saw a look of sheer shock overcome Melowin's fair face.

"Do you realize what you are doing?" Melowin hissed. His tone was barely audible, but the severity was unmistakable.

"*I*," Dalis stressed the word, "am forced to take action. You see the prophecy with your own eyes, and you know the events surrounding it."

"Yes, I do see the prophecy," Melowin shot back. "The question is: Do *you* see it?" He tossed the folded piece of parchment at Dalis's chest. "I have known you a long time, Dalis, but this is lunacy! Those elves out there hunting this boy right now have less to explain than you do. Why, in the fates, are you trying to keep him alive?"

"You must trust me," Dalis urged. "The last portion of the prophecy burned away the night the old woman died."

"And?" Melowin prodded.

"And, she went to great lengths to keep him alive," Dalis continued. "She said this prophecy would give us the chance to make a better world: better than we have ever known."

Melowin laughed. "Well, I am sorry to say that is not the vision I see; not unless that *better world* is a world without elves. You know we cannot suffer another civil war. We have barely begun to recover our numbers. Every last elf would die!"

"We have to find the remainder of the prophecy," Dalis reiterated.

"Dalis, listen to me as a friend." Melowin dropped his voice. "I trust your judgment, immensely. I have always stood aligned with you. But even so, I cannot stand with you in good faith that we are doing what is right. To carry on towards this better world you speak of is to flirt with extinction. Can you justify that?"

Dalis stood silently—or, if he responded, his reply was not loud enough to carry to Ector's ears.

"You have saved my life on more than one occasion," Melowin said quietly. "I will stand by you now. But know that it is against my will and good judgment to do so."

Ector felt a sting in his arm. The prick jolted him back to the happenings of their little circle around the fire. Fenodor was leaning over the fire, sniffing the aroma of roasting rabbit, smacking his lips impatiently. Ector rubbed his arm and looked down to find Meric holding a small wooden dagger. Meric flipped it around effortlessly, so that the safe end was no longer a threat.

"Sounds like you might need this, mate." Meric offered Ector the dagger and nodded towards the two elves. Ector blinked, surprised that someone else might have been eavesdropping.

"You must have been working on this thing all day," Ector commented, trying to change the topic. His tone reeked of insincerity as he tried to return his attention to the two elves. Instantly ashamed at his irritation, he looked back. "What is it?"

"Well, a knife, of course," Meric replied matter-of-factly, blinking back. "You remember? Pappy crafts them for trading."

Taking the smooth handle of the dagger, Ector was flooded with thoughts of the Harvest Festival traders. He had, indeed, forgotten that Meric's old man whittled the daggers for barter. He ran a finger over the sharp end and found it surprisingly lethal for the wooden variety.

"Thanks, mate, I guess you heard," Ector acknowledged. "Not sure how much good it will do though. It wouldn't exactly give us a leg-up in this kind of competition, would it?"

He smirked, hoping to lighten the mood, but immediately he wished he hadn't said anything as Meric's face dropped. Ector felt it, too. The mere hint of a competition brought back more memories of the Harvest Festival, and its downfall. The wounds were opened all over again.

"I'm sure your Pappy made it out," Annalin chimed in.

"Where have you been?" Ector asked, just now realizing that, while he had been eavesdropping and talking with Meric, Annalin had completely disappeared.

"Catching these," Annalin responded merrily, sitting down next to him. She held out three fat fish with slate-teal scales and eyes that were still bright and lively.

"Oh, thank everything that is good!" Meric clapped, relieved at the sight of meat. "I've already finished off most of my rations. They barely lasted a day!"

"I doubt your Pappy made it out," interjected Mara. It was the first time Ector had heard her voice since they arrived; apparently, she had been undertaking some eavesdropping of her own.

Every bone in Meric's body suddenly went limp, and all shreds of delight at the sight of food vanished.

Ector's dislike of Mara took a sharp turn towards hatred. Why did she have to crush any hope that Meric's father may have survived? Annalin responded before Ector could manage a coherent insult.

"Well, how would you have any idea?" she asked firmly.

Her question didn't have quite enough venom for Ector's liking, but it would do. Snakes only learned from the poison of another snake, he thought, and right now Annalin was somewhere between a beaver and a mongoose.

"Your new friends," Mara shot back, throwing an arm towards Melowin and Dalis. "They killed everyone! I saw it with my own eyes!"

The insult drew the attention of both elves as they turned to see the pretty face buried with angry, flowing tears.

"They threw fire on the ones who couldn't escape," Mara blurted, sobbing angrily. "And the ones that ran, they died anyways. They died in their houses, choking on the smoke from the fires. No one made it out. We watched from the forests as they walked all the way up and down the valley, throwing that exploding light onto everything. Look!" She thrust an arm behind her, pointing to the sky. "You can still see the fires!"

The black smoke billowing amidst the icy storm was miles away, but it could, indeed, still be seen from their distance. A peal of thunder rumbled just then, out of the soft, orange glow hovering on the horizon. As much as he hated Mara right now, Ector felt the renewed pangs of guilt for not fighting harder to help. Fenodor tried to put an arm around Mara, but she shrugged it off. Her hair swung wildly, slapping Fenodor in the face as she spun away, turning her back to the fire.

Ector could feel the presence of the elves approaching.

"Take heart, young humans," came Melowin's comforting voice. The tenderness was unexpected, considering the unjust verbal attack laid at their feet. Ector had been bracing himself for the blowback, but it never came. "You three escaped, did you not?" Melowin asked.

The question hung in the air, awaiting someone's response, but none came as they all continued to stare sullenly into the small fire.

"Perhaps it is not so unlikely that others were able to escape as well?" prodded Melowin, trying to rekindle any flickers of hope they might have held onto before Mara had dashed them.

Shocked at Melowin's understanding words, Ector lifted his eyes from the fire to look at him, but the first thing he saw was Dalis: His posture was the exact opposite of Melowin's comforting voice. He looked hostile and displeased, as if ready to attack. But he wasn't eyeing Mara.

Bewildered, Ector made to stand, but before he knew what was happening, Dalis charged him, and Ector felt his feet fly out from under him.

Chapter 7
Seeds of War

"We are found!" Dalis's voice rang out.

In the span of a breath, Ector felt the sharp, bony end of Dalis's shoulder dig into his mid-section. He stared at the ground, struggling to regain the wind knocked from him.

"Follow me!" Dalis yelled over his shoulder to Melowin. "Collect the others, before the attack begins!"

A flash of purple danced across the night from the cliff's edge. Ector's inverted view of Melowin illuminated; the elf beckoned the others to follow with a quick hand. Lightning shot from the clifftop, and Ector felt his rump singed with an unbearable heat that spread up his back and down his legs. His back muscles convulsed instinctively, causing his head to lash in excruciating pain. The bolt lit past, striking the ground just paces away, but the smell of his burning pants registered instantly.

"Put me down!" he cried, squirming to get free of Dalis's grip. "I'm on fire!"

Ector hit the ground and felt instant relief as the cool mud smothered the heat into nothingness. Trying to push past the shock, he stared up at the sky, blinking away the purple flash and dancing stars.

"You will be fine, young master," Dalis said, his voice already several paces away as Ector tried to sit upright. The stout silver sword glimmered in the rising moonlight as Dalis drew the weapon from his back.

"Prepare yourselves for battle!" he cried.

The last word had barely cut through the night before the frosty winds arrived, stealing Ector's breath away. The wind gusted, first at his front, then at his back. His back relaxed enough for him to gain his feet, and he checked for injuries. To his surprise, the only sign of the strike was a lightly blackened area on his hip, where the bolt had seared through his clothes. He touched the exposed skin lightly; it didn't hurt any worse than a burn from working long hours under the sun.

As he looked to the top of the cliff, above the waterfall opening, a giant fog emerged, spilling over the edge. The ominous, gray mist raced to the ground with hail, snow, and ice spitting in all directions. It descended like an avalanche. Another flash of purple seared the night sky, and a lightning bolt flew at the smoldering rabbit still cooking over the tiny fire, incinerating it on contact.

"Quickly!" Dalis urged the children.

His voice rallied them as Melowin sprang through the air, avoiding another menacing flash of light that exploded at his feet. As Melowin tumbled head-over-heels, his arms flew out in front of him, as if beckoning for something, but Ector couldn't fathom what. Ector found himself momentarily frozen, staring at Melowin, unable to comprehend how the elf could just stand there.

"We have no time! Hurry, quickly!" Dalis called to Melowin.

The children raced to the protection of the trees, and at Dalis's silent command, Ector threw himself behind Annalin and Meric into a dense patch of low-growing limbs and dark foliage. He turned just in time to see the fog envelop Melowin, who stood like a rock, unwavering.

Ector watched in horror as the mist completely swallowed everything. Looking for any sign of movement, he jumped as an unexpected hand clasped his shoulder.

"Grab the others," Dalis whispered. "I am taking you with me, into the shadows."

Ector gave a quick nod, remembering how Dalis had disappeared into the corner of his underground dwelling. Ector grabbed Annalin's hand without hesitation, and then placed a hand on Meric's shoulder, but the gestures were unnecessary; they were already piled on top of each other. Just a quick second later, a mysterious tingling began to rush through Ector's spine, seizing him with shivers, despite a feeling of warmth spreading outwards through his fingertips.

Annalin must have felt the tingling, too, because her neck erupted with goose bumps, and she shivered.

"The other three!" Dalis cursed under his breath, looking to Grigor, Fenodor, and Mara hiding in a separate bush next to them. "Ector, can you reach them?"

Ector turned, but the bush was so thick, he couldn't see anything. He tried to extend an arm in the direction Dalis was looking.

"They're too far away," Ector whispered, still trying to navigate his hand through the sharp shrub. His elbow slipped off Meric's shoulder, causing Meric to suddenly pop into view. His skin and clothes stood out terribly. The disguise of Dalis's gift had overcome them so subtly that Ector hadn't even noticed the change until that moment.

"Quickly!" urged Dalis. "Place your hand back on Meric!"

Ector immediately pulled his arm back against the grain of the prickly leaves. But the nicks and scrapes registered only briefly before every bit of attention returned to Meric as he disappeared into the shrub's texture and color once again.

"Their scents are unmasked!" Dalis exclaimed, staring at the other three. "They will find us within seconds!"

Ector saw the fog through the tiny window of their shrub; it crashed to the ground, like a slow moving waterfall with soft edges. The mist blossomed back into the air on impact and began to run along the base of the cliff, creeping gracefully. However, despite its peaceful, majestic appearance, Ector quickly realized the cloud wasn't actually blossoming back towards the sky; it was rolling over onto itself and rushing in their direction with incredible speed.

Ector felt his grip wrenched from Annalin and Meric. Dragged out the bush, he watched helplessly as terrified looks fell across both Meric and Annalin; they knew their disguises had left with Dalis. They were being left behind, clearly visible, and all alone to wait for their execution at the hands of the dark elves.

"What are you doing?" cried Ector, looking at Dalis incredulously. "We cannot leave them!"

He struggled against Dalis's grip, but the elf had an unbreakable grasp.

"I am sorry for your friends," Dalis replied. "It was unwise to settle as long as we did."

"We're not leaving them!" Ector demanded. He would not desert the only remaining Cleargardians, least of all the few friends he had left.

"As you have yet to understand, young master," Dalis responded, eerily calm, "your life is worth more than a few ordinary humans."

He said it so simply that Ector stared, stunned with disbelief.

"Too much has been sacrificed to keep you alive," continued Dalis, readying himself to hoist Ector over his shoulder. "And I will not lose you now!"

As Ector felt his legs swept up once again, an unfamiliar object knocked around in his pocket. Feeling the power in Dalis's torso tensing, preparing to launch full-speed, Ector craned his neck and found the handle of Meric's sharp wooden dagger protruding.

The last thing Ector wanted was to hurt Dalis, but there was one thing he could not re-live: Abandoning the few people remaining of his village, for a second straight time, wasn't an option.

He snatched the dagger and sliced it across the elf's hand. He immediately felt Dalis's grip loosen around his waist. Slipping from Dalis's shoulder, Ector landed in a dead sprint and raced back to Annalin and Meric. He didn't look back; he was sure Dalis would be in pursuit in a matter of seconds, once he figured out what had happened. He had to get there before Dalis knew what had hit him.

Ector dashed past the dense shrubbery and found Annalin and Meric standing behind a sopping wet Melowin. He was chanting, meticulously waving his arms, and shielding everyone.

The fear of Dalis catching him was pushed to the back of Ector's mind, as bodiless heads appeared at the forefront of the fog. The familiar purple eyes flying towards him out of the mist danced, glowing with renewed vigor. Wispy hair blew wildly on their floating heads, reminiscent of the dark elf Dalis had killed outside his dwelling, just a night ago.

Ector clutched his knife, knowing there was nowhere to run. But then the air all around him suddenly became stifling and warm. Struggling to breathe, he dropped to his knees. Panic seized him. Not until the cool air along the ground filled his lungs again was he able to lift his eyes and find the fog already upon them.

The mist collided with the invisible wall of warmth, and the fog thinned, disappearing instantly within a few paces of Melowin's glowing red hands.

Ector stared in awe at the elf. His eyes were closed, deep in concentration, as the air all around his hands began to wave and flex with heat, blurring their vision in every direction. Five purple-eyed elves fell from the vapor, stumbling to keep their feet. Their swampy, spotted faces stood in stark contrast to that of Dalis and Melowin.

Soft cackling echoed as the fog hissed to the sky, forming clouds above the edge of the clifftop. It was difficult to tell which one laughed, though, as all their mouths twisted gruesomely, almost smiling.

"Clever," said an icy voice. One appeared from the rear of their group out of the hazy whiteness. "But a waste, all the same."

He moved to the front as the other four flowed into a wedge formation behind him, approaching slowly.

"You may die honorably among elves, knowing you were the first to dethrone us from our steed." He bowed mockingly, flourishing a hand.

Melowin slapped his hands together in reply, and a wave of scorching heat blasted forth. The river hissed with steam, and the ivy-colored leaves that had yet to encounter autumn smoldered red at the ends, twinkling in the night's darkness.

The newcomers shielded themselves from the blast with their sheening black cloaks.

"This is your one and last warning to depart!" Melowin commanded loudly. "I will not spare you a second time!"

The dark elves seethed, tossing their tattered cloaks that now smoked with holes to the ground, but the group's leader chuckled softly in reply.

"Let us make a trade then, shall we?" his icy voice suggested.

Smoke wafted from his hood as he circled to the side, refusing to drop his scorched cloak.

"Five humans and one elf may go free," he continued, "For the price of one dirty half-breed."

The dark soldiers' grins began to salivate at the mere mention of the word *half-breed.*

"Come now, brother," said the icy voice, soothingly. "You have seen the humans; they are little better than a herd of beasts, wallowing in filthy ignorance. It is more than a fair trade."

The dark leader circled behind the group.

"What are you?" replied Melowin, giving no indication he was considering the offer. "A faction of the delusional Earthen Warriors?"

"Hardly, friend!" replied the hooded voice, cackling. "We are of an ancient lineage, born from a forgotten time." He basked in the words and released a long, satisfied breath. "You may think of us as protectors," he continued, with an air of a teacher giving a lecture. "The true protectors of elf-kind."

Ector felt the eyes of the others turning from their leader and locking onto him.

"You are, unknowingly, I am sure, allowing an especially nasty disease to thrive in your midst, dear brother," he pressed on.

Melowin tracked the elf's movements silently as he came back into view. His dark soldiers meanwhile spread out, encircling them.

"I know it must come as a shock," said the dark elf, smirking ominously. "But take comfort: The cure is at hand!"

A tense silence followed, leaving the dark elf's words hanging in the air, echoing in Ector's mind.

"Give us that one," he demanded, pointing a bony finger at Ector's head. "And the remainder of you are free to go, including the humans."

The promise drew agitated stares from the dark soldiers, clearly displeased at hearing the offer a second time. But they quickly refocused their displeasure squarely on Ector.

Melowin's hands pulsed like red embers as he watched the dark leader pace back and forth in front of them.

"My patience is thinning, brother," the dark elf commented threateningly. "Hand over the abomination, or you all die."

Another tense moment passed, as the children waited to see what Melowin would do. But Melowin continued to stand, unflinching, silent.

A low, rumbling growl was the only warning. Ector shifted his eyes and caught a flash of light. The orb took flight out of the corner of his eye, but it leapt too quickly. It was already upon him, flying for his head before he could blink.

Ducking much too late, Ector stared wide-eyed and breathless at the ball of light hovering overhead, on the verge of exploding. It had stopped, a breath's distance away, trembling. But as quickly as it came to life, the orb left him and began coursing around the encirclement, faster and faster. Melowin's arms caught Ector's eye; the orb was mirroring his every movement.

Melowin stood, rooted, orchestrating the bright ball with complete control until it looked like a ring of solid light orbiting them. Then the bolt cut through the circle and rammed into its owner's chest, exploding. The dark elf soared a hundred paces before crumpling in a lifeless heap.

"No more fire of any kind!" commanded the hooded leader over the furious hissing of his soldiers. "The gift of fire is strong with this one."

The dark elves reached for weapons slung along their waists and hidden on their backs. Ector, dagger still in hand, quickly flung the wooden blade. The unexpected attack stuck in the shoulder of one still seething at his fallen comrade. He dropped to the ground instantly, but not before another dark elf withdrew a long, crooked blade and advanced on Ector with lightning speed.

Melowin made to release another scorching wave, but before his hands connected, Ector felt the cold metal of the jagged blade against his throat. The elf stopped, just long enough to send Melowin tumbling away with a wave of his hand. Watching Melowin crash into a tree, the henchman then reclasped both hands on his weapon, teeth bared with angry pleasure.

Ector closed his eyes. Waiting for the cold metal to end him, he flinched as sparks burned his face amidst a deafening clash of metal-on-metal. Stunned, Ector found Dalis's stout silver sword once again saving his life but inches from his cheek.

Ector rolled from the attack and rose, watching as Dalis struggled to match the assailant's strength. The dark combatant hovered menacingly, his smile widening, as he forced Dalis lower to the ground with all his might.

Dalis, already on one knee, shook with weakness. His hand looked terribly infected, foaming and bubbling yellow, stained with dried blood where Ector had sliced him and growing worse by the second. Dalis cradled it close to his side as he fought the crooked blade from advancing any further with his good arm.

"Retrieve your dagger!" Dalis said in a strained voice.

Ector bolted, but suddenly stopped at seeing Dalis seized with cramps and doubled over in pain. Clutching his stomach, Dalis let the blades slip from each other.

"Do your worst to them!" Dalis rasped, trying to regain his footing and stand straighter. But whatever had overcome him continued to hold him hostage, leaving him bent and cringing.

The dark elf sneered, watching with delight, like a hunter playing with his wounded prey. A rumbling laugh escaped as he started to circle, slowly.

"Hurry!" Dalis ordered. "Retrieve your dagger!"

Ector leapt forward for the wooden knife buried in the dark elf's corpse. But he stopped, nearly tripping over his feet as he found the dead body pussing with the same yellow foam. A foul, putrid stench of acid wafted forth; the wound looked exactly the same as Dalis's infliction.

Ector breathed slowly. His stomach churned, but he pushed onward, latching onto the handle. He closed his eyes and withdrew the dagger to the sound of a slimy sucking noise.

"Stop," came the dark leader's icy voice behind Ector.

Ector turned to see another elf advancing silently, with a thin curved knife raised over his head. "Let Belela finish his work and avenge his brother."

The soldier spat at the command. But he obeyed, letting the short blade slowly drop to his side. He stepped away, rejoining the dark leader to watch.

Swallowing to keep the vomit down, Ector rose and turned. But as he stepped to the two slowly circling each other, he froze: The trees all around rustled with activity. Elves, the fair-skinned kind, began to emerge from the depths of the dark forest.

The lone dark elf circling Dalis halted at the sight of others. His grin turned to a grimace. Quickly regrouping, the dark elves stood, their backs together, forming a triangle.

"We are fortunate to have a few friends close tonight," coughed Dalis, managing to stand a bit straighter, trying to breathe deeply. His body shook involuntarily, but his face looked calm and detached.

"We wish no more spilt elf blood tonight!" the hooded leader bellowed, surprised by the growing number of wary onlookers. "But know now, this very second, you will all die if you interfere further!"

The threat was not well received by the newcomers, all of whom stared upon the creatures with bewildered looks, a few even gasping. Despite their shock, the newcomers began to tighten their circle, slowly withdrawing weapons of their own. The dark creatures scanned the area quickly to the sounds of bows creaking and swords unsheathing.

Sensing their waning control, the dark elves banded more tightly together. The leader cursed, but it was as if a secret command went out, because all three, in unison, reached their arms to the sky. Their eyes glowed even more intensely purple while dark ominous clouds started to form overhead, drowning out the moon and the stars. No sooner had the murky mass formed than it began to churn and swirl with activity.

"No!" cried Dalis, still clutching his stomach. Despite his weakened condition, every last sign of pain disappeared from view. He rose to his full height, his eyes glowing like a blue fire.

Looking at Dalis, one of the soldiers allowed a slight smirk to show; the dark brothers began to pull at the clouds, beckoning for something invisible with all their might, until the hook of a spindly vortex dipped out of the thick cover, and the beginnings of a massive tornado started.

Raging out of control, growing in thickness and lashing from side to side in the sky, the torrential winds whipped violently amidst the sight of shock and disbelief across every elf's face. Shivers ran through Ector's spine as he realized they were helpless against the dark elves' powers.

Ector's eyes shot to Dalis; he stood like the dark elves, reaching for something, but then he cried in a thunderous voice, "Aylo Hadi Im-Harari!"

The last word had barely left his lips when lightning shot across the night. Illuminating the entire forest, the jagged bolt struck the cliffside. An explosion of rock, a deafening peal of thunder, and an avalanche of crumbling mountain, mud, and water rained down upon them. Everyone fled, except the dark elves.

Their eyes glowing even brighter, they maneuvered the vortex closer to the cliff face. The falling rubble slowed as the angry storm sucked the falling debris into its swirling mass, but it only lasted a moment. The tornado rebelled, bending severely at the middle, fighting to go its own way. The dark soldiers' arms strained as they fought the will of the stormy beast, trying to control it.

Waiting until the very last second, their eyes like lanterns in the night, the three leapt out of the way as the tornado no longer had any interest in acquiring the destruction. Their concentration broke, and the tornado swept upon them. The cyclone quickly receded into the churning sky, where the clouds immediately slowed. Then, quite suddenly, everything that had been drawn up came raining back down upon them.

Shielding his head, Ector ran blindly, squinting to keep rock fragments out of his eyes. He reached out, trying to feel for anything familiar as he blocked the overhead assault. Amidst the crashing darkness, a hand suddenly latched onto his shoulder and began guiding him. He squinted one eye open, enough to see the approaching tree line.

As they arrived at the protection of the forest, the roaring collapse of the mountainside began to fade; Ector rubbed the dust from his eyes and found Annalin, Meric, Mara, Fenodor, and Grigor all racing to join him and Dalis.

Dalis dropped to his knees.

"Take these pine needles," Dalis counseled, pointing to a low-hanging branch.

Clearing the last bits of dirt from his eyes, Ector noticed Dalis's color worsening, even through the darkness of night.

"Chew eight times, just as before," Dalis continued, "and give them to the other three. Cover their scents."

"Are you all right?" asked Ector. "I'm really sorry about your hand."

Dalis waved off the apology and called for Meric. With a baffled look, Meric approached.

"Tell me," coughed Dalis. "Of what wood is that dagger carved?"

Meric fumbled with his words for a moment, clearly shocked by Dalis's growing discomfort.

"Uh, well," Meric finally managed. "Mountainwood, I think. Yes, yes, I am sure of it! It is very difficult to sharpen any other wood like that without breaking it."

"I thought so," said Dalis, hacking terribly and fading by the passing second. "There are very few plants poisonous to elves. But wood of the mountain tree is one of them."

Ector grabbed a handful of pine needles and began counting as he chewed. He watched Dalis with shocked eyes. After a few seconds, he retrieved the mess, grabbed Grigor's hand, and slapped the masticated needles into it; Grigor seemed so bewildered, he just held it stupidly.

"Rub it all over your skin," Ector instructed, trying to nudge Grigor into action. He grabbed another handful of pine needles and quickly shoved them into his mouth.

"Uh, thanks, but no," Grigor replied, managing to find his voice. He extended his arm, trying to keep the mash from touching any more of his palm than necessary.

"Fancy another encounter like that one, do you?" Ector managed with a full mouth. "If not, rub it all over your skin. They won't be able to track you."

"You first," replied Grigor, attempting to force the handful back on Ector.

"We've already done it!" Ector shot back, frustrated. He threw a hand towards Meric and Annalin. "Those two have already done it, and so have I. You, Fenodor, and Mara are the only ones left!"

Grigor looked physically pained, and while Ector could sympathize, at this point, if the circumstances were turned, Ector would have gladly bathed in Grigor's vomit if it stopped these dark elves from being able to find them.

"Can't I chew it myself?" asked Grigor, looking to Meric and Annalin as if they were delusional for doing something this disgusting; but the two were kneeling next to Dalis with undivided attention, watching the elf convulse with uncontrollable shaking fits.

"Just do it!" Ector demanded, spitting the wad of half-eaten pine needles into the ground as he cursed himself, frustrated at losing count. He immediately reached for another handful and waved Fenodor over.

At the sound of another ominous peal of thunder that shook the night, Fenodor turned and ran to the protection of their tree.

"Hold out your hand," Ector instructed, once Fenodor was within earshot.

"I don't have a scent!" Mara fired back, looking insulted. "I bathed in the waterfall just earlier today."

While Ector stifled a scoff at the feeble diversion to avoid the disgusting task, Annalin approached, looking intently at Mara's fingertips.

"What's this?" she asked, gently reaching a cupped hand under Mara's outstretched palm.

Mara investigated, searching for the source of Annalin's interest, but she quickly found her palm shoved into her face; her jaw dropped, with blotches of pine needles hanging off her cheeks and nose.

"Do your arms as well," Annalin instructed, flinging clumps of moss-like mess off her hand. She left Mara standing like a petrified stone and returned to Dalis. Before kneeling at his side, though, she turned back and looked directly at Fenodor and Grigor.

"Do you two need assistance as well?"

The boys glanced at each other for only a fraction of a second, and then vigorously rubbed the mash all over their face, hair, neck, and bodies.

Sprinting over to the next tree, Ector snatched a handful of the oily, bitter-tasting leaves creeping up the trunk.

"Here, take these as well," he added, throwing a large handful into his mouth, chewing as much as he could in one bite.

"I... WILL... NEVER!" Mara screamed, wiping large globs of the plastered pine away from her face.

"Do the same thing," Ector prodded, dividing the mess between the three. And despite the outburst, she and the other two eventually undertook a second bath just as Dalis beckoned for him.

"Do you remember the purple vines of the forest?" he asked weakly. His eyelids were half-closed and looked heavier with each passing second. "In the forests surrounding Cleargar?"

"You mean the common purple vines growing everywhere?" Ector asked, nodding sharply.

"I need one handful of their roots, as quickly as you can," Dalis urged faintly.

Ector turned and surveyed the dark forest. It was almost impossible to see anything at a distance. Walking briskly in a random direction, he stopped as a voice called out to him.

"Stay your worries, young Ector."

It was a familiar voice, directly in front of him. Ector searched frantically for the source, but then Melowin appeared, hobbling out of the darkness.

"I have what you seek right here," he continued.

Limping past Ector, Melowin dipped his hand into a pouch concealed beneath his cloak and pulled out a handful of what looked like dried, wrinkly, white worms. He bent quickly and administered to Dalis. Seeing the worried looks of concern from Meric and Annalin, he added, "Do not be troubled; your friend will survive."

Outlines of bodies began to shift in the corner of Ector's eye just then. The movements were eerily similar to the way the dark elves had hovered on the outskirts at the festival. Instinctively Ector tightened his grip on the wooden dagger and turned to see the newly arrived elves emerging from the dark of night. As they drew closer, a few gasped in horror.

"By the fates!" exclaimed one. "These are humans!"

Then another voice from behind Ector challenged the statement. "They cannot be. We would smell them."

Another elf, off to Ector's side, concurred. "And we would be able to hear their thoughts."

"Could you not smell them, and hear their thoughts just moments ago?" asked the first elf firmly. "No, look at them! These are definitely humans. How is this possible?"

The question hung in the air, pressing for an answer from someone, but only silence followed.

"Well, I would rather know what those creatures were," inquired yet another elf, emerging from the depths of the forest; the other voices had all clearly been male, but this one sounded feminine. "They were shaped like elves, but sick-looking and green! Have you ever seen anything like it?"

Discussing the creatures, their voices began to fade as Ector's attention channeled onto Dalis; he slowly chewed the gnarled, white worm-looking roots, still writhing in pain.

"I feel terrible," Ector said, watching Dalis try to cope with the excruciating injury.

"You feel terrible?" asked Melowin, turning immediately to tend to Ector next. "Are you cut as well?"

Baffled, Ector searched himself for an injury that hadn't registered, but then he realized Melowin thought he actually, physically, felt terrible.

"No, no," Ector replied, "I'm not cut. I mean it's my fault. I never meant to hurt Dalis like this! I feel terrible about what I've done."

"Oh!" replied Melowin, waving a dismissive hand. "Do not worry. He will be all right in a few minutes, once the Marduk root begins to work. I forget that Mountainwood is not poisonous to humans."

Melowin turned to check on Dalis before continuing.

"The dwarves are more to blame than you, young Ector. They deserve every evil imaginable for introducing that vile tree into our land."

Melowin's statement was met with an agreeable sort of silence from the other elves, some of whom Ector saw nodding through the darkness. A couple shifted their heads to Dalis, but the rest now firmly fixed their attention on the other baffling sight before them: Humans.

"But Mountainwood makes the best tools," Meric interjected, almost apologetically. "My Pappy uses it for everything! We had no idea it was poisonous."

Ector tried to apologize once more, but stopped as Dalis held up a weak hand.

"It was my mistake, young master," he replied, now sounding stronger. His sickly color, even in the faint moonlight, was noticeably dissipating. Then the shaking stopped, and he gingerly got to his feet.

"I should never have taken you from your friends," he continued, picking his stout sword up off the ground and sheathing it back beneath his traveling cloak. He flexed the fingers on the injured hand; the gruesome pus had stopped, and the wound had closed, but there was a clear scar.

"Well," Meric continued, stepping up next to Ector, pulling another wooden dagger from his trousers as he shook it at Dalis. "I'm not sure what kind of humans you're used to dealing with, but try to take Ector again, and you'll have a whole bunch of these to deal with, eh?"

Meric's support made Ector feel even more ashamed. As he hurriedly signaled for Meric to put the dagger away, Ector heard Dalis laugh.

"Yes, I will heed the warning, young master Meric."

The elves all began to circle closer, and as they came into better view under the moonlight, it became clear, very quickly, they did not share Dalis's light humor. Even though everyone kept their silence, Ector felt several pairs of eyes studying him and the other children with unwholesome interest.

Hearing footsteps, Ector turned and found Melowin walking away from the group towards the rubble of the fallen cliffside. Eyeing the enormous pile of boulders and inspecting the area where the dark elves should have been, Melowin called back to them.

"They are not under here." Melowin wore a frown as everyone continued to stand in silence, watching the children. Ector felt pinned to the spot.

"How can you be sure?" Annalin asked, breaking away from the protection of the tree to join Melowin. It seemed like a good question, considering the mound of rocks now piled right where the dark elves had stood. Ector couldn't imagine anything surviving under the new mountain of boulders, which completely obscured anything of what might be lying beneath. Elves were fast, but not that fast.

"Can you really not smell their stench?" Melowin asked, amazed.

Annalin sniffed the air as Melowin's voice dropped closer to that of a private conversation, out of earshot. Seeing Annalin shake her head, Ector found himself taking a couple of whiffs, wondering if he might be able to detect any traces of something different in the air. But only the scent of fresh cliff debris floated through the night.

"Well, it is not here anymore," remarked Melowin, looking puzzled.

Another flash of light lit the night sky, and Ector lifted his gaze in time to hear another peal of thunder echo overhead. The sky swirled ominously with muted flashes illuminating the clouds from within.

"The unnatural storm is stabilizing," said Dalis, responding to the growing number of eyes looking upward.

"This is forbidden magic!"

Ector lowered his eyes from the sky, searching for the feminine voice in the night. The speaker was standing off to the side. Ector first noticed long, shimmering dark hair, collected tightly in the back like Dalis's. Even in the darkness, the shadowed look of concern on her face couldn't diminish a striking beauty that left Ector almost weak the moment his eyes adjusted. Her skin seemed to glow in the soft hue of the scattered moon rays. The way her elegant hair was tucked behind her ears, a strand hanging loosely down her cheek... Ector felt intoxicated, as if he had taken a deep swig of Grasshopper Ale that had sat around too long. His knees wobbled while her eyes sparkled, searching for a response.

"Forbidden magic, indeed," chimed Melowin, returning to the group with Annalin at his side. "Since when can a shadow-lover command the lightning?"

Ector tore his eyes off the female, wondering at whom the question was aimed, but then he saw heads starting to turn towards Dalis.

Dalis answered with a strong silence. An awkward moment passed, long enough for Ector to suspect they might be communicating with their thoughts again.

"What's a shadow-lover?" Ector asked, summoning the courage to break the silence.

The question was met only with unblinking stares.

"A shadow-lover," Dalis responded finally, "is an elf whose gift manipulates the shadows."

Ector waited for Dalis to continue, but when it became apparent he had trailed off, Ector prodded Dalis with another question. "Like you?"

"Not quite," Dalis answered, keeping his eyes fixed firmly on Melowin. "I manipulate more than just shadows. But it is easier for some to think of me only as a shadow-lover."

"Does that make you a fire-lover?" Meric asked excitedly.

Ector turned to see Meric staring at Melowin.

"Indeed it does, young lad," Melowin replied, breaking eye contact with Dalis and turning to meet Meric with a smile. "Dalis and I were just discussing to whom the power of lightning should belong, if it is, in fact, to belong to anyone."

Melowin slowly returned his gaze to Dalis, locking eyes once again.

"It is forbidden magic!" the female elf said again, but more heatedly this time, frustrated that the other two didn't seem to hear her. "It belongs to neither of you!"

"I quite agree," Melowin replied, giving her a nod. "But if it *were* to belong to one of us, it seems all the stranger that a shadow-lover possesses a greater aptitude than, for example, a fire-lover." He placed his hands to his chest, indicating himself. "That is, of course, the product of lightning, is it not? Fire?"

The look on Dalis's face said he did not appreciate the question, especially in front of the newcomers.

"Our enemies are unmatched," Dalis responded, after another moment passed in silence.

"Know your limits, Dalis of the Wood Elves," Melowin replied, gravely. "I saw a hint of something other than blue in your eyes."

"I see hints of something other than blue in yours, as well, when you try to read my thoughts. Shall I, in turn, worry about you?" Dalis asked sharply.

"You know quite well we are talking about different things," Melowin shot back. "Do not deceive yourself, old friend. You are walking a slippery path."

The children watched on, looking back and forth between the two ensnared in their conversation. But soon Melowin cleared his throat and turned his back on the discussion. Leaving the group, he walked back to the mountainous pile of rubble, investigating one last time for any signs of a dark presence.

Dalis didn't seem to object to dropping the subject as he turned his attention towards the other elves gathered around him, all of whom had been mostly silent, watching everything unfold.

"Thank you for answering my call of distress," he announced, addressing everyone in the group. Ector counted maybe six new faces in total as the clouds began to break apart in the sky, revealing more of the full moon's light.

"What is happening here?" demanded a very serious elf with short, spiky yellow hair. His voice was light, but carried a tone of authority. "These are *humans*."

The obvious statement hung in the air, but the elf's unrelenting stare, and the heavy quiet, pressed uncomfortably for somebody to explain.

"Before I say anything more, we need to move to a safer location," Dalis replied. "Once we are away from here, you will learn what has been kept hidden from you. It cannot be kept a secret any longer."

Everyone waited with mixed expressions, some of curiosity, and others of disapproval—but especially among the children, excitement.

"Let us depart at once, before the dark ones return," Dalis continued, beginning to retrieve a few strewn supplies that had survived the clash. He nodded for Ector to collect his belongings as well.

"We will need your gifts to disguise our movements," Dalis continued, talking over his shoulder towards the other elves still rooted to their spots. Ector felt a hand on his shoulder and turned to see Melowin standing behind him.

"I am with you," Melowin answered, looking towards Dalis. "But I want to hear everything once more from the beginning."

Murmurs rustled between the remaining elves at Melowin's words.

"How long have these humans known about us?" inquired the yellow-haired elf curiously. It was not an innocent curiosity though; his tone was closer to that of a demand.

"Rest your worries," replied Dalis calmly, nodding appreciatively towards Melowin for his support. "Only a few days now."

"A few days too many," responded the elf, again with the same strange tone of authority.

"The time for reprimands is not here or now," said Dalis more forcefully, securing the last remnants of some dried leaves spilled on the ground. "We suffered this attack because we lingered too long in the first place."

Ector saw Dalis steal a quick, almost accusatory glance at Melowin. "It was my mistake," Dalis continued, "but it will not be made again."

Melowin made a noise as if he wanted to say something, but instead he heaved a sigh.

"You did try to warn me, and no, I did not heed your warning," Melowin responded, acknowledging Dalis's statement reluctantly. "The fault is mine. Let us, indeed, move onward before we are ambushed again."

Dalis, in turn, acknowledged Melowin's words with an appreciative nod and waved for Ector to come closer. Ector didn't hesitate as he felt the hostile stares from the new elves latching onto him again. Stealing a look over his shoulder, he found Meric and Annalin following him as well.

Just as Dalis turned to head deeper into the night, a howl broke the silence. It was Mara. She was bleeding. A sharp stick protruding from her shoulder dripped with blood as she stumbled, wailing with panic, to a nearby boulder. Fenodor and Grigor immediately rushed to her side.

Ector looked around, at a loss, until realizing a sharp, splintered branch had impaled her from on high, skimming just inside the protection of the forest cover. It was unfortunate and unlucky, as neither Melowin nor Annalin had suffered any injuries while examining the rubble much further outside the bounds of safety. Ector looked to the sky to see the last remnants of the churning clouds; the high winds were blowing the last of the storm westward.

Mixed emotions washed over him as he dropped his gaze back to Mara: He felt guilty for fighting off the thought that she deserved it. Defensively, he started running through all the numerous reasons why he thought this, and finally settled on her insensitive remarks about Meric's father as the most deserving reason. But he managed to rebuke the hostility as Meric's father stuck in his mind. They had all lost someone close to them. Ector had never felt particularly close to old man Bodock, or his wife, both of whom were the closest thing to family. But Rahms was gone. The one being he would have thrown his life down for had raced fearlessly back into the disaster that no one had survived, to do what Ector couldn't.

A wave of sorrow hit him as he thought about his lost companion. The twang of sadness began to swell, making his eyes water. At least Rahms had initially made it out. Maybe there was still hope.

Plucked from his thoughts, he found a broad, round leaf entering out of the corner of his eye in the hand of Dalis.

"She will be alright, young master," said Dalis consolingly, handing the leaf to Ector.

Ector suddenly realized he had kept his eyes fixed on Mara as the sad thoughts of Cleargar and Rahms passed through him. He quickly wiped the tears away, now even angrier at Mara that everyone thought he was welling up over her. He fought off another wave of hostile feelings.

Well, at least we know they can't hear our thoughts anymore, Ector thought as Dalis moved closer to Mara and knelt by her side. Ector almost wished that, for those few embarrassing seconds, the thought-masking charm had been lifted so that everyone knew his tears were not for Mara.

"Brace yourself," said Dalis, positioning his hands over the front of her shoulder, where the stick had flown into her. "Remember," he counseled, looking over his shoulder as Ector pushed the leaf into his mouth and started chewing, "only eight chews, and only two fingers."

Dalis's instructions drew noisy, awe-struck stares from the new elves, whose looks of mild curiosity changed instantly to disbelief, and even some laughs.

"What does he think he is doing?" exclaimed one. "This only works on elves!"

"Do not worry yourselves," scoffed another in reply. It was the elf with yellow hair again. "He is only wasting his own storages."

Ignoring the comments flying around him, Ector did as instructed and extracted the messy leaf with only two fingers. This was followed by several gasps from the new elves as the mash shimmered bluish-green and pulsed with yellow flecks on the edges. It was the same leaf Dalis had given him to heal the wounds along his gums; he remembered its sweet taste. But he hadn't taken the leaf out of his mouth last time to examine it; he had simply spread it over all the areas of his mouth that hurt and then swallowed it. Had it shimmered this way inside his mouth?

Mara began to howl uncontrollably, without a care in the world that she might be alerting the dark elves to their whereabouts. Dalis swiftly cupped a hand to her mouth, muting the noise as he slowly pulled the sharp, broken branch from Mara's shoulder. She writhed in pain, trying to wriggle free of Dalis's grip, but it was futile. Ector bent down to hand the magical healing plant over to Dalis, but hesitated suddenly at seeing Mara begin to pale from the sheer amount of blood gushing from her wound.

"No, I cannot touch it," said Dalis, scooting away slightly, but still restraining Mara's muffled screams. "Place it inside her wound with your two fingers."

"Do I have to?" Ector asked apprehensively. "I can't just give it to her?"

"The healing properties only work with minimal contact, especially with this leaf," Dalis responded. "Place it in her wound before its magic begins to fade, and before we are forced to use another leaf."

Gritting his teeth, Ector closed his eyes and moved closer. Squinting them open again, just enough to see where he had to put the glowing mess, he felt the warmth of Mara's blood surround his fingers. He drove it as deep as he could into the gaping hole in her shoulder, even against her intensifying thrashing and screaming.

"This is impossible!" gasped one of the elves behind Ector, crowding closer for a better view.

Ector removed his hand from Mara and began wiping her blood off in the grass, as he examined the bloody, broken stick, slightly thicker than an arrow, lying next to him.

Mara's screams dissipated, and Ector looked up again to see all the elves watching with even greater stares of shock: Before everyone's amazed eyes, including Mara's, the yellow flecks, which still pulsed through gobs of blood, suddenly began to turn the whole injury purple. Then barely another moment passed before the purple turned a fleshy color, and she was instantly healed. Not a trace of the injury remained.

Several seconds passed as Mara studied her shoulder. The elves stared with various emotions: disbelief, outrage, puzzlement, but all of them doing so in silence, until Annalin asked a question.

"Why don't the pine needles glow?"

"Yeah!" chimed Meric, next to her. "Or those other shiny leaves. Why don't they glow, either?"

"Not every plant shimmers with its magic," replied Dalis. "But that does not mean it has none." He stood to face the other elves. "As you can see, we are not dealing with any ordinary human here."

"Indeed," replied the yellow-haired elf, looking between Mara and Ector as if he didn't quite know what to do with them. "Perhaps the strangest part about these *dark ones,* as you called them, is their determination to kill the boy. Tell me, Dalis of the Wood Elves, why do they hunt him?"

Dalis hesitated before shaking his head. The sky was clearing and not even a hint of a cloud remained.

"In due time," Dalis responded. "You will all have your questions answered in due time. Now is the time to leave."

The elf with spiky yellow hair ignored Dalis. "This goes beyond mere dislike of humans."

Ector was ready to leave with Dalis at the first step, not wanting another run-in with the dark elves, but he also wanted answers to these same questions. He felt himself torn, hoping Dalis would take just a minute to explain something, anything! But his attention was snatched away as Mara's two fingers, the ones attached to her freshly healed shoulder, jabbed fiercely into his chest.

Ector looked around, reeling at the sudden assault.

"You're the reason everyone's dead!" she hissed.

Ector stood, shocked and silent, as he rubbed at the shot of pain in his sternum.

"Yeah, that's right," huffed Fenodor, deciding that now would be a great time to use his deep, oaf-like voice. "Those same demons were all circled around you at the festival, too!"

Fenodor turned on Meric next.

"Then the fire started flying once you pulled him out of there," he said, reliving their initial escape from the ambush at the festival. "You two are the reason the village is destroyed!"

Ector found his voice again. "I didn't realize Mara granted you permission to speak," he fired back, directing all his Mara-related anger towards Fenodor. "If it so pleases her," he continued, giving a feigned bow to Mara, "maybe you could save your thoughts right now, and bring them up again when we're not running for our lives!"

"Hey, I have an idea," added Meric, jumping into the conversation. "Why don't we shiv you with a piece of wood, and see how long it takes before you're begging for the healing leaf that only Ector can make work?"

"Ector can keep his filthy fingers to himself!" Mara shot back.

Annalin broke in next. "Your shoulder is healed because of Ector! How can you be so ungrateful?" she asked incredulously.

"Well, Annalin," Mara replied, saying her name with complete disdain, "if you had more brains and a little less leg, you might be able to recall that I got hurt in the first place because of Ector. And," she continued, hanging on the word unnecessarily long, "if you could remember even further back to the night our town was burned alive, you'd remember that was because of Ector as well!"

"Look!" Annalin fired back. "Ector didn't ask for any of this to happen. He's surviving it the same as the rest of us! At least you can break off and go your own way whenever you well please, knowing these devils aren't chasing you!"

"And to where would I go?" blurted Mara, rolling her eyes. "To my charred home with a bunch of burnt corpses waiting for me inside?"

Fenodor and Grigor took a step forward and folded their arms over their chests. Towering on either side of Mara, they nodded victoriously as if they had come up with the retort on their own.

"And besides," Mara continued with finality in her voice, turning towards Ector. "I hardly even noticed I had a wound! That silly leaf barely did anything; I could've mended myself much better in my own home had you not brought this curse down on us!"

The seething words of contempt made Ector sorry he had wasted the time even chewing the leaf for her. Before he could form a coherent retort, one of the elves spoke.

"Dare as I may to interfere in the affairs of humans," said the elf with spiky yellow hair, "I am afraid none of you can be allowed to walk away from here. We have a very serious matter to deal with: You all now know that we exist."

Dalis moved to the front of the cluster, just as the elf finished his last word.

"The time is coming," Dalis interjected loudly. "Our two worlds are converging, and it is happening faster than any of you could possibly imagine. There will be unthinkable destruction for elves, unless we can reveal the root of this darkness that plagues us."

The elf with spiky hair looked as if he wanted to say something, but he stopped, affronted, as Dalis ended the discussion by turning and waving for the children to follow. Ector didn't hesitate; looking over his shoulder, he found Meric and Annalin stepping right behind him without a second thought.

After a few steps, Dalis beckoned to the new elves.

"Let us journey together, friends," he said. "We must find this dark root before the race of elves is no more."

"I do not see how we have any choice in the matter," replied the elf with spiky yellow hair curtly. "After you," he said, turning to Mara. "We do not want any stragglers getting lost, do we?"

Chapter 8
The Fireside

After hiking through the night and well into the next day, the entire group of six new elves, plus Dalis, Melowin, and the six children, arrived at a resting point. Ector's feet burned with blisters. The exhausted group plopped down, Ector, Annalin, and Meric against a fallen tree, while Mara, Fenodor, and Grigor all landed back-to-back adjacent to a stone fire pit that Melowin was building.

Meric struggled to remove his tall, deer-leather boots, stained with muddy, melted snow. "Sure wish we had some of that Grasshopper Ale right now." He paused, finally removing the first boot. "Our new *friends,*" he continued sarcastically, nodding towards the new elves, "look a bit bothered that we needed to stop for a bit, don't they?"

Ector nodded. Their *new comrades,* as Dalis liked to call them, had remained mostly silent during the trek northward out of the golden mountain range. They had just crested the last of the mountains covered in twinkling aspens, yellowed from autumn, and were now facing a view of enormous peaks breaking through in the distance. The mountains before them were covered in snow, and the mountaintops whipped with a ferocious wind that, even from a distance, could be seen blowing the white right off the peaks.

A gust like the one Ector had just been watching assault the faraway summit suddenly leapt through the trees all around them. Ector grabbed the Mountainwood dagger lashed to his belt, preparing for the worst as he hurriedly got to his feet. The shuffling on either side of him, followed by tense looks of fear on the faces of both Meric and Annalin, confirmed that they, too, were readying themselves for another attack.

"Do not worry," came Dalis's voice. "It is just a natural breeze. Nothing slows the winds in these higher parts."

Seeing them hesitate, Dalis took another, more visible whiff and nodded with a slight smile to put the children at ease.

Ector hadn't realized he was holding his breath until he released a sigh of relief. The sudden jolt had used up what little energy remained, and an extreme exhaustion washed over him as he plopped to the ground, resting against the fallen tree again. Relieved at the false alarm, he worried that he was too tired even to fight. Based on Meric's and Annalin's ragged appearances, he wasn't alone. None of them would be able to put up much of a fight if the dark elves discovered them this very second. But thankfully, Dalis looked as fresh as ever.

As Ector glanced around at all the elves making preparations for the evening, he couldn't find a hint of fatigue in any of them! The trek had lasted all of last night and had consumed the entire day. But to see them continue working as if it was nothing more than a mere pasture crossing was unbelievable! Ector's worry heightened even more; he didn't trust the new elves. They weren't as threatening as the dark elves, but he sure wouldn't dare venture off without Dalis.

"I think that pine scent is wearing off, mate," Meric commented, sniffing his arm. "I can't smell it any more. It might be time for another dose; what do you think?" He held out his arm for Ector to smell.

"I believe you," Ector replied, pushing Meric's arm away with a tired laugh. "If you're anxious for another helping of spit-covered pine needles, I can oblige."

"Well, I'd rather have an extra helping than an extra skirmish with those green things," Meric retorted. "At this point, I'm so tired, I'd probably just lie down and let them have me."

Ector gained his feet, silently agreeing with Meric, and reached for a handful of short pine needles on a limb branching over them. Before he could bring the needles to his mouth, though, Dalis was suddenly before him, knocking the pine needles out of his hand in a flurry of movement.

"Neither of you paid attention earlier," Dalis scolded. "Do not meddle with your skills outside my instruction. Do you understand?"

Shocked, Ector glanced at the fallen pine needles now scattered on the ground.

"Wouldn't it be safer to make sure our scents are still masked?" he asked, still reeling at the sudden confrontation and beginning to feel perturbed at Dalis's lack of confidence in him.

Dalis shook his head. "I will tell you if the charm fades," he replied firmly. "But I assure you; your scents are still masked."

Dalis must have noticed Ector's disgruntled look, because he beckoned for Ector to sit, and then he too sat down against the tree in the midst of the other elves still making preparations. Melowin arrived with a bundle of dead forest wood and arranged the pieces in his freshly completed stone fire pit.

"The smell of pine is irrelevant," Dalis began, to the sound of a crackling fire that sprang to life at the beckoning of Melowin's glowing red hands. "It is the magic within the pine needle itself, combined with your gift, Ector, that removes one of the signs of your human presence. Do you understand?"

They all nodded, including Ector, as he watched Dalis procure a few slices of dried cheese and flat crunchy bread from a small pouch within his traveling cloak. Ector took a modest portion as Dalis handed out rations to him, Annalin, and Meric.

"Is that how they found us?" Meric asked, nodding towards the other elves now traveling with them. "Did they track our scents? Well, not our scents, but the scents of the other three?" He nodded towards Mara, Fenodor, and Grigor.

"No," Dalis responded, "but I do suspect that is how the dark elves tracked us down. We were very unlucky." He paused for a second as he looked at Ector suspiciously. "But then again, we were lucky to walk away for yet a third time, unscathed."

Feeling unsure of himself, Ector opened his mouth to prod for an explanation, but Dalis continued before he could ask.

"I am not sure if our new comrades were able to smell Mara and the others or not. But remember, we elves tend to stay away from humans, so even if our new companions were close enough, the scent of humans would have kept them away, not drawn them closer."

Dalis paused, taking a bite of food.

"Well, how did these other elves know we were in trouble?" Meric asked.

"Because I called for them, in distress," Dalis explained. "It is every elf's responsibility to respond to the call if they are close enough to hear its ring. Even if we heard the call right now, we would be obligated to respond to it."

"I don't remember hearing anything," Meric commented.

"I do not suspect you would have," replied Dalis. "The call does not register to the ears of humans. We were already outmatched, both in numbers and ability, but once I became poisoned, and after seeing Melowin collide with the tree, I had to send for help. Our only hope was to see if others were in the area. And fortunately, they were." Dalis nodded gratefully towards the new elves. But Ector sensed hesitancy in him.

"But?" Ector asked.

"But," Dalis continued, more quietly, "by adding more numbers to our group, we make our situation more complicated. We will encounter yet another problem before long." He shifted his eyes to Mara, Fenodor, and Grigor.

Ector glanced at them too. "Yeah, I'd say the problem has already surfaced."

Dalis gave a laugh. "Yes, it seems so, but I was rather referring to our food situation; we seem to be gathering more and more mouths to feed. And Elmondove will not allow any of you to depart with knowledge of our existence. So, it seems we have an ever-increasing amount of demands to deal with, in addition to keeping you hidden from the dark ones."

The name *Elmondove* caused the children to exchange confused looks. Dalis nodded towards the elf with short spiky yellow hair. "He is not one to unnecessarily challenge," Dalis continued, "as he has connections high within the Elvish Council and could make this journey more difficult than it already is."

A moment passed before Ector scoffed and shook his head, looking back at Mara, Fenodor, and Grigor, his thoughts returning to the problem of the food shortage. "They caught themselves a nice, fat rabbit earlier and had no qualms about keeping it all for themselves. That's one less problem for you to worry about: I'm sure they'll manage."

"Quite," replied Dalis, "but the hunting of animals will not be tolerated in the larger presence of elves. My sympathies to the ways of humans are not shared by my peers."

Annalin spoke for the first time, pulling herself up straighter.

"But the dark elves called us animals," she interjected. "They called us beasts, when we were first hiding inside that bush in the forest. Why can they hunt us, but we can't hunt for food?"

"Well," replied Dalis, looking impressed with her, "that is precisely why this whole ordeal has gone over as well as it has with our new companions."

Annalin shared a confused look with Meric and Ector.

"Our new friends *do* look at you as animals," Dalis explained further. "As animals that are being hunted, and our comrades feel it necessary to investigate."

The look of offense on Annalin's face was followed with a soft whisper from Dalis. "It means they are not our enemies, which we already have plenty of at the moment. So we will use it to our advantage, until you are all safe."

He took one last bite of bread and encouraged them all to do the same. "Eat up, you will need your strength. Tomorrow will not be easier. And, if the dark ones manage to track us down again, I can promise it will not be the handful of novices that found us this last time."

"Novices?" exclaimed Meric. "You mean, there are dark elves even more powerful?"

"Think of the ones yesterday, again, as newly joined," responded Dalis. "But yes, there are much more powerful ones. And I suspect if you had tried to down a darker elf with a Mountainwood dagger..." He shook his head at Ector, indicating that it probably wouldn't have worked. But he let a small smile through at seeing Ector's shoulders drop in disbelief.

"I do not know for certain, of course," Dalis added. "But at the very least, it was a most excellent idea, young master, and even better execution!"

Ector nodded, appreciating Dalis at least acknowledging he had killed one of the dark elves, no matter how unlikely or bizarre the circumstances.

"How could you tell they were only novices?" asked Annalin.

"For one, their skin was still blotchy, and had only begun to transform," Dalis answered. "But even so, the spots on their skin were still relatively light. The dark elves that came for the old woman, and later hunted down your parents, Ector, were almost completely emerald green. The most obvious sign of their inexperience though, was their struggle to control the tornado they summoned. A darker elf would have effortlessly shifted the vortex... by himself."

Helplessness washed over Ector as he wondered where the limits to their dark magic might end. These elves had killed his parents, and now, after nine years, had finally picked up his trail again to finish what they started. Compared to what he had seen so far, even Dalis was no match for these dark elves.

Seeing Ector lost in thought, Dalis prodded him. "Go ahead, I can tell you have many questions."

A series of frustrated noises prefaced Ector's reply. "How are we supposed to beat them? Our luck won't last forever."

Meric nodded fervently, apparently glad Ector had put words to it. Annalin, too, awaited Dalis's answer with a hopeful look.

"It starts with knowledge," Dalis answered, nodding. "Elves are almost as old as the Earth Herself. We have existed together for centuries, and we have a deep wealth of knowledge concerning our gifts. But you must remember, this realization of your gift is only a few days old to you."

His answer was nowhere close to what Ector hoped for, and despite his efforts to control the frustration, he felt his temper rising.

"I'm well aware we are outmatched," he fired off. "I don't need another reminder how inferior we are! I just need to know how we can beat them."

"Patience will serve you well, if you can manage to keep it, young master," Dalis replied calmly. "Listen to my words again: If you want to defeat your enemies, it starts with knowledge."

The words simmered in Ector's ears as he felt another wave of hot anger towards Dalis, but he kept it contained this time. He heaved a sigh, considering Dalis's words in earnest. It was an obvious statement: It starts with knowledge. *Yes, of course, the elves have more knowledge of magic. Consequently, I'm running for my life. Of course it starts with knowledge. The elves know all the magic, and I know none of it.* Ector shook his head, feeling the waves of anger begin to roll over him more intensely. *Brilliant!* he thought condescendingly. *Now I can defeat the dark elves knowing I'm a complete twit! Masterful advice.*

"For example," continued Dalis, seeing Ector's frustration about to boil over again, "the pine needle charm you were about to so graciously offer Meric for a second time would have, in actuality, removed the charm's effect. Meric's scent would have returned instantly and begun filling the forest with the odors of human."

Ector took a deep breath, finally understanding what Dalis was trying to say.

"It starts with knowledge," Dalis reiterated.

"Alright," Ector replied, still frustrated, but now in better control. "No more meddling with magic. I will consult with you first."

Dalis nodded. "Well done, young master. I can no longer hear your thoughts, but it is not difficult to see you are frustrated. This is not an ideal setting to learn magic. If you three are feeling rejuvenated, come help finish the preparations," he said, getting up and heading towards the edge of camp.

Ector's legs were stiff, but he willed his body into a standing position. Just as he finished struggling to his feet, he stopped to watch Dalis approach Mara, Fenodor, and Grigor. The three looked like hostages being dragged along against their wills. Dalis dug deep into his traveling cloak and extracted more of his rations. Handing each of them a helping of dried cheese and crumbled bread, he gave enough for all of them to get a couple of decent bites. The gesture seemed to surprise Grigor as much as it did Ector.

Mara, however, turned her nose up at the food.

"We don't need any of your disgusting demon food!" she hissed, turning away from his outstretched hand.

Ector considered hollering for Dalis not to waste his time or food, but he was somewhat glad to see Fenodor take it and sneak a mouthful while Mara wasn't looking.

As Dalis walked away, Ector kept his eyes trained on Mara, thoughts beginning to spiral around about whom he disliked more: Her or the dark elves? His thoughts slipped away though as a heated voice registered.

"Do you honestly think myth-telling is helpful right now?" asked one of the elves. Turning, Ector found Dalis intercepted several paces from Mara's group; the elf had shorter, black hair, but beyond that, Ector couldn't distinguish much in the dusk quickly descending on them. "You were caught traveling with humans, and the punishment will not be light!"

"You saw the dark ones!" came Dalis's incredulous, albeit soft reply. "How can you deny a supposed myth when it stands in front of you?"

Ector made himself look busy, clearing out a small area to make a suitable sleeping space as he continued to listen.

"Dark elves do not exist!" the other elf shot back. "If you were better versed in your myths, you would know the stories tell of a deep evergreen skin color after partaking of the dark magic. These elves, misguided as they are, were more or less like us."

"Did you not see the first signs of the change? The green spots? The blotching?" Dalis asked, looking bewildered at needing to defend the notion that these had been dark elves.

The elf scoffed and ventured a laugh. "The first signs of the change? According to whom? You? Do you have some secret knowledge, privy only to yourself, about these so-called *dark elves*? If dark elves were ever real in the first place, they became extinct hundreds of years ago!"

"Barely over one thousand years ago did they disappear," Dalis confirmed, nodding. "Not due to extinction though. To dormancy."

The other elf shook his head, now at a loss for words.

"I do not pretend to have all the answers," continued Dalis patiently, in the face of the elf's cynicism. "But their practices and mannerisms match perfectly with the old woman's description of the dark elves."

Something he said seemed to soften the elf's attitude, but only so much as to drop the conversation.

"Elves cannot change their scents," mumbled the elf, throwing out one last comment before turning and walking away. Ector couldn't see Dalis's reaction, but Dalis hesitated for a moment, clearly watching the elf walk away.

A few moments later, Ector finished constructing his sleeping area under the enormous pine, and he looked up to find Dalis working his way closer to him, moving around the edge of the camp. Ector watched intently as Dalis moved his lips, silently uttering some foreign tongue as he moved methodically. Ector wondered if perhaps Dalis was placing some kind of incantation or spell on the area to protect them, but the thought was interrupted as Melowin approached Dalis from the rear. The two began to talk in barely audible voices.

"Are you sure you know what you are dealing with, Dalis?" Ector heard Melowin ask seriously. Ector started gathering pieces of firewood scattered close by, but as he piled the branches in his arms, he lingered to hear a bit better.

"They sent me flying through the air with a simple wave of a hand!" Melowin continued softly. "There was nothing I could do to stop it!"

"That is precisely why the boy has remained hidden!" Dalis replied, apparently still heated about the last encounter. "The dark ones have been hunting him from the moment the High Council got wind of his existence. The old woman managed to last three years keeping this prophecy a secret, before it almost poisoned her. Do you think he would have survived beyond a few days had the proper channels been used?"

"I agree. He would not have lasted long," Melowin paused for a moment. "But you have yet to reveal to me why you do not think him a threat."

Ector couldn't believe they were talking this openly about it so close to him; perhaps they had forgotten he was there.

"Truth be told," Dalis whispered, dropping his voice even lower, "we are forced to choose between two evils, and this darkness spreading through our ranks is more threatening than the boy. If defeating it means allowing Elvish knowledge into the hands of humans, so be it."

He raised his arms and uttered the final words of whatever he was doing. Ector wanted to steal a glance at him, but he dared not give any hint that he was listening. He placed the sticks quietly on the ground and pretended to search for something in his pack.

"The old woman went to great lengths to protect the boy, and I will do the same," continued Dalis, dropping his arms back to his side.

"But blindly?" Melowin stressed the question so that his voice rose, making it easier to eavesdrop. "Without knowing the missing part of the prophecy?"

"The old woman's gift of foresight was significantly enhanced in the presence of elves," Dalis responded. "Before dying, she foresaw a better world, for both our races. Somehow, this young halfling is the key to making that happen."

Melowin placed a hand on Dalis's shoulder, and the two exchanged a few more indistinguishable words, before walking in opposite directions to resume their chanting on the other edges of the camp.

As the night wore on, most of the children and some of the elves drifted off to sleep. The stars popped brilliantly against the clear, dark sky, but Ector found himself unable to sleep, lost in thought once again. The fire had faded as Melowin arrived out of the forest with a fresh batch of wood. Ector watched Melowin chuck three large logs onto the flames, and immediately it roared to life again, sending its light to all sides of the camp.

Fantasies of the Harvest Festival floated through Ector's mind as he tried to divert his mind from his stomach; they had eaten only enough of Dalis's rations to take the edge off the hunger pains. As he watched the flames dancing higher, images of Cleargar's large, grass-covered fields filled his mind; he could see their spacious magnificence glowing, lit by the tall fire poles just as it had been on that last evening. The stage was set for his final jump in the Top Hopper competition. He saw himself downing a pint of delicious Grasshopper Ale as he took the starting line. Feeling the lunge back and then a heave forward, the vision was so real he could almost swear the wind was racing through his hair right now.

Ector breathed deeply, feeling a peace settle over him as he flew through the air, sailing well past the Bellington boy's mark. But the peace was short-lived, and the fantasy dissipated. The reality of his loss crept into his mind. The Bellington boys celebrating floated through his mind after that, and he was half-glad he hadn't had to witness their victory in its fullness. He still couldn't believe he had lost; Meric's jump was perfect!

Ector sat up from his leaning position against the log, feeling silly that he was still upset over losing the race. He reminded himself that a much bigger race was in progress.

Heaving another sigh, he attempted to recapture the elusive tranquility, when Annalin's always quizzical voice suddenly reached his ears. As he listened, straining to understand her words, the wind shifted and billowed the smoke into his eyes. He rubbed at the pain and, sitting up a bit straighter, searched blurrily for Annalin.

"I've been thinking about that leaf," came her voice again, distinguishable this time.

Ector wasn't quite sure how long they had been talking, or if their conversation had only just started, but he listened, hoping for a new distraction from his stomach.

"You know, the one used to heal Mara?" Annalin asked.

"Yes, I remember," Dalis replied.

"Well, I'm just confused, I guess," Annalin continued. "I thought you had the gift of disguising yourself?"

Dalis nodded. "Yes, I do."

She pointed at Melowin, who was retreating back into the forest after warming the fire with his hands. "And Melowin has the gift of fire?"

"Yes, he does," confirmed Dalis, nodding once again.

"Well, the healing leaf," Annalin continued, "it doesn't really belong with either of those gifts, does it?"

"Indeed, it does not." Dalis sounded astonished. "I am really quite impressed with your savvy, young lady Annalin!"

Ector couldn't see Annalin's face through his watery eyes, but he couldn't help but think she was blushing, seeing her head dip slightly.

She had a knack for asking all sorts of questions that never occurred to Ector, but Ector always found himself excited to hear the answers.

"The healing leaf is from a time long forgotten," explained Dalis. "It was born in a time that saw the rise of the dark elves: The time before the Pact of Tommas. The leaf is one of the only remaining magical plants that works, regardless of gift."

As Ector made to move into a better position, a twig snapped underfoot. He froze as both Dalis and Annalin looked in his direction.

"You may as well join us, if you will not sleep," came Dalis's voice. He continued with the tale as Ector moved guiltily closer to the fire.

"Since that time," Dalis continued, "the magical gifts of the healing leaf have steadily deteriorated." He patted a small leather pouch slung on his belt. "I dare not even touch one right now to show you, because our touch is what diminishes its healing power. One might say it is our curse for breaking the Pact of Tommas. Only use two fingers, like this..." He demonstrated by picking up a dead leaf off the ground. "Let it touch your skin as little as possible, and then immediately into the mouth. The more it is handled, the faster its magic weakens."

"Like this?" Annalin asked, picking up a yellowed leaf and imitating Dalis's movements.

"Yes. Then you would proceed to chew it, eight times precisely. The mouth is most effective at releasing the inherent magic, but eight chews is the balance at which contact begins to disintegrate the healing properties." He performed a mock chewing motion and then proceeded to remove the imaginary leaf from his mouth. Annalin performed the motions right along with him.

"It worked instantly, once upon a time," said Dalis, with a hint of remorse. "As I said, the potency has faded over the centuries. But there is a lesson here, Ector: This process of using only two fingers, and only eight chews, is the most fundamental way to unlock the magic of something. Unfortunately, this recipe is the only method that works anymore when it comes to the healing leaf. But this fundamental method works on everything, when you have a gift such as yours."

Dalis laughed suddenly, apparently noticing that Annalin was still imitating his every movement. "Yes, if you were an elf, that would be perfect technique."

Ector could see Annalin's shoulders drop slightly with disappointment.

"Traditionally," continued Dalis, replacing the brown maple leaf on the ground, "the healing leaf has only worked on elves. But with Ector's unusual gift, the magic is now transmitted to you humans."

Ector felt their eyes lock onto him.

"It is a rare gift, indeed," Dalis continued very seriously. "One that many elves would feel threatened by if Ector was common knowledge to our masses. The Earth granted these gifts to elves a long time ago, and to us alone. She favored us far beyond every other creature that tread through Her forests and swam through Her rivers. A gift such as Ector's, which allows our abilities to seep away to the other creatures of the Earth, is very taboo among our kind."

The words drew a silent nod from another of the elves whom Ector hadn't realized was still awake, until he saw the bobbing motion from the corner of his eye. Seeing that Ector's attention had been drawn to him, the elf spoke.

"That is about the only thing that is true from what has been said this night," he remarked. The voice was heavier than any of the other elves Ector had heard thus far; he was one of the silent ones that hadn't spoken a word since arriving to their rescue at the foot of the cliff.

"The only reason you have been allowed to carry on with this mythical nonsense is because it is exactly that," continued the voice. "But keep revealing more about us, and the gallows will find you, friend."

Dalis turned his head to address the new voice.

"Mythical nonsense?" Dalis asked curiously. "The dark assassins killed the great prophet by the cover of night; I witnessed it with my own eyes. They intended the same fate for me, along with this young one here. Nine years they have hunted him. The gallows are of no concern in a secret war that is about to rage into plain sight, for all to see."

"Are you sure others will see the truth, as you see it?" asked the voice.

"Why would they not?" asked Dalis without a moment's hesitation, turning to face the voice. "When the old woman's last prophecy is finally revealed to the masses, the High Council will reap what they have sown through these dark wars waged in secrecy."

"I have a hard time agreeing," replied the voice calmly. "Regardless of your views on the High Council, and these *dark elves*," the voice couldn't hide the mockery, "your plan, if I understand it, is to openly defy the Council, by way of associating with humans, and then you hope to gain followers by professing your unfounded beliefs in old myths about dark elves?"

Dalis didn't respond.

"These tales are rarely remembered," the voice continued. "And even fewer take them seriously. You will amass only eccentric, zealous fools to your side. That is the truth."

Melowin, arriving with another batch of wood out of the dense darkness of the trees, joined the conversation. "Perhaps you are right." He set the logs down several paces away from the fire, and settled next to Annalin. The flames illuminated his unruly appearance, his hair dangling with twigs and looking knotted, as if it had gotten tangled in some thick brush. Ector fought to keep a smile hidden.

"But I, for one," Melowin continued, nodding in support of Dalis, "am inclined to revisit the old stories after this whole ordeal. Who says the legends cannot be true?"

The voice chuckled lightly in the darkness, and Ector couldn't help but see why: Melowin's untimely, ragged arrival certainly gave credence to the voice's remark that only eccentric, zealous fools would stand behind Dalis. From what Ector had seen so far, Melowin was none of those things, but the elf's appearance, at this very second, said otherwise.

"Point proven," answered the elf's voice from the darkness, not bothering to respond further to Melowin's comment.

"Just because I look the part at the moment," replied Melowin, "does not mean I am, in fact, any more or less foolish than the elf to my left or right. Might I ask who the greater fool is: The elf who entertains an improbable idea, or the elf who only digests what the masses find acceptable?"

There was a slight pause, which allowed Ector to consider the question.

"Well, fear not," responded the elf, chuckling again. "If you do not want to be counted among the masses, I doubt anyone will make that mistake before long."

Ector was sure the elf meant it more as an insult, but Melowin seemed to take it as a compliment, nodding appreciatively. The body of the deep voice shifted on the outskirts of the camp and settled into a sleeping position, turning his back on them.

"Come," said Dalis, returning his attention to Annalin and Ector, "let us all sleep. The trek tomorrow will not be as easy as it was today and last night. Tomorrow, we ascend through the Gray Mountain passes." He pointed into the darkness in front of them. The night left only a dim outline of the mountain range awaiting them, but Ector vividly remembered their tall, windy, snow-capped peaks from the last hours of sunlight. In his mind, "easy" would not exactly describe their last day-and-a-half's trek.

After staring at the mountains for another silent moment, Ector finally stood up, along with everyone else, and returned to his sleeping area, exhausted. He settled a few paces away from Meric, who was already fast asleep, twitching with dreams and mumbling softly. Before Ector drifted off into the depths of a dreamless slumber, the last thoughts of the golden mountains floated through his mind; the twinkling, yellow aspen leaves shimmered just like Ms. Weely's clover fields as the wind rolled through them. But the vision dissipated, and he didn't stir even a muscle until the first rays of the sun crested the treetops that next morning.

Struggling to lift a single, groggy eyelid, Ector tried his best to ignore the commotion tugging him back to consciousness.

"We want answers, now!" demanded one of the elves. They all stood, huddled together a short distance away, looking at Dalis.

Ector cracked open a second eye, just enough to see the group circled around each other. He shifted his eyes to his toes and saw Meric and Annalin still fast asleep.

"Silence, or you will wake them!" responded another voice in a terse whisper.

Elves really must think we're stupid animals, Ector moaned in his head. The last thing he wanted was to be awake, but their ruckus was unbearable. Their discussion would have woken a bear a league away. He shut his eyes hurriedly, to avoid any attention.

"They have slept for almost six hours now!" exclaimed the same voice. "It cannot be long before they stir. Be quiet!"

"Have you not watched them from afar?" asked the female voice, which Ector had heard speak only briefly before. "They sometimes sleep twice that long! And a little more than occasionally, I might add," she finished with a laugh.

Ector couldn't believe Meric and Annalin were sleeping through this. He stole another glance down through shaded eyelashes, and it was perfect timing: He caught an involuntary twitch in Annalin's eyes. She was keeping them forced shut. Meric had to be pretending, too, Ector thought. Thankfully, Mara and her two guards had removed their little circle to the edge of the encampment, where the elves' discussion was probably too faint to hear.

"Everyone be silent!" Dalis commanded in a softer voice.

In the pause that followed, Ector could only assume the elves were making sure the dispute hadn't woken them. He slowed his breath with his eyes firmly closed, breathing deeply to imitate the rhythms of sleep. The silence continued for another few moments.

"Alright," whispered Dalis finally. "I understand your concerns."

"Do you really, Dalis?" replied another voice heatedly. "I have already lost count of the number of decrees broken since we encountered you." The voice sounded familiar. It was that one with the spiky yellow hair. *What was his name*? Ector thought, trying hard to remember. Then it popped in his head: Elmondove.

"You said you would tell us everything," said another voice in an accusatory tone.

"And I will," responded Dalis calmly, "But not here. We might wake the humans." There was another pause, before he continued. "Somira is correct about the humans and their sleep habits."

Ector squinted an eye open just enough to see Dalis gesturing towards the young, beautiful female elf with long, caramel hair. That must be her name: Somira.

"Especially after yesterday's trek," Dalis continued, "the humans should remain asleep long enough for me to tell you what I know. Follow me, if you please."

Ector heard soft footsteps padding away from them. He waited a moment longer for the footsteps to become fainter, and then opened his eyes. Annalin held a finger to her mouth, gesturing for Meric to remain quiet, but she jumped at seeing Ector already awake.

She took a calming breath and nodded towards the elves, indicating she was about to follow them.

Ector nodded his agreement and looked towards the last sounds of the elves; the long, wispy branches of a nearby bush had just settled back into stillness as he silently gained his feet. Looking back to make sure Mara and the other two were still asleep, Ector made eye contact with Meric just in time to see him signal to follow Annalin, who was leading the way in stealthy pursuit. The idea of sneaking up on elves seemed less than wise, but Ector was tired of all the whisperings.

Annalin pointed to the ground, indicating she wanted them to step exactly in her footsteps. She took special care to walk only on patches of fallen pine needles and soft foliage that wouldn't crunch. It was a great idea. If they were able to get close enough to hear, the charms already in place would leave the elves none the wiser. Ector felt a twang of guilt as he reminded himself the charms were meant to keep them hidden from the dark elves, not from Dalis. But he quickly dismissed the thought.

Annalin stopped abruptly in front of a dense ring of bushes concealing the elves from view. She shot up a quick hand, indicating that both Ector and Meric should stop. She pointed through the bushes, but it was unnecessary; Ector could already hear the voices just on the other side. Chatter and soft, indistinguishable clamoring shot back and forth, before Dalis's voice broke through with the first discernible words.

"We need to move the children to an Elven Circle," Dalis said.

"Absurd!" exclaimed another elf, interrupting him. "That is absolutely out of the question!"

"Why do they need to go to an Elven Circle, Dalis?" asked another with rising temper.

"Stop!" said yet another voice. This one sounded like Elmondove. "Before we discuss any of that, first matters first." A pause followed. "The prophecy, Dalis: Give it to us."

Ector couldn't see what was happening, but tension followed in the wake of the silence. The discussion had died on the spot as he, Meric, and Annalin looked at each other nervously. Ector couldn't help but wonder if the elves could smell them. The silence was so thick, he held his breath, fearing that even the slightest noise might give them away.

Then a light crinkling of parchment from the other side of the bush reached his ears. Ector released a slow, grateful breath; the elves were still located in the same spot.

Annalin craned her neck higher to see what was happening. She had barely looked for a moment before Meric began prodding impatiently for an update. She waved him off with a quick hand and continued peering through the thin hole in the bushes. She mouthed the words, *"reading something"*.

Ector, too, felt impatient; he rose to a higher squat and craned his neck around to peer through Annalin's peeping hole. He had to see what was happening.

Ector saw Elmondove first; the elf held a piece of faded, yellow parchment in his hands. It was tattered at the edges, and charred black at the bottom, and his lips moved as he read whatever was on it. He looked confused as he reached the end.

"Where is the rest?" he asked, bewildered. "I can clearly see the top-strokes of at least one more line that has been burnt off."

"Let me see it," said another elf, snatching the paper out of Elmondove's hand. Ector watched the new elf's eyes widen, moving faster from side-to-side as he, too, reached the end of the note, confused.

"By the fates!" he exclaimed, a dumbstruck look overcoming him. "Why is this boy still alive?"

Dalis didn't answer immediately.

"How can you justify protecting this abomination?" demanded the elf, losing his temper.

"Quiet yourself," hissed Dalis, "before you wake them."

"So what if I do?" demanded the elf again, making no effort to control his voice. "Clearly you have read the prophecy, and yet you still protect him?"

"I protect him," responded Dalis, cutting him off and raising his voice in kind, "because as you can clearly see, this is not the entire prophecy. There is more!"

"Well, what is it?" asked Elmondove, jumping back into the conversation. "What is the rest of this prophecy?"

"That is what I have to find," replied Dalis, dropping his voice again. "The only other record of the prophecy lies within the libraries of the High Elvish Council."

There was a brief pause; Ector could see a few of the elves simply staring at each other before Dalis continued.

"That is why the humans must be taken to an Elven Circle," Dalis continued. "The protection charms already in place around the Circles will grant the humans sanctuary from the dark elves, and just as importantly, will give me enough time to travel to Lannonoir and retrieve the full prophecy."

Another brief silence followed before Melowin's voice broke in.

"But you said you thought these dark elves were the High Council's henchmen? If that is so, what makes you think the Council has not already destroyed the last remaining copy in the libraries?"

"That is absurd," came Elmondove's voice. "It is against decree number 643 to tamper with or otherwise alter any prophecy once it arrives from its source."

"Oh, my mistake," Melowin replied mockingly. "Yes, I feel much better knowing there is a piece of parchment somewhere, with a decree on it, standing in their way."

Elmondove shifted out of Ector's view, but the awkward silence that followed clearly indicated the tension brewing amongst them.

"Tell me, Elmondove," Melowin continued, "what decree prohibits the High Council from forming secret armies?"

There was another awkward silence. Elmondove didn't respond.

"Enough," came Dalis's voice. "Venturing into the libraries is a risk I must take." The finality in his tone made it evident that his mind was already settled on the plan, regardless of their bickering.

"Dalis," pleaded the same, unfamiliar voice that had been so critical of Dalis's decision to let Ector live. "This is madness! Where is your reasoning?" Before Dalis could answer, the elf pressed on. "This one single boy threatens to destroy all elf-kind!"

"Nay," interrupted Dalis. "Read the last two lines again."

The elf took a step towards Dalis, coming into view. His shorter, black hair was collected in the back today like that of the others. He had fierce sage-green eyes, and a scar running along his cheek. Ector wondered if the elf had encountered a poisonous Mountainwood weapon; the scar had the same rugged damage now featured on Dalis's hand. The elf glanced down at the parchment and read it a second time.

"That is your reasoning?" asked the elf belligerently. "Read the lines preceding it!" He threw the parchment back at Dalis. "You know we cannot survive a war like this. Our numbers have barely begun to recover from the last Great War!" He shook his head in disbelief. "And that is not even mentioning that the remainder of the prophecy could say anything!"

Ector's frustration was building as thoughts of simply charging through the bushes and lunging for the paper entered his mind. Although he felt excited and almost willing to do it, a voice of reason reminded him that the elves were impossibly faster. *Argh!* If only they had some of the Butterfly Honey Drub! But even then, the thought of racing to the paper with lightning speed faded quickly as he remembered that it worked better on girls. Stealing a quick glance at Annalin, he decided he wouldn't have to sell the idea very hard. She looked anxious to see the parchment, too. *Argh!* he thought again. It made no difference; they didn't have any!

"Nay, again," Dalis responded. "The last two lines show that there is another possible ending as to how these events could unfold." He retrieved the piece of parchment from the ground, refolded it, and placed it safely back inside his chest pocket. "Moments before the old woman died, she said this prophecy foretold of a new world, more glorious than anyone had ever imagined, for both elves and humans."

"And tell me, Dalis," came another voice; this one sounded like the one from the fire last night. Ector suddenly realized how unaware he was of so many of their traveling companions. They had been together for two nights now, and yet they might as well have not existed until this moment. With the exception of Dalis and Melowin, all the elves had trekked along behind him, presumably to make sure none of them wandered off. And Ector hadn't looked back, even once.

"How long have you believed in a dark elf reemergence?" asked the voice, sounding condescending.

"Since the night they assassinated the old woman," Dalis replied simply, waiting for the elf to continue.

"Ah ha," continued the elf, acknowledging the answer, but still with the same condescending tone.

"They used magic that no elf should possess," Dalis added, clarifying his reasoning in the silence that followed, which the other elf seemed happy to let happen by saying nothing. "What are you aiming at?" came Dalis's voice. "You might not have seen them descend over the cliff, riding the wind and mist, but surely you saw the tornado they procured, did you not?"

He waited for a response, but none came.

"If you doubt its darkness," Dalis continued, "I am sure Somira will be happy to enlighten you to its signs. And perhaps Elmondove here can give us the decree number forbidding the use of such magic?"

Elmondove cleared his throat, apparently uncomfortable at suddenly being used to support Dalis's position.

"The weather is unpredictable this time of year, as we all know," replied the voice, sounding agitated by Dalis's response.

"Unpredictable?" remarked Dalis, now with a hint of mockery. "And was it also a coincidence that the storm descended at their beckoning?"

"Well, if that were the case," answered the voice, going on the offensive, "perhaps you are among their legions? Did you not command the lightning to destroy that cliffside and rain down upon your enemies?"

Ector could see the tips of Dalis's ears beginning to turn red, but Dalis said nothing. Stealing a quick look at Melowin, Ector saw regret on his face, presumably at saying as much earlier in front of everyone.

"That would be decree number 29: The Orxon doctrine," Elmondove's voice responded, as he stepped partially back into view. "The Orxon doctrine prohibits the practice or harnessing of any Earthen magic," he recited. "That is to say, any magic that belongs solely to the Earth, and which should remain solely with Her."

"Tell me, then," replied Dalis. "Decree number 29 is a result of the dark elves and their times, yes?"

He waited, but no one responded.

"And that specific decree was in response to the darkest of elves to have ever graced us, no?" he continued, shrugging for someone to challenge him.

Still, there was no response.

"Yet you scoff when I suggest such times may be upon us again," he went on. "You see the forbidden magic before you, but you deny its presence even when the physical signs of its reemergence are clear?"

"If I remember the old tales correctly," responded the same unknown elf, "their skin should be evergreen, darker even than these trees, yes?"

"Yes, but the first signs of that change," answered Dalis, "are blotches on the skin, which they had."

"And how might you know that?" inquired the voice.

"The old woman was among the oldest, even among elves. She lived in those dark times and had first-account knowledge of their dark transformations."

"Ah ha," said the voice, once again condescendingly. "Quite convenient for you to have such a knowledgeable resource on the matter, would you say?"

Dalis nodded. "Convenient, indeed, for recognizing a reemergence before the masses realize it too late."

"Perhaps you are imagining what you dwelled upon in your centuries of solitude with her?"

"Did I imagine the vortex as well?" Dalis pointed to the sky.

"As I said, I saw nothing of the sort. Yes, the skies did darken, and yes, a tornado did emerge, but at their foolish beckoning?" The voice paused for a second. "The foreign tongue that leapt from your mouth concerns me more. You remember? The words that coincidentally coincided with that lightning bolt, which then struck the mountainside and, coincidentally, crushed your enemies to death?"

Melowin cleared his voice. "I do not believe they were crushed to death," he interjected. "As unlikely as it sounds, I think they somehow vanished before the rubble hit them."

"Did you verify that as fact?" asked the voice inquisitively.

"Of course not!" scoffed Melowin. "We had to flee; time was of the essence to ensure escape!"

"Ah ha," said the elf, whose tone was starting to compound Ector's frustration with annoyance, and judging by the permanent state of Dalis's reddened ears, Ector wasn't the only one.

"Perhaps it is possible that their peculiar scents simply vanished upon death?" asked the voice, his tone reeking as if reasoning with the simple-minded.

"Peculiar stench, you mean?" Melowin looked at the elf with sheer disbelief. "And have you ever heard of an elf's scent disappearing the instant they pass?"

"Well, as a matter of fact, yes I have," came the elf's reply, without the least hesitation. "There is a tribe within the Woodland Elves that developed such a skill during the last Great War; I believe the intent was to mask any clues left behind from the dead as they fled. It was to protect the ones who lived and to prevent them from being tracked."

"I know the skill of which you speak," said Dalis. "That is a gift of my tribe."

His response seemed to surprise the elf into silence for a moment.

"But I assure you," Dalis continued, "the scent does not dissipate immediately. It takes several moments before all signs of existence are completely gone."

"Ah ha," said the voice, condescension multiplying. "Yet *another* convenient coincidence. You just happen to be of the tiny Woodland Elf Tribe of which I speak? I think I have heard enough."

"Very well," said Dalis, forgoing the opportunity to rectify his reputation. Ector couldn't fathom why he chose not to engage; it was clear he was losing support among the elves. *Why doesn't he fight back*?

"We leave when the sun fully clears the tree line," Dalis continued. "And we will trek to the northernmost Elven Circle."

Ector suddenly looked to the sky to see how much time they had; the sun had already cleared halfway over the tree line. They would be leaving very soon.

"Indeed, we will head north," came Elmondove's voice. "But it will not be to the Elven Circle; we will head to Lannonoir so that you may give an account of your breaches."

Dalis responded only with silence at first.

"And what of the humans?" he asked finally. "Do you deny that the boy is being hunted?"

Ector didn't hear a response from anyone as Dalis waited for an answer.

"We will be offering them up for slaughter if we do not safeguard the innocent humans first," Dalis added.

Just then, a twig snapped next to Ector. Fear seized him, freezing his blood. He dared not move a muscle, nor even to breathe, but it was too late. The horrified, apologetic look on Meric's face said everything, as several pairs of hands reached through the bushes.

Chapter 9
Elven Circles

Forcefully pulled through the rough shrub, Ector found himself pinned with several sets of eyes as he emerged on the other side. The hands released their grip on his shirt, and he stumbled slightly. The elf with vibrant sage-green eyes and the scar on his cheek had grabbed him. Meric and Annalin popped from the bushes as well, at the hands of two other elves.

"Where are the others?" demanded another.

Ector recognized the voice; it was the one who'd sat a short distance from the fire last night, talking with Dalis. He had a mane of tawny copper hair, which, unlike that of the others, moved unbound with the gentle breeze. He held Ector captive with severe, dark indigo eyes, his jaw muscles flexing with tension as he surveyed Ector silently from head to toe.

"They are still sleeping," replied Melowin, returning out of the bushes from where Ector, Meric, and Annalin had been hiding. "There is no one else here."

"You are quite sure?" asked Elmondove. "It seems it was unwise to grant them an unscented charm," he added, throwing an accusatory look at Dalis.

"I am afraid it was unavoidable," Dalis replied simply, "but as they would have discovered much of this information soon enough, it is of no concern."

"It is of great concern!" Elmondove fired back, turning on Dalis. "With every passing minute, you draw us deeper into your gross violation of decrees, which continues to reveal more about us to them!" He nodded towards Annalin, Ector, and Meric as if they couldn't understand.

"Perhaps you dislike being spied upon," Ector interjected, unable to control his temper that had been building since waking. He supposed some of it was due to hunger and sleep deprivation, but whatever the reason, he'd had enough. "How long have you watched us from afar? I was also promised the whole story," he continued, ignoring the hostile looks aimed at him. "And I have just as much of a right to hear about this prophecy as anyone else here. Maybe more of a right, since it's about me!"

"Patience, young one," interrupted Melowin, shaking his head disapprovingly. "Losing your tongue will not serve you well, as I have heard Dalis tell you before."

"I've stayed my tongue long enough. We've listened to everyone talk like we're a pack of wild boars." Ector felt the fire inside him burning hotter. The female elf with glowing caramel hair shrugged; she seemed to think the example an apt fit and apparently found it odd the humans thought of themselves otherwise.

Her reaction did nothing to improve Ector's mood, but he managed to halt his words and take a deep breath. An inner voice convinced him that it wasn't worth trying to change their minds; he just needed to figure out a way to better use his newfound gift, and that wasn't going to happen if he continued upsetting the only ones who knew its secrets. If he could just manage to learn enough to protect himself, or better yet develop some sort of weapon to discourage further attacks, it wouldn't matter how much the elves hated him. There would be nothing they could do except leave him alone and go their own way.

"Never mind," Ector said decidedly, as the elves continued to gaze upon him with either scathing or curious looks. "We appreciate you warding off the dark elves, but we'll go our own way from here. We'll forget we ever saw you. No decrees broken."

The shocked looks from both Annalin and Meric reflected how Ector felt inside. He was just as surprised to hear those words come out of his mouth, but even if he could take them back, he wouldn't. The brews were an accident, but this time he had something he didn't have before: The knowledge that it was his gift. He felt a rising confidence—no, a rising excitement—that he could find different ways to turn his gift into a weapon against these monsters.

"If we agree on nothing else today," Dalis responded in a patient voice, "it is that you cannot be allowed to go your own way from here."

To Ector's amazement, all the elves nodded their heads in agreement, even the one with a mane and severe blue eyes who looked ready to attack him.

"Prepare to move north to the Elven Circle," Dalis said, looking at Ector and then at Meric and Annalin. Ector locked eyes again with the elf from last night's fire to see if he would object, but he said nothing.

"Go wake the others," instructed Dalis. "We eat briefly, and then leave."

Ector didn't want to turn his back on the dangerous stares, but the pressure of Dalis's silence, waiting for him to obey, finally forced him to turn back towards the camp.

"At the risk of being redundant," came a whispered voice from somewhere behind Ector, "perhaps it *was* unwise to grant them those unscented charms."

Ector couldn't tell which elf said it, but he shook his head irreverently. He regretted not choosing his words more carefully, but he still did not regret a single word he'd said; the elves held all the power, spied on humans in secret, and hated the idea of a non-elf possessing one of their gifts. Now, because it was used against them, in a rather harmless yet deserved way, they wanted to undo everything! *Of course they do,* Ector said to himself. *But they can't undo anything, can they?*

He continued to shake his head as he thought about it more; they could try to undo the charms, yes, but he knew how to mask their scents and their thoughts again.

Knowledge can't be undone, Ector continued to think daringly. Dalis was right: Knowledge was the key! If the elves wished to push the issue and remove the charms, he would, of course, have to bend to their will; the elves were too powerful to confront head on. But Ector could place the charms back on, once the timing was right. And this time he would do it when it benefited him, Meric, and Annalin the most. He would just need to get a plan sorted out, before the elves removed the thought-masking charm and regained full access to his thoughts.

He worked through his ideas, crunching slowly on a forest root he had stumbled upon. It was bitter and tasted more like dirt than anything else. But at least it was something to fill his stomach. As he chewed and pondered, he heard the others return to the subject of the dark elves. Based on their broken chatterings, none of them agreed on what the swampy creatures might be exactly. If these things were in fact the returned dark elves from some forgotten past, Melowin was the only one even remotely open to hearing it. But Ector discerned one consistent thing amongst the clamoring: A sense of unease.

Pouring steaming hot pine needle tea down, Ector finished the last bit of root and spent the remainder of the morning waiting for Dalis to say it was time to remove the masking charms, but Dalis never even hinted at it.

"They don't look too happy about letting us go to that Elven Circle place, do they?" chimed Meric, noticing the undeniably hostile looks.

Ector shook his head as he scattered burnt logs amongst the forest foliage. Meric took the cue and started hauling in piles of dead leaves to cover the flattened areas where they slept. It was another moment before they had a discreet word.

"I have no clue what an Elven Circle even means," Ector whispered, pretending to drop a pouch off his belt. He bent slowly to retrieve it, and then checked his bootlaces, making sure they were tight. "Do you want to go there?" he asked softly.

"I don't think we have much choice," Meric whispered back, slowly reaching for another burnt log. "At least we'll be safe, right?"

"Yeah, right!" replied Ector, a bit more loudly than he intended. He stole a glance around him to see if he'd drawn any attention, but all the elves were continuing to work their magic, muttering incantations and weaving their arms and hands intricately around the borders of the camp. Ector couldn't tell if they were adding more protections to the area, or removing any signs that the magic ever existed. The thought hung with him for a moment, as he wondered if magic left any traces. He made a mental note to ask Dalis later and brought his attention back to Meric's comment.

"Almost all the elves we've met hate us," he said hurriedly. "If that keeps up, I doubt there's anywhere safe for us, at least where elves are involved."

Meric raised his eyebrows. "Yeah, but at least it won't be this dark elf variety. This lot here seems satisfied just to hate us."

"Don't be too sure," Ector continued ominously, stealing another glance around to see if anyone was watching them.

Don't worry, he thought. *If they're looking, they probably just think our thumbs are inferior. They won't suspect a thing!* He let a slight smile show. Yes, if the elves wanted to think of them as some sort of brutish beast, he would use it to his advantage and play dumb when it served him best.

A ruckus sounded off to the left, distracting Ector from the amusing mental banter. He turned, half-ready to engage in yet another battle, but it was just Fenodor: The oaf had tripped over Grigor, who had disguised himself rather well under a huge pile of dead pine needles, leaves, and sticks.

Ector breathed a sigh of relief and loosened his grip on the wooden dagger clutched within his white knuckles. The commotion had apparently caught some of the others' attention as well, as Ector saw the female elf shaking her head at the two continuing to fumble over each other, both trying to stand.

Ector let another small smile show as he wondered if perhaps the elves had only been spying on people like Fenodor and Grigor this whole time. If that was the case, at least he could understand how such ideas about humans took hold. *Well, I guess it's their fault for only watching the stupid ones,* Ector thought, feeling the simmering excitement about one day being able to defend himself against the elves rekindled.

"It is time to move," Dalis called, waving all the children over.

"Where are we going?" asked Grigor groggily, having just woken up.

"We are taking you somewhere safe," replied Dalis.

"And where might that be?" asked Mara, with the same sourness from the previous night.

"We are starting our trek to an Elven Circle; it is located in the far Northland," Dalis answered. "It usually only takes a day or two by an elf's stride, but I imagine it will take closer to five or six days with all of us. The sooner we leave, the sooner you will all be safe."

Ector took count of all the elves for the first time as Meric dumped the last pile of forest foliage over their sleeping areas: Melowin and Dalis, both of whom were already beginning to trek away from the campsite; Elmondove, with the short, spiky blonde hair, who appeared very knowledgeable on Elvish law and, of all the elves, seemed most noticeably displeased that humans had discovered their existence; and then the sole female elf, whom Dalis had called Somira.

Ector had a hard time getting a good read on her, but she seemed to be somewhere between indifferent and mildly turned-off by humans. However, she didn't seem innately hostile like some of the others. Ector suspected her dislike of humans was at least open to change, as evidenced by her surprised reaction that Ector and the others thought better of themselves than a pack of wild boars. While his gaze lingered on her a moment longer, her lean confident frame shifted ever so slightly. Every subtle movement drew his eye like a bee to a flower. Her beauty was unsurpassed by anything he had ever seen, to the point that it was distracting. She turned her eyes towards him, and Ector quickly diverted his attention to the trees.

Clearing his throat rather clumsily, Ector returned his attention to the next elf in line, or rather the next two. They were undeniably the youngest of the bunch and both lads. One had short, wild red hair, similar to Ector's, but the dark red variety. He also had deep, cobalt eyes and a bit more muscle on his frame compared to the other elves. But he had the same pointy ears as the rest. The second younger elf had long blond hair gathered in the back and lighter azure eyes that seemed to jump right off his face. He was a bit shorter than his companion, and much leaner. Ector hadn't heard them utter a word yet.

Behind the two lads stood the elf with short black hair pulled tightly in the back. His scar and his forest-green eyes seemed more pronounced as the sun struck him in the face. This one still looked none too pleased about how their secret meeting had ended; he scowled at the ground, occasionally bending to pick a few pieces of wild weed and stuffing it somewhere deep inside his traveling cloak.

Finally, behind him, stood the elf from the fire last night: the one who'd tried reasoning with Dalis, but had then devolved into subtly mocking him at the botched secret meeting. He had long flowing brown hair and intense, metal-blue eyes that were now studying the surrounding forest. Ector wished he hadn't provoked him. Wariness bubbled up at the idea of something bad happening to Dalis or Melowin. Allowing this elf to trek at the rear of the group struck Ector as a supremely bad idea, especially after the way the secret gathering had ended. The elf looked dangerous. And Ector had no clue as to what powers were lurking in this one.

OK, six new elves, plus Dalis and Melowin, and then five humans plus me, thought Ector, trying to shake off the warning. *Fourteen in all.*

"We are definitely going to lose if the elves turn on us," he whispered to Annalin and Meric, watching Mara and her two bodyguards collecting their boots and shoving down the last crumbs of bread.

"Yeah, I don't care how fast Dalis and Melowin are," Meric agreed. "Two versus six are not good odds. And no offense, mate," he said with a wry smile, clapping a hand on Ector's shoulder, "but your magical brew-making abilities wouldn't be my choice weapon against this crowd."

"No offense taken," replied Ector.

"They won't let anything happen to you." Annalin nodded reassuringly towards Melowin and Dalis who had stopped to discuss something. "Dalis has been watching you since you were born. He'll get us to this Elven Circle, if it's the best place for you."

"Well, as long as we stick to you like sap on a tree," Meric continued, "between Dalis, Melowin, and these Mountainwood daggers, maybe we'll have a chance."

Ector signaled for them to stop talking as suddenly he realized all eyes were on them; Mara, Grigor, and Fenodor made their way over to join them while the elves waited impatiently for the humans to pick up the pace and start trekking. Ector released a deep breath, fighting the feeling that they were being herded away. Dalis was right: His rebellious thoughts were going to get him into trouble if he couldn't control them better. He needed as much time as possible to learn how to use this magic better. He took solace in promising himself that the rebellious thoughts could flow free again, once they had what they needed. Ector took another calming breath and followed Annalin and Meric, as they caught up with Dalis and Melowin.

The day turned cooler in the face of clear, sunny skies. The golden forests faded away behind them, and the colors of fall began to return in pockets along the rising, rocky mountainsides. The group crested a steep ridge a short distance later, and a new view of wave after wave of mountains awaited them, with white peaks as far as they could see. Ector didn't know if the journey would end somewhere in their depths, or somewhere beyond, but either way, it was absolutely beautiful. There was no possible way they could reach the other side in just five or six days though; their destination had to lie somewhere in the mysterious recesses.

They continued to trudge forward without stopping, down the other side, up another smaller ridge, and down again, until after a while the overwhelming sense of the trek ahead began to ease. Ector even started to enjoy the journey, especially the solitude as they marched along in long periods of silence.

Lost in his thoughts, he found himself wondering again about the brews and if there was any method to their magical effects. *Oats must produce a springy effect, like with the Grasshopper Ale,* he thought. But the Original Brews contained dashes of oats, too, and there was no bouncing, only a glow. Both types of Original Brew had lots of corn, though. *Maybe the corn is the key to glowing.*

He went on like this, analyzing ingredients and their possible effects, until they reached a long, sloping forested area. The group had spread out, causing their once-organized line to appear more like a moving blob. The elves seemed irritated at the slower pace and had all moved towards the front of the group. But to Ector's great relief, he could now see everyone with a simple turn of his head. He was still defenseless against any one of them, if they decided to turn and attack, but at least being able to see them put his mind a little more at ease.

Taking a deep breath of the sweet mountain air, his thoughts began to drift back to the magical brews again. But his mind didn't linger there very long as a strange sight suddenly caught his eye: The two younger elves were off to his left; the one with red hair trekked along like everyone else, but the one with long yellow hair had suddenly disappeared, right under the full sun! One second he was there, walking next to the other, and then the next, he was gone! Ector turned to see if Meric and Annalin were watching the elf effortlessly flash in and out of view, hiding behind nothing except the thinning air. They weren't, but Ector didn't want to draw any attention at the moment. He turned back to see if the elf had reappeared yet, and had to search for a moment, but then, *boom*! There he was again!

Ector rubbed his eyes, wondering if the light was playing tricks on him, but he found the rest of the surrounding forest behaving normally. Suddenly he realized he'd been watching too long and was startled to see the elf staring back at him. The elf gave a wink, and a smirk began to widen on his face, just before *boom*! He was gone again. This wasn't like Dalis's gift at all.

Ector gazed through the empty forest, astonished. He remembered Dalis in the shadows of the corner; Dalis needed the shadows, and had only really disappeared after they looked away from him. This elf could disappear regardless, and in the full afternoon light.

"Psst!" came a voice on his other side.

Ector jumped, instinctively reaching for the dagger on his belt. The young elf reappeared next to him, laughing.

"How did you do that?" Ector asked incredulously, a bit shaken. Meric and Annalin both looked back, apparently confused, assuming the question was meant for them.

"How'd I do what?" asked Meric, looking over his shoulder. "Hey, wait a second." He suddenly realized the elf with long, yellow hair was now walking beside them and pointed towards the other young elf with red hair, still trekking a short distance away. "How did you get here so fast? You were just over there a minute ago; I saw you!"

The elf laughed again, clearly pleased with the attention.

"It is my gift," he answered.

It was the first time Ector had heard him speak; his voice was confident, but much younger-sounding than any of the others, confirming the suspicion that he was, indeed, younger than the others traveling with them.

"But how did you disappear?" Ector asked, still in disbelief. Then he told the elf about Dalis's gift, and how Dalis needed the shadows to disappear anywhere remotely close to what the elf had done. "But you vanished under the sun!" he finished.

The elf nodded, still pleased with himself.

"Dalis and I are of the same color, but we have different abilities," he said, paying respect to Dalis by way of a slight bow.

It was a strange comment; the elves all appeared pretty much the same color to Ector, except for the dark elves, of course, with their mossy blotches everywhere.

"Dalis is a shadow-lover, whereas I am a light-lover," the elf continued. "The stronger the light, the more easily I can bend its rays around me, making it seem as if I have disappeared!" He smiled proudly. "Watch."

Boom! The young elf vanished again before their eyes.

"If you had been listening carefully," whispered the elf's voice out of the thin air, "you would have heard my footsteps approaching."

A soft pattering rustled the ground next to Ector, as the elf shuffled his feet in the fallen leaves. But after the leaves stopped flailing along the forest floor, Ector found the elf's footprints gently pressing down with every step. It would have been nearly impossible to tell if the elf was sneaking up on him. Ector looked down, feeling a bit embarrassed at the loud crunching his own steps made.

Boom! The elf reappeared again.

"I can almost vanish completely under a full moon, too!" said the elf, glowing with pride.

"No, you cannot," said another voice, surprising Ector from behind. Ector whipped around to see the other young elf with dark red hair closing in on them.

"Quamas likes to fancy himself a Leighmoor," said the red-headed elf, with a slight smirk.

"And I suppose you do not?" replied the yellow-haired elf, turning to face the new arrival. "I am closer to mastering my skill than you are yours, Unair!"

"What's a *lay-more*?" asked Ector, struggling to pronounce the foreign word.

"Bending light is barely even a real skill!" Unair taunted, shaking the red hair away from his face, ignoring Ector's question.

Quamas's large, crystal-blue eyes widened with anger; he stood taller, trying to make his lean frame tower over the thicker-built Unair, albeit unsuccessfully.

"Everyone can bend light!" Unair continued to tease, staring back with an equally defiant dusky night-sky gaze. His auburn hair glistened in the afternoon sunlight, and his eyes danced excitedly at poking fun at the leaner, yellow-haired Quamas.

Meanwhile, Ector's question continued to be ignored, or at this point had been missed altogether.

"Well, let us witness your great light-bending abilities, then, if everyone can do it," dared Quamas, beginning to walk again, stretching his arms out wide in a welcoming gesture, before folding them across his chest confidently.

"Fine, I will," Unair shot back, readily accepting the challenge.

A look of concentration suddenly fell across Unair's face, and to Ector's amazement, the elf did indeed begin to fade from view. But it was nowhere as good as what Quamas had done; Quamas had disappeared completely, without a trace, while Unair looked closer to a ghost with wispy, faded strawberry hair. Ector wasn't sure which would have been more frightening: An invisible voice, rustling through the forest, or a ghost-like figure doing the same.

"Pitiful!" said Quamas, victoriously. "I am surprised you were even allowed to advance to the next Circle!"

"Do you mean the Elven Circle?" asked Annalin, quickly jumping into the conversation.

"Of course," answered Quamas, taken aback at her sudden interest. "Is there any other kind? Humans do not have Circles, do they?"

"Well, to be honest," replied Annalin, "we're not really sure what an Elven Circle is."

"Well, you have no need to know, do you?" Unair was clearly perturbed that the conversation had switched away from his light-bending abilities.

"Do not be sour, or I will tell Dalis," Quamas said reproachfully.

Unair's skin tinged red at the threat, but his demeanor changed after that, and he was more polite.

"If I remember right," Quamas continued, "I believe we learned in our human studies circle that you have something close called a *sa-kool.*"

Annalin suppressed a laugh. "Yes, but we pronounce it *school.*"

"Ah yes," said Quamas, nodding. "That sounds closer."

"So an Elven Circle is a school?" asked Meric, looking for clarification. "Why would a school be any safer for us?"

"Well, it is not like a human sa-kool," Unair interjected, also struggling to pronounce the word. "Elven Circles are of the utmost importance for our survival."

At the children's odd looks, Unair continued.

"The Elven Circles were created centuries ago," Unair explained, but Quamas cut in.

"No, millennia ago," he corrected, looking annoyed.

"Right," Unair continued, conceding Quamas's point with a nod. "But the Elven Circles became something entirely different after the second Great War. The dwarves began strategically targeting the Elven Circles at that time, so the Circles had to adapt. They needed more protections placed around them, and a greater focus on competition and battling. You know, in case the dwarves managed to break the barriers!"

At the children's confused looks, Quamas jumped back in to clarify.

"The war supposedly dragged on for ages, both sides refusing to bend to the will of the other. Eventually, the dwarves got the idea that they could gain victory by destroying our passage of knowledge from one generation to the next." He shook his head disgustedly. "When the dwarves began targeting the Elven Circles, we had to change everything about them. How they were built, what was taught, and so on. Since that time, the Elven Circles have grown to become some of the safest places the Earth has ever seen."

The curious, lost looks on the children's faces drew a surprised reaction from both Unair and Quamas.

"You mean you have never heard this history before?" asked Unair with disbelief.

"Before a few days ago, we didn't even know you were real," Meric replied, equally perplexed at their ignorance of human ignorance.

"Hmm, I had always thought it was wasted effort trying to hide from humans, but I guess not." Unair raised his eyebrows and nodded with shock. "You are, indeed, shaped like us, but you truly have more likeness to animals to have not discovered us."

The never-ending human-animal comparisons were beginning to push Ector well past annoyance, but he managed not to show any signs of it this time.

"Well, if every elf can bend light, what's your real skill, then?" he asked, aiming the question at Unair.

"I, unlike my good colleague here," replied Unair proudly, "am a water-lover."

"Here we go," mumbled Quamas.

"But you see, a skill is something all elves share, like being stealthy, bending light, and so forth," Unair explained, sounding like a teacher.

"But," interrupted Quamas, "very few can push the boundaries to complete invisibility, like Dalis and I can!"

"However," Unair continued, ignoring Quamas, "that is the true difference between a skill and a gift. There are elves who have heightened skills," he stressed, looking directly into the fuming crystal eyes of Quamas. "Things all elves can do, albeit some to a higher level. And then there are those of us with gifts." Unair placed his hands on his stout shoulders, indicating he was talking about himself.

Quamas began to protest, but all Ector could catch were incoherent noises as the two argued over each other, before Unair raised his voice louder and said, "Although, there is really no difference between the two... If you want to know the real distinction between gifts and skills though, there you have it," Unair finished, making the subtle difference between the two terms explicitly known.

"Alright, you want a turn?" roared Quamas, suddenly disappearing. Ector watched his footprints zoom around behind Unair, who was left searching for the invisible elf. A loud smack suddenly resonated somewhere behind Unair's stout backside, and his deep dark eyes widened with shock as he howled with pain.

"Be careful what you start," he warned, rubbing his rear tenderly, while he looked around slowly.

Worried that they were drawing too much attention, Ector looked towards the other elves, but none of them seemed to care about the young elves' antics; they all carried on as if this was completely normal behavior. Ector finally caught at least some sign of awareness of the scuffle: Somira, the lone female elf, threw a look over her shoulder, followed by a slight shake of her head as she continued to trek on ahead of them.

Just then, a short distance away, Ector's eye caught a stick slowly levitating off the ground. It hovered in mid-air, just behind Unair. Ector thought about warning him, but the sight was so bizarre, he found himself just watching, speechless. Suddenly the stick hurled itself, flying end-over-end, towards Unair's unprotected back. Ector reached out a hand to warn him, but it was unnecessary as Unair turned with blazing speed towards the blind attack. Throwing a hand out, he halted the incoming stick just paces from striking him. It hovered in mid-air, peacefully, as a smile spread across Unair's face. Then the stick began to shake violently. The vibrations intensified until the stick exploded, sending dozens of shards falling to the ground. But, more interestingly, hundreds of tiny water droplets went soaring out of the stick.

"Too easy," Unair jested. "Try something a little drier next time!"

The water droplets continued to race away from his outstretched hand, until about half of them collided with the invisible Quamas, several paces away.

"Prepare yourself!" cried Unair, sprinting to the still invisible but now dew-covered Quamas, who was left momentarily stunned by the splashing. Ector looked around again, amazed that the commotion still wasn't drawing the least bit of reproach from the older elves.

Unair launched himself at Quamas, tackling him to the ground. Quamas reappeared once again, popping back into view as the ensuing wrestling and tussling resulted in Unair rolling into a dominant position, on top of Quamas.

"Surrender?" Unair asked, smiling victoriously.

Quamas looked murderous. He continued thrashing from side-to-side, but it was futile; Unair held him firmly pinned to the ground, and with every attempt to wriggle free, Quamas only made his predicament worse, allowing Unair to tighten his grip further.

"Surrender?" Unair prodded again.

"Surrender," Quamas wheezed angrily.

Unair immediately sprang to his feet and offered a hand to Quamas; Quamas took it reluctantly.

Ector turned to see if Meric and Annalin had watched the whole amazing exchange; seeing Meric standing with a slack jaw, and Annalin also speechless, he didn't even need to ask.

"This must be new for you as well?" Unair asked, breaking them out of their stunned states.

Ector nodded slowly.

"This is how we learn at the Elven Circles," Unair explained cheerily, failing to disguise his pleasure at beating Quamas. "Actually, I think that is how it got its name, is that not right, Quamas?"

Quamas nodded. "Yes, it is a common game we play. All the apprentices within an Elven Circle take turns rotating through... well, we call it rotating through the circle." He shrugged apologetically at not being able to find a better way to describe it.

"Once we circle around," Unair continued, clearly still feeling the excitement of victory coursing through him, "we face each other and wait for the signal. Once given, all the apprentices use their gifts, or skills..." He threw a look back towards Quamas. "And we begin to attack and defend against one another."

Ector's eyes widened. That's exactly what he needed: Practice at defending himself! *And why not go on the attack*? he thought, feeling the excitement clearly visible in Unair beginning to take root in him as well.

The apprehension of going to an Elven Circle suddenly dissipated: Dalis may have wanted to take him there for the protections placed around them, and Ector knew Elvish hostility would probably still exist there, but if he got to see more battles like this one unfold, he couldn't help but think his odds for defending himself would improve.

"The goal is to deflect attacks from everyone else in the circle," Quamas added, striding up alongside them. "But you also want to deliver attacks of your own, while simultaneously defending yourself, until you are the last one standing. If forced out of the circle, or forced to surrender as I just did, you forfeit your position in the circle."

Unair nodded, adding excitedly, "And if you are good enough, when you advance out of the Elven Circles you can become a Leighmoor!"

"What's that?" asked Ector, for a second time. "What is a Leighmoor?"

"First you have to become an Elvish Warrior," Quamas clarified, but more to Unair than to Ector. "Then, once you prove yourself to be among the best warriors, you can be chosen to become a Leighmoor."

Ector nodded as he watched the excitement between the two young elves escalating, causing each of them to try to outdo the other in their explanation. But Ector still wasn't sure what exactly a Leighmoor was, so he continued to wait silently, hoping it would all make sense eventually.

"Only the most elite Elvish Warriors are even considered," Unair continued, throwing a look at Quamas, suggesting he was less than elite.

But Quamas ignored him this time, and finally turned his attention back to Ector.

"Did you know that your friend, Dalis, was a Leighmoor?" he asked.

Ector shook his head, "I had no idea. But I still don't know what a..."

"Aye, he was," interrupted Quamas, nodding with growing interest. "One of the best! His battles are famous, legendary, even among us!"

Ector turned his attention to his unassuming protector, who continued to trudge on, oblivious to their conversation.

"Melowin was a Leighmoor, too!" Quamas added. "He might not be as famous as Dalis, but he is still well known. The two of them fought together in many a battle!"

"How do you know all this?" Ector asked.

"I take a special interest in studying Leighmoor history," Quamas explained with pride. "Their training is unrivaled and very difficult. It is what makes them the best warriors the Earth has ever seen."

"What kind of training do they do?" asked Meric excitedly.

"All kinds!" replied Quamas, reveling in the children's growing interest in his favorite subject of study. "It is even rumored they can talk to each other with only their thoughts, regardless of their gift! Most elves have to be born with a gift like that, but Leighmoors are reputed to have accomplished it! Usually, only the most gifted elves can read minds, but a Leighmoor's training pushes the bounds of their natural abilities!"

"So they *can* read our minds!" exclaimed Meric, confirming Ector's earlier suspicions.

"Well," replied Quamas, dragging the word out with a smile, "it is not exactly hard to read the minds of humans, with the exception of you lot, of course. You can always tell when humans are near. I am still uncertain as to why humans even bother thinking at all; you may as well just say everything that crosses your mind!"

Unair stifled a laugh, clearly agreeing.

"With elves, it is different," Quamas continued. "The gift to communicate only by your thoughts must be voluntary, meaning that both elves must want to have a conversation that way *and* be capable of doing it."

"What happens if one of them doesn't want the other to read their thoughts?" asked Meric excitedly.

"Well, then, it just does not happen," replied Quamas, shrugging indifferently.

"Can an elf force their way into someone's mind?" Ector asked, remembering the peculiar scene between Melowin and Dalis. "Maybe causing them to guard their thoughts?"

Quamas raised his eyebrows with interest. "It depends on how powerful the elf is," he replied finally. "In terms of the Leighmoors, it would be difficult to reach that level of proficiency, unless they were already born with that gift. And remember we are talking about elves here, not humans."

Ector shrugged, not sure why Quamas felt the need to make the distinction. Seeing the lost look in Ector's eyes, Quamas continued.

"I just wanted to clarify that reading human thoughts is not really a gift or a skill. It actually takes more skill to block out the never-ending noise than it does to read them."

"Agreed," Unair added quickly. "Tapping into the thoughts of a human is like collecting water from a river. The thoughts are always flowing and all one needs to do is simply 'go down to the river' and collect whatever you want."

"And," Quamas interjected again, "just as the river is none the wiser when you bend to fill your water satchel, humans cannot tell when we are listening or not."

"Right," Unair said, jumping back into the conversation, talking over Quamas yet again. "However, with elves, it is more like extracting water from a barren ground. An elf cannot just happen across another elf's thoughts by chance, like with humans. It takes real effort!"

"And," interrupted Quamas, "the elf giving up their thoughts will certainly know when someone is trying to read their mind. There is no disguising it."

The heated explanation between the two ended in a silent standoff, both staring daggers, trying to tower over the other while continuing to trek onward.

"The point is," Quamas continued, finally turning back to Ector, Meric, and Annalin, "that it might, *might*, be possible to pry into the thoughts of another elf, against their will, but only if the elf was born with that gift. Cultivating something like that, to that particular extent, with no natural ability..." He shook his head. "Near impossible!"

Unair mumbled something that sounded like "*Maybe for you!*"

Ector saw Quamas's eyes flare with anger, but this was followed by a deep breath and a silent sideways look from the lean, yellow-haired elf.

"Can elves hear that far away?" Ector asked, deciding to change the topic, throwing a nod towards Dalis, who was leading the way a good distance ahead of them.

"Oh, definitely," replied Unair. "The question is: Is he choosing to listen to us? It is not uncommon to ignore the incessant human noise."

Ector squashed his urge to scoff; these two elves were contributing most of the noise up to now, but he kept the thought to himself.

"But with these other elves chasing you," chimed in Quamas, sounding eager to challenge Unair's comment, "I am sure Dalis is listening to every word right now."

Ector stole another glance at Dalis; if he was listening, he didn't show the slightest interest in their conversation.

"So did you two see the prophecy?" asked Annalin.

Brilliant! thought Ector, feeling his excitement leap so high he could have kissed her. He had gotten so consumed in watching the two duel with their gifts and their words, that he'd completely forgotten they'd been present at the secret meeting.

"Yes," Unair replied simply.

Ector's heart skipped a beat. He waited anxiously for Unair to say something more, but to Ector's disappointment, he reverted back to the previous discussion.

"Quamas is right about Dalis's fame," Unair commented, looking impressed. "You should count yourself lucky to have him as your protector."

Quamas nodded, clearly equally impressed. "But I have never heard of anyone except the prophets having protectors," he added, turning to Unair with a look of mild bafflement, "let alone a human!"

"Well, the magic we witnessed at the cliffside was a first, too," Unair commented. "But if those other elves are after you, there is no doubt you will need a protector. And even that may not be enough," he said ominously.

Ector snatched a few strands of the tall mountain grass in frustration as they crossed the threshold into a high plateau area. They continued to trek onward in the wake of the other elves, leaving behind the barren, craggy mountains, dotted with colorful forests, as they now entered a wide, golden, grassy expanse.

"Why do your prophets need protectors?" asked Annalin curiously.

The elves stared back blankly for a few stunned seconds.

"Wow," Unair finally responded. "You really know nothing about us, do you?"

Annalin shrugged. Unair heaved a sigh, clearly struggling with where to begin.

"Uh, well," he started, "the prophets are very important to us. Obviously."

Quamas huffed and mumbled something that sounded like, "*Brilliant explanation!*"

"Well, feel free to give it a shot, then!" Unair fired back, swiping his hand through the air and causing water to leap from a nearby puddle and collide with the side of Quamas's face. "Do you recall the last time we had to give an account of why the prophets are important?" he asked, flustered.

To Ector's surprise, Quamas wiped the water from his face calmly. Was he going to let the incident go? But then Ector saw Quamas subtly flex his hand, and a ray of light popped out of nowhere in front of Unair; the intense flash of light dissipated as quickly as it had appeared, but it left Unair blinking, blinded.

"Ah!" Unair cried, shielding his eyes much too late. His foot snagged somewhere in the tall grass, and he stumbled, flipping forward into a patch of especially scraggly grass.

"The prophets are important to us," Quamas explained evenly, as if nothing had happened, and making no effort to help Unair stand, "because they continue to guide us to dominance over all the other races. They tell us what will happen, and we use it to our advantage."

"Are they always right?" asked Ector anxiously, hoping the answer was no. "Have they ever been mistaken?"

"Oh, all the time!" chimed in Unair, brushing himself off as he returned to the conversation, still blinking. "As a matter of fact, I like a good rebel who defies the prophets!"

"Stay your tongue," warned Quamas. "We are not inside the Elven Circle."

"We're inside the Elven Circle?" Meric broke in, looking around confusedly. Clearly he'd been so absorbed in watching Unair gather himself up that he must have misheard what Quamas had said. But it didn't stop him from pressing on. "How do we know we're inside?" Meric asked, turning to Ector.

Ector stared in reply, baffled. "I think you misheard him, mate. He said we're *not* in an Elven Circle."

"Oh!" replied Meric, blushing slightly at the misunderstanding.

"It is a saying we have," Quamas replied, clearly unsure what intelligence level he was dealing with. "Rebellious comments like that are accommodated only in the learning environment. Once outside the walls of a Circle, we must show the utmost respect to our elders, especially the prophets." Quamas aimed the last words at Unair.

"Right," said Unair lackadaisically. "I forgot."

"But if the prophets are often wrong," Annalin began, "why are they valued so highly?"

"Because," replied Quamas, "when their predictions have been correct, they have had enormous implications! Take the old woman for example." Quamas threw a hand in Dalis's direction. "Her first prophecy put an end to the second Great War. Think about that! It put an end to it!"

"I'm afraid we don't know anything about any Great Wars, first or second," replied Annalin apologetically.

"How is that even possible?" Unair exclaimed incredulously. "The second Great War lasted over one hundred years!"

"That is a rumor!" countered Quamas. "Nobody knows for sure how long it lasted."

Ector exchanged an unsure look with Meric and Annalin.

"You don't know how long the war lasted?" Ector asked confusedly.

"Nobody does," Quamas replied. "We have no histories prior to a thousand years ago. We have rumors about the war, and we know about the old woman, of course, but the details have been lost."

Unair nodded in agreement. "Since it is called the second Great War, we assume there must have been a first as well, but those histories are gone."

"Why?" asked Meric, clearly dejected at the news. "You've forgotten all the stories as well?"

"The subject is rather delicate," Quamas responded, lowering his voice and glancing around quickly.

"Well, we have plenty of other stories," Unair added excitedly. "Like the Battle of Orleum! But you have heard those, I am sure."

Meric shook his head excitedly, hope restored.

"No?" Unair looked perplexed. "Perhaps you know it by a different name."

"They would not have seen any of it," countered Quamas. "The last half of that battle took place deep under the mountains."

"But not all of it!" replied Unair, still utterly shocked at the children's lack of knowledge. "There were still battles that saw the sun!"

Quamas shook his head. "Not anywhere near humans, there were not."

Unair continued shaking his head in amazement at the idea that none of them had any clue about the battle.

"But to answer the question," Quamas said, "we know that the second Great War ended only after the old woman delivered the prophecy that guided us to victory."

"What was it? The prophecy, I mean. What was the old woman's prophecy?" asked Ector, feeling hope beginning to rise once again that he might discover some clues about his own prophecy.

Both Quamas and Unair looked confused.

"Uh, well," began Quamas, "that, too, is unclear. It would have been part of the records that did not survive. But I think you are missing the point; in answer to your question, the prophets are important to us, because they have repeatedly led us to victory. That is why the prophets have protectors." He turned towards Annalin in answer to her question. "And that is why only the very best, even among Leighmoors, are chosen to protect them: It is so they can live a long life and bear as many prophecies as possible."

He paused and stared at the three of them to see if they understood.

"But," Annalin continued, uncertain if she was communicating her question clearly or not, "why do they need protectors? What are they being protected from?"

Quamas gave an exaggerated nod, as if suddenly realizing he had left out a crucial piece to the story.

"The dwarves know of our strength in the prophets," he continued, "but we must take a step back first: The dwarves revealed their truly vile nature when they started to target the Elven Circles. They knew that our strength stemmed from the passing of knowledge there, so they began to target the Circles, trying to eradicate our future. And as with the Circles, the dwarves had also managed to learn of our strength in the prophets. Once they discovered it, the dwarves attacked, and they have continued their attacks, trying to assassinate all of them. Dwarves are sneaky. They like to wait until they think complacency has settled on us, and then they strike. That is why only the best, even among the Leighmoors, are chosen to protect the prophets; it could be years, even centuries, of nothing and then *wham!*" Quamas slapped his hands together, startling all of them. "You are under a Dwarvish attack!"

Annalin blinked away the shock, trying to regather her thoughts. "But you said the prophets were not always right," she countered, finally managing to collect herself.

"Well, the biggest thing is finding a prophet that has been right once," Quamas clarified. "Once they deliver a good prophecy, we know they are a real prophet. The effort to weed out false prophets ended several centuries ago, and our group of prophets nowadays is very reliable."

Unair nodded. "Yes, we have not had a serious challenge in, well, almost two centuries." He sounded almost disappointed at the lack of activity.

"Well, how many prophets are there?" asked Ector, deciding to gradually work the conversation back to the topic of his own prophecy.

"Hmm," said Quamas, looking to the sky while he counted. "Maybe fewer than ten."

"Only ten?" Ector exclaimed, surprised.

"And the old woman was by far the greatest among them," Quamas added. "All elf-kind mourned her passing from old age just over ten years ago."

"Old age?" asked Ector suspiciously, distinctly remembering Dalis's story of the dark elves' ambush and assassination by night.

Quamas nodded. "And Dalis was her equal among the Leighmoors; no one has ever matched him in battle."

Ector stared at Dalis with new appreciation as the protector continued to trek onward, still either oblivious or uninterested in their conversation.

"So that's why the others haven't attacked you," Annalin commented, with a look of dawning realization. "The others don't want to challenge Dalis, do they?"

Some of the elves tilted their ears slightly at her remark.

"We should stop talking," Ector interjected, suddenly feeling wary at provoking the other elves.

Better get used to it, said a voice inside. Ector heaved a sigh, knowing the sentiment was true. From the way things had gone so far, he doubted they would ever amass more than a few elves to their side. As it stood right now, Dalis and Melowin were the two rarities. Ector wondered about Unair and Quamas: He liked them, and they certainly didn't seem as hostile as the others, but he didn't know if he fully trusted them.

"Wait," said Meric. "I want to hear more about this battle! I didn't know dwarves existed, either!"

"Well, they may as well not exist anymore," said Unair, with a hint of contempt. "After we finished them off this last round, they have not been heard from or seen since."

Ector had completely forgotten about Mara and the other two, until she slowed and asked, "If you all hate us so much, why did you care about one old woman?"

Ector cursed himself for being so blatant in their talking; if Mara could hear them, then that meant the elves probably could too, even though they were at a much safer distance ahead.

"Well," Quamas answered, nodding politely at Mara's entry into the conversation, "there is a bit of a controversy surrounding the old woman, especially within our Circle. I am not sure how it is elsewhere, but some believe that she was not entirely human."

He paused, as if about to deliver some amazingly profound piece of knowledge.

"She was believed to have been one of only two halflings ever discovered!" He looked expectantly at everyone, waiting for shock and excitement to fill their faces.

When he was instead met only with blank stares, he continued, "What I mean is half human, half elf!"

Still not connecting with any of them in the way he had hoped, Quamas didn't bother waiting any longer for a reaction. "And," he pressed on, stressing the word, "she strangely chose to embrace her lowly human roots!"

"That is ridiculous!" Unair interjected, dismissing the idea with a scoff.

"I said it was a controversial belief," countered Quamas defensively.

"It sounds like you believe it, too!" gibed Unair mockingly.

"Well, then, who is the other halfling?" asked Mara, interrupting their bickering with her usual arrogance.

Ector wasn't sure why Mara was suddenly so interested; usually she was more than pleased to keep as far away from him as possible. *Maybe she's bored,* he thought, feeling discouraged; he was never going to be able to steer the conversation back to his prophecy again.

Quamas stared stupidly in response to the question, looking between Mara and Ector several times before finding the words to say, "Well, he stands before you, of course; the other halfling is your companion, Ector!"

He continued to cast unsure looks between all of them, clearly reevaluating his initial assessment of their intelligence.

"Dalis also mentioned that," Ector finally responded, ignoring the quizzical stares from both Quamas and Unair. "But how did you know I was half human, half elf?"

Quamas's uncertainty devolved into amazement as he stared back in reply; presumably he was having another internal argument about what animal humans were closest to, but Ector decided just to wait patiently for an answer.

"Well," Quamas replied slowly, "it is stated quite clearly in the prophecy, of course." He continued to stare at them, clearly struggling how to break it down for them further. Then a dawning realization fell across his face.

"You mean to say you know nothing of your prophecy?" he asked hopefully.

Ector nodded. "But we would very much like to know. Would you mind telling us?"

"Oh, thank the fates!" Quamas said, shaking his head, his voice returning to normal. "I had begun to think your thinking-capacity was the same as a forest turkey! Do you know, when it starts to rain, those turkeys stare straight up at the sky, trying to drink it down, and sometimes drown?"

"No, I did not know that," replied Ector, fighting the urge to fire off a clever retort.

"Well, I did not memorize it, but it started something like this," Quamas began. But before he could even get a word out, Elmondove interrupted their conversation.

"Have you been discussing the Elvish ways with them?" he asked accusingly. His once spiky yellow hair appeared more disheveled now, as the trek had pushed onwards.

"Well, yes, of course," Unair replied, looking surprised.

"That is strictly forbidden! Get back to your positions!" Elmondove ordered.

"Could you not hear us talking this whole time?" asked Unair confusedly.

"Yes, of course I could!" sputtered Elmondove, looking as if he was about to explode with anger. "But I stopped listening to your immature ramblings about a mile ago! You both have your Circle Provings coming up soon, and I know you need the practice, but this is absurd! It serves me right, I suppose." He grabbed Unair and Quamas by the elbows and began guiding them away, muttering, "I never should have let my guard down around humans."

"Argh!" Ector turned to Annalin and Meric. "We were that close to hearing the prophecy! That has to be our first mission going forward. Agreed?"

Annalin and Meric both nodded.

"Yeah, let's not get distracted anymore until we find out what it is," Annalin added. "We'll try to ask Unair and Quamas again, when we stop to rest tonight."

She leaned in closer to Ector as Elmondove, Unair, and Quamas settled back into their positions a good distance away. She whispered so softly, Ector had to lean in even closer.

"We need to find a plant that quiets our voices, so they can't hear us talking." Her voice was barely audible, but Ector was able to fill in the pieces he had missed by reading her lips.

"How are we going to do that?" he whispered back. "I don't know which plants do what. The brews were all accidental. We might set off a beacon for the dark elves to find us, like what happened earlier with Meric."

Annalin shook her head. "Dalis has good intentions for us," she whispered. "But I do not believe that about the others. What if something happens to Dalis? We need to take action."

The concern had been burning in Ector's mind, too. He knew he didn't stand a chance if the elves turned on him; Quamas's playful disappearing and reappearing all afternoon had fully convinced him of his inferiority. He hadn't been able to hear a single footstep, even when staring right at the elf's feet making marks on the ground. If one of them wanted to sneak up on him and slit his throat, they could do it whenever they well pleased.

"Nothing will happen to Dalis," Meric said in a quiet but confident voice. "Didn't you hear what those two said about him? No one has ever beaten him in battle!"

"Yeah, but that doesn't mean it can't happen," Annalin countered. "And the other elves don't have to beat Dalis. They just have to beat Ector, which won't be hard."

It was tough for Ector to hear somebody else put words to it like that, even though he knew she was right.

"But regardless," Annalin continued, "we have to be able to talk without the threat of them constantly eavesdropping on us. I'm sure they'll be paying more attention to us after what happened just now."

Ector agreed with everything she was saying, but it didn't change the fact that he didn't know how to competently wield his magic. "What do you want me to say?" he asked finally, in answer to Annalin's silent prodding for him to take action. "I wouldn't even know where to begin!"

"Maybe it's less about the plants you touch," Annalin suggested encouragingly, "and more about your intention behind the touch?"

Ector and Meric both replied with confused stares.

"I've been thinking," Annalin continued, not really paying attention to them anymore, but discussing the matter with herself, "a number of things could have gone wrong with your brew making. Right?" She turned, reengaging them, waiting for them to follow her line of thought.

"Yeah," replied Meric. "And?"

"And," she continued, "why didn't it? Why didn't a single brew cause someone to get sick, or smell bad, or... I don't know!"

Ector thought for a moment; she did have a point. Ector had almost removed Meric's unscented charm by accident. And except for the magic he had produced by Dalis's directives, every other crazy magical thing had been sheer luck! So why hadn't any other accidents happened yet?

"All I'm saying," Annalin continued, "is it's rather incredible, if you think about it! Maybe it's your intention behind the touch. Every single brew you made was perfect for a festival!"

"But I've already told you," Ector replied, momentarily forgetting they were whispering, "I didn't make the brews! I just harvested the ingredients."

Annalin waved an annoyed hand at him, signaling for him to talk more quietly. "But that's what I mean! You were probably thinking about the festival while you were harvesting, right?"

Ector thought back for a moment, and he did have to grant her that; dreaming about the festival was the only thing that had made the long hours in the fields enjoyable.

He shrugged. "What's your plan?" he asked, resigned to see if there was any truth to it. He knew he would have to make the leap at some point and experiment with his gift. And further convincing himself, there was absolutely no guarantee that his plan to pick up more knowledge at the Elven Circle was even going to work. Maybe they would try to lock him away in a dungeon. Or worse!

The fearful thoughts began to run wild through his mind, creating all sorts of terrible ways the elves might turn on him and prevent him from escaping. It didn't take long before he was sold on Annalin's idea.

"Pick a plant you've harvested before," Annalin suggested, pushing the plan into action.

Ector looked around as they continued to trek onward; there weren't any of the usual oats, corn, or barley. But there were some very interesting violet-blue mountain tulips with a fluffy white center scattered throughout the field. He had picked a variety of flowers for the brews before, but he had never seen one like this. The next forest line was quickly approaching; if he was going to use this particular flower, he needed to pick one fast, and without the elves seeing.

"You think it's safe to try this one?" Ector asked, touching one of the tall flowers. "I don't see any of the usual plants around here."

Annalin shrugged her approval, and Meric's anxious nodding did little to conceal his excitement to see what would happen. Ector stole a glance at Dalis and the other elves, to see if they were eavesdropping. It was impossible to tell. None of them paid any special attention at the moment, but it proved Annalin's point even more strongly: They needed a way around the elves secretly overhearing their every word.

"What should I do with it after it's picked?" he asked, looking for ideas.

"Try chewing it, just like you did with the pine needles," offered Annalin. "Dalis said that was the most potent way to unlock the magic, remember? Eight chews, two fingers."

"Right," said Ector.

He waited for the next flower to come within reach, and closing his hand around the bud, he let his forward momentum snap the blossom from its stem. He dared not look around, in case someone heard the noise. Holding it cupped in his hand, out of view for a few more paces, he slowly placed the flower in his pocket and kept walking.

Throughout the rest of that day's trek, they didn't stop at all. But it didn't matter. All Ector could think about was the flower. He hadn't received any suspicious looks, and no one tried to inspect his pockets. A few of the elves' voices did manage to ride the wind back at different points in the day, but most seemed preoccupied with the dark elves' whereabouts. They ascribed various names to the green creatures, but a worried tone was the common thread between everyone. The most interesting words came from Melowin's distant voice; he wasn't worried so much about another dark elf encounter, but rather, why the dark elves had yet to find them again. Ector heard Dalis dismiss the concern, saying the charms in place were more than sufficient to disguise them. The dark elves could not possibly know of Ector's gift, which meant it would not even cross their minds that the humans' most telling signs might be subdued. Ector also heard Dalis comment that if the dark ones tried to track him like a regular human, they could spend the rest of Ector's life looking for him and never see his face again. Ector hadn't caught any more of that particular discussion, but as the day pushed onward, Melowin's unease persisted.

When they did finally arrive at a stopping point, it was later that afternoon, just as the sun was dipping towards the distant mountain range. Mara's incessant complaining about hunger pains had forced them to stop a bit earlier than the day prior, as she fell dramatically against one of the trees in the never-ending Mountainwood forest.

As Ector started to sweep away a flat spot to sleep, he took special care to make sure his sleeping area was next to a fallen log: He planned to use it to block himself from view when the timing was right and pull out the blueberry-colored flower. But as he cleared away the debris, the prophecy suddenly popped into his head; he looked around for the two younger elves, hoping that now might be a good opportunity to reignite their earlier conversation.

But Elmondove had quickly put them to work. Ector watched them toiling away busily and couldn't help but wonder if Elmondove had held true to his word and listened in on their plan.

Both Quamas and Unair stayed busy the entire waning afternoon, placing different enchantments on the camp, hauling in dead wood for the evening, or carrying out some other task cooked up by Elmondove. Melowin had already started a fire, and Ector decided to warm his hands against the chilling autumn air. He sat with Annalin and Meric, playing with a piece of straw, waiting impatiently for an opportunity to arise. He'd offered to help with tasks several times before sitting down for good, as had Meric and Annalin, but the elves didn't want any human help. As Ector watched Unair and Quamas continue to work, he was torn between whether he felt more like a prisoner or a baby.

Deciding to take advantage of the elves' neglect, Ector retreated back to his sleeping area just as the elves started to settle for a brief spell. Of course, Unair and Quamas were still occupied. The other elves had all divided into smaller groups, scattered around the campsite, talking indiscernibly amongst themselves. The sun still hadn't completely disappeared, but the soft rumblings of Fenodor's snoring reached Ector's ears. He gave another quick glance around, debating whether to extract the flower from his pocket or not.

His stomach suddenly gave a loud, painful lurch. Realizing he hadn't eaten anything all day, he scanned the area and found almost everyone idly talking, watching the fire, staring out into the darkening forests, or sleeping. How much longer could he endure without food? He tried to force his thoughts back to the flower. Through sheer will, he focused on the possibility of magic hiding inside the flower, rekindling the excitement that had carried him through the day.

He reached into his pocket and extracted the flower, being careful not to draw any attention to himself. Keeping his eyes on the ground, he listened for the slightest noise of an approaching elf en route to snatch the plant away from him. But after a few seconds, he remembered that it did no good to listen for their impossibly stealthy movements. Unassumingly, he lifted his head and looked around, making sure everyone was still in the same place. But at the slight movement of his arm, Meric and Annalin suddenly glanced over with knowing looks; apparently they had been waiting all day, like hawks, for him to retrieve the flower.

Ector invited them over with a subtle nod. Annalin and Meric both stood up and walked over, sitting down strategically to block Ector from view of the elves.

"Wait," Ector whispered, before bringing the flower to his mouth. "What if it's poisonous?"

"Just do it, you ninny!" Meric replied in a hushed voice, barely able to contain his excitement. Ector opened his palm hesitantly, still debating the dangers of doing this without Dalis's supervision, but he never had a chance to voice those concerns before Meric, just as Annalin had done with Mara, shoved Ector's hand to his face. Before Ector knew it, he was chewing the curiously flavored flower; it tasted like a very potent spice that burned his nose.

"Stop, stop!" whispered Annalin after a moment. "That's eight chews!"

More than glad to get the flower out of his mouth, Ector abruptly stopped chewing, and efficiently extracted it with two fingers, just as he had done several times before.

"Are you sure it works this way?" he asked, trying to get the taste out of his mouth. "Dalis said this was only necessary for a few plants, like the healing leaf."

"You did this same thing with the pine needles, remember?" Annalin replied, growing frustrated with Ector's reluctance as she craned her neck to try to see the masticated mess hidden in Ector's lightly closed palm. "And the other vine-leaves as well," she added. "Dalis said it's the most fundamental way to unlock the magic!"

"It's not going to hurt to give it a try, is it?" Meric prodded.

Ector wasn't so sure; he could imagine several disastrous scenarios, but he found himself equally curious as to what would happen. He had already begun to resign himself and open his palm, but not before he saw Annalin silently gasp. She reached for the mashed-up blue petals and plucked a piece away before Ector even had a chance to look down.

"Ector, look!" she whispered with awe, holding the slimy flower between her fingertips; it pulsed with an orange glow.

Chapter 10
Tongues and Eyes

"Something's got to happen!" Meric exclaimed, reaching past Annalin's awe-struck stare and grabbing a small chunk.

"What are you going to do with it?" Ector asked, unable to hide a gruesome look. The pine needles hadn't exactly been a pretty sight afterwards, but this flower was decidedly worse. Hungry as he was, the shiny, goopy glob made Ector's stomach lurch as he watched Meric happily rub the mess all over his face and neck.

"That's horrifying," commented Annalin. But then she, too, began to flatten the mash out between her palms, preparing to spread it over her face.

"Don't do it," Ector pleaded, cupping his other hand over his mouth to stop the vomit from rising. "I mean, shouldn't we wait to see if it works on one of us, before we all start bathing in this stuff?"

"Blegri eltri buttom," Meric blurted out incoherently.

Ector stared, stupefied, at the nonsensical string of sounds, but Meric was clearly pleased with whatever had just left his lips; it had the typical tone of an insult. But it was just a bunch of noises. It didn't make any sense.

"Flergi abu hotim rob," Meric continued, at which Annalin burst out laughing, hiding her face apologetically. Ector could see her turning red with fits of giggles, as whatever had been said was clearly aimed at him.

"Shrevy irtum rob," Annalin gasped between giggles.

Looking back and forth between the two, and deciding the gibberish had undeniably been one of Meric's insults aimed at him, Ector witnessed a sight never to be forgotten: Meric and Annalin, both guffawing and giggling with mashed-up, spit-covered flower all over their faces, making incoherent noises at each other. Ector didn't know whether to laugh or just continue staring stupidly.

He looked down at the last piece of violet-blue glob in his palm that continued to pulse orange. Reluctantly shaking his head and ignoring the protests inside him screaming not to do it, he brought his palm closer and commenced smearing the now cold, mushy flower all over his face and neck.

Annalin and Meric continued to giggle as Ector almost immediately regretted the decision. But to Ector's surprise, the sounds of their conversation transformed mid-sentence, as Meric said, "Blergi fodo tropim hop ox dung. I mean, no offense, mate, but maybe try chewing on some mint leaves next time. Maybe it's the flower, but I doubt it. I don't remember the flower smelling like that before it went into your mouth. Your breath is dreadful!"

Annalin continued to laugh uncontrollably, trying to hide her ashamed red face.

"Well, now that you two aren't talking in your made-up language anymore," Ector retorted defensively, "maybe I'll wipe my rear with it next time and see if that's more to your liking!"

It was too much for Annalin; she rolled onto her side, clutching at her ribs.

"There's nothing made-up about anything I just said, mate," Meric replied, still cracking a smile. "I'm just telling you as a friend: Your breath is awful!"

Ector couldn't help but notice the extra attention suddenly coming from the elves. He looked back at Meric for a moment, considering if it was worth pressing the issue, and deciding that it was, continued. "No, that was definitely gibberish coming out of your mouth."

He turned to Annalin, who had finally started to recover her breath. "You were speaking it, too," he said suspiciously; Annalin usually wasn't one to fake ignorance. "It was like you could understand him."

"What are you talking about?" she asked. "Why would I not be able to understand him?"

"You even spoke the same kind of gibberish back to Meric," Ector continued, a bit frustrated at their shiftiness on the matter.

"Ector," Annalin replied, finally returning to her usual self. "We've been talking like this the whole time. I mean maybe a bit louder now, but..."

Ector stared uncertainly between them; both seemed completely unaware of the strange exchange. Ector signaled for them to hush, seeing Melowin approach from a short distance.

"Well, whatever this flower did, I don't think it quieted our voices," Ector added, quickly wiping his face clean of the wretched-smelling mastication.

"What an interesting dialect you three are speaking," Melowin commented, inserting himself into their huddle cheerfully. "I do not believe I have heard it before."

Ector's mind began to race. The magical substance definitely hadn't muted their voices, but he had heard the same garbled tongue coming from both Annalin and Meric just seconds ago. Realization began to dawn as Melowin stared at Ector, too. Apparently the gibberish was now coming out of him as well.

"Well, thank you," Meric replied, jovially, oblivious that anything mysterious was afoot. "I think we Cleargar folk have a very distinct accent. You really can tell when we talk with travelers!"

Annalin looked uncertainly at Ector, waiting to see what Melowin would say next. Ector remembered back to her words about the intent behind his touch: He hadn't put it together at first; he had watched for some sign of stealth to emerge, as when his thoughts had suddenly flowed lighter after the thought-masking charm. But quieting their voices hadn't been his true intent, now that he thought about it. Keeping the elves from eavesdropping on them was.

Ector felt a shock surge to his core. The charm had worked! They were speaking gibberish to the ears of others: a different language even! For the first time, he felt capable of competing against the elves. His gift had protected them, unbeknownst to anyone outside their little circle.

"Well, yes, you do have a bit of an accent," replied Melowin. "But I was more referring to that local language you all were speaking."

All four exchanged bewildered looks for different reasons: Meric was still oblivious that something extraordinary had happened; Melowin had clearly heard the strange tongue, the same as Ector; but perhaps most unexplainable, Ector couldn't help but notice that Melowin understood them all just fine now. The gibberish hadn't made any sense until his face came into contact with the flower. How was it possible Melowin understood them now?

"Maybe we were just talking softly?" suggested Ector, curious to see if the strange language would come out again.

"Perhaps," offered Melowin, though clearly unconvinced, pausing to see if the children would add anything else. "Well, sorry to bother," he said after an uncomfortable moment had passed with everyone looking at each other confusedly. He returned to his spot on the other side of the fire and busied himself with something that Ector couldn't see. The early evening rays blinded him as the sun now touched the treetops.

"Are you thinking what I'm thinking?" Ector whispered, looking at Annalin.

"Maybe," Annalin answered. "You think this blossom disguised our voices so he couldn't understand us?"

"I thought so at first," replied Ector. "But he seemed to understand us just fine when he came closer."

"Ah ha!" Melowin interjected, zipping over with unnatural quickness. "Right there, what were you two just saying?"

Annalin and Ector exchanged another bewildered look, although this time it was partly feigned on Ector's part as another realization crept into his mind.

"It's an old, old township language," replied Ector, offering a made-up explanation before the other two could answer.

"I knew it!" Melowin exclaimed excitedly. "There are not too many languages unfamiliar to my ear, but that is definitely one of them. Perhaps one day soon, I will be able to converse in your native tongue with you." He bowed politely.

"That would be lovely," replied Annalin, sharing a lightning-quick wink with Ector.

"Tell me, how do you say goodbye?" asked Melowin, perking up with sincere delight at the opportunity to learn the new language.

"Blergi flurgi," Ector replied, recalling some of the words he had heard before undergoing the charm.

"Well, blergi flurgi!"

The three children exchanged a silent moment, simply looking at each other, as Melowin walked off, satisfied.

"What... just... happened?" Meric asked, looking utterly lost, as Ector and Annalin shared a look of sheer amazement.

"It's even better than what we tried for!" Annalin exclaimed quietly. "He can understand us when we talk directly to him, but he can't understand a single word when we speak amongst ourselves!"

"Couldn't have said it better," replied Ector with growing excitement, not even bothering to keep his voice down. He looked around at the other elves; most of them were noticeably displeased, presumably at hearing the same indiscernible gibberish that Ector had first heard.

Brilliant! he thought, even as Dalis gave a quiet glance at the three of them.

"I knew they had all been eavesdropping on us!" Ector exclaimed, feeling vindicated at the sight of so many displeased faces.

"Quiet!" said Meric, trying to shush them. "I'm pretty sure they can still hear us."

"Haven't you figured it out yet?" asked Annalin impatiently.

At Meric's continued look of loss, Ector began to explain how their speech had become magically garbled, once they had rubbed the flower all over themselves. All the while, Ector didn't give a second's thought that the elves might be capable of overhearing anything intelligible, and he confirmed it by ending his explanation with, "And elves are stupid!"

He paused, and then looked around at them. There was no reaction.

In the minutes that followed, if there had been any lingering doubts about the magic of that single, little blue flower, they were now completely gone. Ector struck up another conversation with Melowin, and even gave an evening greeting to Somira to further prove his suspicion that not a single elf had a problem understanding him: That is, when he desired for them to hear and spoke directly to them.

"I noticed something earlier today," Annalin commented, once Ector had returned and revealed the results of his little test. Their group of three had repositioned closer to the fire and were now sitting next to Unair and Quamas; the two young elves had just plopped down as Elmondove finally ran out of things for them to do. The hunger pains were intensifying, causing Ector's stomach to clench down on itself, but he listened determinedly to Annalin's voice, trying to take his mind off the growling.

Suddenly the older elves rose from their various groups and gathered together a short distance away from the fire. Ector strained his ears to catch anything discernible, and after a few seconds, he caught one of them murmuring about the food shortage, which apparently was now beginning to affect all of them.

Ector listened intently to one of them criticizing Dalis's decision to go this deep into the Mountainwood forest. Then one of their voices rose slightly, enough for Ector to clearly hear.

"You saw the extent of this forsaken Dwarvish forest before you entered it!" the elf cried; it sounded like the one with the scar on his face. "It stretches northward for at least four more ridges! There is nothing to eat here!"

The intensity of the murmurings rose even higher after that, drowning out anything discernible. He continued to struggle for a few more seconds, but he felt his attention drawn towards the cold, penetrating eyes of Mara boring into him. Fenodor had risen from his short nap, and was now sitting on one side of her, with Grigor on the other; the three sat close enough to the fire to feel its warmth, but apparently their anger that Ector was still breathing disrupted their ability to enjoy the flames.

"When you made that stick explode earlier today," Annalin continued with her series of questions, looking at Unair, "your eyes turned really blue. Is that normal?"

"Yes, it is," Quamas replied, looking a bit exhausted but also keen to field the question before Unair had a chance to open his mouth.

"But," Unair interjected, "it does not flare nearly as bright for those without a gift." He looked around at the children and gave a subtle nod towards Quamas, throwing a silent jab at his apparently meager skill of manipulating the sunlight.

"Does it mean anything when the eyes flare?" Ector asked, trying to stop another battle from erupting between the two, now that they finally had a chance to talk again. "Or is it something that always happens when you use your magic?"

"It does actually mean something," Unair replied, sounding more serious. "But let me explain something first: The color of an elf's eyes indicates what type of magic lives inside them. So when you see the iris flare blue, for example," he said, pointing to his own, dark peacock-colored eyes, "it is a sign of the gift's heightened use."

"But," began Annalin, pointing at Quamas, who was noticeably frustrated at Unair's comment, "I saw Quamas's eyes flare, too, when he caused that bright light to pop in front of you."

Ector tried to think back to the magical exchange between Unair and Quamas; he had been so awe-struck at the sight that if anything remarkable had happened with their eyes, he must have missed it. "But shouldn't Dalis's eyes flare, too, if it's a sign of using magic?" he asked, trying to remember back to their time in his dwelling. "I mean, his eyes are really, really blue, but have you ever seen them flare?" He looked at Annalin, unsure.

"When you reach Dalis's level of proficiency," Quamas explained, perking up at the support from Annalin, "your eyes are in a constant state of flare! That is why his eyes look like ice!"

"The color blue," expanded Unair, "is what we call the Earth's favored color." He nodded with a hint of smugness, and for once, Quamas looked as if he wholeheartedly agreed with something Unair had said.

"Why?" asked Annalin.

"Because blue is the sign of the gift that manipulates the elements of the Earth," Unair answered. "Those of us with blue eyes can bend light, absorb the shadows, repel and attract water and rocks, and even create fire and ice. We manipulate the Earth Herself!"

To his obvious delight, a sound of awe escaped from Meric.

"We call it the Earth's favored color," continued Unair, "because it is the closest to Earthen magic, which is forbidden by Elvish law to manipulate. Earthen magic is magic that should only belong to the Earth, but some of us naturally cross that line a little bit."

"But why does that make blue the favored color?" asked Annalin, clearly not making the connection.

"Because," replied Unair, sounding exasperated, "our magic is the closest to the magic that the Earth uses! Earthen magic is the magic that could destroy the Earth if not cared for properly. To have gifts so close to Hers is a great responsibility!"

"What about the other eye colors?" asked Annalin. "Does that mean they have weaker gifts?"

"Well," answered Unair, dragging out the word, "we tend not to characterize the gifts of green and brown eyes as weaker. Just different. Actually, their gifts can be quite powerful; I have a few green-eyed friends who are just as formidable in the Circle competitions as anyone. And we have one brown-eyed colleague, too! Wow, is he good!"

"What sort of gifts do green-eyed elves have?" Ector was excited to hear the secrets of those with shamrock eyes, like himself.

"Yeah, and what about brown eyes?" interjected Meric, his dark cider eyes suddenly shining with excitement against the reddening sunset. "What kinds of gifts do they have?"

"Well, as you probably could have guessed, Ector," replied Quamas, taking a turn at explaining, "your green-eyed kin have a gift with plants. Those with green eyes make medicines, potions, elixirs, poisons: all kinds of interesting things."

The unimpressed, letdown feeling running through Ector's mind must have been apparent on his face, because Quamas added, "Do not discount the value of the green-eyed gifts. Those are the elves who build the Elven Circles!"

"I don't suppose any of them make magical brews," Ector muttered, disappointed to hear he would essentially be a gardener compared to what the blue-eyed elves were capable of doing.

Unair laughed. "Why are you upset? I told you, green eyes can be just as fierce in competition as blue eyes!"

"What about brown eyes?" asked Meric excitedly, ready to jump out of his skin.

Unair laughed even louder. "You remember, of course, we are talking about elves, right? These colors do not mean anything for humans." He continued to laugh, while Quamas picked up the question.

"For elves," Quamas said, "brown eyes indicate the gift of communication. They can decipher messages in the wind, understand animal speak, even transfigure into different beasts, if gifted enough."

"That is right," agreed Unair, finally allowing his laughter to subside. "Certain brown-eyed elves can be a real problem to deal with, like when they transfigure into wolves and rally a nearby pack! Nasty competitors, those brown eyes." He shook his head.

"And can they communicate using only their thoughts?" asked Annalin, trying to confirm what they had heard earlier. "Just like you were telling us before?"

Quamas and Unair nodded.

"But only some of them," Quamas clarified.

"Is there anything else the green-eyed elves can do?" Ector asked hopefully.

"Well, you can always expand outside your gift," said Unair. "However, it is quite difficult to do."

"You mean like Melowin and Dalis?" Ector asked, suddenly making sense of how the two could have been talking with only their thoughts although neither had brown eyes.

"Exactly!" Quamas nodded fervently. "It is very common in Leighmoor training to expand outside your color, beyond your native gifts. It is also very difficult, but again, that is why only the best are chosen. You must already show exceptional talent."

"How do you do it?" Ector asked curiously. "How do you expand beyond your color?"

"Well, for most, it is forbidden. By Elvish law, we are required to stay within the bounds of our color," said Unair. "For example, blue eyes cannot cross over into the realm of brown-eyed talents, and so forth."

"But for Leighmoors, the laws are different," said Quamas, picking up the explanation. "They are charged with some of the most difficult missions imaginable, and for that reason, they are afforded every advantage."

"Why is it forbidden for other elves?" Ector asked.

"Because," answered Quamas, looking hesitantly at Unair, "some believe it can lead to very dark things if one is not careful."

"Rubbish!" scoffed Unair.

Quamas ignored him. "And if an elf does manage to expand into a new color, some even say you will see their eye color change!"

"That is not true," countered Unair. "It only adds flecks of color; I saw it happen once. My friend broke Elvish decree; he was a blue-eye and branched into the realm of the green-eyed elves. Tiny flecks of green appeared, but the color was still undeniably blue, no matter how much he practiced."

This time Quamas was the one who scoffed, rolling his eyes disbelievingly.

"Why would someone want to change from blue to green?" asked Ector bewildered. "I mean, it seems like blue would be the better color to inherit."

"Well, I quite agree," said Unair without hesitation. "But again, do not underestimate the power of the green-eyed elves. I mean, you are one, right? To do so is to underestimate yourself. You must have confidence in yourself, certainly before anyone else will."

Ector shrugged, agreeing after thinking on it for a moment.

"For example, your thoughts are currently masked from us," Unair continued. "If you had blue eyes, you could not accomplish that. Even if you had brown eyes, you would have to be incredibly gifted to block your thoughts from us, considering your human weaknesses. All colors can accomplish many of the same ends, albeit through different methods. But I will say it again: Green eyes are not to be underestimated."

Maybe Unair was right? There was the unscented charm, the thought-masking charm, and now that mysterious dark violet flower that had garbled their private conversations from undesirable ears. Maybe his color wasn't so bad, Ector thought, beginning to wonder what else he was capable of doing.

"Well, what about the dark elves?" asked Annalin. "Their eyes were purple. What does that mean?"

Unair and Quamas exchanged a curious, confused look. "I have never seen, nor even heard of such a thing," Quamas replied, shrugging the question away.

"You didn't see them at the waterfall?" asked Ector, taken aback. "When they descended over the cliff in that fog?"

"Well, descending in a fog would definitely be dark magic." Unair raised his eyebrows. "But I did not see the fog come over the cliff. It was already spreading throughout the forest when we arrived with Quamas's uncle, Elmondove."

"That's your uncle?" asked Meric, turning to Quamas, shocked.

Quamas nodded. "Yes, why? You do not think we look alike? Besides our hair, almost everyone thinks we do."

"No, you most definitely do," said Meric, nodding fervently in agreement. "Your uncle just seems a bit *in love* with the Elvish law, if you know what I mean." He struggled to finish the sentence, clearly trying to change what he'd initially wanted to say.

Quamas shrugged. "Well, as the Secondary Minister of Elvish Decrees, I suppose you would have to at least have some interest in the law," he said matter-of-factly.

It was hard to imagine someone better suited for such a job than Elmondove. The way he quoted the Elvish laws at will, he had to have them all memorized. If Elmondove was the Secondary Minister, Ector wondered what the first-in-line Minister of Decrees was like.

"No, there are only the three eye colors," Unair said, confirming Quamas's initial reply. "Blue, green, and brown."

"Well, now there's a fourth color," replied Ector.

"We were the last to arrive, so I did not get a great look, but I thought it was some kind of blue," commented Unair, unconvinced.

"No way," said Ector. "They flared purple, just like your and Quamas's eyes flared when you were wrestling with each other."

"The light can do funny things," Quamas remarked. "See?"

Just then, his eyes began to sparkle cerulean as the light from the fire swelled and intensified all around them. Before Ector had to shield his eyes, Quamas's skin started to shine like a glare off a lake.

"That's definitely not what I saw," said Annalin, siding with Ector. "Your eyes were blue that whole time."

"Yes, but did you not see how my skin appeared different? The light can do funny things," Quamas reiterated.

"Ector is right," said a voice, startling them. It was Dalis coming to join them, while the other elder elves continued their discussion at a distance. Ector had become too comfortable and let his guard down; he realized that he'd assumed this entire time that no one outside their circle could hear them. The new charm seemed to work sporadically, or at least, Ector had yet to discover the subtleties of when it was working and when it wasn't. He hadn't intended for any of the other elves to hear their conversation; maybe because they were already talking with elves, it negated the charm?

"There is, indeed, a fourth color," continued Dalis. "One that, of course, would not be taught in the Circles because of the darkness that follows it."

The two young elves sat silently and respectfully as Dalis settled in amongst them.

"Unair is right, though," Dalis continued. "When an elf expands into the realm of new gifts and abilities, the eyes only reveal specks of the new color within the iris. It is not a true color change. However, there are those who have, indeed, achieved true color change: It is a sign of the dark elves, who are growing in number."

A moment of silence passed with the young elves and children weighing Dalis's words.

"What gift does it foretell?" asked Quamas.

"It does not foretell of a gift, but of a darkness," Dalis answered. "Purple means the thorns have overtaken your mind and blocked out the light."

"Where does it come from?" asked Unair, taken aback at the sudden discovery.

Dalis shook his head. "It comes from somewhere else," he said simply.

He rested a moment before looking towards the two young elves and asking, "How are you two doing?"

"Fine, of course," said Unair proudly, lifting his stout shoulders a bit.

"How are you doing on food?" Dalis asked, clarifying his question.

"We will be alright," reassured Quamas. "We should be arriving to the Northland Elven Circle soon, yes?"

Dalis nodded. "Yes, hopefully in four days time."

"We have had to go longer on just tree bark," Unair replied dismissively.

"Yes," replied Dalis, "but the bark of this forest is not good for eating; in fact, nothing in this forest is useful."

"Are we not entering the purple moss forests tomorrow or the next day?" Unair asked. "That will give us plenty of sustenance."

The idea of eating moss sounded terrible to Ector, and judging by the look on Quamas's face, he was less than pleased about the idea as well, although he nodded.

"It really hurts to say this," Ector interjected, "but Mara is right: Our food is gone, and we barely made it today. We have no storages for tomorrow. There's no way we can make it another day like this."

"Take this," said Dalis, breaking a tiny morsel of dried bread in half, and then breaking that piece into three, one each for Ector, Meric, and Annalin.

"This is the last of your food," Ector replied, refusing to accept it. "I've been keeping track. Everyone is completely out!"

Dalis gestured for him, Meric, and Annalin to take the bread anyways.

"Elves can manage much better foraging off the forest than humans can," he replied.

"But you just said nothing is good for eating around here," Annalin countered.

"We will be fine," Dalis responded, trying to quiet her concern.

"Is the other half for tomorrow?" asked Meric, looking disappointedly at his meager ration.

"No," replied Dalis, "This remaining piece is for your traveling colleagues over there." He nodded over his shoulder in the direction of the miserable-looking Mara, Fenodor, and Grigor; Ector had been so engrossed in his conversation with Quamas and Unair that he hadn't seen the three move away from the fire. Grigor looked like half the person he had been just a couple of days ago. The long treks and little food had whittled him down considerably. He still looked like an angry bullfrog, amazingly enough, but closer to a sickly bullfrog that had picked the wrong side of the pond with no flies.

"Ector, come with me," Dalis continued, getting to his feet.

Reluctantly, tiredly, Ector began to follow, but he stopped as Dalis approached Mara's group; he didn't want to get any closer than necessary and risk another outlash. He was too tired to deal with her right now. But to his great surprise, Mara quietly accepted the bread from Dalis's outstretched hand without a word. To Ector's even greater surprise, he thought he heard Grigor mumble something that resembled, "*Thanks.*"

Dalis waved for Ector to follow as he turned and headed for the main group of elves.

"I need you to help me with something," he whispered as they arrived beside the rest of the elves, circled a short distance from the fire.

"What did you want to show us?" demanded a hot-tempered elf. Ector couldn't help but notice yet again the scar running along his cheek. The evening sun turned his eyes a heavy olive-green color, which accentuated the injury further. "You think handing out your last few crumbs solves the problem?"

Dalis didn't respond but instead placed a hand on Ector's shoulder. "For those of you who doubt me, witness the gift of this halfling."

Ector felt their eyes turn to him, several of them even more hostile than before. Why was Dalis insisting on putting him in the middle of their feud? These elves clearly did not like humans, and were even less pleased after learning he was the prophesied one. Nothing was going to change their minds.

"Dalis." The scarred elf turned away from Ector. "When you gave the signal of distress in the forest, we came to your aid, did we not?"

Dalis didn't ignore his question this time. "Yes, you did."

The elf nodded. "We were all journeying along a different path, but we gave up those paths to come and help you." It was the first time he'd spoken in a gentler tone. The sudden change in his voice made feelings of guilt start to grow in Ector; all of these elves had, indeed, given up their time over the past couple of days to help them escape, even the ones who didn't want to be here.

"Do not flatter yourself, Labri," replied Dalis, shrugging off the elf's softening words without hesitation. "You came because your duty is to help an elf in distress. Your arrival deserves no more praise than any other required duty we have to each other. And you chose to stay because you wanted to observe the prophesied boy, not because you wanted to help."

His unflinching rebuttal was an unexpected slap; clearly he hadn't felt the same burden of guilt growing in Ector. As Ector looked quickly back at Labri to see what he would do next, he saw the olive-green in Labri's eyes leaping like a fire. But the ensuing silence suggested something closer to anger than offense. Ector watched Labri carefully, and it dawned on him that Dalis was right. The feelings of guilt transformed instantly to violation; Labri had been trying to manipulate him.

"The point is we are all ill-prepared for this journey," continued Labri heatedly. "Never minding the humans, we have no more food!"

"Well, yours is the gift with plants, is it not?" prodded Dalis. "Why do you not produce the sustenance we need?"

"That is impossible, and you know it!" exclaimed Labri, looking truly insulted this time.

"No, not impossible. It is the old magic from the last Great War, before the Pact of Tommas was broken."

"Rubbish!" spat the elf with long, untamed hair and midnight-blue eyes. "That is nothing but an elfling tale for the evening fire."

"Which part is rubbish, Norias?" asked Dalis curiously, continuing to keep his calm. "The old magic? Or the Pact of Tommas?"

"All of it!" roared Norias, his flowing tawny hair turning into even more of a mane.

"Patience," said Melowin, placing a gentle hand on Norias's tensing arm.

"I will not have patience!" Norias spat, suddenly turning on Melowin, yanking his arm away. "My patience is gone for this madness!"

"We should show respect," offered Melowin, absorbing his belligerent words calmly.

"I had respect for your name," said Norias, and then he turned back to Dalis. "And yours, as well: The greatest Leighmoor of our time, I know! But you have very much gone mad!"

Dalis nodded, not in agreement but rather with a look of understanding at the challenge that faced him.

"We will see," he replied. "You may be right concerning my madness, but the more important question is, if you are wrong, will you be open to a history hidden from you?"

Norias scoffed. "If you are right, I will be open to the Earth splitting Herself wide and casting me into the depths with the dwarves!"

"Mind your tongue!" warned Melowin severely. "Or you may find yourself reaping your careless words!"

Norias brushed off his warning with a smile. "Clearly your madness is contagious, Dalis. Were I not concerned for the fate of elf-kind, I would be wise to leave now. Your superstitious beliefs make you weak."

"You are free to go your way whenever you please," replied Dalis, not responding to the insult. "Your duty is done and has been much appreciated."

Labri barged back into the conversation. "Even if I could procure suitable food for us, it would not matter. The humans require hordes of food just to survive; it would be impossible! Not that I would grow any food for them anyways..."

"Not impossible," answered Dalis for a second time, pausing. "But there is also the unsavory way: We always have the animals of the forest to ensure our survival."

"Meaning what, exactly?" asked Somira, interjecting for the first time since Ector had arrived, wearing a rather disgusted look. "While the humans still eat like savages, it does not solve the sustenance problem for us."

"Yes, I quite agree," said Elmondove, also chiming in for the first time. "I hope you are not suggesting we eat their meat!"

"I shall feel better if you could tell us the decree number forbidding such things," said Melowin, mocking Elmondove.

"You want a number, do you?" Elmondove shot back hotly. "How about decree 412, which lays out all the manners in which one might be found guilty for degrading the building blocks of Elvish society? I am sure I could find something to your liking in that list. You seem less than worried about your fate, when in fact you were found aiding these humans, along with Dalis."

The usually calm, detached demeanor of the elves had vanished, and Ector began to notice that, when faced with hunger, the elves became very grumpy.

"Well, if you are unwilling to utilize decree number 487, which accommodates the consumption of animal flesh for survival," replied Dalis, showing a sudden, surprising knowledge of the Elvish decrees, "then it leaves us little choice but to delve into the old magic."

"Yes, please, let us see this old magic," Norias teased, his eyes dancing wildly. "Use your gifted pet to procure the impossible for us."

Dalis had remained calm up to this point, but this triggered a change in him. His arctic eyes glowed brighter, and the shadows drew closer. The evening was already starting to wane, but the lightless depths of the shadows stretching across Ector's face felt unbearable. The emptiness had no end. Fear snatched at him, leaving him unable to see anything in any direction.

"You may think me mad," came Dalis's dangerous voice out of the darkness. "But tread carefully."

The bottomless shadows couldn't have lasted more than a few seconds, but it felt as if the darkness would never end. In that moment, light completely disappeared from existence. Not even time could find its way through the brutally silent absence. Not until the hopeless fear finally released its grip, and the glow of sunset returned, did Ector realize it had gone.

There was another world out there, so dark, so void and massive. Ector shielded his face from the barrage of light; the evening now shone like the noonday sun in his wide-open eyes. The elves seemed to handle the transition more easily, but even Norias had to brace for the sudden impact. Only Dalis remained unaffected.

"Ector, I believe you can help us all," Dalis continued calmly, as if nothing had happened. The others stood, uncertain and apprehensive, as Dalis moved Ector into the middle of their circle. There was no more bickering. There was only silence after witnessing the greatest Leighmoor wield his gift. Dalis tolerated differing opinions, and even insults against his name, but they all found a clear line where his patience ended. Judging by the look on Norias's usually confident, borderline arrogant face, not even he would venture to make the mistake of calling Ector a pet again.

"When we arrive to the Northland Elven Circle," Dalis continued, almost daring anyone to protest against the idea again, "you will notice the area surrounding the great forested city is laboriously cultivated year round. This provides for our sustenance needs, even in the cold of winter."

While Dalis looked around at all the elves, the explanation seemed intended for Ector; Elmondove made a sound as if he wanted to stop Dalis from revealing any more Elvish insights in front of a human, but he stopped himself short of saying so.

"Many an elf would have you believe it is of their own skill or gift that such food abounds during the winter months," Dalis continued, now turning his full attention to Ector. "But they would be only partially correct. It is true that an elf, such as Labri here, would be far more skilled at providing food for our people than I."

"Because of the green eyes?" asked Ector timidly. He didn't want to interrupt, but he had to be sure he understood.

"Correct," Dalis responded. "However, no one among us can make a plant sprout from its seed, any more than we can breathe life into the dead. Those gifts belong to the Earth alone."

Ector saw a few subtle nods of agreement from the others.

"But the secret that allows us to farm throughout the winter lies in the soil," Dalis continued. The nods of agreement from the others stopped abruptly. Whether Dalis noticed or not, he continued, oblivious to the silence.

"The soil, a very special soil, was a gift from the Earth." Dalis held a respectful hand over his heart and bowed ever so slightly. "Its fertility was a token given to the race of elves as a sign of the Earth's love for us. It was revealed through the first prophecy, from our greatest prophet. The same old woman who delivered just one other prophecy: Your prophecy, Ector."

Sadly, Dalis let his hand fall and drifted deep into thought for a few moments before continuing. "The entire land existed this way for a brief time; fertile, lush, never-ending. Until the Pact of Tommas was broken."

Norias's confidence was returning as Ector caught a noticeable shaking of his head.

"And now," said Dalis, lifting his head again, "we must dedicate an entire legion of elves just to preserve the drastically diminished greatness of this beautiful gift: Our soil."

Soil? thought Ector. He suddenly felt very lost. What was so important about the soil? Farming through the winter was, in a way, amazing, but why couldn't they simply harvest like the humans to get them through the winters?

"Sorry, I'm not following," he said, confused.

"Imagine if you will, young Ector," replied Dalis, apparently seeing the disconnected look in Ector's eyes, "that you are marching into battle against your greatest enemies, who pillage the Earth of Her minerals and precious materials, mining the very life from Her. You arrive at war, and because of Her gift to you, you can procure immediate, wholesome, invigorating foods that have never graced the mouths of the other races. Days, weeks, even months of constant battle would have worn little on us. We endured without resting long into the night and well into the coming days without even the hints of fatigue. Can you imagine?"

It did suddenly seem incredible as Ector began to nod his understanding.

"This is the old magic of which I speak," Dalis said with reverence. "We enjoyed these graces for but a brief time; it started when Tommas forged the promise on behalf of all elf-kind. And then it ended when that promise was broken. The goodness was a taste of what was to come, had we not betrayed our dearest friend."

Uncertain how any of this affected him, Ector asked, "What is it you would have me do?"

"I was with the old woman when she briefly spoke of you," said Dalis. "She expected great things from you; more than what we can glean from the piece of paper she left behind."

Ector's heart jumped. Was it finally time? Was he finally going to see what everyone else standing around him already knew? He waited for Dalis to reach into his chest pocket, where he knew the prophecy was kept hidden.

"I suspect you may have a connection to the old magic," said Dalis, giving no indication that he intended to retrieve the parchment. "I also suspect that is why she said you can lead both of our races to a more glorious and wonderful world than either of us has ever known."

Ector began to feel the pressure of Dalis's expectations weighing heavily on him. What if he couldn't deliver what Dalis believed him capable of doing?

"We will see if I am right," said Dalis, "and hopefully, at the same time, solve the crisis that hinders us this evening. Place your hands out like this." He held his hands out in front, with his palms facing down towards the ground, and squatted. "Do it with me."

Ector did as Dalis said. Dalis held a hand up, indicating he wanted Ector to wait a moment.

"Your gift may not be developed enough yet to make this work. But if the old magic lives within you, we might be able to see a glimmer of it. Once your hands make contact with the ground, do not break your touch with the soil until I say so. The old woman stressed this point when she told her stories; it is very important." Dalis sounded serious. "Do you understand?"

"I understand," Ector replied, feeling suddenly nervous and apprehensive at what might happen. He looked over his shoulder; Meric and Annalin were watching him carefully, from the distant fire.

"Crackpot," whispered one of the elves—probably Norias or Labri.

"OK, now," instructed Dalis. "Very gently, but with purpose, place your hands lightly on the soil."

What does that mean? thought Ector. *How do I place my hands on the soil with purpose*?

As he brought his hands closer to the ground, Dalis placed his hands on Ector's shoulders, and it didn't take long for Ector to notice a change. Immediately, images of plants magically sprouting between his hands began to flare uncontrollably through his mind. A strange sensation vibrated within him, drawing his hands closer to the ground against his will. Suddenly he was an instrument being played by something else. He looked up at Dalis, scared. But Dalis gave a reassuring nod.

Embracing the odd vibrations growing stronger, Ector felt wrong to fight it. Then, like being swept away in the current of a river gushing down a mountain, he found himself sucked into a vision. All sorts of colorful, peculiarly shaped plants and fruits flowed through his mind. He felt the soil make contact with his shaking hands, and instantly a force drove his hands deeper into the moistening forest floor. His first reaction was to pull back, but he kept his fingers firmly buried beneath the dead foliage.

The vibrations intensified, and after a few more seconds, he felt sick. Blinking hard, he focused on the ground, refusing to let his empty stomach spew what little it contained. Another second passed. An elf murmured something, but Ector couldn't distinguish the words; the vibrations were ringing so loudly now, he couldn't even tell which elf had spoken.

The shaking spread throughout his whole body, until he heard what must have been Dalis's voice call out.

"Focus! Do not fight it!"

Ector tried to ignore the fearful thoughts rushing through his mind. Could he even pull his hands away from the ground anymore? He limited his breath to his nose, slowing the pace. Mysterious, colorful plants raced through him, until one in particular latched onto his mind's eye much like the soil had latched onto his hands. The colors changed to lights, shining like a hundred suns. He tried to shield his eyes, but his hands stuck to the earth like roots. He closed his eyes as tightly as he could, but there was no relief; the light was in his mind. He couldn't hide from it.

Then something amazing happened. Pure bliss. Relief. Nothingness. His hands were free, his eyes didn't burn from the blinding lights, and the vomitous feeling was completely gone. He tried to blink his eyes into focus, but it was more out of habit than any true need, because he could see just fine. Looking down at where his hands had dug into the earth, he saw a small sky-blue and yellow bulbous plant, fighting the blowing wind.

"What is it?" he asked, unnerved at the strange plant as the last buzzing sensation exited through his extremities.

"This," Dalis hesitated, "is something that has not been seen for a thousand years."

Chapter 11
The Budding Prophecy

Melowin inspected the strange sight. "I have never seen anything like it," he exclaimed with sheer awe. "Which part is edible?"

Dalis shrugged. "My conversations with the old woman never went that far. It looks like it has some sort of root, though."

Meric and Annalin joined the edge of the group, looking on anxiously. As Melowin tugged, the strangely colored plant came easily out of the ground, revealing a deep-purple, onion-like bulb with yellow lines running in a spiral down to the dirt-covered tip. Not even Norias or Labri could conceal their interest as Melowin wiped the plant clean. Mara, Fenodor, and Grigor, hearing the commotion, joined the group as well. They arrived just in time to hear the fresh snap of the bulb breaking away.

"What does it taste like?" Ector asked. "Is it any good?"

Melowin blinked in surprise, chewing for a quiet moment as the elves studied him closely.

"It is amazing," Melowin said, sounding distracted. "I have never tasted anything like it. Here, take some."

He cracked the remaining bulb and handed half to Dalis and half to Labri.

Dalis broke off a piece and passed the larger chunk to Somira. Labri did the same, keeping a chunk for himself and tossing the rest to Norias.

"The leaves are delicious too!" exclaimed Melowin. "Here!" He split the celery-like stalk into pieces and handed every piece of the plant out to Unair, Quamas, and then the six children. Silence was the only thing heard for the next few minutes as everyone chewed quietly.

The stalk tasted like a honey yam to Ector, but it crunched and crumbled like a nut. The rush of nutrients instantly energized his whole body. After only one bite, he felt as if he could trek through the night, even without sleep. An image popped in his mind as he took a second bite: A perfect log landed in a dying fire, stirring the flames higher, burning hotter, refusing to turn to ash. That's what had landed in his stomach. He took another bite, and it was even better than the second. He hadn't realized how miserable Meric looked until seeing that his cheeks were no longer sunken and hollowed.

Ector popped the last bite into his mouth; this one had a small, dark teal leaf on it with spidery yellow veins running to the tips. It was sweet like a berry, but with only a tiny amount of juice. Thoughts of the Harvest Festival sparkled in his mind; he couldn't help but think how perfect this plant would have been in a brew. Although what magical effects it might produce, he had no clue.

"This is absolutely incredible!" exclaimed Somira, looking at Ector for the first time as something other than an animal. Her beauty seemed to intensify in the midst of her sudden new interest. Ector choked, unprepared for such attention. Her sparkling, berry-blue eyes were the equivalent of ten Grasshopper Ales, dancing happily inside him; the wind would have carried him away at the first step. He grabbed Meric's shoulder for balance.

"You all right, mate?" Meric asked, laughing with relief. "Is this food having a funny effect on you?"

"Er," Ector gagged, trying to clear away the food lodged in his windpipe. "Yeah, I'm fine. For the first time in my life, I'm full after only three bites!" he said, trying to throw off any suspicion.

"I know!" exclaimed Meric, slapping him on the back. "It's amazing! How did you do it? Can you do it again, so we can pack it away for the trek ahead?"

"I don't know," replied Ector, considering the idea. "It was pretty painful growing just the one."

"Well, being hungry is pretty painful, too!" Meric commented, his spirits improving by the second. "I mean, I don't want to be insensitive, but if you're going to be in pain either way, you may as well spare the rest of us, right?"

Ector laughed. "Or maybe I'd prefer some company to share in my misery?"

"Alright, fair enough. We'll take turns being miserable with you; I'll take first shift since I'm already full."

"You're a real mate," said Ector, shaking his head, laughing again.

"How did he do that?" asked Labri, finishing his portion of the plant. Ector wasn't sure how to describe Labri's tone, but it certainly wasn't grateful. "What did you do when you touched him?" Labri demanded of Dalis.

"I helped him focus," Dalis answered. "Had his mind wandered aimlessly, sticking to every passing emotion, the old magic could have injured him."

As the last pink rays of daylight finally dissipated from the clouds, Ector watched everyone eventually disperse, discussing the matter in low whispers. As they departed, some of them looked at Ector with disdain and a hint of fear along with the usual hostility. Several took extra care to keep their voices inaudible.

As Annalin peppered Quamas with more questions about eye colors, Ector watched on. He couldn't help but notice Quamas's increased interest in Annalin; the elf had never been unfriendly, but his levels of responsiveness to her had soared. Then there was the laughter. Watching for several more moments from the shadows of the night, Ector wondered why jealousy stirred in him.

"You were excellent this evening!" Dalis said, appearing out of the night and interrupting Ector's envious gazing. His words carried the pride of what Ector imagined a father might say.

"Thanks," Ector said, appreciating the words. "It felt strange. I didn't know what was happening."

"I am not sure if I aided you at all. By the time I recognized you were struggling, the plant had already sprouted from the soil."

"I wish I could have seen it," Ector said, feeling astonished that he might have done most of the work on his own. At Dalis's confused look, he explained the brilliant flashes of color that had blinded him to everything.

"This is all very strange, even for us," Dalis commented, looking around at the other elves.

Glancing up, Ector found Melowin captivating Meric's attention a few paces from the fire, no doubt telling stories of some great Elvish battle. Somira was also in their company, listening; Melowin seemed just as excited to recount the adventure as Meric was to hear it.

As Ector scanned the campsite, he saw the chilly demeanors of Mara, Fenodor, and Grigor, continuing their silent treatment in the midst of the whole group.

Shaking his head, he then saw Labri and Norias also sitting removed, engaged in quiet conversation. A small fire of their own glowed between them.

"They're still upset with me," Ector remarked, nodding towards Labri and Norias. "Why?"

"If you asked me that question yesterday, I would have said because they do not want humans inside an Elven Circle," Dalis responded.

"Would I learn magic there?" Ector asked, unable to stop the question before it raced out.

Dalis nodded slowly. "After today, the answer is, almost certainly. Even if there was no formal teaching, you would learn just from watching the others."

"And Norias and Labri don't want me to learn. Do they?"

"Correct. But today has complicated the matter."

"How?" Ector asked. "Because of that plant? They're not happy to have something to eat?"

Dalis shook his head gravely. "Master Ector, what it took to make that plant crop up today is beyond Elvish skill. If I had to answer your question yesterday, I would have said they are upset with the idea of allowing anyone except a full-blooded elf into the Circle, even if it was just for your protection."

Ector nodded. "But answering that question tonight?"

"As I said, it is more complicated now. I suspect intolerance has transformed into fear." Dalis paused for a moment, allowing his explanation to seep into Ector.

"We overheard one of the others say you couldn't sustain another war," Ector commented, breaking the short silence. "Is there another war coming?"

"Yes," Dalis said, after much silent deliberation. "There is almost certainly another war coming."

"Because of me," Ector pushed, wanting to hear Dalis confirm it.

"No," Dalis replied quickly. "Regardless of you. They will use you as an excuse for battle, but the conflict is coming either way. Do not ever let yourself fall into the trap of thinking you brought this on."

"We're all out here suffering because of me!" Ector stressed in a whisper.

"We are all out here suffering because of elves like those two over there," countered Dalis, nodding towards Labri and Norias. "This war is coming because of our jealousy. It runs deep in our blood and feeds our pride. I have watched your kind long enough to know you are capable of understanding much more than we ever expected. So I am sure you can understand this: The Earth chose us. She blessed us with gifts that no other creature possesses. And then, Her greatest gift was taken from us because of our pride. Once we thought ourselves just as great as the Earth Herself. And we were severely mistaken. We paid a strong price and continue to pay it today, but it does not lessen our pride." Dalis discreetly pointed towards Labri and Norias again. "Yesterday, their jealously wanted to keep anyone but a pure-blooded elf from learning our ways. But today, their jealously consumes them. You have a gift that exceeds anything we are capable of doing, and that alone is clearly maddening for them."

Ector stole a long look at Labri and Norias.

"To answer your question more fully, though," continued Dalis, "I think it is a number of things upsetting them. My belief in the old stories, for one. Much of what I have told you is largely considered false—material that is only suitable for elflings as a bedtime story."

"We were starting to gather as much," Ector interjected.

"They do not wish to follow one who believes such things. Nor do they respond well to seeing the truth of it with their own eyes. What you did tonight should not have been possible, and yet, it should be cause for celebration. The magic you performed tonight has only ever been seen at the height of Elvish power, and you can take us back there!"

"If I could do that, why do they hate me so much?"

"My belief in the old stories has traveled beyond mere annoyance and now infuriates them," responded Dalis dejectedly. "They are not even open to hearing it now."

"But that doesn't make any sense!" stressed Ector. "Why would they fight it, if they see it is true?"

"You are young, even by the humans' estimation." Dalis smiled. "As you age, I am afraid you will see that much of the world does not operate based on what is logical or true."

"I don't understand." Ector shrugged. "There's no reason why it can't."

Dalis chuckled. "I hope you are right. Today's world is very different from the world that existed during the time of the old magic. And there are some who think we should base our reasoning only on the world we see today, rather than the histories that have led up to this moment. My beliefs come from an elder who was over one thousand years old. Times were much different then, as you can probably imagine. We had no decrees; no limitations on what we tried to pursue magically.

Even if the old woman's accounts were skewed, as all individual accounts are to some degree, would it not still seem logical to believe her stories, in order to better understand where we are today?"

Ector shrugged and nodded. "It seems reasonable to me."

Dalis laughed. "Point proven, young Ector. It would follow, then, that the world does not operate based on what is logical or true." He paused. "The masses find it laughable that there are those who still believe these stories to be our history, beyond just the evening tales that everyone commonly believes them to be today."

"Why do they find it laughable?"

"Mostly because the tales are far-flung from the realities we see today," Dalis replied. "And to hear the old woman talk, it is almost as if the High Council wanted us to forget those times. Elves today are not taught the true history at the Circles. What happened in the second Great War and in the times before it, we do not know. Any record dating back to that time is extremely rare and difficult to find. She never said a blemishing word against our kind, but she also made it no secret that the elves wanted nothing more than to forget the memories of the second Great War. One thousand years later, that is essentially what has happened. We are all ignorant of the true events that have brought us to this day."

"What kinds of stories did the old woman tell?"

"She told of the elves' rise to power. But she also told of the devastating effects after the Pact of Tommas was broken. The High Council could not stop the natural discussion about such events between grown elves at the time, but they could certainly strike it from the Elven Circle curriculum and attach a social stigma to it, which they have."

"Are there others who believe in the old stories, besides just you?" Ector asked.

"Few. Like our dear Melowin; he may not necessarily believe the old stories to be fact, but he is open to the truth revealing itself, unlike our other two companions." Dalis nodded, once again indicating Labri and Norias. "We all saw the same thing today. I have met many like them who would base their reasoning solely on what the world reveals today, which as I said, is a very different world from what existed centuries ago. As you can see, they have great difficulty accepting a truth contrary to what they knew just moments ago. But it makes perfect sense if you are willing to believe in the old stories. The magic you just performed has not been seen in over one thousand years. I believed in it, you believed in me, and together it was brought to the surface again. The truth of the old stories was revealed this evening, but even after seeing, they cannot accept it. It challenges everything they have seen up to this point in their lives. Their reasoning is based on what the world has revealed to them today; not what history has revealed to us over the ages. Seeing something as outrageous as what happened this evening, the only way for them to move forward is to reject it."

"Why can't they accept what they saw?" asked Ector. "Didn't you say that's how they form their reasoning? Based on what they see?"

Dalis shook his head. "Sometimes even when you see, you are still blind."

"How?" Ector pushed, still unable to fully make sense of it.

"It was difficult for me to believe the stories in the beginning, too," Dalis answered patiently. "Sometimes it takes time for the roots of truth to penetrate a hardened heart."

"But they saw it!" Ector whispered with disbelief.

"To believe in such things nowadays borders on forbidden. The stories and beliefs are acceptable, if told in jest or as a teaching tool. But to actually believe in them..." He trailed off. "One extraordinary event will not change their thinking. The only records of that time are buried deep within the Great Elven Libraries. And most are not even aware the records exist."

Ector summoned the courage to broach what had been on his mind for many, many hours now. "Is my prophecy stored there as well?"

Dalis didn't answer at first, but he gave a slight smile. "Do not think I have forgotten about your clever attempt to eavesdrop on us and discover the prophecy back there," he said. "Be glad I have not revoked those invisibility charms."

"Well, I would just put it back on once you walked away, now that I know how it works," Ector replied, instantly cursing himself for spilling his plan so easily.

"I expected as much, which is why I have not even bothered."

"Why haven't you revealed the prophecy to me yet?" Ector asked, refusing to allow the opportunity to slip away. "Everyone else knows, except for me."

"No, not everyone. I do not believe your other human colleagues know, either."

"That's not what I mean," said Ector, beginning to get frustrated. "All the elves know, even Quamas and Unair. The prophecy is about me; why should I be the last to find out about it?"

The playful banter dissipated as Dalis searched for an answer. "The prophecy is a burden, young master; a burden you should not yet have to bear. The day will come when you have no choice but to carry it, with all the consequences tied to it. Do not rush it."

Ector's patience thinned instantly; grateful for the charm blocking his thoughts, his mind immediately turned to using his newfound magic to somehow obtain it.

"Your skills improve by the day," continued Dalis. "I hope any doubts you may have about your greatness are long gone. No human has ever shown this kind of ability."

"Well, I'm not human, am I?" replied Ector shortly.

"True," Dalis conceded. "But no elf in the past thousand years has accomplished what you achieved tonight, either. Be proud of who you are, young master."

Ector nodded. "So I guess this means you won't tell me about my prophecy?"

"Not tonight," replied Dalis, getting to his feet. "We are closing on the Northland Elven Circle; it is maybe a four-day trek from here. Bathe in your rest, as you humans like to do, and we will start our journey early tomorrow."

"Goodnight," said Ector abruptly. He waited for Dalis to make his way to the other side of the encampment before heading over to Meric.

"Having fun?" he asked, sitting down beside Meric, just as Melowin and Somira departed to join Dalis.

"Oh wow!" exclaimed Meric. "You won't believe the stories I've just heard!"

"Yeah?" asked Ector, feeling instantly better at seeing Meric's enthusiasm.

"I don't even know where to begin!" replied Meric excitedly.

"Well, I've learned some rather interesting things myself," came Annalin's voice as she appeared out of the darkness on Ector's other side. She pulled herself close to the fire and sat next to Ector.

"Well, before we begin sharing, I may as well go first and get my disappointing news out of the way," Ector continued. "Still nothing on the prophecy."

Meric and Annalin waited for him to continue, but he just stared back blankly.

"That's it?" Annalin asked. "You and Dalis were talking for a good while; he didn't say anything else at all?"

"Nothing we didn't already suspect. I wouldn't trust Norias or Labri to pick up Rahms's droppings."

It was a phrase Ector used all the time in Cleargar, when he didn't trust someone, but hearing Rahms's name rolling off his tongue so easily made his heart hurt. For the first time, Rahms wasn't by his side; suddenly he missed his old friend severely. Wondering what Rahms would think of his newly discovered skills, he gave an inward laugh; he'd probably be scared skittish.

"Did you learn anything else?" Annalin prodded.

Ector thought for a moment. "The other elves apparently think Dalis has gone mad for believing in those stories he's been telling us."

"Yeah, but we guessed that already," said Meric. "I mean, it wasn't exactly hard to see that coming."

"Exactly. So in short, I have nothing. What did you two find out?"

"Oh, let me go!" exclaimed Meric quickly, as he saw Annalin beginning to answer. "Dwarves are nasty mean!"

They waited a moment, letting Meric revel in what he clearly thought was an excellent summary of Melowin's tales.

"Alright, then, well done, Meric!" Annalin interrupted with false cheeriness. "So, Quamas and Unair gave me some more information on the green-eyed elves, Ector."

Ector tried not to laugh at Meric's anxious twitching, as he waited for a chance to jump back in.

"You really shouldn't be put out about having green eyes," she continued. "They can do some really amazing things!"

Ector nodded, pretending not to be distracted by Meric.

"But the best part of all," she said breathlessly, forcing Meric to close his mouth for a third time, "is this: Are you watching?"

There was a quiet rustling on the outskirts of their little circle just then, and Ector jumped to his feet.

"Did you see it?" Annalin asked excitedly.

"See what? The rat?" asked Ector, searching for the thing.

"Oh, wow," said Meric, releasing a pent-up breath. "I thought it was a snake!"

"No, it was this," replied Annalin, holding out a thin stick in her hand.

"I don't understand," said Ector.

"This stick was on the other side of Meric just a second ago!" Annalin replied excitedly. "I drew it over to me!"

"What?" Ector exclaimed, clapping a hand to his mouth, realizing he had just drawn everyone's eyes to their little circle.

"Don't worry, they still can't understand us," said Annalin. "Quamas asked me a little while ago about our strange human language, so the charm is definitely still working."

Ector felt another twinge of jealousy at hearing Annalin say Quamas's name, but he released a relieved sigh.

"Wait." Ector held his hands out, stopping the conversation from moving forward. "You drew the stick over to you?"

Annalin nodded excitedly.

"Magically?"

Annalin nodded even more excitedly. "I think so!"

"How?" Ector prodded, stealing a glance at Quamas and Unair. "Did they teach you?"

"Inadvertently!" Annalin replied, with a sly smile. "I don't think they saw while I was sitting with them, but a large piece of bark fell off the tree the first time!"

"How did they teach you?" Ector asked again, excitement rushing through him.

"Quamas said you have to focus all your attention and picture what you want to happen in your mind," Annalin replied. "He said the clearer the picture, the more powerful the result!"

"Did you picture the bark falling off the tree?" Ector asked, baffled as to why she would chose that as her first target.

"Well," said Annalin, a little sheepishly. "Not exactly. I sort of just looked into the darkness and focused really hard. But I felt something inside change just before it happened!"

"What changed?" Meric asked, no longer interested in changing the conversation back to the Elvish battles.

"I don't know how to describe it, exactly," replied Annalin, thinking back. "You remember Mr. Bullberry's ox?"

"Uh, yeah. The red and white one, r-right?" Ector stuttered, surprised at the sudden shift in conversation.

Annalin nodded. "You remember when Mr. Bullberry would load down a full wagon and then strap that old ox to the front? He would strain for what seemed like an eternity, you remember?"

"Yeah, he had a rough go of it," Ector responded. "What about it?"

"Well, the change I felt inside was like that first moment when the wagon wheels would begin to turn; it felt like that first slow creak forward."

"And then the bark fell off the tree?" Ector asked suspiciously.

"Well, if you don't believe me, I just did it again!" Annalin countered.

Ector definitely heard something rustling through the foliage. And Annalin definitely didn't have a stick before. Ector's heart jumped into his throat.

"Can you do it again?" he asked, wanting to see it one more time.

Annalin didn't answer at first. "Maybe tomorrow," she said, after stealing a couple glances in both directions. "We're drawing too much attention right now."

It was true; inquisitive stares were absolutely trying to pry into their encrypted conversation.

"Something tells me I wouldn't wake up tomorrow, if some of the others knew what just happened here," Annalin continued, getting to her feet.

"OK," Ector said, agreeing wholeheartedly, "let's steal some time tomorrow evening before the sun goes down; I want to see you do it in the light!"

"If I do it in the light, it will be easier for the others to see, too," Annalin replied.

"Alright, fair enough. We'll find some time away from the others at some point. But if this is real, our situation just got entirely more dangerous."

"Why?" asked Meric. "Why is our situation more dangerous if Annalin can do magic?"

"It was something Dalis said to me tonight," replied Ector, realizing he also hadn't done a very good job summarizing what he learned.

Annalin quickly sat back down, anxious to hear more.

"Not everyone here wants us to go to this Elven Circle," he continued. "Elves are jealous of their gifts; they don't want other creatures to possess them. How do you think those two," he threw a thumb in the direction of Labri and Norias, "would respond, knowing they suddenly weren't so special anymore?"

A dawning look of realization fell on Meric's face, and Annalin also seemed to fully understand at that moment.

"You think they'll still go quietly north, knowing we're headed to a place where we can hone our skills into weapons?" Ector asked, pausing to let them answer. But their silence was confirmation enough. "I don't think so either. Excluding Norias and Labri, everyone else seems open to helping us, so long as we are perceived to be weaker. I say we keep it that way."

Meric nodded. "That's not a bad idea, mate."

"At least for now," continued Ector, "we'll keep their attention focused on me. Who knows when we might need to spring a surprise on them with you, Annalin?"

Annalin nodded. "OK. I mean, I don't know how much use I'll be, but..."

"Keep practicing," Ector encouraged. "But do it quietly. It can't make you worse, right?"

Annalin shrugged.

"Alright, let's get some sleep," Ector said, turning towards his sleeping area prepared with a nice, thick pile of pine needles waiting for him to crawl under. "Dalis says we should be at the Circle in four days."

"You think we should sleep in shifts to make sure they don't try a sneak attack or something?" Meric asked.

"That's not a bad idea," Ector mumbled, thinking aloud.

"What would we do if they tried?" asked Annalin. "We couldn't stop them if we wanted to."

She was right; even if they called for Dalis, the others were so quick it wouldn't matter. Sleeping in shifts wouldn't achieve anything, other than leave them all exhausted. And if the dark elves did manage to find them again, they would all need every last drop of strength.

"Let's just sleep," said Ector. "All of us. They haven't tried anything underhanded yet. Dalis will keep us safe."

"Ha!" said Meric. "Dalis will keep *you* safe! What about me and Annalin?"

"Well, like I said," Ector replied, "as long as they aren't wise to Annalin, we shouldn't have anything to worry about."

"I hope you're right, Ector, about getting better with practice," said Annalin nervously. "I don't like the way they're looking at us right now. I know the charm is garbling our conversation, but I have a really bad feeling."

"Just keep practicing," Ector reiterated, turning to look Labri and Norias full in the face.

After a long, unblinking stare that made the seconds grind to a halt, Norias broke eye contact and then whispered something to Labri. Ector had avoided putting words to the idea, but now that Annalin said it, he had a really bad feeling, too.

The night passed uneventfully, and Ector got a surprisingly good sleep, compared to the past several days. In the morning, he rubbed at the tingling sensation in his hands after procuring three more plants for the group to eat. His hands were numb after producing two that looked exactly like the one from the previous evening, plus one very odd, red and purple, wart-like plant with orange leaves. The odd one was the last to surface; Melowin grabbed the base of the large-leafed orange stalk and pulled it out, revealing the wart-like, lumpy underside. Ector stared for a moment; if it wasn't poisonous, it might actually be easier to divide into equal portions, as each nodule was roughly the same size and resembled a small potato.

Melowin broke the first node off and handed it to Mara for her breakfast, but she held it away ungratefully between her forefinger and thumb. *What a shock!* thought Ector sarcastically, shaking his head.

He was glad to see Grigor growing tired of pandering to her every whine. Grigor took his lump of purplish-red root and bit fearlessly. Two chews in, and he looked immediately healthier. Ector watched him carefully for an extra second, wondering if perhaps his skin was glowing orange.

Melowin made his way around, until a small, purplish-red root landed in Ector's open hand, oozing with a clear, sticky syrup.

Looking around at the others before taking his first bite, Ector found everyone shining. He bit off a tiny section: It crunched like an apple, but tasted like a perfectly roasted bird with sugar juice.

He took another bite, much larger this time, but stopped for a moment as the first swallow hit his stomach. Strength returned like an avalanche down the muscles in his legs; suddenly he felt ready to trek for days—maybe even run for days if he had to. Finishing the small helping, he searched in vain to see if anyone else didn't want his or her portion. But as expected, everybody's was gone, even Mara's after she'd eventually changed her mind.

"This is amazing!" Annalin said, swallowing the last of her bites. "How did you make this last one? I think it's my favorite!"

Ector shrugged. "It's just like the brews; I've no control over what comes out. Or crops up, in this case."

But then his thoughts returned to Annalin's idea about putting intent behind the gift.

"What?" Annalin asked, seeing him deep in thought.

"Nothing. I was trying to remember what was going through my mind when the last plant popped out. I was thinking about the uneven portions everyone got last night and wishing I got to taste some of the root..."

Annalin's eyebrows shot up. "Guess what everyone got to taste this time! I'm telling you," she said excitedly, "I think your thoughts influence what comes out."

The others started packing up their belongings just then, so they dropped the conversation to do the same, but as their trek stretched onward through the day, Ector's mind returned to the idea again and again. The sun shone brilliantly, and the morning felt amazing, partly because of the satisfying breakfast, but also because it was as warm as the first days of the harvest. Either way, this day was starting out immeasurably better than any they had had so far. That was, of course, until the sun began arching high into the late-morning sky, and a small group of ragged-looking elves suddenly appeared out of nowhere, directly in front of them. The trees were spread a good distance apart, so it came as quite a shock to see the traveling group appear so close without warning.

"What an odd party?" said one of the traveling elves by way of a greeting, slowing to a halt in front of them, blocking their progress. He had a spindly bow strapped across his back, and wild, knotted yellow hair. All were lean and looked roughly the same, just with different shades of hair and different colored eyes.

"Greetings. Can we help you?" Dalis asked, deciding to stop and not force his way through the group of four, who were spreading out in a horizontal front.

The elf who had spoken blinked stupidly—or at least, that was how it struck Ector.

"This is not how it appears, friend," came Elmondove's voice from somewhere behind Ector. "We are escorting these humans to Lannonoir, where they will face trial."

"And the party gets odder," said the same unknown elf, continuing to blink. "Forgive me, but since when do humans stand trial in Elven courts?"

Elmondove made a series of uncomfortable noises before starting to explain. "Well, you see," he fumbled, pointing a noticeably shaky hand at Dalis. "This elf here was discovered fraternizing with these humans. He is the one we are escorting. He is to give a full account of his breaches."

Dalis shot a glare at Elmondove, but Elmondove responded by simply turning his nose a bit higher.

"Really?" said the new elf with a delighted grin. "Well, it seems this is our lucky day, comrades." He turned to the others, all of whom also began to smile deviously. "Why waste your time, good civilian?" he continued, turning back to Elmondove. "Let us have a trial, here and now." He unhooked the bow strapped across his back.

"Well, um," stuttered Elmondove, "I believe we should follow proper procedures for a case like this."

"Proper procedures?" asked the elf mockingly. "I will have you know we are granted full authority to handle matters of treason."

"You are granted full authority to continue on your way," Dalis replied.

Elmondove's image as a weasel solidified in Ector's mind, but his thoughts turned to Norias and Labri; both were more likely to join these new elves than to help Ector ever again.

"Perhaps if we..." Elmondove began.

"Guilty!" roared the new elf, his smile growing with satisfaction. "We find you all guilty!" He savored the echo, turning to look Dalis straight in the eyes.

"Guilty of what?" Dalis asked.

"Associating with humans," answered the elf, as though Dalis were slow on his reasoning. He spoke more slowly with a mocking tone. "You see, the punishment for interacting with humans... is death."

A quiet moment passed as Dalis nodded. "It seems so," he said at last.

"So you *are* aware of the penalty," the elf stated, apparently glad to be making progress, while the other three began to spread apart, forming a crescent-moon shape around the front of the group.

"Either I will die for associating with humans," Dalis continued, "or your ignorant hatred of them will lead us to defend ourselves, and consequently, to your death."

The words seemed to stun the elf, and his smile faded a bit.

"But either way, you are correct," Dalis continued. "My friendship with these humans will lead to someone's death today."

The elf nodded slowly, all traces of his foul smile gone. "Indeed it will. Might I inquire before you die, do you even know who we are?"

"I suspect the Earthen Warriors," replied Dalis. "It is a disgrace you even call yourselves elves."

Raising his eyebrows, the elf took the insult with a half smile. "Odd of you to say such a thing. I was just thinking the same of you."

A ball of light flashed in his palm and leapt at Dalis's chest. Dalis's sword glistened in the morning sun as it whistled over his shoulder. A mere breath's distance from crashing into his stomach, the ball split into two streaks of light, streaming around his torso. It struck the trees on either side of him.

Sickening memories of Cleargar's destruction flooded Ector, as Mara's screams filled the air. Turning, he found the other three closing on them. To Ector's dumbfounded amazement, Norias looked ready to engage, but he didn't bother moving Mara to safety as he raised a hand. Fenodor ducked and tackled Mara around the waist. Driving her forward and then losing his balance, he stumbled to the ground with her.

A fleet of small pebbles rose from the ground and raced to Norias's outstretched arm. They swirled menacingly around his forearm, obeying his silent command.

An elf charged the floating stones just as Norias opened his palm; every last swirling rock exploded into coarse sand. Flying into the elf's eyes like something possessed, the wall of sand might as well have been a wall of stone. The elf dropped instantly, scratching at his face. He didn't even have time to blink.

Norias beckoned a small boulder with his other hand, and with a flick of a finger, he sent it soaring, mercilessly striking the defenseless elf in the side.

Crumpled in a ball, howling with pain, the elf tried to protect the subsequent blows as the rock pummeled him over and over. Ector wanted to scream for Norias to stop, but his tongue was in knots.

"Stop!" he finally managed.

Sprawled along the ground, and now limp, the elf didn't move. Norias glanced disgustedly at Ector, but then turned his attention to the group's leader who was trading blows with Dalis. A slew of arrows flew at Dalis from within ten paces as he whipped his blade from side to side. His sword moved so fast, only flashes of light could be seen as it caught the angles of the sun. Arrowheads and feathers rained down, scattering in all directions.

The last arrow had barely left his string before the leader drew a sword of his own and advanced. His sword was long and thin; bulging fatter towards the sharp end, it looked more like an elongated cleaver, with the sheen of some black metal Ector had never seen before.

"No!" Annalin screamed.

Turning, Ector found her staring at an arrow aimed at Dalis's back. Her voice startled the assailant, but only for a second. Grunting at the distraction, he returned his eyes to Dalis's back, taking aim again.

Then a crack sounded.

The arrow wisped over Dalis's shoulder, ruffling his long black hair as it flew past, harmlessly landing somewhere in the tall, golden grass. The assailant was dead, crushed under an enormous limb.

Ector looked back at Annalin; her eyes were wide as she stood with an outstretched arm frozen in place, pointing at the jagged stump halfway up the tree. The thunderous noise caught everyone's attention.

Quick to take advantage, Quamas flashed a blinding flare of light in front of the second-to-last elf. Unair dropped to the ground and swept the elf's legs from underneath him. The elf collapsed, disoriented. Long, thick vines immediately stretched from underneath the forest floor, wrapping around the elf's limbs, neck, and waist. He was left bound and immobilized as Labri's sage-green eyes flared with excitement.

The clang of swords continued as the last Earthen Warrior hacked faster, roaring with anger. But Dalis effortlessly deflected blow after frustrated blow.

Then a rock whizzed out of nowhere, crashing into the last elf's head.

"Stop playing with him," said Norias, walking out of Dalis's blind spot. "Just kill him and be done."

"We did not have to kill any of them!" Dalis roared. "They would have given up in a few more minutes."

"You are more foolish than I ever imagined," Norias replied, all respect for Dalis gone. "You were nearly obliterated because you tried reasoning with them."

"Nearly obliterated does not leave me any worse for the wear," Dalis shot back angrily. "If it buys a few extra moments for them to see reason, it is more than worth it."

Norias laughed condescendingly. "You are, indeed, a fool. You were nearly killed a second time as well!" He pointed to the lifeless elf lying crushed under the fallen limb. "Your refusal to kill him gave them all confidence. Perhaps if you had ended him quickly, the other three might have fled, and we would have only spilled the blood of one elf, instead of four."

"Maybe that was his plan all along," Labri commented. "You heard Dalis yourself: What a disgrace they even called themselves elves.

Apparently, the blood of a half elf is more important than the blood of a real elf."

"Enough!" bellowed Melowin, emerging from the trees with Mara, Fenodor, and Grigor. "This was a clear case of defense-under-attack! Elmondove can attest to that, I am quite sure."

Melowin waited for Elmondove to back him, but Elmondove merely stood off to the edge, reluctant to add anything to the heated discussion.

"A human's blood can be more important than an elf's, in some cases," Somira added, emerging with Meric from the other side of the forest. "Are you not concerned for the human animals when they are poached for fun?"

Labri smiled. He looked as if he wanted to add something, but then decided better of it.

A gasping noise suddenly broke through. As everyone turned, the elf bound in Labri's vines gurgled his last breath. He was wrapped so tightly, the vines had cut deep into his skin, and his lacerations pussed with poison.

Turning, Dalis threw a dangerous glare at Labri. "You summoned Mountainwood?"

"It was in ample supply," Labri responded, shrugging without remorse. "And, since you mention it, you are welcome."

"There was no need to kill him!" Dalis roared. "Nor was there reason to make him suffer unnecessarily!"

"Oh, I understand now," said Labri sarcastically. "You mean like they would have spared you, and the rest of us, from suffering unnecessarily for traveling with humans?"

"We do not have to soil ourselves with their thinking," Dalis replied.

"Right," Labri responded curtly. "Well, next time, you can teach me your lessons from the grave."

Dalis shook his head. "You know their skills were no match for us."

"Well, as Norias said," Labri continued, "perhaps you are unwilling to accept that you needed saving from death twice, once by Norias, and..."

His head suddenly swiveled to Annalin, the gravity of what he was about to say setting in. Vile contempt filled his face as the others began to turn and look at Annalin, too.

"And what?" Melowin asked impatiently.

Staring menacingly at Annalin, Norias interjected, finishing Labri's thought. "And saved again by the human... she brought the limb down."

Norias turned to Unair and Quamas, his sapphire eyes pulsing angrily. "I heard you whispering about this last night around the fire."

"Traitors!" Labri hissed.

Unair and Quamas looked more frightened than Ector had seen any elf look.

"Come now," Melowin interrupted, laughing dismissively. "She has no elf blood; this is ridiculous!"

"Tell that to him!" cried Labri, throwing a hand at the dead elf, his eyes flaring like a frog's glistening back.

"You lied," Norias said, looking at Dalis and then scanning all of the children with untrusting eyes. "You said these were ordinary humans!"

"This limb is rotted clear through," Melowin remarked, inspecting the limb closer. "The violence of the clashing could have caused it to give way."

"No!" Labri shot back fiercely. "It was her; I witnessed it!"

Somira joined in, with a skeptical grin. "Well, let us say we are willing to entertain the idea for a moment. You are a hypocrite to be upset; you tortured his comrade with Mountainwood, but you stand in judgment for how the others died?"

"Pray tell, how exactly is death deserved when it comes at the hand of a human?" Labri was seething with disbelieving anger.

Somira raised her eyebrows, shocked by the sudden hostility aimed at her. "He had his arrow leveled at Dalis's back, yes? He would have deserved death at the hands of a dwarf!"

Labri unsheathed a dagger with lightning speed. The greens of his eyes flared so wide, they threatened to blot out the whites as he lunged at her.

She sucked in, just before the blade penetrated her midsection and skirted to the side. Turning the corner, Labri roared, his arm descending a second time. Closing the distance, she rushed at him and snatched his wrist. Wrapping her other hand around his back, and hoisting him high, she brought him crashing in a heap to the ground. His spine crunched, as a cry escaped him.

Standing gracefully, Somira walked to the dead elf wrapped in the Mountainwood cocoon and drove her heel into the bed of vines. Pieces of thick, woody splinters broke off, and she grabbed a sharp piece just as Labri struggled to his feet.

"Perhaps you would like to experience your chosen instrument of death more intimately?" she asked, raising the splintered dagger to his neck just as he straightened up.

"Come at me again," she continued, "and I will drive this so deep in your back, the poison will take you before you ever dig it out."

Labri's eyes pulsed with fury, but he let the dagger slip from his hand. As it dropped to the ground, Somira shoved him away and kicked the knife deep into the forest. Watching it soar into the canopy, Ector waited for the distant crash, but it never came.

The rest of the afternoon dwindled away in cautious silence, with Ector frequently checking his surroundings, until they arrived at yet another resting point for the evening.

The elves grumbled amongst their secluded groups that night. The attack and subsequent skirmish had severely slowed their journey to the Northland Circle and added almost an entire day, by Dalis's estimation. Labri had remained quiet since Somira's dismantling performance, but he looked nowhere close to pacified. If anything, time and festering had made matters worse.

Ector took the opportunity to try another piece of magic as the idea weighed uncomfortably on him; deciding that he might need to defend himself much sooner than he'd like, he surveyed the different groups one last time before starting.

With an idea firmly in his mind, he picked a couple of bright red vine leaves, and as he chewed eight times, trying not to draw the attention even of Annalin or Meric, he imagined hearing the tiniest of whispers. He spat the reddish mash into his hands, pretending to sneeze, and then waited a moment for everyone's attention to dwindle away from the sudden noise. Casually wiping his nose, he opened his hand just enough to see the mess pulsing in the recess of his lightly closed palm. The red glowed golden around the edges this time.

Seeing the familiar signs of his magic, he stole one last peek at each of the groups before resting his head against his open palms, faking exhaustion. Then he listened.

Excitement rushed in as he turned his attention to Labri and Norias. He could hear everyone in the camp!

"Her skills are weaker than a young elfling's," came Norias's voice.

Labri whispered something indiscernible in reply; frustrated, Ector focused harder.

"No, my friend, not yet," came Norias's voice again.

Slowly Ector wiped his face clean of the reddish mash, pulling at his face with feigned fatigue while doing so.

"It is not the level of skill she possesses," Labri's voice replied, finally loud enough to hear. "But that she possesses any signs of magic at all is disturbing."

Melowin's hushed voice tingled in Ector's ear, all the way from the other side of camp. "I just do not understand how it is possible."

Looking up, Ector caught Melowin sitting with Dalis, shaking his head. "Ector I understand; his mother was an elf. But how can Annalin possibly have a gift?"

"So your worries about the dark elves are no more?" Dalis's distant voice asked. "I can barely keep pace with all the things troubling you tonight."

"No, my worries of them amplify by the hour!" Melowin replied, not sharing in Dalis's lighter mood. "My biggest worry is why they have not found us yet! A traveling party of our size simply begs for trouble, and not surprisingly, trouble continues to find us! It is only a matter of time before we are discovered again. Luck has favored us so far, but it is unwise to rely on it any further."

"Trouble does continue to find us," came Dalis's voice again, "but it also continues to leave us unscathed."

Melowin's distant head nodded fervently in the pause that followed.

"Perhaps we have been fortunate," Dalis continued. "Then again, perhaps it is more than fortune." His voice paused for a moment. "If I share something with you," he whispered, lowering his voice even more, "do not tell the others."

"Of course not," replied Melowin, his voice dropping so low that, even with the charm in place, it was difficult to discern.

"You remember those two lines in the prophecy?" Dalis asked.

A jolt of excitement dashed through Ector's spine as he glanced at Dalis.

"Which lines?" Melowin replied.

"The lines forewarning of a human uprising against the elves."

Melowin nodded. "Yes, go ahead."

"Until today," continued Dalis, "I could not fathom how that might come to pass. But I think I now know."

"Do tell!" Melowin urged. "I, too, thought it extremely unlikely!"

"Ector is the key. We know he unlocks the magic for the humans to experience, as it was with the brews. But it has gone a step further now."

"Meaning?"

"He has progressed. He no longer only unlocks the magic for them, but he enables them to unlock the magic on their own, as evidenced by Annalin. Ector is the key to this uprising."

"You think that is what happened today?" Melowin asked, dumbstruck.

Dalis gave a slight nod. "Ector has no clue what he is capable of."

But I'm beginning to... Go ahead and keep thinking we're stupid beasts, Ector thought.

The whispers started to fade after that, becoming quieter with every passing second. Ector cursed silently, straining to regain his advantage, but apparently the charm didn't have any sort of longevity compared to the other ones he had discovered. The last traces of discernible words dissipated into nothingness after a few more fruitless seconds as he watched the slight movements of their mouths continue.

Ector got to his feet, unable to control the rushing excitement.

"You won't believe what just happened!" he said, sitting down beside the others. Meric looked mildly curious, but Annalin didn't even seem to register his presence.

"Don't you want to know?" Ector asked, staring baffled between the two of them.

"Oh, yes. Of course I do," Annalin replied, but still distantly.

"What's the matter with you two?" asked Ector. Annalin had looked miserable all day, ever since the skirmish, but Ector hadn't gotten around to talking about it yet.

"Listen," Ector continued. "What you did was amazing!"

"Huh?" Annalin replied, confused. "Oh, I'm not thinking about that."

"Oh," he replied, equally confounded. "Well, what's wrong?"

"It's Unair and Quamas," she whispered. "I feel terrible for getting them in trouble."

"Why are they in trouble?" asked Ector, now even more confused.

"Didn't you see what happened earlier? The way both Labri and Norias tore into them for teaching me?"

Ector scanned for the two young elves. They sat huddled, removed from the others, solemnly staring into the dirt.

"I tried to talk with them," she continued, "but they won't even look at me. They're afraid the dungeons are waiting for them."

"Well, I may have good news for you," Ector responded. "News you'll want to share with them, once I tell you."

Annalin suddenly perked up with interest. "What's the news?"

"First," Ector began, pausing to add suspense, "I found a new charm, one that allows us to hear their whispered conversations." He nodded towards the elves. "Here's what I found out: Quamas and Unair didn't teach you how to do magic. I mean, they might have nudged you in the right direction, but..." He paused, shaking his head. "Think back to the brews."

"What about it, mate?" Meric asked, shrugging.

"My touch was necessary for the brews to work like they did, right?" Ector waited for both Annalin and Meric to nod. "Dalis thinks something new is happening. Annalin, you unlocked the magic by yourself! And it sounds like you're only the first of many to come."

Annalin's eyes darted back and forth, processing the revelation.

"And Dalis also thinks I'm the key to something coming true in the prophecy," Ector added.

"You don't say," Meric replied, pretending to have a revelation.

"Shove it," Ector said, smiling sarcastically. "Dalis said the prophecy foretells of men rising against the elves."

"Whoa!" Annalin gasped.

"Right? Can you imagine what would happen if we went to war against the elves? We'd be annihilated!"

"That's putting it lightly, mate," agreed Meric.

"So you're saying... or Dalis is saying... that I unlocked the magic on my own, and because I can do it, others might be able to do it? Enough to create a human uprising?"

Ector nodded. "That's what it sounded like."

"I guess that explains why Labri and Norias hate you, if you're the key to this happening," Annalin commented, still thinking.

"Wait," said Meric, holding his hands out, looking offended. "You said you discovered a new charm. Why didn't you let us in on it?"

"I would have if you'd been sitting next to me," Ector urged. "But I didn't want to draw any extra attention. I had a feeling they were talking about us, and I didn't want to lose the opportunity, in case I could make it work."

"Well, can you still hear them?" Meric asked eagerly. "What are they saying?"

"I can't hear them anymore. The charm worked exactly like I intended it, but it only lasted a few minutes. It wasn't like the unscented charm."

"Well, what did you do differently?" asked Annalin.

"I don't know. I guess we'll get a handle on it once we get some more practice, but I have no clue right now," Ector answered, shrugging.

"Flergi blergi!" Melowin said, startling the children as he passed by. "I am off to get firewood for the night. You know, that local language of yours is one of the most complicated I have ever heard! I still cannot determine any rules based on your private conversations thus far."

Ector smiled politely and nodded. "I'm sure you'll catch on. Flergi blergi!"

As Melowin waved and disappeared into the forest, Annalin returned to their conversation.

"I don't know," she commented. "If you're the reason I can do magic, why is it just now surfacing? All of us have lived our entire lives together in Cleargar. What's different now?"

"Well, like Dalis said," Ector replied, "more elves are constantly around now, so I guess it's becoming more pronounced."

"Let's start from the beginning and make sure I understand," said Annalin. "First, you made the magical brews by accident." She held up a finger. "And that happened because you're half-elf; the magic was already inside you."

Ector nodded.

"Second, the elves closed on your location over the years, and your elf part became more pronounced, which made the brews stronger over the seasons." She held up a second finger.

Ector nodded again. "Or because Dalis was always close by, but either way, yes."

"Alright, third," she continued, holding up the next finger. "Now that you're completely surrounded by elves, your elf-half is becoming even more pronounced, and because of that, I can do magic?"

"Makes sense to me," Meric commented, shrugging. "It's like Dalis said: Your real gift brings the magic to us. Like the brews, the charms, they all have an effect on us. Maybe Annalin brought down half the tree today because that part is getting stronger, too." He paused. "Wait, if you're showing signs of having a gift, maybe another one of us is next!"

Suddenly he looked over his shoulder at Mara's group. "I'm not sure I'd want everyone in that lot gaining too much ability though," he added. "Grigor and Fenodor would probably join those two, before they'd help us." He threw a nod towards Labri and Norias.

"Ha!" Ector exclaimed, noticing Meric had conveniently forgotten to list Mara's name.

"Right, I know," Meric continued. "Labri and Norias allowing humans to join them is pretty laughable."

Ector stifled a second outburst as Dalis approached.

"I have noticed you three talking in your foreign tongue much tonight," he said. "Anything I would be interested to hear?"

Ector, Annalin, and Meric shared a silent look, waiting to see if anyone would speak first.

"Yes, actually," Ector finally replied. "Some of the other elves don't seem to like us so much."

"Today was a tough one," replied Dalis, settling in. "For all of us."

"Some of us, more than others," interjected Annalin. "Is Somira all right?"

Dalis gave a laugh. "Yes. I would not pick a fight with Somira on my best day!"

"But you're a Leighmoor!" exclaimed Meric, astonished. "And the best by the sound of it!"

Dalis laughed again. "I see you are enjoying your discussions with Quamas and Unair." He shook his head for a moment as his smile faded. "Despite how the world may appear to a young elf, there is much more to life than being a Leighmoor. I have fought with the best, and I have watched the best die by my side. Anyone can fall on any day."

"But you're still alive," Meric responded.

"I am still alive, because it is not my time to go yet," Dalis replied. "I should have died many times before this night."

Melowin arrived out of the forest just then, carrying a load of firewood. As the sun took its warmth below the mountain range for the evening, the children watched Melowin arrange the pile, so that the tops all leaned against each other around a handful of smaller twigs and debris piled in the center. As Melowin placed his softly glowing red hands along the edge, smoke began to rise. A crackle and a spark flashed somewhere within the center, and then a healthy fire sprang to life.

"There is a tabooed history with elves," said Dalis, reemerging from somewhere deep in thought, "of mixing elf and human blood-lines. Few embrace the mixing as a sign of peace; most say it is a disgrace to the name of Elf, polluting the Earth's favorite race. Foul prophets even proclaim the Earth will exact revenge on us if we embrace the idea too much. And some of the more zealous believers take it to heart, even killing in the name of the Earth. You met a few of them today."

"You mean the elves who attacked us today?" asked Annalin. "You called them Earthen Warriors."

"That is what they call themselves," responded Dalis.

"Is that what the dark elves are?" asked Ector. "Are they part of this group?"

Dalis shook his head. "The dark elves are something different. Far worse. The zeal of the Earthen Warriors is usually held in check by their love for the Earth. And when they do become violent, like today, they justify their actions as for '*the greater good*.'"

"You've met them before?" Meric asked, astonished.

"Several times," Dalis replied with a smile. "They tend to be misguided and lacking in their Elvish studies. Many among their ranks have left the Circles early in search of righteous adventure, wishing only to exploit the gifts they were born with."

Suddenly Somira approached and joined their little circle.

"I could not help but overhear your discussion," she chimed in.

Ector felt his heart jump into his throat as she sat down next to him. She locked eyes with him for a moment before continuing.

"About the foul prophets," she continued. "I, too, have heard the warnings about mixing bloodlines. Before you dismiss them as false prophecies though, some might say an impending civil war among the Earth's chosen race is proof of the revenge awaiting us. And according to your prophecy, this will not be just any civil war, but the greatest ever seen. What do you say?"

Ector shot a glance at Annalin and Meric.

"The last four unknown lines of the prophecy are the most important," replied Dalis. "The foretold boy is undoubtedly before us, but the war is not."

Somira nodded. "How do you know four more lines exist?"

"As a protector of the prophets," Dalis responded, "we are trained to watch for subtle signs. In all the history of Elvish prophecies—the true ones, I mean—subsequent prophecies always follow the pattern of the first. In the case of the old woman, we are looking for seven paired lines. We currently only have five pairs, which suggests the remaining two pairs burned away the night she died, leaving four unknown lines."

"But you do not know what the last four lines contain," Somira stated, pressing the issue. "Every step forward with these humans tempts our destruction. You do know that?"

"The greatest prophet in Elvish history believed in this boy," Dalis answered. "She died to keep him alive. And I will do the same."

"But Dalis, you must see reason," she urged. "How do we know the old woman held the best intentions for us? The idea she was half-elf is very suspect, but if you say she was, I have no reason not to believe you. But in that case, the old woman was not a woman at all, or an elf. She was one of only two, Ector here being the other. Are you certain you are not blinded by your love for her? Are you certain she did not feel a higher sense of loyalty to this boy than she did to us?"

Ector could see Dalis's ears beginning to redden.

"Can you say for certain if she really wanted to see the survival of elf-kind?" Somira pushed.

"I vowed to keep this boy alive, and I will until the full prophecy is retrieved," Dalis replied evenly, although struggling to keep what looked like anger from boiling over.

"If you cannot answer my questions honestly, Dalis..." she countered, somewhat surprised that her words had caused such a reaction. "You do realize what you are asking of me? Of all of us here?"

Dalis released a slow exhale. "If you knew how much she contributed to elf-kind. How much she sacrificed. You would barely be able to entertain such questions, even quietly within yourself. I have never questioned her allegiance nor will I start now. She believed Ector could bring about a new world more glorious than you or I have ever known. And after seeing the old magic hidden within this boy, I see her vision as well."

It was strange listening to Somira and Dalis speak as if he wasn't there; Ector didn't want to interrupt, but he decided to try his luck once again.

"Would now be a good time to show us the prophecy?" he suggested innocently, as if he hadn't been trying to weasel it out of Dalis for days.

"You have not shown them?" Somira asked, astonished.

Dalis shook his head without a word, his eyes boring into Somira's.

"No, he has not." Ector replied for Dalis. "But nothing would make us happier," he added hopefully.

Somira stood up.

"Goodnight, humans," she said, incidentally brushing against Ector as she stood. The warmth of her touch resonated through him like a bolt of lightning, leaving him tingling. He pretended not to notice, but it drove from his mind the disappointment of yet another failed attempt. As she walked away, she was the only thing he could think about.

"Can you do something for us, please?" Annalin asked, just as Dalis made to stand.

"Absolutely, lady Annalin," Dalis replied, slightly taken aback.

"Will you talk with Unair and Quamas?"

"About what?" he asked, stealing a look in their direction.

"Labri and Norias came down hard on them for teaching me magic, and now they won't even talk to me," Annalin explained. "Will you tell them it's not their fault?"

A look of understanding dawned on Dalis's face. "Thank you for saying something. I will straighten that out right away."

He said his goodnights and immediately headed off to the lonely side of the fire where his silhouette disappeared behind the flames as he sat down next to the two.

Ector, Meric, and Annalin continued discussing all the revelations long after, until distant laughter caught Ector's ear. Turning his head, Ector saw both Unair and Quamas in much better spirits, still talking with Dalis.

"So, what do we know?" Annalin asked, a relieved smile spreading across her face at the sight of Unair and Quamas. "Let's start from the beginning, once again."

"We know it has fourteen lines in total," Ector began. "And we also know there's a possible war coming."

"A civil war, amongst the elves," Annalin added.

"Right, but is it really a civil war if humans are involved?" Meric asked.

Annalin shrugged. "Good point. But Ector will be at the center of uniting us."

The weight of Annalin's words suddenly felt very heavy. How was he going to unite the humans? He didn't even want to have a war. Especially against the elves. Dalis's words echoed in his head again: *Ector is the key to this uprising.*

"Then, there was something the dark elves said to you the night they attacked," continued Annalin. "What was it again?"

"Oh, something about a mark," replied Ector. "I don't know if that's part of the prophecy, though. I don't really have any marks. I mean, there's this scar from where Meric's mule kicked me..."

He lifted his shirt, revealing a U-shaped mark on the back of his ribcage.

"No, I don't think that's it," said Annalin, not even bothering to look. "It was something about a sunset."

"Oh, evening's light," Ector replied, remembering the dark elf hovering over him at the festival. "He said I bore the mark of evening's light."

"Yes!" Annalin exclaimed. "That's it."

"What exactly does that mean?" asked Meric, confused.

Ector shrugged. "I have no idea, mate."

Chapter 12
A Restless Night

The fire had dimmed to a red glow by the time Melowin stood up to make another trip into the forest for wood. The excitement from the day dwindled, as Mara, Fenodor, and Grigor had already prepared their sleeping areas for the night, away from everyone else, as usual. The elves, of course, did not require the same amount of sleep; their quiet conversations continued as strongly as ever.

Ector, propped against a large tree, waited for his mind to settle, as Annalin slept next to him. So much had happened, it was hard for his mind to let it go. Thoughts of the prophecy, the attack by the ragged-looking Earthen Warriors, the new eavesdropping charm... everything kept replaying over and over in his mind.

Thankfully, Meric was having difficulty sleeping, too.

"Have you got any more of that stalky plant?" he asked, his stomach gurgling so loudly that Annalin stirred.

"Yeah, hang on." Ector rummaged around in the sack attached to his belt. He snapped a piece off and tossed the bluish celery-like stem to Meric.

"You know what's strange?" Meric remarked, taking a bite. "These things are really amazing, but when you get hungry again, you get really hungry."

"Yeah." Ector decided that a small snack wasn't such a bad idea. "You know what else is interesting?"

"What's that?" Meric asked, amidst the sound of a fresh snap as he took another bite.

"The moment the sun goes down, these plants won't grow anymore," continued Ector. "They need direct sunlight."

Meric made a thinking noise. "Well, that's good, right? At least we're not stuck here hungry all night, trying stupidly to grow more of these plants in the dark when it won't work."

Ector shrugged. "It's just interesting. Every day we're learning so much."

Meric nodded slowly. "That I can definitely agree with."

Ector was about to continue the mindless talking, in the hopes it would encourage sleep, but he felt a sudden unease growing within him. He glanced around. Everything was silent and peaceful under the glimmering stars. Scanning the campsite, looking for any signs of movement in the darkness surrounding them, he noticed that Melowin still hadn't returned with the firewood yet. But besides that, nothing looked out of the ordinary.

"You all right, mate?" Meric, having finished the last bite of his meal, began searching for what had caught Ector's eye.

"It's nothing," Ector replied, trying to shake the feeling. He watched Dalis for a long moment to see if he showed any sign of concern, but he was deep in discussion with Elmondove on the far side of the encampment; he didn't even seem aware that Ector was watching him. If something were wrong, surely the elves would know long before Ector.

Meric drifted off to sleep after that, and Ector let his head droop, hoping that if he imitated a sleeping position, it would lead to actual sleep. But the annoying tension clung to him, refusing to let go.

He settled down slightly lower, allowing his head to rest against the log as if it were a pillow, but he opened his eyes just enough to see Dalis through shaded eyelashes. Dalis still didn't seem concerned. Ector panned his eyes to the next group; Quamas and Unair were laughing with Somira, while she drew something in the dirt. Just looking at her face, Ector felt a fierce desire to keep her safe. He simmered, reminding himself that a feeble leaf blowing in the wind could keep her safer; at least the leaf probably had some useful bit of magic hiding in it.

A twig snapped somewhere behind him. Ector jumped, turning slightly towards the sound; it was probably Melowin, returning with fresh logs. He was due back any moment now. A voice inside said to stop being so jittery, but it did little to reassure him as the edge started intensifying.

The tingling that suddenly jolted him to his feet shot through his spine as he turned to see Labri and Norias coming out of the darkness behind him. The two stopped dead in their tracks, their eyes glowing emerald and midnight blue, staring directly at him.

"I didn't see you two move away," Ector commented, balanced somewhere between surprised and vindicated, knowing they would come for him.

The eyes shifted slightly, suddenly looking over Ector's shoulder in Dalis's direction. Norias's eyes narrowed with anger, just before raging river blue. Then the faintest movement caught Ector's eye: something hurtling through the darkness with ferocious pace.

He ducked, instinctively, as a medium-sized rock ruffled his hair and crashed into the fire, causing an explosion in the camp.

Labri's emerald eyes emerged out of the darkness, but as Ector stepped back, a wiry vine slithered around his ankle, trapping him in place. Labri charged, withdrawing a short, silver dagger from a hidden sleeve on his waist.

Ector fumbled with the Mountainwood knife strapped to his belt, but his heart dropped as he heard it thud to the ground. He lunged into the oncoming attack on instinct, vaulting forward just as Labri reared back to thrash at his neck; the incredible pace didn't leave any time to adjust. Ector's outstretched hand crumpled painfully as Labri's foot landed squarely on it, but he quickly pushed the agony to the back of his mind as he felt Labri collide with his shoulder. Looking up, he found Labri flying head over heels into the bushes.

Ector flexed his hand, forcing the pain away as he strained every last finger towards the knife accidentally kicked closer during the collision. It was almost within reach. He flattened out on his belly, struggling against the vine binding him.

Suddenly, the sound of rock on metal began to clang throughout the camp. Glancing over his shoulder, Ector found Dalis and Norias engaged, trading blow for blow. Ector flipped onto his back, hoping the new position would give him the extra reach, but he froze, momentarily mesmerized by the sight of rocks raining and zooming at Dalis from every direction. Even though all eyes were on Dalis, the elf danced with the darkness, disappearing and reappearing before their very eyes. Rock after rock clanged off his sword or sailed right through as the shadows shifted around him. Dalis was in striking distance within seconds, and then blows with their fists and bodies began.

Ector had been in plenty of tussles, but never had he witnessed such intricate movements. The concentration required to deflect incoming fists from all directions, followed by knees and elbows to the midsection and stomps to the feet, must have been why all the rocks en route to the center of the fight suddenly plummeted in mid-air, dropping back to the ground. Dalis and Norias maneuvered in and out of choke holds, eye gouges, and every sort of unexpected attack imaginable.

Dalis rolled atop Norias, ready to rain a fist down, but Norias planted both feet firmly on Dalis's chest and gave an incredible push, sending him flying end-over-end through the night. Dalis landed as if he had sprung of his own accord, though, and immediately charged the barrage of rocks screaming towards him like a wall.

Labri reemerged from the camp's edge, looking shaken. It had all happened so quickly; the sudden explosion had left everyone stunned as they searched for an unfamiliar attacker in their midst. But finally seeing that the attacker was one of their own, Somira formed a barrier in front of Ector, with Unair and Quamas on either side. She signaled for them to stay back, but they ignored her, spreading out on her flanks with a fierceness Ector had yet to see from them.

Quamas cleverly blocked the light emanating from all the fires, causing the campsite to go black. It was only for an instant, but when the light returned, Unair was behind Labri.

Suddenly Melowin came running out of the forest, dazed at the sight confronting him. Upon seeing Labri quickly disarm Unair and then unexpectedly charge through Somira at Ector, Melowin caused the remaining red embers from the fire pit to shoot like a firework towards Ector. Ector covered his face, bracing for the searing pain. But to his amazement, every last coal landed next to the wiry plant restricting him. Within seconds, the smoking taut vines snapped away.

The forest floor came alive, vines latching onto Melowin, Somira, Unair, and Quamas, from all directions. Labri dove around Somira and sprang at Ector, but Ector tumbled forward, face first into his dagger, and rolled away. Gaining his feet with the knife in hand, Ector turned to face Labri one on one.

Labri charged, enraged, striking with unfathomable speed; Ector felt the sharp metal enter his shoulder before he could react.

Pain. His muscles were tearing away. Unbelievable pain.

An evil grin spread across Labri's face as he pulled Ector closer. "Try to get out of this one," he whispered darkly.

Holding Ector pinned, chest-to-chest, Labri held a hand to Ector's neck and pushed himself up, strangling Ector with all his weight. Ector couldn't breathe. Panicking, he squirmed violently.

The Mountainwood dagger flashed in his mind. It was still clutched in his hand.

As the metal knife swiftly and excruciatingly retreated out of his shoulder, preparing for one final blow, Ector stopped trying to pull the elf off him. In the fraction of a second it took to gather himself, Ector drove the dagger as hard as he could into Labri's back. He felt the knife slip in between the elf's ribs, down to the hilt.

Labri's eyes widened.

Dizzy and fading, Ector felt air seeping down his throat again. The elf's stranglehold had loosened. Leaving the dagger in place, Ector pushed the elf away just enough to raise a leg. Labri tumbled backwards with a ferocious kick.

Landing on his back, Labri howled as the force of the ground drove the Mountainwood dagger even deeper. He writhed with Dwarvish poison coursing through his body, gasping for air, reaching awkwardly for the knife just out of reach. As he began to sputter and cough, the vines constricting Somira, Unair, Quamas, and Melowin released their hold. Labri lashed uncontrollably, trying to stand, but his legs gave way, unable to support his weight.

Norias, seeing his comrade clinging to the last strands of life, disengaged with Dalis and sent Unair soaring through the air with a small boulder to the stomach. Not even Somira could defend against the sudden attack of rocks assailing her. She blocked a host of blows as Norias weaved through the swirling campsite.

Ector watched, rooted, waiting for Norias to turn on him next. But instead, he plucked the dagger from Labri's back, and then withdrew a handful of the familiar, white Marduk roots: the same that had cured Dalis from the fatal Dwarvish poison before. Labri loosed a searing cry as Norias forced him to his feet, shoving the roots into his mouth.

The two quickly retreated into the darkness as the assault of rocks continued to berate them.

"Enough!" cried Elmondove, throwing his hands out. The rocks transformed instantly to harmless aspen leaves and floated gently to the ground. All eyes turned towards him.

"So, you can transfigure," came Melowin's voice. "I was wondering if you had a gift."

An ominous threat echoed out of the night, before Elmondove could respond to the sarcastic comment.

"You will have your civil war!" came Norias's faint voice.

The last word seemed to echo forever, and then everything went quiet again. The fire had rekindled, but it now flickered in several places all around them, burning small pockets of foliage and wreckage from the fighting.

Chaos erupted.

"We must move immediately!" commanded Dalis's voice, amidst the scrambling of everyone trying to collect their sparse belongings. "Erase all evidence we were here. Two minutes! Ector, come here." He dropped his voice lower and handed Ector a healing leaf.

"You know what to do with it," he continued. "Their plan almost worked. Move quickly."

Ector went to work releasing the magic from the healing leaf and hurriedly shoved it into his shoulder, despite the severe, sharp pain tempting him to vomit.

Quamas and Unair began tearing down the site with ruthless efficiency, stuffing packs, stamping out fires, and strewing fresh foliage everywhere. Meanwhile, Melowin performed the customary enchantments always left behind as Somira and Elmondove collected the other children, all of whom besides Meric and Annalin had taken refuge in the darkness of the forest. As Dalis began snuffing out more fires with Annalin and Meric, Ector joined them, feeling the immense relief of the healing leaf spreading throughout his shoulder.

Not a second past two minutes and the group was hastening through the forest, cutting a trail. Spindly branches scraped and stabbed them as the attack site disappeared far behind in a matter of moments.

"I am sorry," Dalis whispered, running alongside Ector. "But you will not be able to sleep tonight."

"That's fine," gasped Ector, already winded and struggling for breath. "What are we going to do?"

"We have to reach the Northland Circle as quickly as possible, before those two find the dark elves. They know our whereabouts and our plans."

"We will never make it," came Somira's voice from behind them. "We cannot travel anywhere close to the pace required with the humans. They have position on us already; they retreated north."

"I agree," came Melowin's voice from their left flank. "The Circle is no longer an option."

"Wait," said Unair, speeding effortlessly in the rear. "If we continue east, there is another Elven Circle..."

"An Eastern Circle?" asked Melowin skeptically. "I have never heard of such a thing."

"Unair is right," agreed Quamas, easily closing the distance on the main group. "A new Circle, a decade old, perhaps."

Even in the dark of night, the worried look that befell Dalis's face was evident.

"I have to rest!" came Mara's voice. "I can't run anymore!"

"We've barely been running at all," came Annalin's frustrated voice. "I've seen you run further for fun at the Festival. We're running for our lives, in case you've forgotten!"

Mara's whining turned to sobs as she dragged her feet, slower and slower.

"I can carry her," offered Unair, lifting her in one fluid motion and hoisting her over his shoulder without even breaking stride.

Witnessing her sobs turn into tantrums and flailing, Ector felt embarrassed for all humanity that Mara had to be among the first humans the elves encountered. Fenodor looked ready to offer to carry her, but he was just as winded as the rest of the humans. His attempt at chivalry died feebly amidst his heavy breathing, and Ector secretly thanked him for it.

"Has anyone else heard of this Eastern Circle?" Dalis asked.

"Yes," came Elmondove's voice, "although I did not realize it was already operational." He looked to Unair and Quamas. "Explain how you know of it. It is not common knowledge."

"Rumors are all, really," replied Quamas, suddenly sounding unsure. "Just another Circle."

"No, not just another Circle," interjected Unair. "An experimental Circle."

"Experimental, how?" asked Melowin.

"That is enough, no more," Elmondove cut in.

"No, that is not enough," Dalis replied. "We need to know if the headmaster can be trusted."

"You mean persuaded to break Elvish decree?" asked Elmondove, accusingly.

"We have enough enemies," replied Dalis, slowing to a walk and stopping the entire progression to confront Elmondove. "You have seen the old magic with your own eyes. Do you deny it?"

Elmondove looked furious for being singled out.

"I take your silence as confirmation you do not deny it," Dalis pressed on, after a tense moment. "Ector will deliver the life stolen from us. If that same life comes to the humans as well, and if that means we break decrees, then so be it."

"This is where our paths part, then," said Elmondove. "I am outmatched and will not challenge you, but mark my words, Dalis of the Wood Elves. You will pay for your transgressions."

"I am not leaving, uncle," Quamas added quickly, barely mustering the courage to say so.

"What did you say to me?" Elmondove responded, almost daring Quamas to say it again.

"I s-said," he stuttered, "I said, I am staying."

Elmondove shook his head, severely disgusted; he threw a murderous look between Dalis and Quamas.

"So be it," he said threateningly.

In a blink, Elmondove turned, and running northward, he disappeared in the same direction as Norias and the wounded Labri.

"You think he'll join those other two traitors?" Meric asked, turning to Ector as he huffed, still trying to catch his breath.

"I doubt it," Dalis interjected, not even slightly winded.

Ector had plenty of doubts, but he held his tongue.

"The other two want blood," Dalis continued. "Elmondove does not want to dirty his hands with our deaths. He wants the Council to do it for him."

"Will the Council really kill you?" asked Annalin.

"I do not know," he replied gravely. "There was a time not too long ago where reason and sense prevailed. A time when the High Council would not sentence another to death simply for interacting with humans, especially if the old magic was discovered, waiting to be reignited. The old woman feared a darkness spreading throughout our ranks, and I am afraid she was right. Elves today are not the elves I remember."

Ector was confused as to why Dalis would be ignorant to this shifting amongst his own people, but then he remembered: Dalis had been secluded for...

"How long did you live with the old woman?" he asked. "You didn't contact any other elves while you protected her?"

"Until the night she died, no. I did not have much contact. I was there for too long. This should never have happened." Dalis turned towards Unair and Quamas, both of whom seemed completely dumbstruck and hurt at Elmondove's sudden departure, especially Quamas.

"That was very brave of you, young Quamas," Dalis said. "Standing for what is right can be very painful sometimes." He moved to put an arm around him. "But know this: You will make a very fine Leighmoor someday with that kind of fortitude. In the end, our fortitude to remain loyal to what is true is all that matters."

Quamas released a troubled sigh, but he looked comforted at Dalis's encouraging words.

"You two are the only ones who can save us now," Dalis continued, looking between Unair and Quamas. "Tell me the rumors you have heard about this Eastern Circle."

Quamas and Unair looked at each other for a moment, trying to gather their thoughts.

"Well," Quamas began, "it is definitely further from here than the Northland Circle."

"How far?" Dalis asked.

"If we run," chimed in Unair, "maybe three days."

"If we run at an elf's pace, you mean," interjected Melowin. "Remember we have to travel at the humans' pace." He aimed a displeased look at

Mara. "By the look of things, it seems our journey from here will include a fair amount of walking."

"No, three days by a human's pace," clarified Unair.

"How do you know where it is?" interrupted Quamas inquisitively.

"We ventured that way last summer, during an exercise," Unair replied, shaking off the question.

"You ventured three days from the Northland Circle?" Quamas exclaimed with disbelief.

"Of course not. There were no humans with us," replied Unair impatiently. "It would have only been about a day's distance at full speed." He exhaled, apparently annoyed at having to explain himself. "We were traveling by night, trying to outflank a team from their rear, but needless to say, we got a bit turned around in the dark and found the Eastern Circle by accident."

"Did you outflank them?" Quamas asked, excitedly.

"No," Unair replied, perturbed. "We went too far and ended up facing them head on. And then we got in trouble for venturing out-of-bounds."

"Let us discuss this down the trail a ways," suggested Melowin, trying to get the two back on topic. "What is the matter, Dalis?"

Dalis's eyes worked frantically in the moonlight, as he tried to figure something out. "What do you think, Somira? Can we make this Eastern Circle?"

"Maybe." She shook her head doubtfully. "It would be very close. Our numbers are dwindling, our enemies growing..." She paused to think some more. "You feel quite certain Elmondove is not interested in joining with the other two?"

"I would be surprised," replied Dalis, but he looked as if he were considering the question again. "I suspect he is en route to Lannonoir."

"It could go either way," Melowin offered. "Let us not waste any more time guessing what others will or will not do. We must take action, and very soon, if we want to avoid a blood bath."

"It is coming either way," replied Somira ominously. "Either today, tomorrow, or many months from now, but the humans' presence will not be kept secret for long, even if we reach a Circle."

"A Circle will buy us more time," Dalis reminded them.

Somira nodded. "I agree. And with time comes the possibility of a different path forward."

"Right," said Melowin, clapping Ector on the shoulder. "So what is our plan?"

"Norias and Labri still expect us to head north," Somira continued. "They know reaching a Circle is crucial to our plan. We must hope they are oblivious to this Eastern Circle, like Elmondove was."

"He was not oblivious," Melowin corrected. "He just seemed surprised it was operational, apparently ahead of schedule, or something."

"Either way," Somira continued, "if a Council member is unaware of its activity, then the odds are good that the average elf is also unaware."

"Agreed," said Dalis. "But if an ambush lies for us on the northerly route, and we never pass it, they will widen their search for us. And if they are aware of this Eastern Circle, they will surely guess it and be able to cut us off well beforehand."

"I was considering that," replied Somira. "But I do not see any other options before us."

"We will simply have to push the pace," Melowin said, giving a lingering look towards the humans. "It is better than continuing on north."

"We can do it," said Annalin.

"We'll do whatever it takes," agreed Ector.

"We still do not know if the Eastern Circle can be trusted, though," warned Somira.

"We have no other choice," Dalis replied. "Once the dark elves find Norias and Labri, and they will, we will not be able to fend them off. Not this time."

Just then, a heavy, unexpected rustling approached out of the darkness of the forest. To Ector's bafflement, it was not coming from the direction where Labri, Norias, and Elmondove had departed; it was coming head-on from the east, the new direction they had planned to travel. Whatever it was had heard their voices. It was coming straight for them.

The five elves encircled the six children, as the commotion turned into pronounced thudding, like the sound of running feet.

"Wait!" said Meric, pushing through the elves' barrier.

"Meric, what are you doing?" asked Annalin, shocked to see a smile spreading across his face.

"It's all right," Meric continued as Dalis caught him around the waist.

"Young master Meric, stay back," Dalis warned.

"Can't you hear it?" Meric asked, staring, baffled, at everyone as if he were the only sane one in the group.

"Hear what, mate?" asked Ector, pushing closer to the elves at the front. "You mean the sound of the dark elves coming for us?"

"No!" cried Meric. "It's Rahms!"

Dalis loosened his grip around Meric. "It definitely does not sound Elvish," he whispered.

"Or it could be a hoard of them," Ector countered.

"There is no stench," Dalis added, still cautiously guarding Ector with outstretched arms.

Meric was now far away from the protection of the elves, continuing to wander forward as the rustling grew so loud it sounded as if whole trees were coming down.

"Meric!" Ector hissed. "Get back here!"

Twigs snapping, leaves crunching: the bushes shook violently before Meric's prediction came true: The hairy beast of a dog barreled out of the darkness. And he wasted no time bathing Meric with slobbery licks as Ector stared stupidly at his best friend in the whole world.

The elves all sheathed their weapons and allowed their dimly glowing orbs to fade into nothingness.

"How did you know it was a dog?" Somira asked incredulously.

"Yes, indeed." Melowin allowed himself a relieved sigh. "I would like to know the answer to that question as well."

Dalis, however, slowly turned to watch Meric with a mixture of interest and disbelief.

"It is spreading," he muttered, barely audibly.

Tree bark shattered from the whipping excitement of the dog's tail as it whacked against everything in sight, including Ector's knee, which made him stumble slightly. Annalin threw her arms up, trying to deflect the drool as Rahms gave her a quick lick; then the dog turned excitedly towards Ector. Copious amounts of foaming slobber dangled from his smiling face as he bounded forward happily.

"Shhh, quiet boy," Ector said, avoiding a glistening web of flying drool as it detached from Rahms's jowls. He placed a calming hand on the dog's head. Rolling onto his back, Rahms waited anxiously for Ector to rub his belly, sweeping the forest floor with his tail.

"Alright, alright." Ector gave him a quick pat. "Listen, you have to be quiet..."

He didn't expect Rahms to actually understand him, of course, but to his sheer amazement, Rahms sprang to his feet and sat still, slowing his huffs to a quiet breathing.

"That's incredible," remarked Annalin, staring at the dog in amazement.

"Well, that's a first for me," Ector added.

"Don't worry, I told him everything," Meric chimed in, giving Rahms a scratch behind the ear.

"You mean you can hear him," stated Melowin. It wasn't a question. "Dalis, let me see that prophecy once more."

"Speaking of reading minds," Somira commented.

Dalis handed over the tattered piece of parchment, and while both began to reread the prophecy, Dalis studied Meric.

"I do not understand," Somira said, shaking her head as she finished. "This says nothing about humans. There is no elf in him; he should not be capable of such things... nor should she." Somira pointed a finger at Annalin, undoubtedly referring to the limb-crashing incident again.

"As I have said," Dalis replied slowly. "The old woman's gift heightened in the presence of elves."

"What does that change?" replied Somira. "We are not talking about Ector."

"This is part of Ector's gift," Dalis explained, studying all the children. "He is a conduit to the humans; he allows them to express their natural potential beyond their current limitations. The gifts of humans have apparently been dormant, until now. This is what they would be, if they were more like us."

While Dalis and the others discussed the situation amongst themselves, Ector turned to Rahms.

"Where have you been, boy?" he whispered, giving the dog a good ruffle. Rahms responded with an appreciative lick across Ector's face, but he continued to sit without making a sound.

Then, Ector couldn't help but notice Meric become rigid and tense.

"What are you doing?" he asked, watching Meric's tightly trained eyes follow the dog's every twitch and pant. "Have you lost it? Your mind, I mean..."

Meric gave a bewildered, speechless look upwards, and then immediately returned his awestruck gaze back to Rahms.

"He says, he went back to Cleargar the night we left," replied Meric.

"Mate," said Ector, trying to be delicate. "Look, I don't know what happened back there, but this is crazy."

"He says there are three more," Meric continued, still looking stunned.

"Three more what?" replied Ector, asking himself why he continued to feed the madness.

Meric locked eyes with Ector. "Three more of us."

"From Cleargar?" Ector pressed, feeling a strange mix of dread and hope mingling inside.

Meric nodded. "He says he returned to the village that night we left Dalis's home, and led three children through the forest, away from the dark elves. He felt your urge to go back and help, so he went in your stead."

"You're not joking," Ector replied, feeling his doubts slipping away entirely.

Meric shook his head. "I'm dead serious, mate."

"Why were you the only one who knew it was Rahms?" asked Annalin, looking equally perplexed. "Why did none of the elves know?"

"Because," replied Dalis, approaching them, closely followed by the other four elves, "Meric is the only one here with the mark of communicating: Brown eyes."

He paused.

"Your gift is getting stronger, Ector," he continued, almost sounding worried.

"Can you hear other things?" asked Annalin, surprised by the sudden arrival of Meric's gift. "Other animals?"

"No," Meric replied, "but I heard Rahms before. You remember that night of the Hoppy-Brew tryouts?" he asked, turning to Ector.

Ector thought back. "What about it?"

"That's how I found the stores hidden underneath your floorboards. Rahms showed me."

Meric turned to the elves closing still more tightly around them.

"Rahms rescued three others," he continued, looking at Dalis. "He left them hidden that way, about half-a-day, I guess, at a dog's pace." He pointed in a generally eastern direction, but it was out of their way towards the south.

Dalis immediately began to shake his head. "We simply cannot. I am sorry."

"Then tell us where this Eastern Circle is, and we'll meet you there," replied Ector firmly.

"Ector, the more humans we drag into this, the more we endanger their lives," interjected Somira. "Our Elvish allies are shrinking by the hour, and Dalis is right; we simply cannot take on any more humans. It is a miracle you are all still alive, especially you."

"Rahms says they haven't eaten since the village was destroyed," continued Meric, listening intently to the dog again.

"What if I go and retrieve them," offered Melowin. "That is, if you have some food to spare, Ector?"

Ector immediately reached into his food sack, ready to compromise.

"No," replied Dalis, squashing the idea. "I need you here, in case we fall under attack again. We have more than just dark elves hunting us now."

"With this new food, we could travel the entire distance tonight and arrive by sunrise!" offered Ector. "I'll be able to grow more food for everyone in the morning."

Silence followed.

"It is only a half day," Melowin added quietly to Dalis. "And it may be to our advantage: It sounds as if this mysterious Circle is due east of us. If our enemies discover the new plan, they certainly would not expect us to head this new direction first, and then approach from the south."

Somira nodded, seeming to suddenly like the idea, despite her earlier objections. "Especially if we move at an elf's pace, or at least closer to it, with this new food. Our position would be far beyond anything the dark elves might gather from Norias and Labri."

"Can you three make it?" Melowin asked, turning to Ector, Annalin, and Meric.

"We'll be fine," Ector answered for all of them; he saw Meric and Annalin nodding their support out of the corner of his eye.

The group, almost in unison, turned and looked at Mara, Fenodor, and Grigor. They looked miserable, resting on the ground; Ector was fairly certain Grigor was half-asleep.

"Technically, we do not need to bring them along anymore, now that Elmondove is gone," Unair chimed.

Somira shook her head at the idea. "They have to come with us now. It will not be long before many know what has happened here over these past few days. It will be known that there were six humans who traveled with us, and if we turn up with only three at the Eastern Circle, the remainder will be hunted and tortured into revealing everything they know."

"We are not far from the Eastern Circle," Unair added. "I saw its section of the wood from a distance today, when we cleared that last ridge."

"We have enough elves to carry them, too, if needed," added Quamas, puffing his chest out slightly as he tried to imitate Unair's thicker build.

There was silence again as Dalis considered the idea. "The direct path gives us the advantage on the Circle," he said, shaking his head apologetically.

Ector couldn't believe it.

"I left them once already," he interjected. "I have regretted that decision ever since. I will not abandon them again."

Dalis turned to Melowin with a knowing look that quite clearly said they didn't have enough time for this much dissension in the group. He turned to Meric next. "Ask Rahms if he will guide these humans to the Eastern Circle and meet us there."

"They are too weak to walk," Meric replied, immediately trouncing the idea. "They've been resting, exhausted for two days now, in the same spot."

"It is amazing they are still alive," remarked Melowin, astonished. "With nothing to block their thoughts from screaming out through the forest, those children should have been a beacon to the dark elves."

"I will not leave them," stressed Ector. "The sooner we leave, the sooner we can get to them, and then to the Elven Circle."

"It is time to move," Dalis said, turning decidedly.

Ector watched as Dalis began to lead them due east again. He didn't want to challenge Dalis and defy him, but leaving those survivors out there, helpless, was simply not an option. He'd rather die trying to save them, than flee and live. But then Dalis veered to the right, walking in line with where Meric's outstretched finger had indicated that the children were hiding, sparing Ector from the decision.

"We must move as quickly as possible," said Dalis, starting to run. Ector immediately picked up the pace, sprinting full speed after him. Exhilaration rushed through his spine, knowing they weren't going to leave anyone else out there to die because of him.

"Eat your last rations," Ector called out in a soft voice over his shoulder. He dug into his pouch and threw the last bulbous nodule into his mouth, beginning to chew vigorously as he sprinted.

The energy was immediate and forceful. Ector's legs felt as if they were running by themselves, and his breathing slowed once he swallowed the last remnants of the magical food. He felt like he could run forever.

Looking over his shoulder, he found Annalin and Meric doing the same with their own rations; as they ate, the spring in their steps jumped significantly. Annalin easily passed Meric, and then a few seconds later she passed Ector and closed the distance on Dalis's lead.

Stealing a look over his other shoulder, Ector couldn't suppress a gleeful feeling at seeing the young elves forcefully shove the last bits of their rations down Mara's throat.

Chapter 13
The Broken Pact

The night wore on, turning colder. With only a few false alarms along the way, spurring Ector to run even faster, the group suddenly, and unexpectedly, arrived at a place devoid of any vegetation. The sun was just beginning to peek over the rolling, sandy hills, which stretched as far as Ector could see. The landscape was terrifyingly empty.

Ector wasn't sure if he or Dalis had begun to slow first, but he felt his legs slowing to a walk as Annalin and Rahms did the same just ahead of him.

"Where is Meric?" asked Dalis, turning to search for him. "Where are these children hidden? I cannot hear or smell them anywhere."

"What is that?" Meric exclaimed, suddenly popping out of the forest behind them and seeing the vast, sandy expanse for the first time. Apparently he hadn't heard Dalis's question, but Ector couldn't blame him, as he turned back, staring with awe; winds swept away the scorched landscape, causing the hills to change before their very eyes.

Dalis accommodated their stunned silence and waited for the rest of the group to take in the strange sight.

"This is the desert," Dalis commented, taking a moment to look back at the sandscape in silence. "These lands were not always this way; they used to be just as fertile as any other."

"What happened?" asked Ector, unable to hide the shock in his voice.

"According to the old woman," replied Dalis, "the barrenness overcame these lands after the Pact of Tommas was broken."

Ector watched the wind gust across the tops of the dunes, forming tiny whirlwinds that sucked the sand up to the sky. As the sand devils raced down the slopes, the dusty earth fell back to the ground, dissipating into nothing while fresh vortexes formed anew in their wake. It was a continuous cycle that repeated itself over and over again, making the land look like a living thing.

"I've heard you talk about the Pact of Tommas before," commented Meric. "But I'm still confused about what it is... or was."

"The Pact of Tommas was our promise to the Earth," Dalis answered. "It was a promise made on behalf of all elves, and broken by one. Just as the desert stares back at all elf-kind, it stares equally at you, and the dwarves, and every other creature that comes here; today, we all bear the punishment of that broken promise." He pointed to the empty landscape. "No one, of any race, can make use of this land now."

"Some elves would find pleasure in that," remarked Melowin ominously, having arrived silently out of the forest behind them. Dalis threw a grave look at him but didn't argue with the sentiment. Finally Mara's group came barreling out of the forest, followed by Quamas, Unair, and Somira at the rear.

"In the days of old, young Ector, the gifts of good elves far surpassed anything you have witnessed of these dark ones," continued

Dalis. He pointed to the ground at their feet, which bore sparse, brittle shrubbery that faded quickly into the desert. "Life here struggles to flourish even to this day," he continued with sadness in his voice. Ector couldn't help but compare the lush forest behind them to the wasteland before them; the contrast was stark.

"Just as you see life diminishing on the edge of this desert," Dalis said, "so, too, have our gifts and abilities diminished every year since. Our gifts today pale in comparison to what they once were."

"Dalis," came Somira's voice from behind them. "I would talk with you for a moment in private, please."

Dalis didn't waste time joining her. They moved away from Ector, Meric, and Annalin, and the other elves took this as an invitation, walking a short distance back towards the forest line and forming a tight circle so their voices were inaudible to the children.

As Ector looked around again, he received an unpleasant glare from Mara's group; apparently they were still upset at having been force-fed the magical food, which allowed them to run through the night. Ignoring them, Ector tapped both Meric and Annalin on the shoulders as something caught his eye.

"Look here!" he said, pointing to the ground just behind the brittle vegetation sprawling out into the desert. There was a patch of the same red vine-leaves that Ector had dared to experiment with earlier.

"These allowed me to hear the elves' whispers last time!" he exclaimed, bending to pick a large handful, enough for the three of them. Annalin's eyes widened, and excitement brimmed on Meric's face.

Just as he had last time, Ector focused all his attention on hearing the tiniest of murmurs, blocking all other thoughts from entering his mind. He turned his back to the elves and threw the whole stash into his mouth. After eight chews, the same golden glow pulsed between his two fingers, shimmering vibrantly. Ector divvied the wet mush using only slight movements between himself, Annalin, and Meric, and then each, in turn, turned away from the elves.

The magic was instantaneous. If possible, it was even stronger this time. Ector wondered if the potency had something to do with the amount of leaves, or perhaps it was because these leaves were a few days further into the autumn season. A twinge of frustration assaulted him that he didn't have better control over his gift. But the thought died away as the elves' conversation became as clear as the sun cresting the distant, sandy hills.

"If you take them to the Circle," came Somira's voice, "they will undoubtedly learn how to better use their gifts."

"I thought the plan was to use the Circle only for its protection," came Melowin's voice, sounding a bit confused. "To give you more time to further investigate this bizarre series of events. Has that changed?"

Before Dalis could answer, Quamas's voice broke through. "Would it be so bad if they did learn to harness their gifts?"

Ector saw Dalis place an encouraging hand on Quamas's shoulder.

"I agree," came Dalis's voice. "Training them to use their gifts will lead to a better life for them. Perhaps they can avoid the mistakes that have cost us so dearly."

It seemed as if Somira shook her head in disagreement, but Ector didn't want to turn and draw any attention.

"Dalis, we are all involved in this now," came Somira's voice again. "It will not be just you that pays the price. Four elves will hang by your side if we are discovered."

"We *will* be discovered," Dalis assured her. "This prophesied halfling will cause a revolution, but like a seed, we must give him enough time to grow. After that, the decrees to which Elmondove and his kind cling to will be no more. A new world will take shape. Hopefully, a better one."

No one said anything for a long moment after that. Wondering if the charm had already begun to wear off, Ector stole a quick glance at where the elves were huddled. No mouths were moving. So Ector waited patiently to see if any more of their conversation would register.

"It will be an opportunity for us to study them, too," came Melowin's voice, just as Ector was about to give up. "If this shift is destined to happen, we will have the upper hand knowing their capabilities ahead of time."

"Is there a reason we cannot be allies?" came Quamas's voice.

"Not inherently, no," responded Dalis. "But after this ordeal—first the dark elves, then the Earthen Warriors, and now Labri and Norias—if you were a human, would you trust us enough to be allies? Would you want to be friends with a people that seek your death at every turn?"

Quamas didn't respond; no one did for another long moment. The idea was well stated, Ector thought, because that was, in fact, exactly how he felt.

Annalin took a step closer to both Ector and Meric.

"We have to find out what that prophecy is," she whispered intensely, "regardless of whether Dalis wants us to see it yet or not. If the elves we've met over the past few days tell us anything, it's that we're going to be hated. Everywhere."

"I don't know," Meric commented quietly. "Quamas and Unair seem to like us alright. Maybe there are more like them?"

"Count the number of dark elves that have tried to kill Ector," replied Annalin. "Then add elves like those Earthen Warriors, and elves like Labri, Norias, and Elmondove; it's just like Dalis said. We really don't have many allies. If it's anything like what we've seen so far, it will be little safer for us at this Elven Circle."

"Shhh," hushed Ector. "They're talking again."

"Take Meric's gift with animals," came Dalis's voice, trying to persuade the group of something. "Melowin has an excellent point: Aside from Ector, the Circle will be an ideal place to study the other humans' innate abilities. It was puzzling to see Annalin's gift start to come through, but when Meric showed the signs as well, it means there might be hosts of humans out there with dormant gifts."

"We will be called human-lovers," Somira responded with great concern. "Does that not bother you?"

"Once Ector is old enough to embrace his true purpose, the perception of humans will be re-written," Dalis replied. "Once the masses see how wrong they were, you will be counted among the first to have realized it."

"And how do we counter those who accuse us of polluting the Elvish bloodlines?" asked Unair.

"It will be difficult at first," replied Dalis. "Perhaps simply to endure the insults in the beginning will be the best response, until the humans start to prove they are not the animals commonly thought to be."

"But regardless," Melowin interjected, "some elves will not change their opinions on the matter. Remember our mission: We have to find the missing piece of this prophecy. Do not trouble yourselves with persuading those who will not be changed. The purpose of the humans being at the Circle is to buy time. If the others want to continue thinking of the humans as savages, simply say they are here to be studied and evaluated. Say whatever you need to, in order to keep the peace."

Silence followed again. Ector stole a quick glance at Meric and Annalin to see if the charm was still working on them, and he couldn't help but smile; if their stares could start fires, the ground would be burning.

"There is one other point I want to bring up, specifically for you, Unair, and you, Quamas," came Dalis's voice again. "In addition to their elf-like abilities that are starting to bud, I think the humans may possess a very different kind of magic entirely."

"What do you mean?" came Somira's outraged voice.

"Yes, why are you just now mentioning this?" Melowin sounded almost upset.

"I am still evaluating its likelihood," replied Dalis, "But the Earth seems to... how do I say it..." He paused for a moment, which dragged on forever.

"The Earth," he began again, "seems to accommodate their desires, you could say."

A blast of frustrated scoffs emanated so loudly that no charm would have been necessary to hear it. Ector wiggled a finger in his ear, trying to calm the ringing.

"And what do you mean by that, exactly?" came Melowin's voice again, over the murmurs of simultaneous questions.

"Whatever the humans focus their attention on, the Earth seems to reposition the pieces already in play to deliver it to them," continued Dalis, clearly struggling to articulate the idea.

"Reposition?" asked Somira.

"Yes. What I mean is, the humans attract whatever their minds are bent over," Dalis continued, trying to better describe the idea. "It is a gift more powerful than any other, if it is so. I have been wrestling with this uncomfortable thought since the night their village was destroyed."

"Speak plainly," said Melowin, who was beginning to get frustrated.

"Alright, an example," said Dalis. "Ask yourselves why the dark elves would choose to reveal themselves as they did in front of a whole village of humans."

Dalis paused to let the others consider his question.

"Well, clearly, their hatred of humans is unsurpassed," offered Quamas.

Melowin nodded in agreement. "The humans were all herded together. In terms of convenience, it was an easy mass execution."

"Agreed," replied Dalis. "But slaughtering the humans was not why they came."

Another silent moment passed between the elves as they further considered Dalis's question.

"What are you saying, Dalis?" Somira asked finally.

"What I am saying is that I narrowly escaped their clutches nine years ago, and I have seen these elves execute a mission, both when they assassinated the old woman, and then proceeded to hunt the halfling's family. Their skill and organization is extraordinary. Yet the night they attacked the village makes no sense! All they had to do was wait for the boy to pass into sleep. It would have been an easy, clean, single execution. They could have demolished the village afterwards and kept our entire race's secrecy intact, which they do still value, as most elves do. Why did they not wait?"

Again, silence followed as the elves pondered the question.

"I saw their relentless pursuit of this boy that same night nine years ago," Dalis continued. "Their resolve and their savvy are unmatched by anything I have ever seen. But they were negligent the night they attacked the village. They allowed their hatred of humans to blind them to their true target, and that is what bothers me. It is too great to ignore: They festered for nine long years after the night Ector escaped the first time, and they have since been searching in vain for him... the prophesied one!"

Out of the corner of his eye, Ector saw Dalis check over his shoulder to make sure they weren't being overheard. Meric and Annalin were facing different parts of the desert with their backs to the elves, pretending to be captivated by its awesomeness. Ector froze, not daring to move as he kept his sights trained along the forest line that stopped abruptly against the desert's edge. It gave him enough view of the elves to notice if they became suspicious, which clearly they had.

Apparently satisfied the humans weren't eavesdropping on them, Dalis turned back to the group.

"Finally, at last, the dark elves have him on the cusp of their grasp," he continued, "after almost a decade of unabated vigilance. And they lose him! Not because of luck or the boy's only budding capabilities, but because it was unnecessarily risky and sloppily executed."

He let his words rest on them for another moment, but no one said anything.

"We are faced with two possibilities, when we consider the unlikely events that took place that night. Either it was the dark elves' doing, through sheer negligence, or it was the humans' doing, through some undocumented ability to attract from the Earth what they desire."

Dalis paused to let the elves think through the two possibilities he had offered.

"These dark elves that revealed themselves in the village," he pressed on, "were not newly joined, as evidenced by the exceptionally green color of their skin; and one does not advance to that depth of darkness and still retain the gross level of negligence displayed that evening. These dark elves have remained hidden from even our own kind for who knows how long. Their secret existence is proof of the exceptional savvy required to deceive us for as long as they have. A savvy that mysteriously disappeared at the most crucial point of their mission."

He paused, again, momentarily speechless with incredulous disbelief.

"You do not think luck has played a factor?" Somira asked, sounding somewhat lost and doubtful.

"If you, Somira, had been hunting feverishly for this boy for nine years, would you have made the mistake of letting him escape?" Dalis asked in reply. "Or what if Melowin or I had been that negligent in allowing our emotions to overcome us in that most crucial moment, had that been our target."

"I see your point," came Somira's voice again.

"It would be unforgivable if that happened on a Leighmoor's watch," Dalis added. "And the dark elves' skill and prowess exceeds what is common among the Leighmoor ranks."

"But do you not think their underestimation of the halfling played a role?" asked Somira.

"I *do* think it played a role," Dalis responded, "but I do not think it was a random act of arrogance. I think the Earth gave a nudge to the dark elves' predisposition to act that way—perhaps even encouraging it to happen as part of something larger. What if the humans attracted their desired outcome, naturally, through the Earth rearranging the pieces already in play? What if the Earth gave a nudge to the dark elves' predisposition to be overconfident, which ultimately allowed Ector and these humans to survive?"

"Perhaps it is simply destiny," Melowin offered. "Prophecies do not sprout for common happenings, of which these past few days have been nothing of the sort."

"Even so," replied Dalis, "destiny uses more than luck to bring about its ends; it also uses pieces that have taken years, even centuries to fully develop, which now converge perfectly on this moment in time. Ector would not have survived without the aid of a Leighmoor... and a common Leighmoor would never have even dreamed of using the Elvish gifts and knowledge to protect a human... nor then, would Ector and I have survived without your help these past many days, Melowin. Can you think of any other brother in our ranks who would have been better suited to aid in a journey like this than you?"

"True," said Melowin, "you would be hard pressed."

"It has taken an Elvish lifetime to develop the way we two have," Dalis continued. "To credit chance and luck with where we are at this very moment is to place fine jewels on a filthy boar. They simply do not belong together. The events that will unfold, and that have already begun to unfold, surpass mere luck and chance. There is a method and consistency in all of these exceptional events, pointing towards design, not chance."

"Perhaps," Melowin commented, taking Dalis's words into serious consideration.

"Let us consider the possibility, for just a moment, that it was somehow the humans' doing," Dalis continued. "The humans show signs of possessing gifts that, just a few days ago, were thought only to exist within elves. They show exceptional reasoning and deduction skills compared to what we thought them capable of doing. They also show compassion, to an even greater extent than we do, evidenced by Ector's call for Norias to stop torturing the very elves whom, moments earlier, tried to take his life." He paused to take a breath. "Now, let us consider which is more far-flung. The dark elves lose their bearing on a fundamental level at their most crucial moment, something that has never before been even remotely witnessed. Or the humans, in a series of unexpected surprises, surprise us yet again with a talent that has gone unnoticed because of our misconceptions, which have been proven wrong, again and again, over the past few days."

"And what talent might that be, again?" Somira asked.

"This. Consider the words that left young Meric's mouth the night preceding the incident: 'I hope the old man chokes on his silly festival.'"

Ector heard a gasp, and he couldn't help but turn instinctively. He found Melowin with a hand to his mouth.

"Did you hear Mara's account of what happened?" Melowin asked. "She said the people fled back into their homes, where many of them choked on the smoke and fire that raged through their village that night."

Dalis nodded. "The old man would have been among them. I saw him, with my own eyes, taking shelter in his pub just before the fires consumed the front side of the building. I did not confirm his death, but Melowin's three humans said a great many people perished in the smoke of those fires."

"That is astonishing!" said Somira with disbelief. "Young Meric really said that to you? He really wished the old man would choke to death?"

"I do not think he meant it in earnest," replied Dalis. "But he said it passionately; I was standing outside their room after the old man had locked them upstairs in his pub. The dark elves were closely tracking Meric after he had foolishly drawn attention to himself, leaping unnaturally high after drinking one of Ector's brews. Again, I do not think young Meric meant the words in earnest; he was angry at being secluded from the festival, as was young Ector. But nonetheless, the humans appear to have the ability to draw in the things on which they focus, not with magic, but with passion!"

"Come now, Dalis," scoffed Somira. "You cannot possibly be serious. You think flippant words from an angry young human caused their village's destruction?"

"By itself, I know, it sounds outrageous," replied Dalis. "But then consider all the other unlikely events that have also unfolded since that moment: That same passion that Meric spewed in anger also exists in their will to survive against a far superior enemy that should have achieved its mission years ago. The humans should be dead. And yet they endure."

"Because of the prophecy," Melowin added.

"No, not because of the prophecy. The prophecy is meaningless. Everything that exists within these humans would still exist, even if it was not being forced to the surface right now by their current predicament."

Dalis paused again, and Ector could hear him take another labored breath.

"In analyzing how Ector has survived, and now, how all of these humans continue to survive against incredible odds, it is their will, their passion, their refusal to die. They expect to survive, and the Earth gives them the means to do it!"

There was another silent moment as the elves considered Dalis's words, and then Ector saw Dalis hold his arm out.

"This scar on my hand is where Ector slashed me with the Mountainwood knife," Dalis continued. "I should have died from this wound, considering how long it took to ingest the Marduk root." Dalis paused to let the others examine his hand in detail. "A dark elf fell almost immediately to this same, exact Dwarvish dagger, once it stuck in his shoulder." He paused again to collect his thoughts as the others listened intently, still studying his scar. "Yet I survived, by some unknown fortune, to stop Ector's neck from being sliced open."

Another long silence followed.

"As I said," Dalis finished, "it is a gift more powerful than any other. And if this is the case, the more concerning thought is that this gift seems to exist in all of them."

Ector could see Dalis shaking his head again.

"All I know," Dalis continued, adding one last thought, "is that the dark elves botching this boy's execution a second time because of a sloppy operation is beyond improbable."

"The humans have surpassed all our expectations many times thus far," added Quamas, sounding open to Dalis's analysis. "Especially Annalin."

Ector stole a quick glance at Annalin just in time to see her blush and try to hide a smile.

"At this point," said Dalis, forging on, "I consider it more likely that the humans have an undiscovered gift to attract whatever they focus on."

"Well, based on what I have seen these past few days," Melowin interjected, "this makes an even stronger case for keeping an eye on them under the protection of a Circle. For both their protection and ours."

Looking over again, Ector caught a peek at most of the group nodding—all except Somira.

"Maybe your estimation of these dark elves is overdone," she suggested. "Perhaps in reality they do not live up to your decade-old memory of them; time has a way of embellishing the truth, would you not agree?"

"My analysis is not based on one decade-old memory, but on several memories that fill a decade," countered Dalis. "Surely you must realize the dark elves had combed the area around the human village several times before they actually discovered him. Without my gift of stealth working in his favor, Ector would have been discovered merely months after his arrival to the village. I know what it has taken to conceal his existence from them for nine years, and I assure you, it has required every drop of my skill."

The voices began to fade, getting softer and softer. Ector couldn't stop his head from whipping around to see if they were still talking. And they were. Ector cursed quietly as he realized the charm was wearing off.

"That's exactly what happened last time!" he said, looking at Annalin to see if she could still hear anything, but her attention had turned solely to Meric. His face was pale, almost horror-stricken. Ector searched him for signs of an illness, wondering if maybe the vines had somehow made him sick.

"I... destroyed... Cleargar," Meric said faintly. His knees buckled, and he collapsed to the sand.

"Somira's right," replied Annalin, dropping to his side to console him. "It's absurd to think something you said caused all that!"

She grabbed Meric's shoulders and shook him violently to snap him back into the moment. She also made no attempt to keep her voice down, despite Ector trying to *shhh* her with his hands.

"We weren't supposed to have heard any of that!" Ector reminded them in hushed tones. "Meric, come on, mate. They're going to look over any second!"

"You heard Dalis," replied Meric, staring up at the sky. "I was the first... the first full human to show signs. I couldn't control my thoughts. I destroyed our village..."

"NO, YOU DIDN'T!" shouted Annalin.

Ector helplessly dropped his hands, turning his thoughts towards any sort of believable story for how they might have overheard the elves. They were drawing too much attention to expect anything short of a disaster.

"I couldn't hear animals talking until the elves showed up," Meric continued aimlessly. "Maybe part of your gift makes our thoughts come true, too!" He threw a terrified look at Ector.

"I doubt it, mate," replied Ector, feeling a slight relief that Meric was at least still talking. "If I had the gift of making our thoughts come true, I would just passionately think these dark elves to death, and we'd be done with it, right?"

"It's crazy!" Annalin added. "You heard Dalis yourself; he just can't figure out how the dark elves let Ector get away again. That's all!"

"What's crazy?" exclaimed Meric. "Elves are real! They can do magic! We can do magic!"

While undeniably upset, Meric did have a point. *Crazy* was a word that had lost all value.

"Listen," continued Annalin, refusing to give up. "The Elven Circle will keep Ector safe from the dark elves. Has it occurred to you that Dalis might be exaggerating for the sake of urgency so we can get to this Circle without any more incidents?"

"Now that is a bit far-flung," replied Ector. "He had almost everyone's commitment before he added that last bit. You heard him the same as I did. There's no reason to make up a story about us having a special gift all to ourselves, unless he really thinks it. They're all sufficiently worried about us as is without needing to invent more reasons to be concerned."

"Unless he wanted complete and total commitment from everyone, including Somira!" replied Annalin.

"OK, look," replied Ector, dropping his voice and trying to *shhh* Annalin with his hands again. "If they keep hearing their names, they're going to come over and start asking questions."

"Remember the charm?" yelled Annalin, raising her voice even more. "They can't understand us, Ector!"

Ector had, indeed, forgotten about it, but was now extremely thankful it was still in place.

"Fine," he said, waving his hands of the unfolding disaster.

"I'm sure Dalis knows that if we lose anyone else," continued Annalin fiercely, "we're done for. He didn't even want Melowin traveling ahead to rescue these humans that Rahms found."

This charm apparently didn't work on dogs though, as Rahms gave a tired bark and meandered over at hearing his name.

"I should give him more of the food," Ector commented, more to himself than anyone else, as he watched his exhausted friend plop down at his feet. That reminded him: He needed to grow more plants.

Now that the sun had fully crested the desert's horizon, Ector washed his hands of the discussion and walked a few paces deeper into the forest where the soil was more fertile. As he bent down, he wondered if the close proximity to the desert would affect what came out of the ground.

"Is it so unbelievable Dalis might be making something up to get their commitment, so we can make it to the Circle?" Annalin continued, unrelentingly, a short distance away. "Cleargar is *not* your fault, Meric!"

Stealing a look over his shoulder, Ector found poor Meric looking as if he wanted to eat a whole basket of the magical food and run as far and as fast as he could into the open desert. Deciding this was one of those battles better left alone, Ector returned his gaze to the ground in front of him. As he placed his hands out, the familiar vibrations started to resonate through his palms, and then throughout his entire body. He was beginning to like the sensation more and more; the ground sucked his hands into the sandy soil like a current sweeping him down into the earth. It was only a few moments before thick, waxy leaves started to protrude. Ector stared, amazed, as a plant sprouted around each hand; this was the first time more than one thing had grown at once.

The vibrations continued to intensify until the shiny leaves gave way to a rough, armored-looking bulb. As it broke the soil, Ector felt the earth loosen its grip on him, and he pulled his hands away. No matter how many times he performed the magic, the amazement and fascination never diminished.

Staring, awestruck, at the sight before him, Ector reached to retrieve the firmly rooted plant. It required all his might, but eventually an enormous oblong root emerged from the ground, fully armored. Ector studied the bizarre plant, wondering how they were going to open it. Undecided, he proceeded to stuff the awkwardly shaped bulb into his largest pouch located on the back of his belt. He worked to extract the second, which featured the same, armored nodules poking through the ground. Between both plants, there was no doubt enough food for everyone thrice over, with extras, but this new variety didn't look as easy to divvy up as the last round of food.

"Wait, stop," came Melowin's voice. Surprised, Ector turned to see what was happening; all the elves were still gathered in their little circle, but Melowin was holding his hands out for everyone to be quiet.

"Do you hear that?" Melowin asked.

"Humans!" exclaimed Dalis, relieved. "They are close."

Rahms gave a bark and immediately leapt into a full sprint, heading back into the forest. Ector shoved the second, slightly smaller root into another pouch alongside the first and began running while trying to secure the top flap so it wouldn't fall out. He'd only taken three sprinting steps before he was painfully aware of how difficult it was to breathe; the fatigue in his legs threatened to bring him to the ground. It suddenly dawned on him that not only had they not slept all night, but they'd also replaced it with hours upon hours of running as fast as possible. He needed more of the food, and he needed it now.

Looking at Annalin and Meric, he could tell their energy was significantly diminished, too. They did little better at keeping up with the elves, all of whom were tearing through the forest as fast as possible. The elves quickly passed a tired Rahms as well, apparently no longer needing the dog's guidance.

"Wait!" said Unair, throwing up his hands for everyone to stop. In the silence that followed, everyone watched him as he listened intently.

"Yes, lad, we hear them!" exclaimed Melowin, perturbed.

"No," replied Unair, shutting his eyes and concentrating even harder. Seconds passed as everyone watched him uncertainly, and then his eyes flew open. They were filled with fear.

"Elves are approaching," he said.

Dalis immediately closed his eyes in concentration just as Unair had done and covered his right ear, apparently trying to block out the humans' screaming thoughts that must have been bombarding them.

After another second, Dalis cursed. "He is right. We must move quickly!" He leapt into a sprint, running even faster, but then he stopped again, smelling the air carefully. His face suddenly twisted with disgust as a familiar, foul smell wafted gently along the forest's edge.

"It is but a few more paces this way," Somira yelled over her shoulder. She had continued to run, oblivious to the new threat. But the putrid stench, as evidenced on the faces of the other elves, was unmistakable: Dark elves were approaching.

The fatigue in Ector's legs was too much; he knew he wasn't going to be able to outrun them this time. Dalis, savvy to Ector's extreme state of exhaustion, was already sprinting back towards him.

"Can you carry me?" Ector asked, feeling no shame in asking the question this time. "Just for a little bit?"

"For more than a little bit," replied Dalis, sweeping Ector off his feet and hoisting him effortlessly over his shoulder.

"I just need... enough time... to break up... this root," Ector said through difficult breaths as his midsection was smashed firmly against his spine from Dalis's shoulder bone. He inhaled several, stilted breaths and tried to hold them as long as possible. Reaching behind his back, he began frantically searching for the root.

"Unair... Quamas!" he blurted out. The pounding of Dalis's quick-paced strides made it almost impossible to get another breath for several agonizing seconds. Facing backwards away from the two elflings, both of whom were already running ahead of Dalis, Ector didn't have a clue if his voice had reached them, but all he could do was hope and point a hand back towards Meric and Annalin, who were both being left behind. They grew smaller with every step.

To Ector's great relief, he managed to suck in another deep breath and hold it for a few seconds just as the forest floor kicked up all kinds of debris on either side of his limited vision. Relief washed over him as he caught sight of Unair and Quamas almost hovering above the ground, racing back for Meric and Annalin. Then Melowin flashed by, following close behind the two elflings. Holding something in his hand, he fidgeted with it as he raced on past even Meric and Annalin. Ector suddenly realized he had forgotten about Mara, Fenodor, and Grigor.

He lifted his head higher to see Melowin discussing something hurriedly with the three of them. He placed whatever he had been fidgeting with into their hands. Ector saw Fenodor break the thing into three pieces, and then all three of them immediately shoved it into their mouths. As Ector watched them pick up speed, running almost at an elf's pace, he knew Melowin must have given them the last of his rations.

Sucking in another breath, he reached behind with all his strength to find the armored plant stuffed into his back sack. It only took a moment to realize it would barely budge, no matter which way he tried to turn it. Releasing his breath, he immediately tried to suck in another before Dalis's jarring shoulder knocked it out again. As he unlatched the buckle to create more room for his hand, his heart dropped: The waxy leaves of the armored plant flashed before him. He watched helplessly as the food rolled away behind Dalis's churning feet.

Slamming his hand against the other pouch, Ector pinned the last root to his back, not a second too soon. The plant was already more than halfway out of the pouch. It had been flopping around unsecured. Ector gripped it, curling his fingers tightly around the plant's rough body. He made sure he had it firmly in his grasp before bringing it around to the front.

Suddenly feeling dizzy, he realized he had held his breath too long and was forced to exhale. He couldn't stop the impulse to take several breaths to try to recover, but the result was bad as Dalis's shoulder banged relentlessly into Ector's midsection. Everything was painful.

Seeing spots and flashes of light float across his vision, Ector brought the root to his mouth and tried to bite off a chunk. His teeth threatened to crack and splinter from the impenetrable skin.

"I found them!" cried Somira's voice, somewhere ahead of them. Then terrified screams rang out, and Ector felt Dalis's pace begin to slow.

"It is all right," Ector heard Somira say. "We are here to help. Your dog found us."

Rahms barked as he sped past Dalis, apparently heading to where the children were left hidden.

"Dalis, I need help," Ector said through tense breathing. "I can't open this thing."

"You can eat once we are safe," replied Dalis, slowing even more to let the others catch up, but still holding onto Ector firmly.

"There are too many of us to carry," said Ector, trying to fight his way down off Dalis's shoulder. "If you can figure out a way to open this plant, some of us will be able to run with you."

"No," replied Dalis shortly. "We need to travel at an elf's pace right now. We have either been baited, or these humans are drawing the dark elves closer with their scents."

"Then let me put a stop to it!" cried Ector. "It will only take a few seconds to get the pine needle charm ready."

"Unfortunately, a few seconds may be all the dark elves need to corner us," said Dalis. "We cannot hold them off with our numbers."

Mara, Fenodor, and Grigor arrived alongside Melowin, huffing for air, even though the magical food was coursing through their bodies. Unair and Quamas appeared a few seconds later, carrying Annalin and Meric.

"Let me talk with them," Annalin said.

Quamas obliged by setting her gently on her feet, and she didn't waste any time tracking down Rahms's wagging tail to explain the situation.

Frustration was growing inside Ector; he could run, if only Dalis would put him down and help him open the cursed root.

An idea struck him.

"Oy, Meric!" he called, tossing the root to him. "Slam that on the rock over there. See if it opens. We need food!"

Nodding, Meric dashed to the angled rock protruding from the ground and slammed the plant onto its sharp edge. The root cracked immediately, spilling large, black seeds all over the ground.

"Do we eat the seeds?" Meric looked confusedly at the mess scattered on the ground.

"I don't know," shouted Ector, still trying to recover his breath. "Just try them both."

Meric shrugged and took a huge, heaping bite out of the inside. It looked fleshy, almost wiggly. Meric coughed and sputtered as he tried to keep the bite inside his mouth, but the liquidy interior of the plant splashed all over his face.

"No good?" asked Ector, shocked.

"Oh, no it's good!" replied Meric, still coughing. "Maybe a little too good!" he laughed.

Ector felt relief wash over him. "Good! Take the other half over to the three new ones."

"Right," said Meric, scooping up the other half of the root. As he ran past, Ector caught a better glimpse of the plant. It jiggled wildly as Meric ran with it, looking as if the opaque inside might just spill over like a bowl of water.

"Whoa!" cried Ector, seeing where the inside of the root had splashed onto Meric. "Look at your face, mate! It's turned your skin fair, like the elves!"

Meric's olive-colored skin was becoming lighter by the passing second, spreading outward from his mouth and covering his whole face and hands. But he didn't pay any attention, as he dashed out of Ector's view at an elf's pace, running towards the children, who were now screaming belligerently.

"I can run if you'll just let me take a couple of bites!" said Ector, unable to hide the frustration as he craned his neck backwards to make sure Dalis could hear him.

"You will go faster if you just stay put," replied Dalis. Raising his voice, he called to the others. "We have to move, now!"

As Ector scanned the ground, he realized all the food was going to be left behind if someone didn't grab it: Annalin was still busy trying to calm the humans, whom Ector had not even glimpsed yet. Meric was talking over her, trying to get them to eat. They were probably ready to explode with fright, thought Ector. Elves and magical food had descended upon them in seconds, after days of being isolated and starving. And in addition to all that, it would have been a miracle to understand even half of what was being yelled at them.

"Fenodor," cried Ector, hoping he had been wrong about Mara's bodyguard. "Grab the seeds there on the ground. We need all the food!"

Fenodor hesitated for a moment, staring back as if a stag challenge had been issued to obtain his doe. Unblinking, Ector waited, hoping Fenodor would just do it. He felt his blood beginning to boil, but then Fenodor finally bent to help. That is, until Mara reached out to stop him.

"No, leave it," Mara said, throwing a menacing look at Ector while he remained helplessly slung over Dalis's shoulder. "We don't have enough time. Those murderers will be here any second looking for the rest of us who escaped." She hung on the words with disdain, almost enjoying Ector's helplessness.

If Ector knew how to make curses, he would have placed the worst one he knew on her.

"Annalin!" he shouted, redirecting his efforts to see if she could help, while staring daggers at Mara. "There is food back here!"

The children's screams intensified, drowning out his voice. Ector couldn't see what was happening, but he could hear Annalin's voice still trying to calm them. By the sounds of the flustered cries for help, they were all going to run out of time.

In that moment, the forest around them suddenly became brittle with frost. The temperature dropped in the span of a breath, and Ector could see a white haze leaving his mouth. He shivered. Time had run out.

"We leave now!" commanded Dalis, running full speed away from the others. Everyone suddenly came into Ector's view as Dalis sped past them: Meric was pulling a boy from the brush, and shoving a piece of the strange, liquid-like root into his mouth. Weakened from hunger, the scrawny boy looked much shorter and maybe a couple of years younger than Meric.

Ector saw Meric yell out to Unair, "Carry this one, I can run."

Meric lifted the boy with elf-like strength onto Unair's back.

Unair secured him tightly with both arms and began sprinting away as fast as he could with the child, departing the fog spilling out of the forest. Quamas grabbed another of the humans and did the same.

The dark elves are going to track us the whole way, unless I can mask their scents, thought Ector. *If only Dalis had listened! Wait...*

Trees were passing by all around. Pine trees! Ector reached an arm out, waiting for the sharp prickling to register, but it only took a few seconds before his wrists and forearms stung, turning bright pink from all the thin branches whipping him. They were passing by too quickly to grab. He recoiled but shook the pain away. Forcing his bruised arms back out, he waited for the stinging pine needles to register again.

Entering another piney patch, Ector clasped his hand as tightly as he could around a random branch, and as Dalis forged ahead at full speed, a sparse handful of needles ripped away. Immediately, Ector brought them to his mouth, but then he stopped as another thought struck him: The thoughts of these new humans were still running wild. He would need to mask them, too. Even if the group did manage to escape and hide, the scent-masking charm would be useless. The blaring thoughts of the new children would lead the dark elves right to them!

Maybe not, said another voice inside; Ector suddenly remembered the dark elves' failed attempt to discover them hiding in the bushes. *But the one dark elf had managed to hear something*, said another voice in rebuttal.

Ector cursed silently; they couldn't take that chance again. All it would take was one newly joined dark elf with the ability to still hear their thoughts for the entire legion to descend on them, wherever they went.

He lifted his head, craning his neck, determinedly searching for the waxy leaves that had blocked their thoughts before, but everything was moving too fast. He wondered if he might be able to rake in a handful by luck, but after a few seconds of letting the different kinds of forest foliage brush in and out of his other hand, he realized the waxy leaves didn't feel distinct enough to find by touch alone.

Dropping his head, discouraged, he watched the ground race by underneath Dalis's feet. Then Annalin's idea suddenly echoed in his mind: Dalis had said the pine needles were not a good tool for quieting thoughts, but what if his gift could overcome that? What if, through sheer focus and concentration, he could combine the scent-masking charm and the thought-quieting charm into one?

Throwing the meager handful of needles into his mouth, he began to chew: *One... two... three... four... five... six... seven... eight...*

Despite the jarring of Dalis's steps, Ector did his best to carefully remove the needles with two fingers.

"Dalis, stop!" he suddenly cried. "The prophecy parchment is blowing away!"

The sudden jerk, as Dalis slowed and turned, allowed Ector to slip from his shoulder with a violent twist.

"Where?" Dalis asked, reaching instinctively to his chest pocket as Ector's feet hit the ground. A confused look spread across Dalis's face as he found the paper still tightly secured right where he had left it.

Ector sprinted back towards the others, and seeing him approach, the others slowed, confused as to why the group was stopping.

"Unair, Quamas!" shouted Ector, splitting the handful of pine needles between both hands as he ran towards them.

They stopped with baffled looks, and as if this ordeal hadn't been enough for the new humans, Ector rubbed the slimy, chewed-up pine needles all over their shocked faces. One squirmed, trying to get away, but Unair kept a firm grasp on him. Ector did the same to the other one hanging over Quamas's shoulder.

"Oh, wow!" said Quamas, rubbing his temples with his free hand. "My mind was ringing with his thoughts. You have the best gift ever! Thank you."

"Can you smell him anymore?" asked Ector, shocked that the pine needles had worked to quiet the boy's thoughts.

"No scent whatsoever," Quamas confirmed. "No thoughts. No scent."

Ector couldn't believe it. It had worked! He had done two charms in one, regardless of any limitations of the actual pine needles. He had willed it to work. And it had!

"Do you know where lying gets you?" asked Dalis, less–than amused at Ector's stunt to wriggle free.

"Wait, there's one more," replied Ector, hoping to delay Dalis's reproach just a few more seconds as he reached for more pine needles. "It won't do us any good to run if the dark elves can still track the last one."

But Dalis picked Ector up off the ground against his will once again.

"As I have said multiple times," replied Dalis, turning on the spot and gaining speed, "the protection of the Circle is the only thing that can stop these things. It does not matter if the dark ones know where we are going now, only that we manage to beat them there. I will not lose you to them."

"Do not worry, Ector," Unair cried encouragingly. "Everything is quiet now. And I smell nothing!"

Ector started to take a relieved breath, but then suddenly realized that didn't make any sense: There was still one remaining human who hadn't gotten the charm. Meric had clearly said that Rahms had hidden three humans.

Ector held his head higher to account for everyone in the group: Unair and Quamas both had one new human each; Annalin and Meric were trailing a short distance behind them, struggling to keep up. Melowin had... Mara? *Why is Mara not running*? thought Ector, almost angry. She had eaten the last of Melowin's rations; regardless of being exhausted, she should have had more than enough to sustain her! Shaking the thought away, he looked at Somira, running alongside Melowin in the rear. She was carrying Grigor! Fenodor was the only one of the three running of his own accord.

"You have to run!" Ector heard Somira's faint voice call out to Grigor as she placed him down. She turned and hoisted a fledgling Fenodor over her shoulder, straining only slightly to lift his large frame off the ground.

"I can't!" Ector heard Grigor whine from a distance. "I didn't get enough to eat!"

Ector cursed them again for not grabbing the seeds off the ground; he wished Melowin would put Mara down and let her run for her life since she was the reason they had no food.

"Where is the third human?" Ector called back to Unair. "We're missing one! You can't hear his thoughts?"

Unair shook his head. "Not a thing," he yelled back, continuing to sprint several paces behind Dalis.

Ector lifted his gaze towards the rolling mist that now consumed the forest like a cloud of smoke chasing them. Out of its thick whiteness came a distant bark. Rahms emerged, pulling away at a full gallop. Even from this distance, Ector could see Rahms's whiskers glistening with frost, and his coat covered in icicles.

It's not possible, thought Ector. No way had they left one behind, after starving for days, only to be found by the dark elves. He was on the verge of exploding.

"You're sure you don't hear anything?" Ector asked again, refusing to believe that the last one had frozen to death or been captured.

"He's gone, mate!" called Meric, sprinting just paces behind Unair. "There weren't enough of us to get him out. Rahms tried to save him, but they closed on us too fast!"

"How do you know?" cried Ector, still refusing to believe it. "You weren't the last to leave!"

"I'm listening to Rahms's thoughts!" Meric called back. "It's too late. He's gone!"

Purple eyes glimmered through the dense, rolling cloud as an entire legion of dark elves emerged to the front, seething with gruesome, bared teeth. The mist quickened its pace, rolling over on itself as it closed the distance on Rahms. Ector could see torn limbs poking through as branches spiraled through the air, bashing into other trees. If Ector hadn't been looking directly at the mayhem tearing apart the forest behind them, he would have never known it was there. Sounds of destruction and chaos should have been roaring all around them, but there was nothing. Only an eerie silence.

Then an explosion echoed through the forest. Dalis tripped from the blast, but kept his feet; Melowin, however, fell, as did Somira, neither able to keep their balance against the unexpected force. The sound of the destruction was no longer cloaked as it roared out of control, racing even faster towards them. Cackles projected out of the dense fog, which continued to spill over itself so fast, it looked like an avalanche coming to devour them.

Helplessness crept through Ector's mind; he was held captive over Dalis's shoulder, feeling every last muscle in the elf's body straining to run as fast as he could. But even then, it was no use: The mist was chasing them down, gaining vast amounts of ground with every passing second.

Orbs of fuzzy light began to glow from somewhere in its depths. Ector only just caught sight of them, before they leapt from the mist, arching high into the air. Then the orbs grew larger as they plummeted back to the earth, heading straight for them.

Ector bellowed a warning for everyone, but no one even looked his direction; his voice was lost in the carnage as the orbs came crashing all around them. Fires burst into life as the streaking bolts collided with the forest. Small at first, the fires quickly converged with one another, forming larger blazes. The balls of light continued erupting all around them, feeding on dead limbs and trees tumbling to the ground everywhere. Leaping on the dried wood like ravenous beasts, the flames swirled into one massive, uncontrollable forest fire.

The intense heat caused the mist to dissipate, but unlike before, when Melowin had evaporated their foggy steed, the dark elves kept advancing. They rode the howling wind this time, stoking the fires as they masterfully navigated the dancing flames and collapsing forest with unseen precision.

"You must run, Mara!" came Melowin's distant voice. Ector watched Melowin drop Mara to the ground mid-stride as the elf continued to sprint through the enormous flames that jumped all around them, threatening to consume them. Mara needed no additional prodding; she tripped at first, but then quickly picked up pace as if fueled by a whole barrel of Butterfly Honey Drub, even passing Melowin with quick strides.

Melowin suddenly stopped in his tracks and turned on the spot. Throwing his hands to the sky, Ector watched the flames follow his command, swirling higher into a formidable wall of red and orange. Screams cut through the thick smoke. Then charred, burning green bodies began to fall from the sky. Melowin turned again and ran, just as Somira emerged out of the flames behind him, the fires licking at her heels.

"There it is!" cried Unair, still a short distance behind Ector and Dalis. "The Eastern Circle!"

Ector tried to turn his head, but the jostling made it hard to get a clean look. All he could see was more forest. More trees. More fuel for this fire that had a will of its own.

Then the clouds above began to darken, and a shadow fell across the whole forest, quickly turning the day to dusk.

"Are we going to make it?" cried Ector, eyes wide, struggling for air amidst the billowing smoke, helplessly watching everyone flee.

"I do not know!" screamed Dalis, trying to make his voice heard over the deafening roar of destruction.

"I can run!" yelled Ector.

"Not faster than this fire!" replied Dalis; for the first time in Ector's encounter with the elf, Dalis sounded winded.

The skies blackened, followed with violent flashes of lightning. Ominous swirling clouds took shape amidst the bolts of purple and deafening cracks of thunder. Ector couldn't tell if it was ash or snow falling, but whatever it was, it began to plummet in droves from the sky. It had to be ash, because it wasn't melting in the face of the fires as it started to accumulate on the ground. They were done for, thought Ector, watching everyone's footprints beginning to take shape in the building layers of grayish-white. No matter where they went, their tracks would lead the dark elves straight to them.

As Ector looked up for some sign of hope, he found Melowin turning every few paces to cause walls of flames to erupt high into the sky; but the dark elves were adapting, either staying back long enough to let the fires die down, or flying higher in the air and hurdling the flames altogether.

"How much further?" cried Dalis over his shoulder. But Unair never had a chance to respond.

Chapter 14
Dead and Alive

The forest went quiet. Ector opened his eyes and found the sky staring back at him as he lay flat on the ground. His mind was blank, except for one, quiet question that rose above the ringing in his ears: Had he died? There was no way they could have escaped. He had to be dead. That was the only explanation. He blinked, shielding his eyes from the light as he tried to sit up.

"Ector!" came a familiar voice. It was distant and hazy. It sounded like Annalin. *Oh no! Annalin is dead, too...*

"Ector, you're OK!" she exclaimed, wrapping her arms around him. She squeezed him tight and then helped him sit upright.

"Where are we?" Ector asked, trying to find his bearings.

They were in a forest of trees, but not just any trees: The most gargantuan, gnarly redwoods met Ector's eyes. They sprawled beautifully into a never-ending forest as far as he could see. Studying one of the closer behemoths, Ector wondered why they hadn't seen this forest from the ridge-tops; the gigantic trunks would have taken over one hundred paces to walk around. And it was only one of thousands that stood before him! Ector blinked again, trying to make his eyes focus. "Where are we?"

"You've been unconscious for a while," Annalin replied. "We were so worried about you. Everyone except Dalis. He knew you'd pull through."

Ector stared, confused, trying to make sense of anything. Seeing him struggling to grasp the moment, Annalin grabbed his arms and shook them.

"We made it!" she whispered. "We made it to the Eastern Elven Circle!"

"What?" He looked around again. As his eyesight came into better focus, he saw elves... young elves. They were climbing everywhere through the forest, scaling the enormous trunks holding scrolls of parchment, books, bows, arrows, long sticks, and swords. Some were laughing, popping their heads in and out of the massive, gnarled veins running up and down the trees, which were so large that the elflings could easily fit into their crevices. Ector lifted his eyes higher and found them running along limbs, jumping from branch to branch across the gaps high above. But perhaps most bizarre of all, no one was paying any attention to him or the other children.

"They saved us," Annalin explained, watching Ector's eyes follow the bustling activity. "They saw the fires destroying the forest outside... they saw us running for our lives... and they opened the gates."

"The gates?" echoed Ector.

"I think we're inside a tree." She pointed towards the edge of the gargantuan forest behind them. "You remember Dalis's underground home, and the enchantment that opened the roots for us?"

Ector nodded.

"Dalis says it's the same kind of magic here."

Ector rubbed his forehead, trying to make his thoughts clearer. The haze refused to leave him.

"Where are the dark elves?" he asked painfully. "Why didn't they chase us inside the gates?"

"I don't think they saw us. The fires were out of control: flames as high as the trees, everywhere. All I saw was Dalis running full speed into one of them." Annalin paused and shrugged, looking for words. "Then it opened wide and swallowed you both! He stuck his arm back out to wave us all in. And we followed."

Ector strained to recollect at least something remotely close to what she'd described. "Why don't I remember any of this?"

"You hit your head when Dalis pulled you through," she replied, touching an extremely painful knot on the back of his head. Ector flinched and stifled a yelp.

"We can still hear their voices on the other side of the gate," Annalin continued. "The dark elves are combing the forest, looking for our bodies. They're turning greener, you know."

"The dark elves?" Ector asked.

Annalin nodded. "They were even greener than the ones at the Harvest Festival."

Ector took another second. "Did all of us make it?" But he immediately regretted the question; he didn't know if he could bear the truth.

Annalin fell silent for a moment. "We lost one," she replied eventually. "One of the new ones. He froze to death in the mist. They're pretty upset." She pointed a finger over Ector's shoulder, and he turned to see the two new additions: Two emaciated boys, who were ravenously eating dried bread, cheese, and nuts from a plate, under the watchful eye of Melowin. Mara, Fenodor, and Grigor had all made it as well; they sat huddled on Melowin's other side.

Rahms then broadsided Ector, bathing him with wet licks for the second time that day... or night. Ector blinked hard, trying to remember the last time he'd slept.

"You pulled through!" Meric exclaimed, laughing. He walked up behind Rahms and slapped Ector on the back before plopping down next to him. "Man! Talk about close," he said, with a smile that quickly turned to a grimace as he inspected the back of Ector's head. "That's a nasty lump you've got there, mate. You all right?"

Ector touched the knot tenderly and winced. "Yeah, I'll be all right. All the elves made it, too?"

Meric nodded. "Yep, just barely though."

Ector turned back to Annalin, who was looking off into the distance at Dalis whispering with an elf they had never seen before.

"You said you heard the dark elves' voices?" asked Ector. "What were they saying?"

"Mostly arguing." Suddenly Annalin looked very serious. "They haven't found any remains of our bodies, obviously, because we're still alive. One, with a really scratchy voice, tried to convince the others the fire was burning so hot that we either melted away or turned to ash and blew away in the tornadoes."

"Tornadoes?" asked Ector, remembering the darkening skies.

"Dozens of them fell on us, all at once." Annalin shook her head, horrified.

"Yeah," added Meric. "My feet left the ground, and I was actually being sucked away when Dalis reached out to pull me in. Thank the fates I was the last one through the tree. If there had been anyone behind me, they would've been done for."

"So that's it, then?" Ector asked, amazed. "They think we were sucked away in a pile of ash?"

Annalin shrugged. "They plan to tell the High Minister that you're dead. But they left a small group to search for more signs, to be sure. If you walk in that direction, towards the forest's edge, you can still hear them walking around."

She pointed towards a fuzzy, opaque barrier hundreds of strides away from their current spot. Blurred colors moved on the other side of the barrier, but nothing was recognizable.

"Imagine that," Annalin continued, as if talking to herself.

"Imagine what?" Meric asked, giving Rahms a good ruffle behind his ear.

She laughed. "We managed to find the only safe Elven Circle."

"Why is this the only safe one?" asked Ector. "Didn't Dalis say any of the Circles could protect us?"

"You think with magic like theirs," she replied, throwing a nod towards the blurred, roaming figures, "that we'd really be safe anywhere else?"

Ector shrugged. "Dalis seemed to think so."

"You didn't see their magic at the end. And Dalis admits he doesn't know everything about their dark powers. No, the only reason you're safe is because they think you're dead."

Ector watched their faded outlines start to get blurrier as they moved away from the barrier. "But why is this the only safe Circle? If we had made it to the Northern one, and they thought us dead, how would that be any different?"

"Quamas says the Northern Circle exists in plain sight, for all to see. We wouldn't have disappeared inside a tree, like we did here. This is the only Circle where we could have vanished somewhere unknown to them."

Annalin had a point; if the dark elves knew that Ector was here, alive, they would be launching everything they could muster to get inside. If they eventually did discover him here, the only thing standing between them was a thin, opaque wall. Ector didn't like it. He remembered Dalis's ceiling; the dark magic had deceived it.

"Maybe Dalis was right," Annalin continued, thinking out loud again. "Maybe we humans *do* have a different kind of magic!"

"What do you mean? How?" asked Meric, a look of concern stretching across his face.

Ector hoped Annalin wasn't rekindling the idea that Meric had somehow destroyed Cleargar.

"What are the odds?" Annalin asked, looking between the two of them, astonished.

"The odds of what?" asked Meric. "Being alive?"

"Exactly!" she exclaimed. "We found the only Circle that could have saved us."

"I don't follow," Ector interjected, feeling the fuzziness intensifying. He noticed that his vision become blurrier as he tried to focus on things up close: in this case, a leaf the size of his torso blowing across the grass.

"Not only are we hidden inside a tree," Annalin explained, holding up a finger, "but we're hiding in a place that none of the elves know about. You couldn't dream of a safer escape, let alone stumble upon it by accident!"

"Why do you think none of the elves know about this place?" Meric asked, turning to look at the elves running in all directions towards their different gathering points, which presumably were their version of classrooms.

"Remember Elmondove's reaction when Unair said he saw this place last summer?" Annalin asked. "Remember how surprised he was to hear it was operational already?"

Ector had, indeed, forgotten about it.

"It's like your magic, Ector," she continued. "It manifests in all sorts of unexpected, strange ways, but it always meets our needs! Sometimes better than we initially intended." A smile began to spread across her face.

Ector remembered he had yet to tell Annalin or Meric about using the pine needles to deliver both charms at the same time; he gave a shrug, starting to believe that maybe they were different from the elves. Maybe humans did have a special magic to attract what they needed.

After retelling the extraordinary event, he found that the story fit perfectly with what Annalin was saying. He stared at her, amazed, starting to believe even more strongly that they were capable of... anything. Annalin continued to smile, prodding Ector to ask, "What?"

"If you can attract anything you need," she replied, "that means that Meric and I might be able to do it someday, too."

"Well, I'm not sure if you remember," warned Meric. "But apparently I caused Cleargar's destruction just by thinking about it. So be bloody careful what you think about."

Annalin was about to respond, but tense words reached their ears from Dalis and the new elf. Dalis threw a nervous glance over his shoulder; it looked as if he was pleading with her.

"I know there is a prophecy!" she exclaimed impatiently. "I just received word of it from the Southern Circle yesterday!" She thrust a small, square piece of parchment into Dalis's hands.

Dalis heaved a troubled sigh, and a worried look came over his face as he began to read the parchment.

"What?" demanded the elf. "You look surprised. You were referring to a different prophecy?"

Dalis's confused stare lingered on her for a moment. Then his eyes shot to Ector. Ector felt pinned like a guilty prisoner under the penetrating, icy gaze. Then Dalis returned his attention to the parchment; it looked as if he were counting something.

After a moment, Ector heard Dalis say, "This is not the full prophecy, either."

"What do you mean, *either*?" asked the elf, sounding irritated.

"Look here," he replied. "Three lines are still missing."

She threw a bewildered look at Dalis before she took the parchment out of his hands and reread it.

"This is what the old woman left me," Dalis continued, reaching into his chest pocket, retrieving the prophecy parchment. "The last part of it burned away the night she died."

The new elf looked between the tattered parchment and the note from the Southern Elven Circle several times before asking, "How can you possibly know there is more to this prophecy? Apparently I know more about it than you do! The burn marks stretch all the way into the part about his gaze of grass."

"I will tell you how I know that there is still more. But first, promise me that this boy can stay, under the protection of the Circle."

"Absolutely not!" she roared. "I would be ushering in the fulfillment of this dire warning!"

"It is too late." Dalis shook his head. "That moment has already passed. His gift is blossoming and has been for some years now. Wait until you see him."

The look of disbelief on the new elf's face grew exponentially.

"Here is how I know there are three more lines," Dalis continued, before her disbelief could transform into another outburst of rejection. Turning his back to Ector and the others, he took her gently by the arm and explained something while pointing at the paper.

"Yes, but this warning just arrived from the Southern Circle," she countered, still loudly enough for Ector to hear. "It is from the High Council! They have issued an elf-hunt for this halfling—the one you just brought through my gates!"

While she and Dalis continued to exchange words, Ector—while not really knowing why—got to his feet and approached them. The sounds of scuffling suggested that Annalin and Meric were following close behind him.

As they approached, the new elf quieted and stared intensely at Ector. She had sparkling jade eyes like his, but she was like no other elf he had seen. Her skin was even browner than Meric's, a deep honey-oak color that shone in harmony with the sun, almost glowing. Her hair was also thick and wavy like his, but dark like Dalis's.

"Is that the prophecy?" Ector asked, looking directly into her shimmering eyes. "May I see it, please?"

Before Dalis could stop her, the majestic brown elf handed the piece of paper to Ector, with a mixed look of curiosity and amazement.

How easily she'd handed it over! While Ector's eyes still lingered on her beauty, Meric and Annalin began reading over his shoulders.

"Well, there you have it!" exclaimed Meric, whistling through his teeth. "They've got your age a bit wrong, but no wonder everyone hates you."

Ector looked down and began to read:

A boy of man and mind of elf
Will stir the tides of change himself
The winds have shift, and born this night
He bears the mark of evening's light
Unite he will, the race of man
Against the elves across the land
Elvish will turn against their own
In the greatest civil war known
Though this foreseen will not yet pass
If the halfling with gaze of grass
Is killed before the age of Fact

Be Aware:
The boy has evaded for ten years,
and will be that same age

Ector took a moment to let the revelation settle on him. "Is this what is written on the paper in your pocket?" he asked, looking at Dalis with fear.

"No," replied Dalis, and at long last, he extracted the piece of parchment that Ector had seen him withdraw so many times before. It was beginning to wear thin at the creases where it had been unfolded and re-folded so many times over the past days. Dalis handed it gently to Ector. Taking it by the charred, burnt bottom, Ector unfolded it and found what looked like very hurried handwriting. The words were exactly the same, but as the new female elf had said, the blackened edge of Dalis's parchment ate into the words, *If the halfling with gaze of grass...*

Ector looked at Dalis with a mix of sorrow and fright: Dalis had saved him in the hope that this great civil war might not come to pass. But it was not to be. The warning was as clear as the sky: To stop the coming war, the boy of man with mind of elf must be killed.

"I see the look of fear in your eyes, master Ector," Dalis said, before Ector could say anything. "But take heart, this is not the entire prophecy, either."

Now Ector could see why Dalis was having trouble securing their sanctuary: apparently Dalis had tried to make the same argument with this new elf. But Ector didn't believe Dalis any more than she did. She had the full prophecy; Dalis was mistaken. He had saved Ector, watched over him all those years, on the false hope of creating a better world for both elves and humans. But the only way this could end was either in the greatest civil war the Earth had ever seen... or in Ector's death. Now here he was, surrounded by elves, with no escape. He had no idea how he'd entered the Circle, and he had no idea how to get out. He was trapped.

"How can you possibly say that?" Ector fired off, almost angry at Dalis's delusional faith that this would end any other way than in his death.

"There are three more lines," Dalis answered calmly.

"You said that before," interjected the female elf. "How can you possibly believe you know more about this prophecy than I, when you have less of it than I do?"

Now that Ector was closer, he could hear and see the authority in her every word and movement. She was in charge of this place.

"You know I was with the old woman," Dalis responded, but a hint of something seemed odd to Ector. There was a history between the two standing in front of him. They knew each other.

She exhaled, frustrated, but didn't add anything; they were both doing their best not to reveal anything significant about their pasts.

"Either you believe me, or you do not," Dalis added, with an edge of impatience. "Are we permitted to stay, or no?"

A nervous tension swelled inside Ector; he wasn't so sure an ultimatum was the best play. But his deep gratitude for Dalis's unwavering support solidified even more. The prophecy from the Southern Circle bore the worst possible news Dalis could have discovered, yet he continued to protect him.

"You said no one else knows of this news?" Dalis pressed, taking the prophecy out of Ector's hand and handing it back to the female elf.

She shook her head.

Ector felt the relief weaken his knees. If this prophecy wasn't yet common knowledge here, maybe there was still a sliver of hope.

"Tell me again, Dalis, how you know for sure of these additional three lines," she said.

"The full prophecy will contain seven paired lines," Dalis replied. "That was the form of her first prophecy. And it will match in sound at the end of each paired line."

"What do you mean?"

"Look here." Dalis took the paper from her and held it out, so everyone could see. "Do you notice anything about the last line?"

"It's unpaired," Annalin answered immediately.

"Very good," Dalis replied, smiling his approval. "It is missing its pair. There should also be seven of these pairs, if it is to match her first prophecy."

As he moved his fingers down the prophecy, counting the pairs aloud, he only made it to five, with one remaining unpaired line left over.

"We are missing the other half to this pair, plus one final pair of lines," Dalis concluded. "There are three more lines to this story. The High Council is hiding something from us. Our mission has not changed in the least. We still need to find the rest of this prophecy."

The new elf watched Ector with steely green eyes for a long, silent moment. "You and your traveling group may have sanctuary," she said at last. "The prophecy will remain unknown... for now."

Dalis gave a grateful bow. She replied with a curt nod to the group at large, and turning on her heel, she headed deeper into the mystical forest. Dalis proceeded to move the children away from the spot, looking as if he wanted to talk in quiet. He signaled for Melowin and Somira to bring the others over.

"Thank the fates," Dalis whispered, wiping his brow with nervous relief. While they waited for the others to join them, he turned to Ector.

"Did you really use the pine needles to quiet their thoughts?" he asked, sounding astonished as he threw a nod towards the new humans being herded over by Melowin.

Ector nodded, making Dalis shake his head with disbelief.

"You are advancing at an incredible rate," he commented. "That is very difficult work you did, and under pressure I might add."

"Well," commented Meric in the silence that followed, while they waited for the others to gather their sparse belongings, "I'm surprised how well everyone is taking to us." He laughed and shared a look with Ector and Annalin before looking back to Dalis. "With the way everyone acts around us—Labri, Norias, the dark elves, even Elmondove—we were a little worried that barging into an Elven Circle might create some problems. But it's gone remarkably well so far, wouldn't you say?" He looked at Dalis. "No one's really even said anything to us."

"Keep your voice down," Dalis replied, not sharing in Meric's delight. He waited as the others joined their little circle.

"Bring it in tight," Dalis whispered as everyone arrived. "I want you all to listen very carefully. The reason no one has bothered us much since we arrived is because you all look like elves right now."

The children exchanged confused looks.

"More or less," Melowin added, tossing the skin of an empty root on the ground in front of them. Ector recognized it immediately: It was the root he had dropped.

"I was able to use part of your gift, Ector, touching your forehead while you were unconscious," Dalis explained. "You may all remember that, as you entered through the gate, I touched you in passing?"

Looking around at the others, Ector watched Meric think back while Annalin nodded slowly. A couple of the others were nodding as well.

"Through Ector, I transferred my gift of disguise to the rest of you," Dalis continued. "You now have pointed ears, like elves."

Ector looked around; sure enough, everyone had a slight point to the tip of his or her ears. How could he have missed it? He blinked hard, wondering if his fuzzy vision was obscuring anything else obvious.

"We couldn't manage to change your color, though," Melowin added. "That is why we rubbed all your faces and hands, rather quickly, with the inside of this root here. It is not exactly a charm, but it will do."

Seeing Ector still struggling to grasp what had happened, Melowin rubbed a finger across Ector's hand to reveal that, while unconscious, they had painted him with the watery nectar of the root. His freckled, bronzed skin flashed fair as soon as Melowin touched it, but after a long second, it faded back to its usual color.

"I don't understand," said Ector, staring at his hand as if it weren't his own.

"I completely forgot to tell you," Annalin interjected. "Our skin did turn fairer when it first went on, but so much happened. Once it faded, I just forgot to mention it."

"Oh, it has not faded." Melowin laughed. "You are all still as fair as me."

The children, again, exchanged confused looks.

"No one looks any different," commented Meric, shrugging. Ector had to agree; Meric's olive-colored pigment had fully returned.

"Why do we need to be fair-colored?" Meric asked. "That other elf just now, she was brown."

"The brown tribes come from the desert, and they all know each other," Melowin answered. "The last thing we need is you fielding questions about your kin. She would have discovered our falsehood immediately. But you came through the gates with the juice already covering you; the fates smile on us again."

"Wait, you mean to say," Dalis interjected, sounding surprised, "that, to each other, you still look normal? You do not notice anything different?"

The children continued to stare, shaking their heads.

"Strange," Dalis remarked.

"Yes, quite strange," Melowin added. "You appear like a bunch of ragged-looking elves, but elves all the same."

"It *is* beginning to fade a bit," Dalis said seriously. "None of you are as fair as when the liquid first touched you. I imagine it will not be long before we are discovered."

"Wait," Ector interrupted, still trying to piece everything together. "That other elf, the one we were just speaking to; if she knows I'm a halfling, do I need a disguise?"

"She knows you are the elf-boy mentioned in the prophecy," Dalis explained. "But your kind are such a rarity among us, no one really knows what you are supposed to look like. It would have been harder to gain her sanctuary if you looked like a human."

Ector nodded. "So we all look like elves to you?"

Dalis nodded in reply. "The real problem, though, is that when this plant juice wears off, she will realize there is a collection of humans here as well. We elves come in different colors, but not the variety humans have. Your spots are a dead giveaway."

The news left Ector swearing that someone had whacked his knees with a stick; they had barely secured the elf's permission to stay, and now they were pushing their luck further.

"Can't we just keep ourselves disguised?" Meric asked, almost pleading.

"I don't think so," Ector answered, before even Dalis had a chance to respond. His mind was already working furiously to find a different solution. "That was the first time this root cropped up, and I have no control over what sprouts out of the ground."

"And," Dalis added, "we will be here for quite a period, while we sort out what to do next. This lie needs to die, otherwise we make our situation worse than it already is. We have her sanctuary for Ector; we should deal with these other consequences sooner rather than later."

Ector glanced at the opaque barrier separating them from certain execution. He released a heavy sigh, trying to ease the dreadful feeling settling in his stomach. If they decided to let their little secret die, more than just that was going to die with it: All their lives were at risk if she found out humans were here. He couldn't believe it.

Dalis looked at everyone and landed on Ector last. "Are you ready?"

Not the End . . .

www.ForsakenElvishScrolls.com

www.ingramcontent.com/pod-product-compliance
Lightning Source LLC
Chambersburg PA
CBHW020603310726
48979CB00008B/1329/J
* 9 7 8 0 9 9 7 4 9 1 1 2 8 *